AS THE
HEART BONES
BREAK

AUDREY CHIN

Marshall Cavendish
Editions

With the Support of

NATIONAL ARTS COUNCIL
SINGAPORE

© 2014 Audrey Chin

Reprinted in 2014

Cover art by Coverkitchen Limited
Design by Adithi

Published by Marshall Cavendish Editions
An imprint of Marshall Cavendish International
1 New Industrial Road, Singapore 536196

Other Marshall Cavendish Offices:
Marshall Cavendish Corporation. 99 White Plains Road, Tarrytown NY 10591-9001, USA • Marshall Cavendish International (Thailand) Co Ltd. 253 Asoke, 12th Flr, Sukhumvit 21 Road, Klongtoey Nua, Wattana, Bangkok 10110, Thailand • Marshall Cavendish (Malaysia) Sdn Bhd, Times Subang, Lot 46, Subang Hi-Tech Industrial Park, Batu Tiga, 40000 Shah Alam, Selangor Darul Ehsan, Malaysia.

Marshall Cavendish is a trademark of Times Publishing Limited

National Library Board Singapore Cataloguing in Publication Data
Chin, Audrey, 1957-
As the heart bones break / Audrey Chin. – Singapore : Marshall Cavendish Editions, [2013]
pages cm
ISBN : 978-981-4484-07-7 (paperback)

1. Vietnam – Fiction. I. Title.

PR9570.S53
S823 – dc23   OCN854823027

Printed by NPE Print Communications Pte Ltd

For Minh...

Công cha như núi Thái Sơn
Nghĩa mẹ như nước trong nguồn chảy ra
Một lòng thờ mẹ kính cha
Cho tròn chữ hiếu mới là đạo con

The labors of a father are as heavy as Thai Son Mountain
Like water from its source a mother's love will always flow
A filial son completes the circle
With a devoted and respectful heart

Contents

Acknowledgements

The labors of those who've helped to shape this book are indeed as heavy as Thai Son mountain. I have innumerable people and organizations to thank.

The first of these is the National Arts Council of Singapore, whose support has been crucial.

I am also grateful to my editors at Marshall Cavendish — Mindy Pang, who first saw the story's potential and shepherded it through the publication journey; and Tara Dhar, who provided valuable insight into story structure as well as corrected all my p's and q's.

A writer is not complete with a community of other writers. Meira Chand, that doyenne of Singapore authors, took time from her busy schedule to read my manuscript and encourage me. Other accomplished authors who provided comments are Andrew X. Pham, Sung. J. Woo and Wendy Lee.

I have also been supported by my writing community at www.thewritepractice.com and www.storycartel.com, in particular Kathleen Caron and Kath Unsworth. Viet Thanh Nguyen's www.diacritics.com, website of the Diasporic Vietnamese Artists Association has been particularly helpful in connecting me to other Vietnamese-American writers.

I had many beta-readers, amongst whom were Amy Tan, Mirel Abeles, Ann Stanley, Nguyen-Phuong Lam, my son Sean Hua, Caroline Wood and her editorial board at Margaret River Press, and the ever-generous Joe Bunting of www.thewritepractice.com. Their honest feedback changed the initial drafts of the book significantly and for the better.

Every author needs to be reminded that a book must be readable. Jennifer Chen Tran, my agent, is indispensable in this respect.

Finally, I must acknowledge Marti Leimbach, whose book *The Man from Saigon*, provided the yeast that allowed a simple memoir to evolve into *As the Heart Bones Break*.

Characters

Thong Tran (Tran Van Thong)	A Vietnamese-American aerospace engineer
The Chief Clerk	Thong's adopted father, a civil servant
The Chief Clerk's Wife	Thong's adopted mother, a homemaker
The Commander	Thong's blood-father, an anti-French Viet-Minh guerrilla
The Commander's Wife	Thong's blood mother, dead shortly after Thong's birth
Chu Hai (Mr Trung)	Thong's English tutor and mentor, a journalist
Nina (Marie-Antoine Nguyen Nguyet Nga)	Thong's wife, a Vietnamese-American psychologist
Papa Nguyen	Nina's father, a member of the South Vietnamese ruling class
Maman Nguyen	Nina's mother, a princess of the Hue court
Tri (Tran-Nguyen Tam Tri)	Thong's and Nina's son
Loc	Thong's adopted sixth brother, a South Vietnamese propaganda officer

Huong	Loc's wife, a homemaker
Kim	Loc's oldest daughter
Jake	Kim's Jewish-American husband
Thi	Loc's youngest daughter
Third Sister	Thong's adopted third sister, a homemaker
Third Brother-in-Law (Ba Roi)	Third Sister's husband, a Colonel in the North Vietnamese Army
Oldest Sister	Thong's adopted oldest sister, a nurse in Saigon
Oldest Brother-in-Law	Oldest Sister's husband, a South Vietnamese Police Chief in Saigon
Binh	Thong's childhood friend, neighbor and school mate, a South Vietnamese loyalist
Ly (Hua Cong Ly)	Thong's high-school and university mate, an ethnic Chinese from a business family
Jerry Chung	The CEO of an Asian business front for the US defense industry
Minh (Tran Van Minh)	A party member and employee of a State-owned tobacco company
Ai Nguyet	Thong's first girlfriend, a Vietnamese pianist
Julia Anderson	Thong's first lover, an American intelligence officer
Jules Anderson	Julia Anderson's son

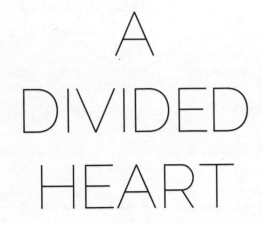

A
DIVIDED
HEART

Part One

BEGINNINGS

01
Original sin

YOU HAVE HIS CONFESSION AT LAST, THE STORY ON
sheets of onion-skin as crisp as rice-paper:

'There was a full moon, a harvest moon. There were two
frightened girls listening behind the wooden door. There
were men shouting from beyond the raggedy fence
overgrown with bitter gourd, lemon grass and peppers.
Quick! Finish with it or we'll be late for the rendezvous
with the new Commander. And I was there—lifting
myself off her, stealing a sideways look...

'She was tiny and very pretty, even with her eyes
red from crying and her mouth swollen from my kisses.
And I regretted it, what I'd done. But we were at war
and her father had to be taught a lesson.

'I pulled on my trousers, tied the drawstrings and ran
out. Ready, I said to the unit leader, my eyes downcast.
Then I hoisted my French carbine across my back and
stuck my elbows out to keep my marching companions
at bay. I didn't want them too close, rubbing against
me with their sweat stained arms and smelly bodies.

I needed to be alone to savor the memory of her lithe brown body under mine, the fruity smell of her thick black hair, the feel of her teeth like pearls against my tongue.

'The man in front of me joked—A little tiger? The man behind said—We all heard her. They chimed together—You tamed her though, didn't you? Was she good in the end?—they asked, their curiosity overcoming restraint.

'I looked away. There was nothing to be ashamed about. Still, it was my first time. I was sorry for myself and for her it had happened this way, and on a Mid-Autumn night too. It wasn't what my father had raised me to do. Even if she had melted into me at the end, sighed with completeness and allowed me to take away her circlet of bone... to remember her by.'

You know he liked to embroider. He couldn't have told the truth if he wanted to, so accustomed was he to double and triple dealing. You know how like him you are... But it's never too late to rid yourself of delusion. There's a circlet you carry close to your heart, a memento from someone who knew you the instant you were made, an oracle bone that knows. In its silence is your story.

02
The house in the delta

YOU WERE EIGHT WHEN HE CAME HOME TO BAC LIEU;
to the yellow stuccoed government house still surrounded
by the fence overgrown with bitter gourd, lemon grass
and peppers, where you lived with your adopted father, the
Chief Clerk.

You had a foot over the stone threshold. He was sitting
at the dining table aiming a chopstick at the Chief Clerk.
Your adopted mother was standing behind them, her fingers
clenched around a pot of stewed fish.

"There'll be war again," you heard him say.

You stood at the front door as still as you could. Was this
one of those times when children should not be seen, much
less heard?

You waited.

Your father looked up finally and beckoned. "Your blood-
father's here to visit," he said, pointing to the unfamiliar man
beside him, pale and square in black farmer's clothing. "You
must greet him."

So, this was the Commander, the swamp fighter the adults
in the house whispered about!

You looked down at the floor and shuffled your feet. You already had a 'Ba', the Chief Clerk. How could you address this newcomer in the same way? You folded your arms in the formal greeting posture and bobbed your head. "Dạ tên con là Thông, respectfully I'm Thong," you said. Then you escaped to the sleeping platform in the back room that you shared with your mother.

This first act of rebellion was hard. But the strategy you'd discovered—to use only self-referencing sentences—would allow you to avoid the Commander's title completely, you congratulated yourself. Even your strict father the Chief Clerk could not fault you, you laughed inwardly.

But you'd fooled no one.

The Chief Clerk was incensed. "We can't let the boy get away with this. He'll think we haven't been bringing the child up properly, that we haven't fulfilled our responsibilities," he said that evening to your adopted mother.

She didn't think so. "What are we going to tell the neighbors if our son starts addressing this visitor as father? We don't need people remembering that my youngest sister married an independence-minded notaire who disappeared in 1946. Or that I went off alone some years ago and came back with an orphan. I won't be the one correcting him. You're the father of the house. If you think it's so important, speak to him yourself," she said, leaving him to seethe as she headed back to the kitchen.

You heard her muttering as she laid out the kindling for the fire. "Commander... hah! Troublemaker's more the word. Older but not changed one bit, still liable to set a house on fire. Just like these old twigs!" she grumbled, addressing Ông Táo, the Kitchen God sitting in a nook above her head. "Soon the local militia will be overrunning the courtyard looking for him, upsetting my pots of mai and chrysanthemums. Trouble, that's what he'll bring."

.....

Ông Táo was still in his nook staring benignly at the world when next your mother walked into the front room and called to you to help set the table.

The Chief Clerk, excitedly waving the pipe in his hand, was tearing into the results of last October's plebiscite. "Ninety-eight percent! That's what the rascal Diem claims he got? Strange, that's what I think. No one I know voted for him."

The Commander pointed to the flagpole at the front gate and the yellow flag with the three red stripes fluttering from it. "It's hardly wise to make such declarations here, in this house. What would it say about your own vote?" he said.

"Doesn't matter," the Chief Clerk said with a laugh. "I'm going to be shot for keeping company with you anyway." He paused, then asked, "So tell me, why are you here?"

Your blood-father began to scratch on the table with his forefinger, illustrating as he talked. "Here's Vietnam cut through its middle, our South controlled by a puppet. This year we're meant to become one again. But the great powers won't have it. Better a Vietnam divided and weak than one united and strong. Diem has American support to back out of the elections. And he will. It's a betrayal we can't allow..."

"Yes, yes, that's the official lecture you give your recruits...," the Chief Clerk interrupted. "But between us, what's the real reason? Why have you actually come back now? And why here?" The Commander looked down at the floor. "Diem's hit us hard and we have to disperse, to recuperate and re-arm.

Most of us are going north, but I have orders to set up
networks for the few men we're leaving behind. I
where's the most dangerous place for me to be? Here
better place to hide? I thought I'd take the chance
of you once more. Get to know the boy. After this, w
when we'll meet again?"

   "More talk of war," you heard your mother
to the impassive Ông Táo as she went back to the
You saw her light an incense stick for him anywa
going to the altar in the front room to set out thre
sticks for the Buddha and another three for the a
As always, she prayed for them to protect all of y
father, your sixth brother Loc, your Third Sister
Brother-in-Law who shared the house with you, yo
Sister the nurse in Saigon and Oldest Brother-in
ambitious policeman, your other sisters and their
you, the youngest—to keep out whatever might th
keep all of you safe.

                    .....

But prayers alone could not keep the war at
Commander was in danger and jeopardizing your f
began to understand as his stay wore on.

   His business—which seemed to you to consist
more dangerous than whispering for hours to y
Brother-in-Law, sometimes crossing the river in
with other peasant garbed men, on occasion leanin
on the jetty fishing, and the rest of the time hangin
the cockfights behind the local army quarters — r
parents nervous, especially your mother.

And then, on a monsoon sodden night in July, just as your mother was braiding her hair in readiness for bed and you were reading to your father from the Confucian Analects, the Commander and your Third Brother-in-Law brought the war home.

They stepped into the front room dripping wet, the Commander's eyes red and wild. "What happened?" your father asked the Commander, who was dressed only in his inner trousers. "He gave them to someone who needed them more," Third answered for him before disappearing into his room to change out of his own wet clothes. "Ah, at your age you should know better," your father said to his friend. "If you knew what was happening out there in the villages, you'd be giving away your clothes too," the Commander said, shaking his head vigorously and spraying droplets of water on your father. "You've no idea, the suffering. The new government's raised taxes again. And Diem's brother Nhu is killing hundreds and displacing thousands in the hamlets. All simple innocent villagers! Life will get more and more difficult. We must resist. And sooner rather than later." His words beat harsh and loud in the living room, overwhelming the sound of the raindrops breaking against the roof.

Your ears perked up at the possibility of seeing some real fighting at last. But your father didn't share the Commander's urgency. "All's well in our town. Look at the latest land redistribution that's reversing those crazy hand-outs you revolutionaries made last year. That's a good thing. The family's gained..." And indeed your family had. Even you, an eight year old going on nine, knew that. Your Third Brother-in-Law's land holdings had increased fourfold. "To fight will only lead to needless bloodshed. Brother killing brother," your father concluded.

You thought about yourself killing your brother Loc. You imagined the Commander shooting your father and raindrops of blood staining your mother's white window coverings. You bit your lower lip. Perhaps war might not be such a good idea after all.

Your father's voice, assured and firm, broke into your confused musings. "It's time you put down the gun, my friend. You're forty-five. You can't carry on much longer. The country can't either, tearing at ourselves and killing each other this way. Which is better, two Vietnams living peacefully side by side or millions of dead Vietnamese? And anyway who are these North Vietnamese you call brothers? Why should I be fighting for them or with them? Our lives are here in our villages and towns, with our families. We should live for these things, not some ideas imported from somewhere else. Give it up."

He'd spoken with such passion you were almost persuaded, but the Commander was not. "Yes, things look alright here in town. But it's different in the villages. Diem's men aren't just taking piastres or chickens or pigs. They're confiscating rice fields and transporting whole communities into walled camps. I can't accept that. And who's behind it all? The American CIA! It's democracy, they say. But whose democracy? And when we get it, who'll guarantee we won't be slaves again, America's this time? We've suffered a thousand years of the same thing. I can't believe that's our fate as a nation."

So true! You opened your mouth to shout along with the Commander, but before you could, your father weighed in again. "I can't say what our fate as a nation is. But if there's blood in the paddies, then you're helping to spill it." The Commander retorted immediately, "And if I don't, then you and

*all your family will continue to sweat for dictators in Saigon
and Washington. How many years of that can you take?"*

*Your father didn't answer. The Commander stood up and
went out to the porch. On the floor, your mother continued to
oil her hair. You sat at her side, picking at the two red spots
under your feet, the ones just like the Buddha's, your mother
had said, the ones that would always protect you and bring
you good luck.*

It was a draw. You breathed with relief.

*You went outside to find out more about the bullying in
the hamlets. The Commander was leaning against one of the
veranda's wooden posts, looking out at the pouring rain. His
big body was shivering all the way from his feet to the tips of
his cropped hair.*

*"He's got fever," you went back inside to report to your
mother. She reached for the medicine chest behind your
father's divan, retrieved her precious herbal oil and porcelain
spoon and went out to the Commander. You picked up the
Analects from the floor where you'd dropped the book and slid
up to the platform beside your father. "Shall I continue?" you
asked. Your father nodded, his face a blank, smooth and hard.*

*You began to read aloud, "Filial piety and fraternal
submission, are they not the root of all benevolent actions? To
be a good son and friendly to his brothers, thus a man exerts an
influence upon his society. How can there be any other talk of
taking part?"*

*You felt your father's hand on your arm. "Do you
understand?" You didn't really. As things were, the two of them
had left you torn. "Con sẽ ráng, I'll try," you said anyway.*

*You looked out to the porch where your mother was trying
to relieve the Commander's fever by scratching long lines of*

medicated green oil into his back with the side of her spoon. You remembered the story he'd told you about Dien Bien Phu and how General Giap had killed 3,000 Frenchmen, precipitating the beginning of the end of French rule. You heard his voice burning into your head, "Always, always it's the heart first. You must have heart to move you along. After that there's the head for understanding yourself, your enemy and the field. If you have heart and use your head, you'll always find something at hand to help you reach your end."

You turned to the Chief Clerk. "Ráng hết sức. With all my heart and mind," you added.

.....

Later that night, after the Commander's fever had subsided, you went to lie down with him in the hammock on the front porch.

In the dark, your arms folded to imitate him, your head on his belly, you dared to ask him, "Do you shoot people?"

"Hardly, I'm sent to win hearts," he replied, his big square hand closing around the bone circlet inscribed with pine needles that was always tied across his chest. He began to sing you a song about a boat woman who rowed defectors across a river into the North, winning hearts one by one. "Something I composed," he told you. "Join in the chorus."

"Winning hearts, one by one by one by one," you sang with him lustily.

But you couldn't block out the sound of your Third Sister crying in the backroom where you usually slept with your mother.

.....

"My husband says he wants to join Uncle in the jungle to fight landlords and win hearts," your Third Sister sobbed, sliding across the sleeping platform into your mother's lap.

You heard your mother draw your sister close and stroke her hair, uncaring that your sister's tears would be wetting her grey silk trousers. "It is a woman's life. You must bear it. You'll learn," she said to your sister. She didn't explain how life could turn even a heart to bone.

You heard the soft slide of falling hair as your mother loosened your sister's bun and ran her fingers through its ebony thickness. "Come. Let me plait your hair for you," she coaxed.

You heard your sister's sobs subside. Her breathing quietened till it was only a sigh of wind. You fell asleep, your head on the Commander's belly, and dreamt once more about your kite, this time circling over the bloated hearts of evil landlords.

. . . . .

Fate had given you the yellow kite.

Abandoned by her owner for the nightly parade of maidens walking to the river, the beautiful golden creature with black eyes and red streamers had offered herself to you like a gift. Left with her string looped loosely around a large can weighted with stones, she'd reared up with the rising wind and shaken her stone weighted mooring free, pulling at the can until it stopped in a hollow at your feet.

Almost breathless with desire you'd taken the can and coiled the string to bring her down and hold her to you. She was unwieldy in your five year old arms. Her tissue, delicate against your face, still held the fragrance of horse glue. You sniffed the perfume in hungrily. You would take her home. She would be yours, all yours.

Your house was at the other end of the kite field across from the town road. The field was crowded. You needed to walk by the road where the kite's owner was standing with his friends. The kite was so large and so shiny and bright you couldn't possibly spirit her home unobserved. You sniffed her perfume in once more and reluctantly walked towards the road to return her to her owner.

He gave you the kite again to keep.

At the time he was a stranger, a tall young man with laughing eyes who chortled when you told him she was escaping and you'd rescued her. "She? You shouldn't be hankering after damsels in distress at your tender age," he said, his eyebrows raised in amusement. Then, giving you a mock bow, he took the kite from you and asked for your name. "So I can thank you properly," he explained.

When you told him you were the Chief Clerk's youngest son, Tran Van Thong, pointing to your parents' house across the field, he breathed out a surprised Aaaah. "So... It's fate we must meet," he pronounced, shrugging, as if some things were just beyond control.

He'd looked intently into your face, making you squirm under his searching gaze. But you must have passed whatever test he set. He patted you on the back and laughed again. "Well, since you rescued the kite, you should have it. Take it home. Don't forget, it's from me to you."

You stammered out your thanks.

"See! I've got a wonderful new kite!" you shouted to everyone as you raced home, the kite held above your head with both arms stretched high.

Once home, you sought out your brother Loc to help you launch her. He let you hold her string as she flew above the waterway behind the family quarters. You were still holding on later at moonrise, after you were called to bed, after you'd threaded her string through the wooden shutters and wound it around the bed post and secured her quite safe.

Lying on the wooden sleeping platform beside your mother you imagined flying with the kite in the aqua sky high above the rice fields, seeing all the way to Saigon where Loc would be going to school, and even further to where the river met the sea, and beyond that... across the ocean to an empty shore with golden beaches.

During the night, the wind rose. In your dreams you heard the kite pulling at her string but could not wake to bring her down. The string snapped. You uttered a cry to call her back, but already she was spiraling down into the dark plantations at the edge of the delta where men with guns hid.

You sat up crying. Slowly you regained your bearings. You were not on your mother's wooden platform but in a hammock. The Commander, not your mother, was next to you. There was a small hollow on his belly where your head had been. You weren't five years old, you were almost nine. The rain had stopped and you were looking up at a full moon. It was just a dream.

But you couldn't shake away the memory. You stared at the Commander's face, trying to make out its contours in the dark. You touched his sleeping eyes, trying to remember their expression. Did they have that sparkle you'd seen in your dream, that teasing humor? Was he the one you'd given your heart to?

A TWO-FACED MAN

03
A family in California

THERE'S A FULL MOON. IT'S MID-AUTUMN AGAIN. But it's thirty years later and you've left your father, your blood-father, the laughing-eyed young man, your tutor, and all their wars behind now. You've sorted out your allegiances you believe. You've followed your yellow kite across the ocean. You've arrived in America.

In America, the autumn moons are bigger.

In America you have a house in expensive Laguna Canyon with a garage, and a linkway joining the two, on which you can perch, and from which you can watch the moon and its reflection in your swimming pool. In America the air outside is fresh, not overladen with the stench of shit rising from the sewers like Saigon, where you went to live after you set aside the Commander and his mad dreams of glory... Where you met once more the man with the laughing-eyes who set you on the path you have been walking ever since.

You breathe in the California air scented with mesquite and sage. It's not the lemon grass and ginger of a Delta courtyard but if your father the Chief Clerk was sitting here with you, how pleased he would be with this holding—the house and its garage, the garden, the pool. Even if there's no ancestral altar in the living room, no *Ông Táo* in the kitchen, he would be proud.

In America, you've finally given your heart away, what's left of it anyway...

You have a highly educated American-born wife; a woman you married in a Catholic ceremony attended by ex-Generals and Ministers from the old regime, a woman who caught you with a high clear laugh that tinkled like a stream of fresh water unstained by war, an unexpected love.

She was waiting for you six years ago at the reception area in Kennedy Airport, holding a big yellow card that obscured the lower half of her face. The card said in Vietnamese — 'Group Leader Tran V. Thong, Group SGP225, Flight 7915' — your name, your group of boat people, the flight you'd just gotten off. Above the card you saw large double-lidded smiling eyes behind horn-rimmed glasses, then a high porcelain-pale forehead and ebony black hair pulled into a crown topping pony tail.

Her eyes scanned your group of tired flotsam sweating in the New York summer, overheating in the new coats and jackets you'd bought to come to America in. They latched on yours. "Are you Mr Thong?" she asked in stilted Vietnamese laced with harsh Central tones.

Overcome by déjà vu you couldn't reply.

.....

The young Vietnamese-American woman had sent you back to your first year in university, to the dance class your crazy neighbor and fellow engineering student Binh organized in the university sports hall.

"Instead of us guys practicing with each other we should ask those girls," chubby Binh had said, eyeing a group of girls clustered on the stage at the other end of the room. *"Good idea, but who's going to ask them?"* you replied. They were elegant girls from the music faculty. Rich girls for the most part, you feared. *"You'll see..."* Binh said. He took your hands and placed them on his shoulders. *"Let me lead,"* he ordered. He began pulling you gradually across the hall and when you reached the empty centre, he let you go, twirled away and shouted, *"Who'll be my partner?"* His voice carried all the way to the other end of the hall where the girls were. As hoped, there was a response. *"Cowboys,"* one of them commented in a Central accent loud enough for all the engineers to hear.

That was when you saw her...

She was in a light peach colored aó-dài that clung to her slight curves. Her long fingers were making a wave to describe something musical. When she concluded with an upward flourish of her hand, her back followed rhythmically, graceful as a willow. Her white silk clothed legs peeking out from between the two long flaps of her aó-dài were long and slender, swelling just a little at her thighs and calves.

You stared, willing her to look back. And miracle of miracles, just when Binh asked her name, she did. Turning away from her friends, she flipped her long pony tail of ebony black hair over her shoulder and looked straight past Binh and at you, the large double-lidded eyes in her oval porcelain-pale face flashing with scorn. "My parents taught me never to talk to strangers," she taunted in a clear high voice, her imperial Hue accent harsh and grating.

Your heart leaped.

Ly, another class mate, an ethnic Chinese boy from a business family, lumbered up behind you to see who was talking. "Way out of Binh's league, that one. She's from one of those snobbish mandarin families. Her father's a congressman, Mother an ex-beauty queen. She's a piano student at the conservatory. I see them at our restaurant all the time. Her name's Ai Nguyet, Beloved Moon."

You hardly heard Ly. You were too busy gawking. Such a beautiful girl, such an ugly accent, and so unattainable... An imperfect circle. Exactly how love with all its pain and bliss should be.

·····

That day in JFK, you felt all the pain of that first love again... After all your training and everything you'd numbed yourself to, your vulnerability to this old sorrow came as a surprise. You remember your eyes closing and your body leaning precariously.

"Mr Thong!" you heard the Vietnamese-American girl with the atrocious accent ask once more, her voice tight with concern. You opened your eyes and steadied yourself. You nodded. "Yes, I'm me," you said ungrammatically.

She reached out one hand, American style, to shake yours. She introduced herself in that accent that added downweights to all the light unaccented Southern tones. "I'm Nguyet Nga. In America, no one can say it. You can call me Nina."

"Ai is a cry of pain. A full moon can only fade," the beautiful Ai Nguyet, your first girlfriend, had said once. She'd warned you but you hadn't taken her seriously then. Here was another girl named 'Moon'. A girl whose Vietnamese accent proclaimed her a daughter of Central Vietnamese mandarins, just like Ai Nguyet. You'd walked that road before and didn't want to go there again. Besides, you were too old and war-weary to fall head over heels in love once more.

But the girl before you wasn't the melancholic moon Ai Nguyet became in the course of the war. She was bright and new, full of the possibilities her country offered. She didn't even use her moon maiden name. She was someone else entirely. You tilted your chin up and reached to take her hand. "Glad to meet you Nina. Please just call me Thong," you showed off in English.

Which she did... And later 'dear' and 'darling' and 'honey'... especially 'honey'. All said casually, in her high voice with its flat Americanized vowels. All said without intention, just like an American would. You wondered against your better judgment how the timbre of her voice would change if she meant what she said, if the words would sound heavier if her feelings weren't casual...

.....

You found out on your thirty-third birthday.

To celebrate it, she took you for a walk around Central Park to introduce you to the duck pond, the castle, even the apparently famous dog statue; every single landmark in her pocket-guide. It had taken more than half a day and now both of you were in front of the Plaza Hotel by the horse carriages, and the book had run out of free sights.

"It's time I went back to my lodgings," you said. The day had been long and hot, the New York summer air muggy. Your feet were sore and your big toe was aching. You were overwhelmed by everything Nina had shown you, overcome by your fourteen days in New York City...

...There was the luxury and unbelievable waste. Like the pair of earrings in the window of a Fifth Avenue boutique, the jade green of rice paddies and the size of pigeon's eggs, the back fastenings fashioned into little cones completely covered by tiny emeralds. You couldn't take it in, their cost, which was almost ten years of your pre-war salary, and the effort spent on those little screws meant to be invisible behind the ear-lobes.

For days afterwards, you stared at the elite of the city as they came out from their office towers and slid into their black limousines, wondering who among them in their grey suits and high heels might be buying those earrings with the extravagant backs. Who, you tried to guess, was the person you couldn't forgive, the person throwing away all that money while millions starved in your homeland?

And then there were the poor in the subways you rode, the tired cleaners and security guards who stank up the train carriages with rank desperation. There was the hunger stalking the darker streets. There were the veterans scarred by your war; befuddled broken men who shambled along the dark alleys, digging in dumpsters for their dinner...

America wasn't quite what you had imagined nor what Mr Trung, your English tutor, had described. But all the same it was fascinating. Just like the girl standing next to you. And you needed to go back to your little room in a welfare hotel in Brooklyn to process it all and the woman you'd spent the day with.

But she wouldn't let you go.

"Come and see where I live." She took your hand in hers. "We'll be alone. Everyone's gone home for Fourth of July. I'll cook you an American dinner for your birthday."

It had been only a fortnight since you met. She was too forward, acting the way a G.I. would in old Vietnam. You felt a pinch of disapproval. Even Julia Anderson, the real American woman you'd gotten involved with back then, had been more measured. But still you followed her home.

She lived in a tiny mid-town apartment with three other Asian American girls. It had a postage stamp balcony with a fat encrusted grill on which she began to make dinner. "True blue New York City hot dogs," she told you with a smile.

More déjà vu...

.....

"Hot dog," Binh had said that day so long ago, jumping down from the wall of his house into your Oldest Sister's front courtyard and pushing a six-inch length of ruddy colored grilled meat in front of your nose.

"Dog?" you'd moved your face away. "Yup, that's what my sister says is on the label—hot dog. Want some?"

You eyed the sausage-like object. It was thinner and longer than a Vietnamese saucisson and seemed to be made of chopped meat encased in skin. "Is it a dog meat sausage?" you asked. "No it's a dog's penis. Can't you see?" he peeled the sausage open for you to inspect.

"Go on..." you were only half sceptical. Half the time Binh's whoppers turned out to be true. "Try it and see," he said. "No. You won't catch me eating a dog's member. I'm no dog eating Northerner, let alone an American."

Binh had shrugged, "Well, too bad. You've just lost your chance to get longer and stronger."

He finished the meat, then leaned over to share the latest tid-bit he'd discovered about the newcomers to the country. "One of my sister's friends married one of them. I heard her telling my sister he's at it all the time, non-stop. And you know why? Because they eat this stuff every weekend grilled over charcoal. They even have thirty-centimeter long hot dogs. Foot-long hot dogs they call them." You gave Binh's stomach a poke, "You're kidding me." He nodded vigorously, "It's the truth."

Maybe. After all you'd seen them in the bars along the main thoroughfares yourself.

"They must have huge dogs over there then," you allowed. "Yes, large dogs and large men. One hot dog a day, that's the way," he had chanted as he climbed back over the wall to his house. "America lover," you'd taunted at his retreating back.

·····

Binh and you couldn't have been more than fifteen then. There hadn't been too many Americans in Vietnam then. Now you were beyond thirty and there were no more Americans in your country. You were in their country now. You could not reveal your prejudices.

You looked at the platter in front of Nina's chest. The hotdogs on it were red and swollen, bursting out of their long bread rolls and slathered with acrid yellow mustard, exactly like the awful hot-dog Binh had tried to make you eat. You steeled yourself, stretched out your hand for one of the repulsive objects, brought it up to your mouth and bit. They were good.

The surprise must have shown on your face. She laughed, wrinkling up her nose; something Ai Nguyet would never have done.

"That was a delicious American meal," you thanked her later.

"Not at all," she accepted, with another wrinkle of her nose.

She was definitely a different girl than your first love.

The two of you sat watching the traffic twenty-five floors below. You talked...

Indeed she wasn't Ai Nguyet. She'd lived all her life in prosperous America. Her questions about your escape from Vietnam, the time in the refugee camp, your life under the Communists, the war before that, were so naive you were charmed. You shared what you could about your life, censoring out the blood, the gore, your sins. She offered you a glimpse of her wonderfully uneventful life—her studies in a women's university in Boston, her academic achievements, her hopes for a career researching the psychology of guerrilla fighters, her reasons for spending the summer volunteering with the refugee service.

It was very late when you got up to go.

"Not before you get all that mustard off your face," she said.

"Oh?" Your hand reached up to wipe your jaw.

But she was there before you. "Let me," she said, bending towards you, napkin ready to dab the yellow off your chin.

Her face was very near yours. She was slightly taller than you and you could look up into her eyes as they focused down on your mouth. They were very dark, the pupils expanded. A single eyelash had fallen onto the perfect skin covering her left cheekbone. There were little flecks of grease on her glasses, a crumb of bread on her lower lip.

You let yourself forget who you really were. You let yourself forget the promises you'd traded for your ticket out of Vietnam. You did not tell her you were flying cross-country the next week to resettle in California with your brother Loc and his wife. You did not tell yourself there could not possibly be a future to this.

"No let me," you said, catching her wrist and leaning in to pick the breadcrumb from her very soft light pink mouth.

"Now that we are both quite clean?" you left the question hanging.

She lowered her eyes.

You kissed her.

.....

It was the first time she'd been kissed this way, Nina confessed. It was a Vietnamese kiss, the merest brushing of your lips against hers, followed by a deep drawn in breath against the side of her nose, as if you were absorbing her essence. It was another manifestation of your exotic otherness, what she'd been intrigued by all fortnight.

She surrendered.

Heftier than her, you were still slighter than anyone she'd known before. Your hairless bronzed skin smelling faintly of incense and the sea... your arms and legs, strong but lithe, what taut flesh there was barely covering your sharp bones... were all exciting and new for her. She was bewitched by how you carefully cupped your hands on her jaw line and ran your lightly stubbled chin deliberately along her collarbone. When it came time, she received you like an emissary from a strange land; letting your otherness imprint itself on her in the same way the ivory circlet you'd fastened on your thigh pressed into hers.

.....

Her body was a new experience for you too. With her milk-fed bones and hard solid flesh around her hips and across her shoulders, she felt entirely different from the bird-boned soft-fleshed Vietnamese women you'd been with before. Nor was she large and unfinished like Julia Anderson, that ample sandpapery American you slept with on and off during the war. Silk-skinned yet strong, with no excess fat, she was how you had always dreamed a fusion of East and West should be.

You worried she might have regrets no matter how much she'd liked it this first time together. There was so much she didn't know about you... You felt her muscles tighten and turned your face to hers. "What is it?" you asked.

She traced a finger up the length of your bent leg to your thigh where your blood-mother's circlet was tied flat with a leather thong.

"One of my mother's wedding bangles," you said, unguarded just then and forgetful of your training. "It's the remaining one of a pair my father gave her, his apology for pawning away her wedding jewelry during the Japanese occupation. By rights, it should have been buried with her when she died, but it was mislaid and they only found it later."

"Pawning her wedding jewelry? Why?"

You wrapped your hand around her finger, guided it around the circlet once more, then up your inner thigh to close both your hands around your penis, which was stirring again. "Because my father was one of those patriotic people who..." you began to reply, not wishing to hide anything from this girl who had so impetuously opened herself to you.

She leaned into your shoulder, waiting.

You turned your head away. It was just the one harmless story. But once you started where did you stop? You were born to a Viet Cong swamp fighter. Like Ai Nguyet, Nina came from a family of French educated anti-Communist mandarins. It was better not to tell, you decided. You brushed your lips against hers, buried your nose in her cheek, and kissed her again... a Vietnamese kiss.

Nina and you fell into bed and in love deluded by both your illusions. Nina expected you to lead her home to her lost motherland. You were ecstatic you had finally arrived in your tutor's America. Illusions can carry you a long way. It's possible to build a whole life on illusions. It's a danger the Buddhists warn against. But America, *Mỹ* the beautiful country, cast such a spell you couldn't resist. Not the country, not Marie-Antoine Nguyen Nguyet Nga, the Vietnamese daughter born on her beautiful shores.

.....

And now, both of you have an American-born son. You squint down from where you are towards the pool where your son is. Tran-Nguyen Tam Tri, that's his name—Tran-Nguyen, Nina's and your family names combined; Tam Tri, his personal name, meaning Heart and Mind—your offering to the Commander to atone for the ancestral sacrifices this son of yours can never make.

Your son is a handsome child, so big for his age no one in Vietnam would think he's just five. A quiet boy with an impassive face, he hadn't started speaking till he was three and even now only manages to do so with the mechanical precision of a highly developed robot. That's because, it turns out from some tests Nina's taken him to, he's extraordinarily intelligent. A genius, in fact.

"Like your name," Nina had said, pleased.

You hadn't corrected your wife about the meaning of your name, how it wasn't part of the homonym *'thông minh'* for 'intelligence' like most people assumed, but something else. "Probably much smarter," you'd simply commented.

But smart isn't normal, you know. And, despite Nina's test results, your son is a worry. You've never encountered a child as opaque as he is. You'd named him 'Heart' and 'Mind' but it seems he has no emotions at all. As for the mind that's so fine, it's more often than not hidden under a thick blanket of silence.

You examine him, squatting by a mesquite bush absorbed by the staring eyes of a toad. Your son, the mystery, says he can hear animals think. You wonder now what he's saying to the toad and what replies he's imagining. You wonder when you and he might have as meaningful a conversation. When if ever you'll be able to talk together as you and your two fathers had? You do not hope for the back and forth repartee your tutor and you shared.

"Thong!" you hear Nina's high exclamation from the house. It's followed by the lower murmurs of Loc, his wife Huong and their children—"What a big den."... "Wow, a walk-in pantry"... "Auntie, is there a Jacuzzi?" This is the first Mid-Autumn festival in your new home. Already Nina will be feeling besieged, your relatives' unspoken envy making her feel guilty. She needs you.

You go down to the garden.

"Mommy says it's time to go up. Say goodbye to your friend now," you tell Tri.

"It is rude to interrupt a conversation. If you must, look for a pause and then say excuse me," he replies, as if reading from a book on etiquette. His body is firmly turned away from you, completely focused on the toad.

You know you ought not to hurry him. You know you must explain the situation slowly and allow him time to adjust. Otherwise, he retreats into one of those wooden silences, from which he won't emerge for two or three days. But it's just a toad, you reason to yourself. You bend over, flick your fingers in front of its bulging eyes and hiss at it.

It takes the hint and hops away.

"Come on, everyone's waiting for us," you say, reaching out to take your son's hand.

He lowers his body onto the ground, crosses his legs and folds his head over his knees. Then he covers his head with his two arms and shuts you out.

"Come on, please Tri..."

There is no response.

You've also learnt you mustn't shout at your son when he withdraws into himself as he just has. But you can't help it.

"Tri! Up! Now!" you shout.

You watch helplessly as he begins to rock himself against the mesquite bush, scarring his face and arms on the twiggy branches. You bend down to untangle his limbs so you can pick him up and carry him to the house, but he rolls himself into a tighter ball and begins to hoot, low and mournful, like an owl.

Shit! At times like this, only Nina can handle him. You sigh, leave him by the bush and go up to the house to get her.

She's in the kitchen with your sister-in-law Huong and the other women, setting out moon cakes and tea on the tiled counter.

"I'm sorry, but I triggered our son," you whisper to her.

She gives you an accusatory look but doesn't say anything.

You watch as she excuses herself, calls to Loc's older daughter Kim and slips out the kitchen door with the girl.

.....

You go into the den where Loc, your brother, and Binh are sitting with some other men from the old Saigon neighborhood. A music video is playing on your new big screen TV—a collection of pre '75 singers crooning plaintively against a backdrop of fake coconut palms and a plastic moon. Some of the men are singing along. The room is smoked filled, the air laden with the sweet smell of light beer, just like an old Saigon working man's bar.

You settle on the floor next to the sofa, pretending nothing has happened down by the swimming pool.

"Sixth Brother," you greet Loc.

"Youngest," he nods back.

He turns to look out your picture window at the white pine, your namesake, standing like a sentinel over the house. It's straight and still now the Santa Ana winds have stopped blowing and moisture's seeping into the bush again.

"Good thing those winds stopped. They're such a fire hazard, the way they suck the water out of the air," he observes, still uncomfortable about your living up this canyon miles away from the Vietnamese community and surrounded by acres of inflammable bush.

"Well, I've been careful to hose down the roof every night. And I even stopped smoking. Just in case..." you assure him. "Don't worry, I know enough not to have all my litigious neighbors suing the shit out of me just because of a cigarette."

"You're not rich enough for them to bother," Binh points out. "Your house is hocked up to your ears, from all accounts."

"You're probably right," you allow. It's rude of him to say it so bluntly but that's how he is. And you owe him. You let it go. "Yup. Nothing for them to get their hands on. Tragic, isn't it?"

Binh won't let up though. "That's not the most tragic part. The tragic part is you giving up cigarettes in the mistaken belief you are rich enough... Ask me to give up my wife, yes; my gambling even. But my cigarettes?" He gives the cigarette he's smoking a slow wet kiss along its length. "No way."

The others laugh. Unlike you, they don't know why Binh changes wives like shirts, and spends every spare cent left over from alimony on Las Vegas weekends. They just think he's a free spirit. The fact he's already been six years in America and is still renting, his only asset a silver Cadillac Seville which doubles as a bedroom when his funds run low, seems to them wild and wonderful. Saddled with wives, children and mortgages, it's a freedom they can only fantazise about.

"What about back in '76?" one of the other men asks.

"Even then I managed. Black markets everywhere and me, a man with an unlimited store of hypodermic needles from that hospital laboratory I worked at. I was raking it in. Do you have any idea how much just one needle was worth then?" Binh arches an eyebrow.

"Then why'd you leave? Why weren't a fortune in needles and all the Soviet fags in the world enough to keep you there?" someone teases.

"I've told you already. I came for chicken dinners, beautiful American chicken dinners."

"Chicken dinners?" Loc asks with a grin, passing another round of beer and cigarettes to prepare for yet another retelling of Binh's story.

Binh obliges. "They transferred a US trained chemist to us. To be re-educated, they said. Well, he just went on and on about how you could buy a whole chicken in the US, a whole damn chicken, for an hour's wages. Just on and on, every damn day..." He looks around, his smile gone. "You remember the rations they doled out then? Three kilos of rice a month and swamp leaves, not even full measure... What was there to stay behind for?" He stops for a second to collect himself and give his cigarette another long lengthwise sniff. "Besides, Marlboros taste better than that Soviet rubbish."

"You're right," you say. "But Marlboros tasted better then. Now they don't taste good enough to burn up a house for. Too much of anything and you don't value it." You turn a morose eye on your cigarette, take a last drag on it, and then flick the butt into the ashtray.

Loc gives you a poke. "Youngest, you're maudlin again. Don't spoil your own party. Get out and get some fresh air," he says into your ear.

Of late there've been more of these exchanges between you and Loc. Is it because you're getting soft or is he just getting more impatient with your bouts of reflection?

You don't know and you don't care, you tell yourself. "Fine," you grunt and stand up.

You leave him to play host and wander back to the kitchen table laden with food. You pour yourself a cup of tea. Picking up a piece of cake you continue out and perch yourself back on the linkway between the garage and the kitchen. Down by the pool you see that Nina and Kim have succeeded in calming Tri and are now walking with him around the garden. Soon he'll be well enough for them to take up to the house, and for Kim, his regular babysitter, to tuck into bed. All will be well, more or less, you breathe with relief.

You bite into the *bánh*. How you love the feel of the thin crispy skin in your mouth, the nutty richness of the filling, the candied melon and sesame oil aftertaste. Nibbling the cake alone this way reminds you of 1979—eating in hiding so you didn't have to share, swallowing slowly to keep the flavors in your throat, to make believe you'd eaten more.

Not necessary now, here, you think. There's so much food in America, too much. As for those left behind over there, you can't do more for them than what you're doing already, you say to yourself as you gulp down your tea, letting its bitterness wash away the grease.

.....

"Too much fat," you tell Nina later, stroking her pale muscled thigh with your index finger.

Everyone has been sent home. Both of you have gone to look in on Tri sleeping quietly in his pale blue bedroom. The crisis is over. It's your time.

"Fat! What Fat?" she's indignant. She crosses her feet, trapping your hand between her legs. "That's all iron, guy," she says.

"No, not there. There was too much fat in the moon cakes. In here." You pat your stomach with your free hand.

"Not tonight darling, my belly aches," she says, mimicking your Vietnamese accented English. She pulls your hand onto her stomach, still hard and flat despite nine months carrying the enormous Tri. "Feel. There's no food in here yet. I'm hungry," she tells you.

Her directness and appetite still shock you. You love it, had loved it from that very first time in New York six years, a lifetime, ago.

You set aside your uneasiness about Tri. "So you're hungry?" you ask as you pull yourself up over her.

.....

You didn't expect your life in America to be easier when you married Nina. But you hadn't anticipated how much harder your marriage made things. Her questions, so charming you once thought, now just seem silly at best and dangerous at worst. For example, this particular night, when you've just come home exhausted from a sales trip to Boeing in Seattle and she's insisting on being inquisitive...

Again, the catalyst is a whisper-thin blue air letter from Can Tho, the Delta city your parents and Third Sister's family moved to after Bac Lieu. Filled with news from your family, it also contains a deceptively worded reminder from your Third Brother-in-Law Ba Roi about your reporting obligations. But Nina isn't able to understand the implied threats in Third Brother-in-Law's enquiries about your health. For her the letter simply triggers an itch to know more about Vietnam and your family.

"I can't believe Third Sister wasn't upset," she says, plopping herself, still damp from her shower, onto your super large bed with its two big mattresses side by side.

"Real Vietnamese women born and raised in Vietnam don't fuss," you reply.

"There must've been a scene," she curls into your side and teases your left earlobe with her little finger, not willing to let go.

You sigh. What you need is sleep, not Nina setting off on an archaeological dig about the war and its effect on your family. But Nina's been fascinated by how Third's heart was won and how he'd gone off to war with your blood-father since she first heard the story. From the set of her mouth you know you won't get to sleep until you slake at least a little of her thirst. She isn't your lost Hue princess Ai Nguyet, but sometimes you can see shades of that same Hue stubbornness...

You sit up against your pillows and light a cigarette. "There wasn't a scene. He was just around the house less and less, then staying out nights. One month's end, it was my Dad and me collecting the rents. And that was that," you say.

You exhale. You're tired. Both of you are... Nina working too hard on her Ph.D., you trying to be everything you need to be at work, at home, and at the rest of it. There's the fallout from Tri too, rushed too early in the morning to day care, ferried home too late and unpredictably prone to breakdowns. But how else can you live here in America? Nina's Papa and Maman, socialites in Virginia's Vietnamese circuit, can't be expected to babysit. Aside from Loc, you have no other family in America, none of the support structures you grew up with. It wasn't something you'd been briefed on when they let you come.

You don't have the energy to let your wife dig further. "The main thing is whether we're going to send them all the three hundred bucks they asked for in that letter, or do we get Loc to send half?" you ask.

She won't be distracted though. "But what did they tell the kids when he left?"

A memory of your blood-father comes to you. His eyes had been lowered under his hairy caterpillar eyebrows. He was saying so softly you almost didn't hear, "Sometimes it's better to hide the truth." And so it is, you've come to learn... You stub out your cigarette and switch off the light. You say, "Whatever they tell kids, I guess."

You roll across the bed and begin to smooth the comforter covering Nina's flat tummy in slow circles. "Sweetheart, *cưng*, it's just too long ago," you murmur into her hair. "Third heard this war cry, he followed it. She was his wife, she must've been upset. But she coped. Life went on. We moved to Can Tho. I went to Saigon to study at Loc's high school. I got on with the things that mattered like work and success. Okay?"

You continue stroking the comforter down the length of her thighs and up towards her shoulders and arms. "Okay?" You peer at her face. Even in the dark you can see she's closed her eyes and her mouth's set in a stubborn line. But she has the most mobile mouth in the world. She's persuadable. It's a question of how.

You take her face in both your hands and kiss her on the lips. She lifts up her right arm to circle your head. Her forearm crosses and tightens against the back of your neck, drawing your face to hers. Your mouths meet.

She bites into your lower lip, a vicious little nip. "Goodnight," she murmurs without opening her eyes, then releases you and turns away.

She can be such an unpredictable cow.

.....

She's a cow about housework too... Predictably so, you sigh to yourself.

You've submitted your body to the Friday night red-eye from the East Coast so you can be home on Saturday morning for your family, and again your welcome is a half-opened and ketchup-stained pizza box by the kitchen door, filled with crusts and soggy fries. As usual, Nina and Tri have gone to bed after their Friday night video marathon, leaving everything for you to clear up.

You drop your suitcase onto the kitchen floor with a thump, unlock it and take all the dirty clothes to the laundry room. Let Nina deal with that, you decide, as you drop the pile onto the tiles before plodding back into the den.

Your big clean up begins with the recalcitrant comforters that always manage to find their way down to the den carpet. Gathering them up, you take them to the sky bridge to whack clean. "Degeneration into chaos is what happens to a house with no head," you can imagine your father the Chief Clerk warning. Rotating heads, in the case of your house, you think peevishly as you beat bits of leftover popcorn out into the mesquite bushes at your feet.

You fling the comforters over the railings to air. Then you go back for the cushions and thwack the life and potato chip dust out of them with an old tennis racquet. Leaving the properly disciplined squares of fluff out to sun, you stamp back to the kitchen door and stuff the pizza box into the garbage can. You thank fate for the dry California weather. In Vietnam, the boxes would have been filled with roaches. But in Vietnam, you huff to yourself, the man of the house would never have missed all the fun and been left to restore order.

How, you wonder, are you going to instill process and order into the house when you're only here on weekends? You pick up the video tapes Tri's left out and slot them back into their cases. Not a single Vietnamese tape in the lot, even though there are now at least ten Little Saigon video-shops with dubbed pirates just half an hour's drive away. Nina allows Tri to pick what he likes, and what he likes is Star Trek, un-dubbed.

You don't regret your travelling job. But in your absence, Tri's growing up into a little baguette, golden only on the outside. Even your simple resolution to speak Vietnamese to him has fallen by the wayside. Your trips are just too packed with back to back product demonstrations and meetings for you to call before bedtime. Travelling cross country to D.C. with stops at the space centers in Houston or Florida, you often leave on Sunday evenings and hardly ever manage to make it home Friday nights. You have no time to talk to your son in English, let alone in Vietnamese.

By the time you're done with cleaning though, you find you've reconciled yourself to the situation.

Sitting down to a cup of coffee, you're almost happy to discover you still have an hour free of wife and son to tidy up the loose ends from the trip—to make expense claims, write trip notes and even finish a report to Ba Roi.

When Nina and Tri come downstairs to give you their sleepy welcome kisses, you're open and loving. You're ready to go back to playing the American husband and father again.

04

The jungles within

IN VIETNAM YOU HAD BEEN an engineer, an interpreter, more... In America you take on a new identity—boat person, new migrant, the man at the bottom of the heap. But you're still the chameleon your life in Vietnam taught you to be. You change yourself to suit the environment, you claw your way into a job with possibilities, you climb the career ladder unnoticed. You become Thong (call me 'Tom') V. Tran, M.Sc. Aerospace Engineering, first an associate engineer testing aerospace fasteners, then a research and development team leader, and finally a technical sales specialist with visiting rights to defense contractors across the country. Just to make sure you're not dreaming about how far you've come, you pinch yourself sometimes.

.....

In 1962, your second year of high school, you were introduced to American machines. The ancient French milling and cutting equipment in the school workshops was suddenly replaced by bright new ones from Chicago. Accompanying the machinery

*were American advisors, huge men with enormous biceps,
pregnant bellies and a wondrous ability to lift the heavy levers
and press down the big pedals of the new apparatus as if they
were dancing. They had the grace of the elephants the Chief
Clerk once took you to see at the circus. It was strength and
agility neither you Vietnamese students nor your teachers
could manage, not even the tallest and strongest among you.*

*"You must try. You'll be working for the Americans on
American machines from now on. You need to get used to it,"
your teachers said.*

*You had refused to get used to it then because you didn't
see why you had to.*

*"Better the old French machines than these clunkers. At
least they were our size," you'd said to Binh.*

*You remember feeling the same about your new foreign
language at school, English. You'd changed from French on
the advice of your Oldest Brother-in-Law, the Police Chief
who dictated yours and Loc's lives in Saigon.*

*"Because the Americans are coming," he had said, like
everyone else.*

*But English was a language filled with grammatical
exceptions you couldn't get your head around. You were
failing a subject for the first time in your life and expecting to
continue failing. It was a prospect that left a hollow panicked
feeling in your gut.*

*At the time, you had not met Mr Trung, the tutor you
were to call Chú Hai or Young Uncle. You had not become
fascinated by the Mỹ. No matter what everyone was saying
about the Americans, what echoed in your head was your
blood-father's long ago prediction that your country would
eventually be taken over by them. All the aid being sent was*

simply so everyone could be trained to be their slaves. Despite their money, what you wished was for them to go home.

But President Diem invited more and more of them to come, advisors who were strangely always at odds with him and seemed determined to undermine his dignity. There was the matter of the monks immolating themselves to protest his harassment of their temples, and the Americans' order to disband the militia forces implicated in the harassing. There was the even more shaming instruction to the President to remove his brother, Counsellor Nhu, from all involvement in government affairs.

"A President shouldn't have to kowtow to foreigners," you grumbled to Loc. You remember Loc's answer. "If you're eating their rice, you need to listen to them."

He'd just given up plans for university to marry Huong, who was pregnant. To make ends meet he'd joined one of the President's militia groups and was hoping to transfer into an American sponsored unit for the higher pay. He couldn't afford to be negative about the Americans.

You hadn't agreed with Loc then. "There's such a thing as a President's dignity," you'd retorted. And when they sent in the CIA and created that coup that killed the President and his brother, the Counsellor Nhu, you'd shouted at your brother, "That's surely treachery!"

.....

Now, you're the one eating their rice, the one who can't afford to be negative about Americans. How the world turns. Not that you are negative anymore. Now, you've just stopped caring. You're just glad you're not disappointing Ba Roi, your doctrinaire Third-Brother-in-Law.

You'd feared in the beginning you would have nothing but inconsequential public information to send Ba Roi. But within five years, you'd learnt enough to provide insightful analyses on developments in US defense technology. Now, following your promotion to technical sales specialist, you've been filling your letters to him with real intelligence gleaned from the many defense companies you visit. You're no longer fretting about the family in Vietnam held to ransom to guarantee your performance in America. Your only worry now is discovery... should one of the coded letters you post randomly across the country get intercepted; should Nina find out who you really are and what you've been up to.

.....

Nina spreads the photographs out once again on the big study table she shares with Tri, shifting them so the sunlight from the windows can illuminate them directly. They stare back at her mute, a mystery she can't unlock. They're her subject, men in black captured for posterity onto black and white Xeroxes. Just images—bony pyjama'd bodies squatting together to keep warm, glassy eyes starring from gaunt grey faces—they can't talk. They're the VC, the enemy. But they've lost their malignancy in the process of being transferred onto paper. What Nina's Vietnamese-American eyes see are just sickly men with rickety bones and sun-starved skin.

"So un-dangerous," she muses to you as she peers into their faces. "It's hard to believe they out-strategized and out-lasted people like my Papa and uncles."

You look up from the floor, interrupting your Scrabble game with Tri. "Too well fed and overeducated, that's your relatives. They spent too long in those French Lycees and forgot their roots. That's why they lost."

"But look at these guys. They're skeletons." Nina picks up a photo for you to look at. "Think. Them against US guns and machinery. Ex-ante, the odds would have been zero to infinity, their victory."

"Infinity? What's infinity?" Tri, who's discovered higher order numbers on his eighth birthday, looks up and asks.

"A number that has no end," you tell him.

"Like a thousand hundred billion million millions..." he starts to count.

"It's your turn darling, play your word," Nina says, forestalling hours of numbers. Then she turns and beams at you, her question still stubbornly shining through her glasses.

It comes back to you, how you made your decision the summer after the *Tết* offensive.

"Let me help," you'd said on impulse to your tutor, Chú Hai.

Because you were sick of the war that had been a constant backdrop to your life for nearly twenty years. Because you'd wanted peace and silent nights filled only with Ai Nguyet's music, whole evenings to stroll the city's boulevards with her, undisturbed by the catcalls of the American GIs and untroubled by worries about getting home before the onset of curfew. Because you wanted a future where you wouldn't have to fret about Nixon's new Vietnamization initiatives, or fear the draft, or anticipate your own death in some skirmish, somewhere, sometime, inevitably. For the war to end, the Americans would have to go, you'd reasoned then. And if you helped get rid of them sooner, all the better, you'd thought simplistically.

Sometimes, all that's needed is a moment and a few words. After that, you're caught and it's too late, you want to tell your wife. But you don't.

"Desperation. When you have nothing, there's nothing to lose, so you can do wild things," you suggest instead.

"But what about my other uncles, the ones my grandfather disowned? They'd so much to lose. Still, they threw everything away to join the other side. And then, they won! They weren't so different from my uncles and Papa on the southern side. What's the explanation?"

Academics, you scoff to yourself. It isn't surprising Nina and her tutors have so much trouble finalizing the details of her dissertation proposal on the psychology of winning guerrilla wars. One or other among them is always coming up with a new way to look at the problem.

"The VC stole your uncles' hearts. First the heart then the head then victory, that's what they believed. That's what happened," you tell your wife.

She rolls her eyes and shakes her head. "You sound like a communist," she says.

"That's unfair," you reply under your breath. She knows how deeply you believe this, you who profess to believe in nothing. It's the reason for Tri's name.

Nina doesn't notice she's hurt your feelings. "They're not talking and everything they ever said is locked away in some secret archive in D.C. There's no data to test a hypothesis about hearts and minds and you've got to show you can crunch numbers for a Ph.D. in psychology nowadays. I'm stuck," she says, stuffing the Xeroxes back into her folder.

She gets up, goes to her big bookcase at the end of the room and begins to re-arrange the bulging files she's stacked in piles there.

You understand why Nina's picked this topic and no other, why she so needs to unravel the mystery hidden behind the VC's glassy eyes. She's a daughter and wife of the war, yet removed from any real experience of it. How can she know who she is if she doesn't know how she's come about, who she's a daughter and wife to?

But it's still too painful a subject for you and her parents, her professors, the others who've lived through the war, to address. Contrary to Nina's assumptions, the war hasn't ended. It's just moved to a different arena. To Washington D.C. where Nina's father and uncles are still trying to fan the Republican Party's anti-communist ardor with polite letters and subtle lobbying. To Little Saigon, where old soldiers like Binh continue to hold memorial meetings dressed up in their carefully preserved uniforms. To your house, where you so resolutely try to maintain neutrality...

It isn't about data. It's simply that no one can bear to confront the consequences of their choices, how they all came to be losers, even when it appeared that they'd won.

"You'll figure," you try to sound supportive.

You don't volunteer that Loc has a huge store of VC capitulation stories archived in his head. It would not be kind to set Nina on Loc and have him relive his past life as a South Vietnamese government interrogator just so she can put 'Ph.D.' after her name. Indeed, it would not be kind to anyone to force them to consider the whys and wherefores of the war's outcome. It continues to rankle even more than ten years after. You know.

.....

But the Tiger won't stop stalking.

"Did you kill anyone?" Tri asks.

It's a question you meant to ask your blood-father and then forgot in the mayhem after President Diem was deposed, while order was being brutally re-imposed on Saigon. Now your impassive too intelligent son is asking you.

It's one of your rare weekday nights at home. You and Tri are working on a family biography, an extra credit project he needs to qualify for gifted kids' summer camp. You've been volunteered by Nina as the subject, another of her attempts to get you and Tri on the same page.

"Nope, never killed anyone. Not even a chicken," you say with a deadpan face.

"Be serious," Nina chides from the sofa, where she's reading a journal. "Your blood-father was a rooster master, a famous one apparently. You must have killed a chicken or two, if only to put them out of their misery after a fight."

Loc had told her that tid-bit about your blood-father, another fact about the cruelties of old Vietnam your wife can't get over.

You think about the chickens you've handled.

"I am being serious," you say, pasting a grin on your face. "Do you know how many chickens were killed to feed the US army during the war? Well, not one of them died at my hands."

"Be serious Daddy..." Tri repeats, his voice imitating Nina's tone for tone.

"Oh alright. What do you want to know then?" you ask him as calmly as if you're just talking about the weather.

"What did you do in the army during the war? What were your assignments? Where did you fight? Whom did you fight?

What battles did you win? What battles did you lose?" Tri reads out his list of questions mechanically.

You give him the edited story, the one you've been telling with eyes straight and heartbeat steady since you were sixteen—the one about studying at the technical high-school in Saigon, being introduced to Mr Trung and becoming an English wiz, choosing to study engineering to make your father and blood-father happy, joining the Army Reserve after the 1968 Tết offensive, getting the plum job in the engineering company because you came first in your university exams, going on assignment with your friend Binh to secure territory in Ban Me Thuot after the signing of the Paris Accords, going back to be an engineering plant manager in Nha Trang until the war's end.

Tri shakes his head as he considers your colorless history. "You're not saying it right," he pronounces.

"Of course I am," you reply.

"No, you're being inconsistent, Daddy," he insists.

Nina tries to come to the rescue. "Tri dear, it's impolite to say that to Daddy when he's telling you everything exactly like he did it. Sometimes, the data is just the way it is. Even if it's boring, you have to work with what you have."

"What Daddy's saying and what he's feeling don't match. He's talking all slow but his heart's jumping like a rabbit. Words and feelings should match. Otherwise, the meaning gets mixed up," Tri insists, making little beeping sounds like a computer going wrong to demonstrate what he means.

You look at Nina in desperation. In your experience, nine year old sons should not behave this way.

"Why don't you go downstairs and make us a cup of tea," she says to you. Then, she turns to Tri. "Maybe you should just send Daddy a letter and ask him to write down all the answers.

That way you don't have to compare what he's saying with whatever signals you say he's sending out. You can just read what he writes and use that data for your report."

You leave her to sort it out. You go down to the kitchen, moor yourself to the bar stool by the serving counter and look out the picture window into the darkness of the canyon. Your reflection stares back at you. Distorted by the shadows of the pine tree outside it looks as desperate and frightened as the sixteen year old you'd been more than half a life-time ago.

.....

You had been running down Ham Nghi Boulevard and towards the Central Market, dodging a gang from the Catholic Boys' Academy, during yet another episode of the internecine battles between your working class school and their elite one.

You could not escape. Alone and on foot, you were easy prey. "Catch the fucker!"... "Beat the balls out of him!"... "Working class prick!"... They laughed as they bore down on you with their expensive Italian and French motorcycles.

They caught up just as you were stepping into the traffic circle in front of the market. Your foot snagged. You stumbled. You looked up to find yourself surrounded by the front wheels of four motorbikes. Four sweat-shined faces, resting on muscular arms folded across the handle bars, stared down at you.

"Comrade Worker, aren't you going to get up and shake our hands?" the smoothest fairest face said.

You brushed off your trouser leg and pulled yourself up slowly, trying to buy time.

They began to dismount.

It was your chance.

When they were half astraddle and unbalanced, you straightened up and dashed through a gap in the circle of motorcycles and out into the traffic, weaving and twisting your way through the honking vehicles towards the market's great gate. Something on your arm was throbbing. A foot felt curiously numb. But you couldn't worry about what those signals from your body meant. You simply had to get into the protective crush of people unbundling their crates and baskets in front of the South Gate.

He was at the South Gate below the bust of the girl martyr killed there the previous year. He'd been amusing himself, letting his still keen eyes wander over the openness of the square, trying to see over the heads of the motorcyclists and bike riders into Avenue Calmette. After the tree-obstructed sight lines of the jungle he had felt good being able to see so far.

He'd just put down the two bamboo cages with his newly acquired and carefully hooded fighting roosters and squatted onto his haunches. Curling his toes into his leather sandals, he'd pressed his feet into the hard concrete pavement below to feel the city sidewalk. And he'd been breathing in the city air, savoring the smoke and sweat, the rot of old vegetables and the dried blood from the butchers.

The traffic had entranced him, the way the two flows adjusted to each other in a fluid give and take. He'd been in a trance almost, until a break in the flow brought him back to full attention. He'd seen the traffic falter, seen the motorcycles slow down and after that one then two then three cyclos veering out from their paths. Then, he'd seen you...

Well, not you. After eight years, he hadn't recognized you. He'd seen a stripling, tall for his age but not fully grown, arms still too long for his body, head not yet caught up with sprouting limbs. You were limping, he saw. And being tracked by a larger boy behind you, another to your right and two more making their way to the island at the centre of the square. You were afraid, he sensed that immediately.

It hadn't taken him any time to decide. A frightened teenager... an untried rooster... an impressionable heart... He'd done it almost without thinking. He stood, picked up the two cages and stepped onto the roadway, dodging the traffic to make his way towards you. When he was about a meter away, just in front of a cyclo laden with caged pigeons, he'd stopped and put down one of the rooster cages, then lifted the door latch and unhooded the bird inside. The rooster had strutted out, its head jerking aggressively, its wings flapping, a sacrifice.

Creating that ruckus hadn't been hard at all, he told you later, his eyes lowered modestly.

You remember what happened next. The cyclo driver pulled on his brake. His cargo of pigeon cages spilled onto the roadway. Suddenly the street was full of fluttering panicked birds flying into the faces of oncoming motorcyclists, bicyclists and pedestrians. A motorcycle collided into another. A pedestrian walked into a bicycle. The large boy who'd been tracking you knocked himself against the side door of a bright new Lincoln Continental. And then he was there, grabbing you by the upper arm, steering you onto Ham Nghi and backing you into a doorway.

You were about to thank him but had barely sputtered "Uncle" when he pushed you down roughly and set an empty rooster cage in front of you. "Squat behind me," he ordered, before placing an occupied cage on top of the first one and taking up a watcher's position in front of you.

Safe now, you took stock. Your throbbing elbow, you realized, was twisted. You'd lost a shoe. You peered out at the road, wondering if it was still somewhere on the street and retrievable. But your view was blocked by your rescuer's cotton-clothed buttocks. You looked up and saw his broad large boned back, then his shock of badly cropped white hair. He stood with an unconcerned air, his head turning here and there as people and traffic passed in front of him, playing to perfection the part of a visiting farmer who'd stopped to smoke and gawk at the city.

When his cigarette was almost finished, he turned around. "Looks like it's safe for you to go your way, young one," he said, giving you his familiar shy yet oddly welcoming smile, his eyes bright under bushy white eyebrows as thick as caterpillars.

How could he have known ahead, the Commander, that the impressionable young man he'd saved would be you? That it would be your long eyes that would widen in recognition? That it would be your untried heart that would fill with a mixture of disbelief and gladness? That you would whisper without any reservations this time, "Blood-father... It's me."

That's the story about the first chicken sacrificed to win your heart.

.....

There was the second, at the villa where Chú Hai gave you English lessons, or conversations, as he preferred to call them.

It was your blood-father who'd introduced you to your tutor after hearing about your troubles with English.

You were both drinking coffee at the Central Market, It was your second meeting after the Martyr's Square incident.

"English is the most important thing now," he'd said, like all the other adults in your family. "All the advanced technology books will be in English. And your job after you graduate will need English. The Army, the new companies being set up, they'll all be run or sponsored by Americans for the next few years."

"I don't want to be sponsored by Americans. I don't like them. They're mất dạy, crass and boorish," you couldn't help snapping back.

He had smiled questioningly, inviting confidences.

The image of Binh's sister hanging onto her GI boyfriend with her butt cheeks swinging in tight American jeans came to mind. It was not a subject to discuss with a parent, how the sluttishness the Americans encouraged among your countrywomen and their own sexuality, displayed so crudely and openly at the bars on Tu Do Street, disturbed and unsettled you. "They just shouldn't be here, they spoil everything," you said, hoping he'd let it be.

He did. He started talking about an English tutor instead.

"A fighter like you?" you asked. You were wary, your responsibilities to the Chief Clerk and your mother and your promise not to involve yourself in the escalating war weighing on you.

Your blood-father shook his head. "Actually, he's on the other side. I worked for his father just before the Japanese war. He did join us in the swamps for a while, the year before you were born. But he changed his mind after a few months. His father was sick in the city, he told us. It was probably an excuse since he joined the Diem regime as a customs officer shortly after. Then he somehow got a scholarship to study journalism in America. Now he's back working for the Americans. He has a real affinity for them. He's the best English teacher you'll find in this city."

You pursed your lips. Not a swamp fighter but even dodgier, an America lover.

"You don't have to like or trust everyone you know. You can just take advantage of their talents," your blood-father said.

True enough. But to sacrifice your precious free time for lessons with an American stooge.

"What about money?" you asked.

"Don't worry about it. He and I, we have a give and take relationship. He owes me a few favors right now."

You didn't enquire how two men from opposing sides could be exchanging favors. By this time, the war had drawn on long enough for you to know that was how things worked. Instead you began to tell the Commander that you would need to consult the Chief Clerk. But then, how would you see your blood-father again if your father objected? It was proving more challenging than you expected, trying to be a good son to both of them. You decided you were better off going along.

You were taken to meet Mr Trung, Chú Hai, at his offices in the servant's quarters of a villa in Saigon's expensive District Three. A laughing man who talked emphatically with his whole body, he was giving you lessons, you were told, because he was a rooster aficionado and an admirer of your blood-father. This in any case was the fiction the two of them wished to enact when you were presented along with your blood-father's gift, a pair of perfectly matched red and black bantams.

You'd thought simplistically then that the real reason for Chú Hai's willingness to teach you was because he was an American loyalist, someone wanting to win you over to the invading side. That was the only way you could explain the method behind the madness of his lessons, which involved you listening to songs, browsing magazines and reading aloud from the labels of the PX-bought American food he forced you to sample; every single activity accompanied by incessant commentary on his part. There was no stopping his chatter, just as there was no stopping the Americans taking over everything in the city. Like the Americans, he intended to seduce you with the sweet richness of American sounds and images, to envelop you in America's plenty till you swallowed it whole and ended up speaking the language like him, from the inside out.

You didn't want that. You wanted to remain resolutely, wholly, Vietnamese. You thought about seeking your blood-father's permission to stop the lessons. But your blood-father had disappeared after your visit to Chú Hai. His regular messenger, the woman who sold sticky rice outside your high-school, had informed you he was busy building a new cockfighting arena for a very important sponsor, the new Prime Minister. An undercover job, she'd implied. You would have to make things clear to Chú Hai yourself, you decided. In the American way he was so fond of.

You coughed.

"Excuse me Chú, I'm only seventeen. I don't have enough money to court girls, let alone American girls. I just need to learn how to speak and listen to English as a technician or an engineer, or if I can't avoid it, as a soldier. I don't need to be an American so I can speak English like you, from the inside out."

You must have hit on something deeply true for he looked intently at you, really looked, as if he was suddenly seeing something new. It was an expression you recalled seeing on his face before, but when exactly you couldn't be sure.

"I'm sorry," you said, hoping you hadn't crossed any non-negotiable limits.

"So you think I'm a người Mỹ, an American on the inside?" he finally asked you in Vietnamese.

It was impossible to know from his face if he was pleased or offended by your observation.

You played with your fingers and waited.

Chú Hai nodded sagely after a few quiet breaths. *"Yes, you're only seventeen. Too young to appreciate all these tips I've been giving you. Although, when I was seventeen, or was it twenty..."* He left the sentence hanging, as if suddenly assailed by an unpleasant memory. But the moment passed. He clapped his hands together decisively. *"Still, I predict that in a couple of years you will meet and even hanker after American girls and you will be sorry you asked me not to bother."*

You must have looked unconvinced.

"Experience is wasted on the young," he said, but didn't pursue the matter further.

He looked at you again, an assessing, weighing look, then closed his eyes. *"Alright, tell me what you want to talk about. Machines? Cars? Motorcycles? Weapons? Military strategy?"*

"Can I choose something else?" you asked, testing more boundaries now that you'd breached the first.

"Sure. Why not?"

"Flight, projectiles, rocket, space, all kinds of flying things..." you said. *"When I was a child I loved kites,"* you explained.

"Yes, I recall that, your loving kites. The yellow and red one, it was your first love, wasn't it?" he asked, leaning over, his bright eyes not quite teasing.

You nodded. How could he know? You must have told your blood-father, who must have mentioned it to him.

He smiled, happy he'd guessed correctly. "Okay then. Let me think about what you've said, and we'll do something different next week."

Things settled now, he was brisk. Getting up from his armchair, he escorted you to the back gate. "See you next week," he said in English, pressing a Hershey bar into your jacket pocket.

You felt his eyes watching until you reached the first turn in the alley. Once out of sight, you unwrapped the candy bar and bit through the peanutty crust to savor the rich caramel filling. Vietnamese candy did not taste like this, so buttery, so thickly sweet. You leaned your back against the alley wall and thought about the afternoon. It was extraordinary how Chú Hai hadn't taken offence, hadn't interrupted you, hadn't ticked you off. He'd simply taken in everything you said as if you were absolutely right. He was so different, so compellingly different, from any other adult you knew. You would come back next week, you decided. You simply had to.

Next week Chú Hai sacrificed the second chicken, although for what purpose you've never been able to determine.

You were making your last turn in the alley when he and a gentleman in a linen summer suit came out of the back gate, each carrying a rooster cage. You saw them take the bantams out, then prime them by repeatedly bringing their heads towards each other until they almost touched, before pulling back.

Unable to make contact, the frustrated roosters become increasingly aggressive and began to flap their wings and crow more and more frantically. When they were sufficiently agitated, the two men threw them free onto the ground. Instantly, the little birds, creatures you'd thought of as merely pert and pretty, reared up and dug their talons into each other.

From the same egg cluster, they were equally matched in weight and girth. But one had slightly stronger legs, jumped just a little higher and struck a mere hint harder. His spur sank into the other's shoulder, deep enough for him to get a second's grip and close his beak around the other's comb. His opponent shook him off, managing a peck at his eye. Claws clicked and clashed, then released. The bantams took to the air again, feet out, talons attacking. A pectoral muscle was struck and a wing fell slack. A bird was shoved down onto the concrete. Surprisingly, it was the slightly stronger one, the one whose eye was injured. Twisting his neck, he pushed his head here and there on the ground, trying to protect his good eye from the aggressive pecks rained on him.

"Time to stop?" you heard the well dressed man ask. Chú Hai waved the question away. "See it through to the end," he said.

The fallen rooster made a final effort to rise on his strong legs and lunge. But impaired by his weakened wing, his attack fell short. The other bird moved his head out and buried his beak into the already injured eye, pulling it out. Squawking in pain, the loser twisted away, trying to escape. But the winner's talons were already in his chest. The two men watched impassively as one brother jumped atop the other, pulled a whole eye loose and tore away at the wattle.

You turned your head into the wall and tried to calm your heaving gut. You heard the winning rooster flap its wings, then crow in victory. From the side of your eyes you saw the two men moving around, clearing up. A cage was opened and then clicked shut again.

"Your luck's not so good Albert. You'll need to be careful. Don't bet on superior air power," Chú Hai said to the other

man. "We'll see," the one called Albert answered before disappearing through the gate.

You felt Chú Hai's arm around your shoulder. "Come on in," he said. You nodded, your head down. As you followed him over the threshold, you couldn't help noticing the fine droplets of blood spattered on the front of his shirt.

Chú Hai could discuss anything and everything. It was you who couldn't confront him about the cock fight. And thankfully he'd treated it quite casually, an afternoon diversion between two adults you'd stumbled onto accidentally. Aside from mentioning that the other gentleman was his benefactor, the owner of the villa, Chú Hai had made no further reference to the incident. He'd simply moved on to discuss the topic set for the day, the US and Soviet space race.

But the fight was still vivid in your mind a few weeks later when you met your blood-father for beef noodles in the famous shop on Pasteur near the villa.

"It was unconscionable," you said to your blood-father. He brushed your complaints aside at first. "Maybe they needed to settle a dispute. It's been known to happen out in the field. Prisoners have been killed or spared on the outcome of a cricket fight."

You were a little shocked by this unwelcome insight into how cheaply your blood-father valued life. "I don't know about what happens out there in the field. But this cockfight to the end wasn't necessary. In fact it was simple bloodthirsty cruelty," you said.

For some reason, that comment triggered his defenses."You think so? Then why didn't you do anything about it? You complained about Chú Hai letting the fight go on but did you think how you might have stepped in to stop it? Sun Tze said, 'biết người biết ta, know others and know yourself'. Why don't you look at yourself before criticizing others?" You muttered, "Well, it wasn't my fight, was it? Weren't my roosters either." Your answer made him even more exasperated. "Not your fight? Then why have you come complaining?" He snorted in frustration. "You're my son but sometimes I think my friend the Chief Clerk has done more to shape you than any blood I gave," he said.

He tapped you hard on your forearm. "You can't continue this way, son, standing on the sidelines the way you did with the roosters. If you didn't want the cockfight to continue, you should have stepped in, even fought your tutor to make him stop. And I'm not just talking about roosters. I'm talking about our country and all the young soldiers being sent to war on behalf of the Americans. If we don't want our young men killed, if we don't want the Americans in the country, then we have to send them home. You have to make a decision and take a stand. It's not right to just eat beef noodles and complain about things being unconscionable."

"But..." You stopped short. He was right. The truth was you didn't want to fight, not for those roosters, nor for the hundreds of thousands who might be killed in the war. You remembered what the Chief Clerk had said about lives needing to be anchored in families, not ideas imported from one far off place or another. You thought about the Diamond Sutra the two of you recited in your childhood, that injunction against the taking of life. To go to war and be responsible personally for ending even one life, no, you couldn't see yourself doing it. Even to save a hundred thousand other ones.

"Surely there must be something we can do other than fight? Surely there must be another way to stop this killing besides

being part of it?" you said to your blood-father. "And what would that be?" he asked, uncharacteristically belligerent.

You chewed on a piece of beef gristle and pondered the question. To demonstrate like the students... to buy up public opinion like the propaganda officers... to set yourself on fire like the monks... To simply be a good son and friend and let the waves of your virtue ripple out into society, like Confucius taught and your father the Chief Clerk believed. The correct answer, you felt instinctively, would clarify everything confusing you about the current situation. But you didn't know what the answer might be and your blood-father wouldn't give it to you.

All he said was, "You think this through for yourself."

You were still thinking as you wheeled your bicycle down the alley towards yet another English lesson. So pre-occupied were you, you didn't ask the question you'd been dying to ask since the cock fight, the question that was buried so deep by subsequent events you forgot you'd even thought to ask it.

.....

Forgotten until this night... You get up from the kitchen stool, wearied by your recollections. You walk out to the living room and the bottom of the staircase. From where you are, you can still hear Tri beeping. The beeps are quieter now, the pauses between them more regularly spaced. But it's not time for you to show your face yet.

You return to the kitchen and settle yourself back on the stool. You examine your hands with their slim long fingers; scholar's hands, your mother had said once to your blood-father, hoping against hope you would not walk his soldier's path.

You hadn't. But, still you had not escaped the war.

.....

The back gate to the villa had been open, the door to Chú Hai's room ajar. All appeared in readiness for your first lesson after the Tết New Year holidays. But the room was in disarray. Chú Hai's armchair had been pushed back in a hurry. A cushion lay on the floor. The standing lamp, which he assiduously turned off whenever he left the room, was still alight with its lampshade askew. The five photographs of American fighter planes fanned out neatly on the coffee table, the promised subject of this session, were soaking in the dark liquid that had spilled from a toppled coffee filter. Chú Hai was nowhere to be seen.

He'd left in a hurry. Whatever the reason, you too should make yourself scarce. Turning off the reading light, you slipped out into the narrow back garden. Someone had kicked over the basket housing the remaining bantam and it was wandering about disconsolately making soft squawking cries. You stepped over it, noticing as you did, noises coming from the villa beyond the servant's quarters... Men shouting orders, doors being kicked open, tinkling glass, gunshots, a woman's screams.

The sound of boots and dragging sandals came towards you.

You retreated back into Chú Hai's room and between his two cabinets, thankful now for their American bulk. Outside, you heard feet scuffling, a body slammed against the wall, a woman whimpering, a man grunting, another man, then the woman begging them to stop. "What the hell do you think you're doing? And to her of all people!" someone shouted. "Get your useless asses back here," someone else called in a familiar voice.

There was more scuttling. Quiet. A woman's soft keening. And then from somewhere to the side of Chú Hai's room, kicks and a crack, like a table leg or bone being broken.

Through the gap between the cabinets you saw a stumbling man with his head covered by a sack pushed into the viewing aperture that was Chú Hai's open door. He was surrounded by three uniformed police corporals who shoved and kicked at him to move on and out of sight. Next to come in view was a tall officer swinging a club. Finally a short stout man made his way across the door frame, one soft white hand on his holster, the other gently stroking the beer belly hanging over the waistband of his policeman's trousers.

"Get him down there onto the floor," Oldest Brother-in-Law said, pointing with a familiar petulant gesture.

Had you seen right? You pressed your face into the gap between the cabinets to make sure. But the pot-bellied man had already moved out of sight. All you could see was the moss covered garden wall. Then a squawking bantam rooster appeared at the threshold. It strutted into the room and walked under the cabinet legs towards you. It was crowing, each crow rising in volume as it made its way to your hiding place until it seemed to you the crowing must not only fill the room but also spill out to the garden. The crowing was all you heard, drowning out the screaming of the man being beaten on the pathway just meters away, the final sharp whack as the club hit his head and then the muffled sound of a gunshot. Your one thought was to catch the bantam and put your hands over its head. To hold its beak shut. To twist its neck around. To keep it quiet, dead quiet.

The bird's neck cracked. Finally the bird was still, so still you could hear Oldest Brother-in-Law say, quite clearly, quite recognizably, "That's it then. Let's take him away."

Months later, after yet another coup, when the Army had re-arranged itself and everything was under control again, you would realize that the man whose brains were knocked out was Albert, the other man in Chú Hai's cockfight. Many years later, Chú Hai and you would finally get around to talking about it and he would confirm that the man was indeed the villa's owner, the government official who was also working for the other side.

Chú Hai would also say that in addition to knocking Albert's face in and tearing off his balls, the perpetrators had raped Albert's sister, a nun. Somewhere in between, you would have found the answer to your blood-father's question. You would not fight, but like the dead undercover agent Albert, you would do whatever one man could.

In the moment, though, all you apprehended was that no one was what they seemed—neither policemen nor villa owners. Not a seemingly benevolent Oldest Brother-in-Law. Perhaps not even an admired English tutor or a much looked up to sixth brother or a blood-father. And like them, you too had to create shades of yourself to survive.

You had witnessed a killing and you had taken a life. Whether you liked it or not, you had stained your hands. You had stepped off the sidelines and joined the war.

.....

You told no one about that afternoon in the villa. Not Chú Hai, not Loc the hero of your youth, not your blood-father. A thing not spoken of could be left behind, like you left the villa behind when you cycled off to the soccer pitch where Binh and Ly were. It could be forgotten, like you forgot when you tackled everyone so hard they wondered what had come over you.

Indeed, you would have buried away the whole incident except that Chú Hai contacted you again.

After a long but not too indecent interval following the villa incident, he'd sent a messenger to Oldest Sister's alley, a pretty straw-hatted young girl peddling guavas."Brother Thong, Chú Hai wishes to meet you," the young girl had mouthed as she weighed out three bright knobby green globes of fruit from the north-western outskirts of the city. Then she'd named the expensive city café Chú Hai frequented.

Chú Hai was on the sidewalk opposite the café, walking a large foreign looking dog when you arrived. "My boy!" he called out. He pulled the dog to a sitting position with a small twitch of his wrist and motioned for the doorman at the adjoining hotel to take your bike. After receiving your greeting, he indicated the strip of green in front of the National Assembly, across from where you were. "Come let's walk there. This great beast of mine needs to do his business."

You crossed the road with Chú Hai and the animal, Chú Hai talking non-stop all the while about the dog's horrifyingly leviathan excretions. You wondered, not for the first time, what might possibly be excluded from Chú Hai's list of conversational topics. As usual with him, the point of the conversation only came near the end, in a few throwaway lines. "I'm sorry I couldn't keep our last appointment," he began to say.

You'd already worked out a counter to that, the story coming unbidden the moment you stepped through the back gate and into the alley after you'd washed away the chicken's dying eruptions. "Oh, you weren't there too? I couldn't go that day as well. I was sick," you said, trying to look innocent and unconcerned. You rushed on, the lying unfamiliar on your tongue. "And then when I went the week after, the gate was locked. I saw that the big gate out front was padlocked too. And of course, I didn't know how to contact you or my blood-father. So I just waited."

"But now you are here," Chú Hai said, looking pleased with the way events had unfolded. Or perhaps just with the story you'd made up.

"You're a lucky chap you were ill that day. There was a disturbance actually. That friend of mine... turns out some people in the present government thought he was stirring a coup. So it's no longer possible to hold our conversations there," he told you. "But I made a promise to the rooster master. And you're such a good student it would be a pity to stop. We'll continue here if you still want to." He pointed to the hotel in front of you. "I work here now with an American magazine. Come after hours. I'll let the doorman know."

You couldn't refuse. You didn't wish to see Chú Hai again, to be reminded of that strangely satisfying feeling of release when you'd killed the chicken. But there was Chú Hai's awful attraction—the possibility he could unlock the secrets of those Americans spreading over the country like khaki green mould, the chance he could help you understand that force which could either be your enemy or your salvation. Your studies with him resumed, now with a new focus—the university entrance exams at the end of the next summer. Your sessions changed from casual far-ranging conversations to detailed analysis of the stories Chú Hai assembled out of the American journalists' discarded drafts; to writing paragraphs from ideas and information provided by Chú Hai; to translating all the material—the ones you wrote in Vietnamese into polished English, the American pickings into fluid Vietnamese.

You worked at it all. Not just with Chú Hai but also alone in your rooftop hideaway in Oldest Brother-in-Law's house. And on all the other engineering subjects as well. As if your life hung on the results. Which it did. You knew very well, if you did not make it to university and gain a deferment from the army, it would be the war waiting to embrace you.

.....

And so, in a sense, the story you've told Tri is not false. For you had gone to university and not become a soldier. The rest of it, the dissonance your son senses, well... there can be no talking about that to either him or Nina at this late stage, not after you've hidden it for nearly a decade. It's a decision you made years ago. You won't change your mind now.

But Tri's perceptiveness is unnerving. You wonder if it's safe for you to go back up to the den, to get physically near him again, when your discomfort is still so apparent to yourself.

You walk halfway up the staircase and peep through the banisters into the study. Nina and Tri are sitting side by side at their work table. He's quietly writing his note to you. Nina has her arm around his shoulders, as if to block out any signals you might accidentally be sending him. They seem a unit, a mother and a son complete without you.

How is it, you wonder, that in an instant, you've been shut out of their world?

05
Facades

NOT THAT YOUR SEPARATION from son and wife actually happened in an instant. The brutal truth is you've never really been part of your son's world. Even Kim, his cousin, knows him better than you do. As for your wife, there have been milestones, particular dates and particular events marking the unraveling of the heart lines between you and Nina, markers you ignored.

There was the Black September stock market crash which bankrupted Loc and Huong and left you with the full burden of remittances to your siblings and their families in Vietnam; which led to Nina's Maman asking you to repay the down payment loaned for your Laguna Canyon house. There was Tri's impending entry to first grade and his need for expensive after school care, a need that overstretched your household's already stretched budget. There was your bigger job in advanced technology sales with even more flying all over the country and longer and longer late night reports to Ba Roi. And finally, there was Nina herself, announcing that she was abandoning her dissertation on the VC. That didn't happen yesterday. It's been almost a year ago...

When Nina tells you she's dropping her beloved dissertation on the psychology of guerrilla wars, to be a clinical therapist at the Veterans Administration, she has all the reasons wrapped up. First, she can't get any data on the VC. Second, the university isn't renewing her fellowship because she hasn't made any progress on the data, meaning a cash crunch. Third, the training pays. Fourth, she's almost guaranteed a Ph.D. and a job if she works with the vets. And finally, there's a staff day care centre she can send Tri to.

"Post-traumatic stress disorder among Vietnam veterans," she sings out the new dissertation topic. "All the advisers think it's a really promising subject. And the patients at the VA are rich with data," she tells you. "I'll be able to hypothecate as many theories as I like," she says, her blinking eyes keeping pace with her running thoughts. "The factors contributing to PTSD... The effect of different treatment modalities on recovery... The importance of pre-existing personality dysfunctions as a causal factor... Whether home country support systems and attitudes influence..." Her right index finger ticks off each possibility on the fingers of her left hand.

She seems happy. But then she presses her lips together. "Writing this dissertation is how I have to play the game if I want a career in academia."

And despite the feeling all might not be right even for Nina, you do not argue. "You've got it all settled then," you say.

You do wonder in passing when the rules of engagement between you and Nina changed? When your worlds drifted so far apart Nina can make such a momentous decision without you having an inkling? What has happened that she's now willing to study the psyche of Americans, to collect data on losers? But you shut out the twinge of worry. You have work to do, new technology to pay attention to, reports for Ba Roi's consumption and Chú Hai's amusement.

And so you've arrived here, a sometime father with a brilliant awkward son you don't know how to help, a drop-in husband with only the faintest idea what his wife does at work.

.....

It isn't even Nina's fault. She would have told you about her patients anytime.

There's the American soldier, only nineteen when he was sent to look for Charlie, the gook in the forest; who could fire only after the gooks did; who'd waited time and again to be killed. And when he was not, had been lifted out again after the carnage and asked to leave it all behind... Except that he couldn't.

There's the USAF Major who flew in from Guam to drop his payload over swathes of green someone had designated as hostile and riddled with supply trails he had to take out; who'd never been allowed to wonder what kind of mules, human or otherwise, walked those supply trails... but nonetheless had agonized about it... And hasn't stopped agonizing.

There's the Lieutenant Colonel at the Military Assistance Command, responsible for the weekly counts, the ones Washington hoped would someday show more than ten VC kills for every American; who wasn't supposed to worry about the lives represented by the numbers... How they died... Who, if anybody, would open the front door to receive news of their deaths. Someone who nonetheless had mourned each number... And continues to mourn.

They're among the thousands who didn't follow orders, who hadn't shut the war out or kept their troubles in; who instead had carried their guilt, confusion, nightmares and more to the VA mental health clinic for Nina to untangle. You would have heard about them and more from Nina, if you'd asked her.

But you don't want to hear. You're having your own troubles keeping everything separate, all your lies and your different realities.

.....

"Did you have a good trip?" Nina asks when you get in from your trip to NASA in Florida.

You hesitate as she kisses you on the tip of your nose.

"Not bad," you say.

She doesn't investigate further, assuming it's not for public dissemination and involves the high-specification screws and pins you put on flying things, some of which are projectiles meant to kill. It's a part of your new high flyer's job she's uncomfortable with. She doesn't need to know if you don't want to tell, her averted back says to you.

It's actually good news you're shy to boast about. The patented aerospace fasteners your team has developed are holding together a Titan rocket sending the first Navistar Global Positioning Satellite out to space. You've been invited to Florida to witness the launch, with family.

"We can make a road trip there, then drive all the way up the East Coast and around to come back," you say tentatively. "It's what Americans do at least once in their lives, and then talk about forever."

Nina isn't convinced. In her youth, she and her Maman, never her busy Papa, had travelled to Massachusetts, Virginia and Pennsylvania to visit the monuments to America's independence and the civil war battlefields. They'd also browsed the Peabody, the MOMA and the Metropolitan, her Maman giving her running commentaries. Every spring and autumn, both immaculately dressed, they went to New York City for a day to buy new clothes. Once, with both parents, Nina had gone to Paris, where her father assisted in the back room with 'the negotiations' and she and her mother attended on numerous Aunts and Great-Aunts in their fussy French parlors. They travelled on trains and planes. They stayed in four star and five star hotels and embassy lodgings. But they'd never driven through the country in their own car, bunking in with barely known relatives and friends, sleeping over in motels.

You see the doubt written all over her face.

"We have a window. I have to wait for my citizenship and security clearance before starting my next assignment. You've got to wait for your supervisors to get through that first draft of your dissertation," you say. You remember Chú Hai reminiscing about the one cross-country trip he made when he was studying in the US, just before he was recalled to Vietnam. "Please. It'll be great," you say to your wife.

The pleading in your voice persuades her.

"Two whole months, the kind of vacation we'll talk about forever," you murmur into her hair as you load up the ice-chest and Tri's car games into the People-mover you've traded-in your BMW for.

Nina makes the sign of the cross in mock prayer. "If we live through it," she says, looking up at the cloudless California sky, trying to hide the worry in her eyes.

.....

The launch in Florida is as beautiful as the outgoings during the war. Better, because the phosphorescent trails of these rockets don't turn back towards the earth to kill. It's a spectacle you can enjoy without reservation. But just as the first stage plume fades and the second stage fires up, the missile makes an angle and swings back towards the observation centre. And, although the room you're in is ten kilometers away from the launch pad, and so insulated the deafening explosions are a mere rumble and the shuddering ground only a deep humming vibration, the slight stumble in the rocket's trajectory sends a tremor through the room.

"Oh," Nina gasps, stepping back from the railing she's been leaning against.

"Not to worry. It's not coming back at us. It's just to adjust the flight path so the GPS will orbit properly," you say to your wife.

You look down at Tri, between the two of you, hoping he's heard your explanation too.

He's standing stock still, his body pressed into Nina's ribcage. One of his fists is crunched inside your hand. You see that his eyes are closed tight and guess he's willing himself not to feel the vibrations coming through the floor and trying to believe he's just at the movies, the noise only a soundtrack.

He's still standing like a sentinel after the flight controller announces the success of the turning maneuver and applause breaks out in the room.

"Everything's fine now," you tell him. "There's nothing to be afraid of." You ease your free thumb into his fist to loosen his solidly clenched fingers and weave your thin ones through them. You rub your other hand against the back of his. You hope against hope that your son will learn that fear can be mastered.

He does learn to be brave, so brave it'll break your heart. But you don't know that yet.

.....

What you know is that even the bravest men can fold under strong enough fire. During the war, the B52s dropping their gigantic dragon eggs into the tunnels north-west of Saigon had shaken even the staunchest of revolutionaries, your blood-father among them.

Your Third Brother-in-Law Ba Roi had told you how he and your blood-father huddled, heads and knees pressed against each other, under their plank bed in their rooster nursery outside Saigon. How they'd involuntarily soiled their pyjama trousers. And how all around them there had been the ringing of the explosions, and the high registers of the roosters crowing their fears into the impossibly lighted up sky. The Commander had mumbled to himself, "To lie under arms and meet death without regret, this is the energy of northern regions and the forceful make it their study. Therefore, the superior man cultivates a friendly harmony, without being weak." Holding onto Ba Roi's shoulder he'd said over and over, "How firm is he in his energy." He would not admit it, Ba Roi observed to you later, but already his resolve was weakening.

For others, there hadn't been a chance for words nor even a thought to mourn their own passing... In a tunnel beneath the ground in Cu-Chi, ten kilometers from the rooster farm your blood-father and Ba Roi ran as a cover for their other activities, the ramparts had shuddered and collapsed and a pretty straw-hatted young girl, an occasional seller of guavas you had met just once, had opened her mouth to scream, then suffocated in the mud pressing against her face. It was an end that haunted your blood-father's messenger, the sticky rice vendor, a story she retold repeatedly in her retirement.

In the city, Chú Hai and you had been luckier. The two of you heard only a distant rumbling, like thunder.

"I did tell the Americans this isn't a good thing, that when the pictures come out, anti-war sentiments will go ballistic," he said to you, "but obviously the message didn't get through to the High Command." He didn't add he'd also warned those in the tunnels that the B-52s would be back soon, his message sent by courier between stacks of brown paper wrappers. He didn't say he'd advised his late friend Albert's patron, the nationalist intelligence director Albert had pretended to report to, that the B-52s should only be used on the supply trails across the border, that every drop inside the South would be a step back for the rural pacification program. "It's hard for them to pay attention, I suppose. There are so many opinions about this war, none of them completely right, none totally wrong," he said. "But I've spoken my truth to those in power. I've done all I can." He opened his hands in resignation. He patted your hand. "That's all you need to do too, the best one man can."

You were confused. What was he trying to tell you?

You'd confessed earlier to him that you would be studying engineering at the university as your father and blood-father wanted; apologizing that you'd wasted his time with the English lessons. He'd brushed your apology aside. "It doesn't matter. As long as you can use your essential qualities, nothing will go to waste. Just do your best," he'd said. "But for whom? Which side?" you'd wanted to know. And then the bombing had started, ending your exchange.

Now, he motioned for you to come and help him with a translation, the technical specifications for a burning agent used to clear bush in the Delta.

As you took the sheet from him and scanned the equations, you noticed that his left eye was ticking, a sign he was troubled.

"It's a fuel mixture of benzene and gasoline. Extremely hot. Burning at 800 to 1,200 degrees Celsius," you began to read. "Then there's a plastic for stickiness and small traces of phosphates to enhance burning. The plastic attaches to the skin, the phosphates burn the flesh to the bone..." You couldn't continue.

"How do they counteract it?" he asked, his fingers drumming against his desk, both eyes blinking furiously now. You searched the document. "Difficult. It's totally different from the old stuff the French used. It burns even in water and because of the stickiness, you can't wash it off. It flows into trenches so you can't hide. Anyway the blasts de-oxygenate the air. If you're not burnt, you suffocate. You have to stop the planes before the payloads are dropped. But anti-aircraft guns don't have enough range to get to the B-52s and the Phantoms. They'll be too high, especially if they're going to drop the bombs with radar controlled missiles. What's needed is surface to air missiles, or air intervention."

"They've just got too much damned hardware, haven't they?" Chú Hai said. His voice seemed uncaring but his elegant fingers were making frantic little tears on the long edge of a piece of paper he'd randomly picked up from his desk. "Flesh and bones can't prevail. The countryside will be empty and we'll all be dead if it isn't stopped," he concluded. A note of resignation had crept into his voice. You were surprised. He was rarely ever despondent. But the darkness passed in

*an instant. His hands suddenly ceased their fidgeting. His
eyes flashed wide open, still and decided. "He was right,"
he said. "There's no other way to make them go except a
new government. We need a general offensive and a people's
uprising to install a coalition government; a government
that will negotiate withdrawal." He nodded to himself, then
grinned, his happy pixie self again. As if some argument he'd
been having with the unknown 'he' had finally been resolved.*

*In a flash, everything became clear to you too. "You'd be
much happier with that outcome, wouldn't you? Although you
would never say so to them," you said, flicking your eyes to the
unoccupied editor's desk on the other side of the room. "You're
a clever one, con," he smiled. He'd taken to addressing you
this way lately, a sign of your growing closeness... "If you
were me wouldn't you rather be earning good money from your
own national newspaper, writing in your own language?" He
lowered his voice. "I would actually have told them. You know
my personal motto is 'speak truth to power'. But in all the time
I've worked for them, they never thought to ask."*

*He looked at you with that same intense assessing look
you'd seen before, then nodded, coming to a decision. "There
are many fronts in a war. One does what one can," he said.
He continued, "It's not so complicated. Like you, I grew up
in the Delta. My father, my mother, my grandparents are
buried there, in rice fields we've owned for generations. I've
had to rebuild their gravestones three times. Once after the
Japanese War, then again when the French came back, finally
last year when the Americans conducted a sweeping operation
through the whole village. To clear communists they said. The
ancestors have a right to peace. We all do. We won't get it until
the war stops."*

He flashed you a crooked grin. "Where their graves are, it must be a particularly unfortunate site. When it's all over, we must get a geomancer to see about moving them." He winked and put a finger to his lips. More could not be said in this office without singularly unfortunate consequences, his gestures said.

He turned to his desk and dug out a report he was preparing, a commentary about a huge cache of Viet Cong weapons destroyed during Operation Attleboro. He passed it to you. "This may be unfortunate news but our comrades need to know. Try rewriting it in Vietnamese for me to send on. If nothing else, it'll get all those awful chemical equations out of your head."

Settling himself in front of his desk, he picked up his dog-eared copy of the Analects, written in the old Sino-Vietnamese characters the French had all but phased out, and began mouthing the words under his breath in the traditional six syllable cadence, "The superior man stands erect in the middle without inclining to either side, how firm is he in his energy. When good principles prevail in the government of his country he does not alter his stand, how firm is he in his energy. When bad principles prevail in the country he maintains his course to death without changing, how firm is he in his energy."

He seemed lost in the verses. In the middle of a passage though, he stopped suddenly to address you. "Never let it be said, that 'Tom' Trung's just an American lackey. Nor for that matter, a simple Marxist stooge. I've travelled the world and drunk from many wells but like you I'm descended from my father's line, from this place and soil."

And looking at him then, sitting under the yellow light of the American standard lamp reading the old words, it seemed undeniably true that this man, whom you once thought had become American from the inside out, was indeed sprouted from this ruptured land; as much a man of tradition as your father the Chief Clerk.

But what about you, you had wondered then. Who might you be?

"If you study English, you'll become an interpreter at best, at worst a spy; do something better, be an engineer," your father had said.

"Do something more. Be an engineer, an interpreter in the course of it. But if your country needs you, also a soldier, perhaps a spy," your blood-father had persuaded.

Chú Hai, though, had asked you to envision it differently. "Be yourself, just yourself," he'd said, trusting you would find your way.

And so you had. You'd offered him your services. In the process, turning yourself into someone too much like him. But yourself, nonetheless.

.....

You look down at your son Tri. He's being very much himself, a statue at your side. You wonder what will become of him. You wonder if you can be as generous as Chú Hai and allow this strange boy to grow up in his own way.

"There's nothing to be afraid of," you tell him again through the corner of your mouth, softly so no one else can hear. It's a lesson you've learnt from your fathers. Even between the closest of kin, it is still important to be delicate about feelings.

.....

Nina's Maman has no such compunctions about your feelings. Although you've shepherded your family half-way across the country to Nina's childhood home in the Virginia suburbs to visit her and Papa Nguyen, nonetheless she will still insist on reminding you how unfit you are to be in her family. Or even at her table...

"My mother's *bánh bột lọt* and my grandmother's *bánh ướt*," she nods at the over-chewy shrimp and pork dumplings wrapped in banana leaves and the snow white rice rolls she hand-pours, carefully garnished with the saucissons she steams herself. "All made following royal recipes," she boasts. Looking down her nose at you, she points to the pièce de résistance, a perfectly executed côte de boeuf. "Learnt at my Swiss finishing school."

You do not allow her to upset your equilibrium. You tell her the food is delicious. You behave. You make sure there's nothing she can fault you for.

Ever the diplomat, Papa Nguyen, flashes you a smile at the end of the meal to apologize for Maman's rudeness before turning to congratulate his wife. "Perfect," he says to her.

He sits back, opens the wooden cigar box already set out to his right and passes it down to his cousins. "Cuban. But still we must have them," he says, with a regretful downturn to his lips.

"Indeed," the cousins agree. But they're only a little shamefaced when they help themselves to the fat brown rolls.

You watch the three older men clip their cigar tops, light up and suck in. They sink into their chairs, fed and at peace.

"To be here in America, living under a democratic government, not at the mercy of a totalitarian regime. It's something to be grateful for," one of them says.

The other two nod, their eyes closed, savoring their blessings.

"Thank God we're not in China. Thank God we'll never have a Tiananmen incident here," the youngest cousin observes.

"Yes," the older cousin agrees. "It was tragic, that incident. But all the same, something useful for the Western world to see. It shows the communists can never change. Black cat or white cat, it doesn't matter, so long as it can catch mice... that's what they say. True. They're still cats, still communist all the way. If you're a mouse, it's something to keep in mind, regardless of whether they're opening up their markets or not."

"But the US is hardly a mouse," Papa Nguyen comments.

"He's not talking about the US," the younger cousin explains. "He's talking about the people at home. The ones we're encouraging to start a general uprising." He turns to the older cousin. "Tiananmen shows the time isn't ripe. If our people rise up now, they'll be killed like those Chinese students. We shouldn't encourage them."

"You mean the dissidents in Vietnam?" Papa Nguyen clarifies, a look of consternation on his face.

"Who else?" the cousin asks.

It is time for you to excuse yourself, you decide. "I'm going upstairs for some cigarettes," you say to your father-in-law.

Craziness, you think, as you mount the staircase. To attempt an uprising nearly fifteen years on, with a population either half starved or dead tired from making ends meet. As for propaganda value... There's no hope in hell the Americans will go back to rescue anyone again, ever. How desperate and deluded can Papa and his cousins be? You can't help pitying them, still fighting that old war in 1989, so many years later.

Back in Nina's old bedroom, you sit down at her teenager's desk and sag into her 1970's swivel chair. Rifling in the back of a drawer, you take out the stack of postcards accumulated from Nevada, Arizona and Florida. With an erasable black ink pen you begin to write over your previous work, now dried and invisible.

Penning the simple English phrases Chú Hai had drilled into you so many years ago—'Having a good time'... 'You just have to see this for yourself'... 'Wish you were here'—is brainless relaxing activity. What's taken work are the original communiqués, written with fast-fade ink in miniscule Vietnamese script during the road trip as Nina and Tri slept—on one card, a short sentence letting Chú Hai know that the schematics for the GPS system and the list of suppliers are in a care package being sent to Ba Roi's family; on three others, a longer review of the American response to the Tiananmen incident, data on the flood of Japanese direct investment into the US and its potential impact on the global power balance; and a last card describing your trip to the Space Centre with a post script about your patented fasteners. They're snapshots of the world through wide angled American lenses, news you're sure Chú Hai will find more interesting than the technical material his and Ba Roi's masters still insist on—technology your countrymen have no capacity to understand, let alone defend against.

It had been different in the past when Chú Hai and you sat late into the night at the office and you'd interpreted the complexities of the blueprints materializing from the mess of his desk. Then your engineering training had mattered. Chú Hai had taken your explanations in, processed them in that multi-leveled brain of his and turned it all into strategy, tactics and battle plans; plans that in one way or another contributed to his masters winning the war. And if you want to be frank about it, to your losing your country.

What joy it would be to sit down with Chú Hai again, for him to see with his own eyes how far along you've gone, pretending to ingest America and turn American from the inside out, as once you thought he had; to hear his wry on-the-mark observations, the best ones thrown in at the end, as if they didn't matter. But it's impossible. Chú Hai's unreachable, stuck behind the bamboo curtain you both helped to build.

You put your erasable ink pen away, pick up another one with permanent ink and sign off with a variety of initials, impulsively dashing off a series of noughts and crosses, kisses and hugs, across one of the cards. Then you address the first two postcards to an office in Hong Kong, another to a post box in Canada, and the last few to Singapore.

You slip the cards into the pocket of the good trousers you've put on for Maman's guests and go back downstairs. Walking out into a still bright summer evening you make your way to the letter box at the end of the driveway, place the cards inside the box and lift up the flag to indicate a pickup. Then you stop to light a cigarette and take a long drag. As if at an altar making an offering, you shut your eyes and pray a greeting to the recipient of the cards.

Still thinking about Chú Hai, you walk back to the house, kicking your uncomfortable black lace up shoes against the gravel. You mustn't forget, you tell yourself, to mention the cousins' futile plans for a general uprising in your next set of reports to Ba Roi.

You don't know that the sound of gravel being kicked up has alerted Maman, who's standing at the kitchen sink rinsing dishes. You don't know that she looks out the window and sees you, smoking and pensive, a forlorn lover openly nursing a broken heart for all to see. You don't know that beyond you, she sees the letter box flag tilted up.

Maman has always been suspicious of you, her unwelcome son-in-law. Notwithstanding yours and Nina's apparent happiness, Tri's cleverness, your obvious success at work, she never lets you forget that she thinks Nina's made a mistake.

It's been that way since Nina showed her pictures of the party your family gave to celebrate the wedding. In yours and Nina's absence, your family had posed around the large color photograph you sent back. A heartwarming acknowledgement of Nina and your new life together, you'd thought. But what Maman had seen was a gathering of thin tired women in glaring synthetics and gaunt men in ill-fitting white shirts around a table with mismatched crockery.

"The type of family from which VC are recruited," she'd said to Nina on your first Christmas visit after the wedding, not caring that you were well within earshot, trying to nap on the crushed velvet love seat across the room. "A family that would've married him off at eighteen to a countryside girl before sending him to college," she'd added. Even if the background checks she had made Papa commission came up with nothing, even if you'd been what you said, a brilliant engineer from a modest countryside background. She remains convinced you're hiding something.

You know about Maman's suspicions. But, as you slouch into her house, you cannot know that Maman will descend to digging around in her own letterbox just to find something to incriminate you with.

06
Faultlines

MAMAN GETS TO THE POSTCARDS before the mailman, Huong calls to tell you.

"It's Sixth Sister. Are you alone?" she whispers.

"Yes. Nina's taken Tri to the library," you reply. "Anything important?" you ask, carefree and ignorant that your world is going to split apart and be blown away.

.....

"It's to a woman," Maman had spat out, flapping the postcards in front of Nina, pointing to the one with the hugs and kisses across the bottom.

Nina knew the truth was more complex. The names on the postcards were androgynous and multi-racial—two Vietnamese, one Chinese, one Western. Notwithstanding the hugs and kisses, the messages seemed strangely generic. As for the addresses, why would you send travel postcards to commercial buildings and post boxes?

The postcards were data needing analysis, Nina decided. Each one hid a message whose meaning, if apprehended, would provide her with an insight into you. But she needed an interpreter. She went to Huong.

.....

"She showed them to me last week," Huong reports. "You were travelling, Loc was out and Tri was at the new kung-fu movie with the children. It was just the two of us in the apartment."

Nina had fished out the postcards from her handbag. Apparently she'd carried them everywhere since Maman forced them on her.

"We were making rice paper rolls for dinner when she showed them to me. They were in English and I couldn't see anything incriminating. That's how I knew what they were," Huong says, skirting around the story.

"What did you tell her?"

You hear Huong suck in her breath against her teeth. "At first, nothing," she says.

"But after?"

"I asked her questions. I wanted to know what you'd told her about your blood-father. She knew his history. But it didn't strike her as strange that he didn't suffer any retaliation despite his defection from the Viet Cong."

Huong hesitates. Then she lets it all out in a rush, "I told her it's because those people thought they could hold you if they let your blood-father live."

"You told her what?!?"

This is the woman you shepherded safely out of Vietnam, the woman you bloodied your hands for. How could she do this to you? You see your life falling apart—your wife and child boarding a plane for D.C., Maman cackling gleefully as

Papa smiles a quiet apology, your house empty and abandoned, sliding down the sides of the canyon and disintegrating into the bush.

"Sixth Sister..." you groan into the receiver.

"She never lived through that war. She has no idea about the complications. She doesn't understand enough to know how to ask you so you'll tell. And if you don't tell, then the misunderstandings will just pile up and pile up. And she'll divorce you. That's the American way. And she's American, even if she looks like us. You should admit that. I had to tell her," Huong justifies herself. Her voice turns accusatory. "Actually you should have told her. From the very beginning, you should have told her everything."

Yes, you should have, you know that. But how could you after what had happened with Ai Nguyet?

.....

Ai Nguyet changed after the Tết offensive. She was no longer the imperious princess you fell in love with. Something had happened while she was trapped in Hue during the siege of the city. But when you tried to ask, she would just raise her hand to cover her face."It's nothing at all," she would tell you.

Yet it was she who complained that you kept her out of too many parts of your life. "Where do you go with those foreigners?"... "Why can't you influence them to write only good things about our government?"... "What do you and your creepy old journalist talk about?" she would interrogate when you came back from an interpreting assignment or a meeting with Chú Hai.

You'd never seen Oldest Sister or Huong subject their husbands to such cross-examination. She wasn't behaving reasonably, you were quite sure. But she was different—more educated and cultivated, an artiste, therefore temperamental. Besides, you loved her. And she was suffering even if she would not tell you why.

You tried to bear it for love's sake. In truth though, there were too many parts of your life you had to hide from her, too many expectations you had to meet.

As the top student in engineering you'd been given a plum civilian job, a posting to the Vietnamese spin-off taking over American jungle clearing operations. It was 1970 and the Americans were already making plans to leave. The spin-off was inheriting not only the Americans' heavy equipment but also the right to lease the machinery to private contractors.

All your friends were envious of your good fortune. "I'd do this anytime over running my parents' fish sauce factories," Ly, who saw the job's commercial possibilities immediately, said. "Our factories actually take work. All you'll have to do is wait till you're senior enough to approve tenders. After that you can just sign contracts and wait for the envelopes to come to your house. Or have your family set up a construction company and lease all the equipment to them at lower than market rates. Either way, it'll be easy money."

You found Ly's typically Chinese excitement about your job's money making opportunities a little distasteful. But it was indeed a heaven sent chance to further your family's interests, provided you kept climbing up the ladder. "Don't waste it," Loc stressed. "Dine with your superiors when they ask you to. Pour for them when they're drinking. Make sure you see them safely home afterwards. And not a word about it in the morning," Oldest Brother-in-Law advised.

Chú Hai was pleased too when you told him about the assignment. "There's no better position for monitoring the Southern Army's land clearing and road building operations. You'll have access to the bulldozing schedules for the whole region around Saigon. There'll be all kinds of interesting pickings in the incoming memos too. The only tricky bit is making the Xeroxes. You'll need to get in before everyone else to do that." He ordered, "Give up your morning coffee with that girl. You have to take full advantage of the intelligence potential."

You cancelled your breakfasts with Ai Nguyet as well as your evening walks before she went home for dinner. Julia Anderson took away more of your time. To break the camel's back, there was the machine...

It was an automated packing machine originally used for filling tubes of toothpaste, an automobile-sized assembly of blackened metal hidden in a warehouse on the other side of the Saigon River.

"It needs re-jigging," Chú Hai had said. He'd lifted up a fat plastic container with a hole through it, about the size of a toilet roll. "We need to put scrap iron pieces into these canisters with the machine, and then have it cap the canisters like this." He'd handed you the closed canister with a hollow chimney sticking out of it. You'd examined the assembled piece. You could guess what it would become when finished, but that wasn't your business. You turned your attention to the machinery. "When do you want it ready by?" you asked. "As soon as possible. It's urgent now the cross border supply bases have been destroyed by the Southern Army's incursion into Cambodia." You thought about the feed hoppers that needed reconfiguring, and the mechanical timer that you needed to

slow down to cater to the heavier loads and larger containers. "A month at least, and even that I can't guarantee," you said.

You were thinner and hollow cheeked when you met Ai Nguyet for ice-cream on a Saturday after over two months of cancelled appointments. She, slighted, failed to notice how fatigued you were. Alternatively mopey and accusatory, she so distressed you with her questions that, just to shut her up, you revealed the truth you'd been trying to hide even from yourself.

"I was re-building a machine to assemble land mines," you told her. "For them?" she asked. She wanted you to lie. But Chú Hai and you had discussed this already. If you chose to marry, it was best your wife accepted you for what you were and was prepared to manage the family in case you were discovered. That Ai Nguyet could not be this suitable woman was another truth you'd been trying to hide from. So be it, you thought. You would not lie to her. You wanted to be loved the way you were. "They're not meant for killing people," you said.

"How could you? How could you?" she began to cry in little sobs, which came slowly, and then faster and faster. She moved her chair nearer you and scrabbled at her shirt and the waistband of her trousers, lifting one up and pulling the other down to reveal the flesh between her ribcage and pelvis. "Do you see?" she asked.

All the while you'd been together, you'd never seen beyond Ai Nguyet's face, her neck, her elbows, her knees. She'd only allowed you to caress her through her clothes. Now you saw that the dip of her stomach and the soft swell of her abdomen were criss-crossed with harsh brown ridges and mounds of rough red. You sucked your breath in and looked away.

"That's what one of those mines that don't mean to kill did to me at Thanh Minh when I was twelve, when we went

to the ancestral graves during the Tomb Cleaning Festival. It's so awful you looked away. But four of our own house servants saw it and raped me anyway last Tết, during the siege. They were establishing a new egalitarian society, they said. They knew about me. I was convenient since I can't have children anymore. Those mines not meant for killing, they took that away too. Did you consider any of that when you were repairing that machine?"

No you hadn't. Chú Hai had taught you the rules of engagement: When the enemy advanced, you retreated; when the enemy halted, you harassed; when the enemy avoided battle, you attacked; when the enemy retreated, you followed. You were on the ground; you were in society; you took the airwaves; you captured public opinion, especially theirs. You used everything and you co-opted everyone. You did whatever it took. You held on to your goals—independence, liberty, happiness. It had sounded simple. It wasn't.

You had kept sight of your goals. You had put distance between yourself and your enemy, yourself and your victim, theoretically. But there was Ai Nguyet, your beloved and your enemy and your victim, sitting a hand's touch across from you, heartbroken because of something you'd done to further a strategy. How was it possible to tell her you'd done it for her? To tell her you believed the machine had been necessary to drive out the Americans, to secure independence and liberty, to bring the peace that would allow the two of you to build a future together?

You forced yourself to meet her eyes, to seek absolution so you could explain. But bitterness had dried her tears and she was flint-faced and unforgiving. Everything between you shriveled in her hard look. Wanting only to hide, you slid the

unfinished dish of ice-cream you'd been sharing towards her,
stood up, and walked away.

About a year later, in 1971, Ly mentioned in passing that
Ai Nguyet's father had accepted a posting to France. Ly's
family restaurant had catered the farewell party at their villa.

You never saw her again. Many years afterwards, when
flipping through a photo album in Papa's and Maman's living
room, you thought you saw her face among a host of bejeweled
women from the old regime. But you have never been certain.

You carried away one thing as you left her—the certainty
that you would never break, never tell, not ever again;
especially not to those you loved the most.

.....

Now of course, you realize, you will have to tell Nina. And the
consequences of that telling, you fear, will be the same.

"What did Nina say, Sixth Sister?" you ask, calmer now
that you know what the worst case scenario will be.

"She couldn't put the two together. What being held to
ransom by them meant. She couldn't believe you'd worked for
them, perhaps are still working for them."

"Sixth Sister, you said that? About my work here in America?"

"Not in so many words. What do you take me for?" Huong
is indignant.

You apologize. Indeed, she hasn't once used the words VC
or communists in your conversation.

"I said that things were complicated in those days and
many people worked for one side, then switched. I said people
did things then that they might not want to talk about now.
I said there are things wives shouldn't ask their husbands.

And then I told her in no uncertain terms that she should understand they'd been part of your life since you were sixteen or seventeen and that you could only break free after your blood-father died. But even then, I reminded her, old ties are hard to sever. The rest of our family is still over there, held to ransom. I told her she should understand you can't refuse if Ba Roi wants a bit of information every now and then. And I told her the less we know about all that, the better. If she wants to poke and pry, we can all be very sorry."

"What did she say to that?" you ask.

"She muttered something about surely this is now the case, surely now your summer holiday will be one she'll remember forever," Huong replies.

"Ah. Okay then." You don't need to know more. You thank Huong and hang up.

You look up at the ceiling fan twirling lazily on its way to nowhere. Shit.

.....

Nina had explained the different stages of psychological coping to you once. How when her patients' worlds turned upside down, they retreated into familiar patterns of behavior. Now you see Nina do exactly that. She heads straight for her most familiar mode of being. She begins to analyse the data—you.

You see her stealing glances at you, appraising you, attempting to re-construct her understanding of this husband suddenly cast in a new light. She brings out your old photo albums, traces her fingers idly through the records of your previous life together, looking for clues that might hint at the you she's just been told about.

From the kitchen window she spies on you down by the pool trying to persuade Tri to put his head under water; getting out first to dry yourself when he refuses; standing at the edge to envelop him with a towel when he struggles out, so he won't catch his death of cold, notwithstanding he's as strong as a horse and old enough to take care of himself. But she won't be seeing anything new, just the father you've always been—attentive, demanding, even obsessive.

"You know when I was doing research for that other Ph.D. topic, I found out that CIA spies are called agents and the people who supervise them are called case officers. Sounds like social workers, doesn't it?" she tells you one night, while you're clearing the dinner dishes. "The FBI designations are probably closer to reality. The supervisors are the agents—the people acting for a larger entity, like a country, or maybe an ideology. The spies are just informants." She stares at you. "Sounds right doesn't it? Informants? Sneaks and tattle tales listening in on conversations, digging in trash cans, building relationships just to betray them. What do you think?"

You turn the faucet on fast and loud. "I can't really hear you darling, *cưng*," you shout over the din. "Later?"

You see her trying to imagine you as an informant. She turns to watch you through half closed eyes as you get up from bed in the dark to glide into the study. She follows. You look up from your desk where you've been reading off your new computer. Her lovely open face shows she's noticed, as she never did before, how you've sensed her and turned around, although she's been so quiet; how, while swiveling your chair to face her, you've managed to power down the computer.

"What is it?" you ask, even though you know exactly what the problem is.

Her courage forsakes her and instead of confronting you she says, "I haven't been able to sleep."

"I noticed," you answer. You go to her and nuzzle her shoulder. "I'll give you a backrub," you say, leading her back towards the bedroom, away from the computer, from your secrets.

She pushes you away. "No I'll be okay. I just need a glass of warm milk from the kitchen."

She walks to the staircase and past your desk. But the screen is already a blank. There's nothing for her to see. By the time she comes back up, the study is dim with only the night light on. You're back in bed.

You feel her looking at you, apparently asleep, your breathing even.

"Who are you?" you hear her ask.

In the morning you tell her you've been reading up for a new assignment, a project abroad. She looks up from the newspaper.

"Classified?" she asks.

"Not actually. Better than that. But it's still tentative. We'll talk if anything more concrete comes up," you assure her.

You exchange kisses.

"What more can come up?" you think you hear her say as you close the front door on her, quiet as a thief.

.....

Nina retreats into a no-man's land you can't penetrate. The chickens have finally come home to roost, the inevitable ending to a story you shouldn't have started in New York those many years ago.

True, you've learnt to love each other notwithstanding, to understand each other somewhat, to live with each other as best you can. You share a good enough life, you've always thought. Yet here you both lie, estranged in the double-mattressed super-king bed Nina has always complained is too big. You'd insisted on it, so you wouldn't wake her when you got up during the night to do this or that. But now Nina's the one using the bed to hide her pains, her straight white back turned against you, lying so close to the far edge you can't even reach over to touch her.

You look at the finger-wide space between your two mattresses, the void between her space and yours. As much as the 17th Parallel, this is a de-militarized zone, a buffer allowing Nina her boundaries even if you've overstepped yours. So you might both keep what passes for peace, an uneasy accommodation neither of you know how to break.

A DOUBLE DEALER

07
The offer

THE LIVER-SPOTTED TAIWANESE AMERICAN does not believe in buffer zones. He attacks immediately. "Something came up in your security clearance application," he says as soon as you sit down at the restaurant table.

It's been months since you received your citizenship papers and signed the non-disclosure agreements for your low grade 'Confidential' security classification. It should all be over and done with. You've revealed everything that needed revealing, even some of the dirty linen. What can have gone wrong?

"Something came up..." you repeat as slowly as you can, stalling for time to think. You curse yourself. If you'd paid attention, you'd have noticed that nothing was as it should be for a run up to a routine interview. You hadn't been able to find the interviewer's name in the company phone book; Human Resources had arranged lunch in a restaurant, not a meeting at the facility. You just hadn't paid attention.

You bring yourself back to the present and the man across the table from you in a nondescript Denny's Restaurant in mid-Wilshire. To the glass topped table with a Western place setting that you're both sitting at. To the bread roll in the bread plate to your left... You reach for the roll, break it apart and butter it, forcing yourself to remain relaxed, very calm and open to whatever comes your way. You're in America, you remind yourself, a free country.

"The only way to get past a polygraph is to be very relaxed, relaxed all the way down to your butt cheeks. Empty your head too, let nothing into it, nothing at all. And remember, when challenged, step back so you seem less threatening," you hear Chú Hai reminding you.

The truth seeker in front of you isn't a machine. All you have to do is pretend to fold.

"What happened?" you ask, your voice trembling; a genuine tremble from an anxious engineer who needs a security clearance to keep his rice bowl. You hope it persuades the interviewer you're a chump, someone who'll break if played a bit longer.

"We'll get to that. Let's get on with the order first," he says, his eyes swiveling to the hovering waiter to pretend a warning.

Asshole. Two can play at that, you decide. You order a rib eye steak. "Rare," you tell the waiter.

You're tempted to add, "Dripping with blood," but you let the Taiwanese say it instead, "Bloody for me."

Having marked his boundaries, he's ready for business. "Now..." he rubs his large flat palms together.

"Yes?" You're suppliant.

"It's a glass ceiling," he says. "Not that important, but still something to think about."

He takes out a leather folder from the briefcase at his feet and removes a sheet of paper from which he reads aloud, "Adopted and brought up by a French civil servant. One brother and brother-in-law on the Nationalist side. Natural father—ex-VC. One brother-in-law—ex-VC. Exempted from re-education in 1975." Then he pulls out another sheet of paper from his folder and turns it around for you to read, "And there's this other thing..."

The other thing is a typed translation of what appears to be an official Vietnamese press statement announcing the appointment of a General Trung to the chairmanship of the Institute for the Study of Foreign Relations in Ho Chi Minh City, a post that can only be occupied by a trusted party member.

"A friend of yours?" the man asks.

"Sorry about that. Never can predict what those party apparatchiks will come up with next," you imagine Chú Hai apologizing.

You push the news extract back at the interviewer. "Everyone thought he was pro-American. You can't hold that against me," you say, projecting shock, injury and betrayal all at once.

Good cop now, the interviewer agrees. "Yes, it's not your fault at all. And it's not a problem for the 'Confidential' classification you already have. But you can't expect them to overlook it come time for upgrading. You don't expect them to let you at the secrets and top secrets, do you?"

You hang your head, the picture of defeated innocence. You let the interviewer take the next step.

He shoves the papers back into his folder, closes it and prepares for a man to man.

"Good thing this is a big company. In a big company, if there's a problem you can't solve, you send it upstairs to people who can take a broader view. That's what happened in your case."

He's in fine flow and you don't interrupt him. You wait for the pitch. For this is what it is—an offer of a new assignment, and not a routine one.

The Taiwanese-American smiles. His liver spots light up. "And those people upstairs, they came up with a solution. If a man can't work on the military side, they said, he can work on commercial affairs. If he can't look at our secrets, doesn't mean he can't go looking at what other folks are up to, what they want to build or to buy. If he's got as good a track record sussing out clients as you have, there's always a way to use your talents."

You let yourself look confused. "You're talking about?"

"My team. Jerry Chung's East Asia commercial team." He flips the folder open again, takes out a card and hands it over. He's the CEO of a company based in Hong Kong, distributors of mechanical equipment. He explains, "We're a fully owned entity by way of Bermuda. The team's engaged in everything in the region—market intelligence, business development, sales, servicing. Not just aerospace fasteners but whole machinery lines, trade financing and anything else they need as well. I run the area but my ground's more Korea, Japan, Taiwan. We've got a guy doing the Islamic countries— Malaysia and Indonesia—based in Singapore, and someone in Bangkok who looks after Thailand and the Philippines plus some side work in Burma."

"Burma? Isn't it embargoed?" you ask.

In full selling mode, Jerry ignores your question.

He rolls on. "Good assignment. Singapore based, with nice tax free overseas allowances and great private schools for your kid. Not dollars and cents or KPI driven like here. Not that much pure engineering I must warn you. But I'd say, looking at your stint in tech sales, you won't mind that. It's more keeping your ear to the ground, making contacts, floating opportunities upwards, oiling the transactions along, that sort of thing..."

"What do you say?"

He leans towards you, his cadaverous frame expansive, eager.

"Indo-China, it's yours if you want it."

.....

"The cold war's over. It's the end of history," Nina had said to you the other day from the deep funk her discovery had caused her to sink into.

If you hadn't felt so guilty, you would've argued with her. "Another meaningless phrase from a slack brained political philosopher," you might have snapped. "History ends when there's no more fuel for *samsara,* the wheel of life. With so much attachment, anger and delusion still brewing in the world, it'll be another hundred thousand lifetimes at least before the world ends." But in the state she'd lapsed into, you couldn't bear to bait her.

Now you wish you had. At least there would be a basis for your going home and telling her, "You see, there'll always be a need for intelligence, for watchers, for front men to move into new territory, for people like me." How are you going to explain what's happened now?

Perhaps, you think desperately, you should bring Jerry home to do the explaining. He's certainly got it all figured out. "So the Berlin Wall's down, the Soviet Union's disintegrating, the Japanese financial system's collapsing. So what?" he's rattling away. "Are the risks to the free world lower? No, they're not! Mongolia, Central Asia, Indo-China—they'll just be easy pickings for Communist China. We're going to stop that. That's why we got openings. We're getting set to win this time...

Take Vietnam. it's the biggest loser in South East Asia if the Soviets collapse. Not going to go to the Chinese if they can help it, right? And they're already playing around with that new life policy, *đời mới,* in the South. There's nothing to stop us beating those Reds from China. We've got more money to lend them, our stuff is better. Communism's just been one bad dream for them over there. Easy-peasy will do it. No guns, no artillery. Just some soda factories, burger and fried chicken franchises, a few sports shoes and electronic assembly lines..." He taps his name card. "Peace, prosperity and co-operation, that's what we're into. We're into business, not death and destruction. And our representatives, their jobs are just to go out and find partners who want to play."

Peace, prosperity and co-operation... No death, no destruction...

"Ha! And your mother's only ever fucked your father!!!" you want to shout back at him. But you disappear instead into polite decorum. "Yes, everything's changing. And you're right, the chances of regaining lost ground are much better than they've been. I'm very much obliged to the company for thinking ahead for me, helping me sidestep that glass ceiling I didn't even know about. But it's a big decision. I've never done anything like this before. I need to think about it. Is that okay?"

"Take your time," Jerry replies. "We're easy."

But you catch the mocking twinkle in his eyes. You know what he is and he knows what you are, the look says. You shouldn't take too long.

.....

You're weary as you drive past LAX and down the 405 Freeway back to the office. All these years and still you're just another one of your blood-father's roosters, running round and round in a cockfighting pit you can't escape from.

You should have known to stop when you discovered Chú Hai's allegiances during university. And despite your promise to help him, you should have stopped that second summer after the 1968 *Tết* incursions, when the truth about the machine killed everything between you and Ai Nguyet. You'd been given another chance when your blood-father died in 1979 and you were allowed to leave the country. But there'd been Ba Roi, hard-core and inflexible, holding onto the leash. And there was Chú Hai to consider as well. Chú Hai when you went to say goodbye — at his most vulnerable, with his ID photo and his enigmatic half un-knotted story full of tangles and loose ends. Chú Hai smiling through moist eyes as he pulled you into his arms in farewell but also in greeting.

Standing out on the linkway later that evening you realize, yes... it always comes back to Chú Hai. Because Chú Hai always welcomed you with open arms regardless of what you'd done with assembly machines, mechanical drawings, chemical formulae or an American woman; because he'd kept faith with you through thick and thin, gain and loss, victory and defeat. How can you desert Chú Hai, he of the same blood, the practitioner of deceit you're cloned from?

You shouldn't beat around the bush, you tell yourself, blowing cigarette smoke from your mouth in quick little puffs. It isn't because your career's hit a glass ceiling. The fact is the axes of global politics are shifting again, the super-powers are re-aligning and Vietnam is once again in play. Son of your father, you're as addicted to the game as he is. It's that simple.

How can you stop now? It's the call of fatherland and blood. Your country and your people waiting to be made whole, that's what's drawing you home.

You haven't discussed any of this with Nina. In fact, you and Nina haven't talked properly since Huong revealed the truth about your double life to her. You should feel abject about this, burdened with guilt. But what you feel is a wonderful certainty. Already you're saying goodbye to your view of the other side of the canyon, already you're breathing in the scent of mesquite wafting in from there as if it's a memory. Leaning against the solid wooden handrail you've smoked from for the last seven years, you see the canyon fading away, the last scene of the movie about your life in America.

Seven—you flick away the ash from your cigarette, it's your number for ringing in changes. And, confirming this, a nightjar begins to hoot from its nest in the stones below you. You hear the sound echo through the canyon seven times.

You stub out your cigarette. It's settled.

08
Adieu

THERE IS NO GOOD WAY to tell a wife you're going back to war.

.....

Your blood-father had offered you this snippet of a story after his defection, as consolation when you found out you couldn't get off the path you'd chosen without endangering him or his new wife, the sticky rice vendor.

"Even before we married, your blood-mother knew where my loyalties lay. Your father and your mother had told her. It's why I took so long to get married. It was the reason I could offer her protection," your blood-father had shared with you. "But she was angry anyway when I asked her to go into the swamps with me. Apparently, your mother, the Chief Clerk's wife, didn't approve. I went to speak to my friend, your father, about the problem. I heard he beat your mother. I hope that wasn't true… But a few days after I spoke to him, your blood-mother told me she'd come along. When I asked why she'd changed her mind, she said your mother had told her it was the right thing to do."

A beating, that's how they did it then.

.....

"There's a new assignment in Singapore," you tell Nina after sending Tri to bed. "It's in commercial. No more flogging weapons of mass destruction, just plain industrial machinery. That should make you happy, no?"

She nods, still wrapped in her blanket of grief. She waits for more.

But more will mean telling her you're meant to open Vietnam to American influence again, to keep your ear to the ground and arrange the flow of US dollars back into the country however you can. More will mean telling her you're now to be a double agent.

You give her the abbreviated version. "They want me to start an Indo-China division." After the postcards, after her conversation with Huong, you hope she can put the pieces together herself.

Nina looks out through the picture window into the canyon, then back at her reflection in the glass, gaunt as a ghost. She listens, only half taking it in, as you recount your conversation with Jerry Chung.

"I thought Indochina was embargoed," she murmurs.

You gloss over that just as Jerry had with Burma. Instead, you try to tell her how this new adventure will be so good for all of you, not just the tax and schooling angles but the fact that you'll be living in Asia, grounding both her and Tri in their Asian heritage. Can't she see the advantages?

She shakes herself alive. "Thong, I don't have a basis anymore to assess the rightness or wrongness, truth or fiction, of what I see, what you say, what I hear," she says, alluding finally to the years of lies she's recently discovered. She looks you in the eye for the first time in nearly a month. "How can I be in any position to either argue or agree?"

.....

"I'll stay behind till next summer, until the end of Tri's school year," she tells you a few days later. "I've got the final revisions of my dissertation to complete. And there's the house to rent out. You go first to set everything up. We'll visit at Christmas and join you when you've got everything ready."

"It's the best way for you and me and Daddy," she tries to assure Tri as you look on, helpless. "It's best this way for us both," she says to you.

Finally, she confronts you with what Huong has revealed, facts you don't deny but whose truth you won't acknowledge directly. Even now. Instead you ask stupidly, "Are you still holding on to those postcards?"

She laughs a bitter un-Nina cackle. "After Huong told me what they were, I posted them immediately. I wouldn't want to be responsible for screwing up whatever great conspiracy you were working on. According to Huong, these are life and death matters for your family over there. What it means for you and me is irrelevant in her books, I guess."

"That's not fair to Huong..." you begin to protest.

She nods, conceding the fact. "What I really wanted to say was I don't know who you are anymore. And because of that I don't know myself either. Let's give ourselves six months. Gain some distance. Maybe I'll be better then. Otherwise..." She leaves it open.

You're unwilling to leave it to chance that way. "Come at Christmas," you say.

She doesn't reply.

Both of you look past the linkway towards the far canyon wall, green this year from the unseasonal rains. It's almost Mid-Autumn again.

.....

Except for Binh, who's made it known vociferously that your decision to collaborate with the communists is treason, everyone else is there to see you off at LAX.

"Keep well then, Youngest," Loc says, slapping your back.

"Take care," Huong tells you as she rubs your forearm.

Their children—Thi the youngest girl now a bashful sixteen, the boys who all tower over you, assured sophisticated twenty-two-year-old Kim—come up to hug you in turn.

"Don't forget we're always here for you," Kim says, open and American with her emotions, her eyes beginning to tear.

"Thank you," you reply.

You watch her compose herself and turn to Tri, her charge, the one she'd voluntarily adopted as her youngest sibling the moment she saw him at the hospital.

"Say goodbye to your Dad then," she instructs.

Tri steps forward and sticks out his right hand. "Bye Dad, then," he says, correct and formal.

You take your son's hand in both yours and rub it hard between your palms. You lean down and whisper into his ear. "You take care *con*. Be brave and take care of your mother."

He nods twice, his face emotionless.

"Good," you tell him.

Why is it your son can't give you the heartfelt hugs Loc's and Huong's children have, you ask yourself? Why can't he tear up like Kim, you wonder? Foolish questions, you decide. You turn away from him to Nina.

She gives you a long hug, rubs her lips against yours and sniffs the side of your nose—a Vietnamese kiss. It's the same kiss she gave you at your first farewell in New York City, just before you flew cross-country to California. Then, after a week of nights in her apartment, you hadn't been sure she would follow. But she'd clung to you, her firm-fleshed Vietnamese-American body pressing against your bones, and promised that you would see her in Orange County at Christmas. And true enough, there she'd been at Loc's and Huong's on your first Christmas in America.

Now you're flying away from her again, across the Pacific to where it all began and will end for you. Your bodies pressing against each other are fleshier now, softer. Again, Nina is whispering that she'll see you at Christmas. And again, you're wondering if she'll follow.

RECOVERING

A

LIFE

Part Two

THE PRODIGAL

09
In transit

THE AIR IN THE SINGAPORE AIRPORT is heavy and moist. Stiff leafed orchids with long flower spikes scent the air-conditioned corridors with the smell of newly cut grass. Succulents you don't know the names of, fringed with thorns and pointed like fiery yellow and green dragons' tongues exude a thick odor of decay. A trace of fermented shrimp, stealing in from an open window somewhere, drifts through the salt and soap aroma of the citified equatorial bodies pushing past you. This is a different time and another country, but as you glide on and off the automated walkways towards baggage claim, it seems you're within smelling distance of home.

Home is still weeks away though. There are formalities to be completed in Singapore and government procedures to be followed. Your employment pass must be processed, your driver's license converted, your signature added to the list of approved signatories for the Singapore subsidiary of Jerry's company. There are people Jerry wants you to meet, your colleagues and the rest of his network. A visa has to be processed in Bangkok before you can be allowed back in your birthplace. Despite the smell of home wafting in from the sea through the port-facing windows of your service apartment, you have to wait.

.....

Nina calls you every other day, spending unwarranted amounts of money telling you the most inconsequential details about life in Orange County, overlaying her words with all kinds of insinuations. "The Santa Anas are blowing again, cleaning out all the bad vibes in the house," she says... or... "I'm sorting out your things, trying to sort you out while doing it."

How does she expect you to reply? An apology can't be enough. As for the truth, you don't know where to start.

"I've been clearing your desk," she begins on this particular call. You imagine her peering in the drawers to look for clues that might unlock the secrets of your VC heart and explain your treachery. But the desk won't reveal anything. You've emptied it. The only clue is the desk itself—the reproduction of Chú Hai's Mid-American classic you'd picked over the Scandinavian table she preferred. A curious choice, she'd commented then. To which you'd replied that you knew someone who had one just like it. If she'd asked that day who you knew with such a grand desk in wartime Saigon, perhaps you might have told her something more about Chú Hai beyond the fact he was your English tutor. But she'd merely nodded and handed her credit card to the saleswoman.

You wonder if she recalls that throwaway line of yours now and if she's curious who that 'someone' might have been.

"You cleaned out the computer. There's nothing left, not even the word processing and Lotus spreadsheet programs. You could just have got rid of the incriminating evidence and left the rest. Now I'll have to take the machine down to Loc and have his boys set up the whole thing again," she complains.

You don't bother to excuse yourself. Cleaning out that computer had been pure reflex. You wouldn't actually have put anything incriminating there in the first place. Surely, by now, she realizes that.

"*Cưng*, this call is costing money. None of this stuff is so important we need to discuss it right away. If you like, write it all down in a letter," you tell her.

"No, all of this is important. It's only in the little things that I'm seeing you at all," she snaps. She rushes on, not letting you interrupt. "I was sorting out the suits you wanted me to send, those Korean greys with that horrible blue tinge. I figured out today why you like those suits so much. It's because they look like communist uniforms."

"I told you before, they were the only ones that fit, at a reasonable price," you say. "Your problem, *cưng*, is that you think too much."

This conversation is beginning to wear you down.

"Just forget about the suits, okay. They dress more casual here. And I'll get some new ones made for business trips. I'm going to hang up now," you tell her.

"Not yet," she pleads."I pre-booked this call. There's two dollars more. You wouldn't waste that, would you?"

When she wants to be, she's still her ancestor's wily daughter. You grunt and remain on the line.

"I went to pack up your tools," she starts again. "I never noticed before how well you had them organized in those stacked plastic bins—screwdrivers, wrenches, your six electric hand drills, the nails and nuts and bolts—all sorted by size. It was really obvious, your obsessive need to have everything separate, in different compartments... But you can't, you know. It's spilled out all over the place anyway." Her voice rises. "You can't insist on keeping it in and shutting it out. We have to talk, Thong."

"Not like this," you say.

"Then when?"

"Not now, Nina. Not over the phone. Soon... When you come."

You don't wait for her reply. You hang up.

She doesn't call for a few days. Then on the weekend she phones to tell you she can't find your bone bangle anywhere.

"I have it," you tell her. You've taken it with you, on your body, as you did when you left Vietnam. It's your parent's history, a protective talisman from your blood-mother. "Why would I have left it behind?"

"We can't get rid of your absence. It fills up the house, the hours..." she answers, a beside the point observation.

She begins to tell you about Tri. "He poured hot wax down the washbasin after an experiment on lava lamps. It cooled into a solid plug. Then he just went and brushed his teeth in the clogged sink. I had to get Loc to come fix it, which upset Tri because Loc wasn't you. He refused to talk for nearly half a day. If you were here..."

She sounds like she's about to cry.

"Get him on the line then. Let me talk to him now," you say.

"He's asleep."

"For once go wake him. Please?"

Tri comes on. He's subdued. But then he's always subdued.

"What was wrong with Uncle Sixth's repair?" you ask.

Tri repeats what Loc said word for word, properly transposed into reported speech. "Uncle Sixth said I couldn't hold the tools and help. He had to do it quick so he could take Aunty Huong to their new nail salon in Los Angeles. I would be a nuisance and slow him down." He goes on, "Minus one of you it can't be the same. To fix it, you should come back."

Your mind races, searching for appropriate words to re-assure him and re-assure yourself.

"We'll see each other in Singapore at Christmas. We'll have fun. That will add back the one and correct the balance, won't it?"

"Alright then," he replies. He's eager to get off the phone. "I need to go to bed now. Mom says I must sleep early tonight. Goodbye."

You say goodbye and set the receiver down. You'll give Nina half an hour to settle him and then call back.

The boy's normal, Nina insists. She's done the tests. He's scored near the ends of the single standard deviation but is definitely not certifiably deranged or even dysfunctional. Just a little bit off normal along the autistic spectrum. Nothing to worry about, you tell yourself.

You go to sit at your rented desk and stare at your rented bed with its monogrammed service apartment linen. You watch the anonymous red-eyed digital clock on the television measure the minutes passing. You're sorry you didn't argue against Nina's decision to stay behind, if only for half a year.

"He's fine. He went off like a light when I sent him back to bed," Nina reports when you call back later.

"Why's he sleeping so early though? Are you punishing him for something?"

"Not at all. We go to church tomorrow, don't you remember?" She knows you have no use for church. But it isn't up to you, is it? Now you aren't there...

The seconds tick by as you wait each other out. She begins to tell you about her dissertation, which will be approved once she changes its title and adds two more tables and six citations. She doesn't know why the new title or the six citations are necessary but if...

You interrupt her. "Darling if that's all, I'll hang up then. Like I said, write the rest down for me to enjoy slowly."

You hear an ominous pause. Then she asks, "Do you have anything else?"

"Oh yes. I didn't manage to say, I got my visa for Vietnam. I'm going to Bangkok Monday morning to collect it," you inform her. "I don't think I can call the US from Vietnam. I'll only manage to get to you the week after, when I'm back in Bangkok."

"Right," she says.

"Love you. Bye now," you whisper.

"Just like that! One of the most important journeys of your life and you compress it into two sentences," she manages to edge in before you can escape. "I seriously don't know how I can miss you so much. You don't leave anything but question-marks and holes to indicate you've been."

This is not the time to start an argument, you tell yourself.

You smack a noisy kiss into the phone. "I miss you too," you say.

.....

You fly first class to Bangkok... To entertainment in red and gold pavilions and blinding neon bars... To massage parlors with numbered girls you can order up like quick-pick lottery numbers, girls you refuse politely.

.....

"The secret to maintaining a relationship is never to commit the unforgivable" Chú Hai had told you after the Dalat vacation you took following your breakup with Ai Nguyet.

Binh, who'd finagled a posting as assistant laboratory supervisor in the Military Academy was your main reason for going there. You'd hoped he would distract. And indeed he had tried his best. He'd sneaked you into his laboratory to see its wind tunnel, the only one in Vietnam. He introduced you to his favorite hostess bars, one each night for the six nights you were in town. He arranged the trysts after, more women in a week than you'd had in your whole lifetime before. But you weren't distracted.

Binh's cushy job in the up-to-the minute army laboratory, the smartly uniformed cadets around town, and the honeymooning couples the mountain city drew year round, reminded you that you could have chosen a different life — a military appointment Ai Nguyet's parents might have approved of and Ai Nguyet in your bed for a lifetime, not the 'clean' girls Binh fixed for you every night...

.....

You have too many sins for Nina to forgive already... An evening in a Bangkok brothel, you're certain, would be the last straw.

"I'm just out of America and still tied to my wife's apron strings. Give me time," you make your excuses to your Thai counterpart, an embarassed grin on your face.

Escaping back to your hotel, you lie in the massive bed and spend the rest of the night fretting over what might happen next, once you set foot again on Vietnamese soil.

10
Return

EVERYTHING IN VIETNAM SEEMS older and dirtier.

The semi-circular concrete bunkers used to protect the helicopters in the old days are sitting where they always sit, by the runway in the wind whipped grass. But the mottled green camouflage they'd been coated with has long peeled off. They're now a nondescript grey, spattered with beige rings of fungi. Despite being spruced up for the new economy, the tiny terminal building is decrepit compared to the last time you were there in 1974, when you'd said goodbye to Julia Anderson. What has not changed is the rows of unsmiling armed personnel inside the terminal. As you walk between them you feel the old frisson of excitement and unease, the quickening of your pulse in case you're uncovered and taken. And now the stakes are higher, with Nina and Tri to be accountable to.

Your visa has a note appended to it, stating you left the country without an exit permit. If they take you in, who will know you've been on their side? There's Chú Hai... But you've been communicating with him circuitously for so long you aren't sure how to find him if you need to. And since Jerry Chung's pitch, you've stopped sending reports to Ba Roi.

Expecting to be watched, you sent news of your homecoming to Third Sister in an ordinary pale blue air letter. You'd written— 'I've been offered an assignment in Singapore. I'll be near home and expect to visit, perhaps in about three months. I'll telegraph when everything is confirmed.' You'd added a postscript for Ba Roi and Chú Hai— 'It's such a good opportunity for learning, I accepted without even asking my wife's opinion,'—a defiant justification for your abrupt departure from orders.

You believe Chú Hai would understand. As for Ba Roi, you can see his thin lips tightening, his eyebrows drawing together. Who's prevailed? Will you get a returning hero's welcome or be taken in as a prodigal AWOL? You square your shoulders and stride forward to immigration to find out.

You're cleared unexpectedly quickly.

Out on the concourse, a wiry man with unruly hair and the rough accent of Northerners from Ho Chi Minh's Nghe An birthplace is waiting for you. You typecast him as a dyed in the wool party member, but he's friendly enough.

"I'm Tran Van Minh, just call me Minh," the handler introduces himself before steering you into an old Toyota van. He notes as you settle in your seat, "You're Tran Van Thong. You and me, Thong and Minh... intelligence, we shouldn't do badly together then."

Tran Van Minh is making the mistake everyone makes about the meaning of your name. But it isn't necessary to correct him if that's the link he needs to get to common ground.

"I hope so too," you say, reaching out to shake his hand.

Minh is on loan from the state tobacco company, your Thai counterpart has briefed. You're to treat him with respect, as the representative of a potential client. If possible you can develop him. What development might entail, though, your colleague in Bangkok hasn't explained. Minh, it turns out, will introduce you to the business opportunity of your life. But just then, you aren't concerned how your relationship will evolve. You're more interested in everything else happening outside your vehicle, in your city.

It's dusk and the city is preparing for night. Through the van's open windows, you smell burning charcoal overladen with roasting pork fat, fish sauce and the sweetness of rotting vegetation. From the black waters of the canals and sewers the rotten-egg stink of hydrogen sulphite rises to assault your nostrils. In contrast to the smells, the city looks wan. The buildings you pass are faded, in need of new paint. The people too are colorless, dressed in washed out beiges and blues or wilted flower prints, a grey pallor on their skins.

The children are eerily thin, matchstick bones sticking out from sharp knees and elbows. They move carefully, like old people, not the running jumping street children you used to shout at and dodge. The van passes a little girl squatting on the side of the pavement, relieving herself. She has a pale heart shaped face and enormous clouded yellow eyes that stare without expression at the Toyota sliding past her, a mere thirty centimeters away.

"Blind from Vitamin A deficiency. There's a lot of that these days," Minh says.

The city is less crowded than you remember, quieter. As the van honks and toots its way through the half deserted streets, the buildings and people begin to merge into the twilight, and then disappear completely into blackness. There's no light from the street lamps to break the gloom.

"Oil shortages. We can't generate enough electricity," Minh explains.

The van's headlights are the only illumination cutting a swathe through the pot-holed street bisecting Tao Dan Park, where Ai Nguyet and you used to walk. On the left and right of the street, the blackness is interrupted by oil lit cigarette booths where, you surmise, both the tobacco and the girls are for sale.

Although evening has just begun, the powdered and lipsticked faces of the girls, each spot-lighted by a flickering yellow lamp, are already bone tired. Haggard and hopeless, the girls seem to expect nothing from the night before them.

Even the whores have given up.

This is not the future you and Chú Hai had anticipated as you walked through the city on the last night before Liberation.

.....

After arranging Huong's and her children's escape from the invading Northern Army, you had left the Delta and rushed back to Chú Hai's office in Saigon. Your journey northwards had seemed such a fool's errand that no one still standing at the remaining road blocks had tried to stop you. You weren't even asked once for a bribe. Still, it took you two days to get back to the centre of Saigon and the hotel.

Chú Hai was working on a story, his fingers flying over the typewriter, a cigarette dangling between his lips. He swivelled around in his chair when the door clicked open. "Ah, you're here at last to see it happen..." The two of you exchanged smiles. Nothing else needed saying.

He was the only one left in the office. Everyone sensible had already left the country. As for the diehards, they were out on the streets trying to cover the story of their life, the last moments. Or the first moments, from Chú Hai's and your perspectives.

You sat down in the armchair near the editor's desk, a huge overstuffed monstrosity like the ones Chú Hai used to have in the room behind Albert's villa. When was that, you thought drowsily? So long ago...

It was night when he shook you awake. From outside you heard the thrumming of helicopters and underlying that sound, a dull roar, as if the whole city was gathered beneath the hotel's windows, muttering. "It's tonight, I can feel it in my bones," he said. "Let's take a walk to see it all with our own eyes. So we'll never be fooled by what's reported in this or that newspaper, by anything I might have written over there," he pointed to his typewriter.

Chú Hai never lied in his reports but he did edit for his audience. The story of the Nationalist soldiers he and you met stripping in an alley before melting into the darkness went into the photo-essay the magazine published about the last days. So did the one about the children fighting over a pile of guns and ammunition left under a tree. Others know the images because of the pictures in the press. It's the originals that remain in your mind's eye, etched there on the night of April 29th 1975 during your walk with the man closest to your heart.

There were other images and sound bites that didn't make the cut. But they too remain in the archive of your memories.

You remember the transvestite in the barber shop famous for its blow jobs. Oblivious to any observers, she was transforming herself back into a boy, her hip long hair falling in dark clumps onto the floor as she snipped and snipped. You remember her mascara'd eyes and her lipstick smudged lips when she turned for a second to look out into the dark, right at the two of you. You remember yourself shouting a warning through the broken shop window. "Be sure to wipe all your makeup off, Comrade."

*There was the conversation Chú Hai and you overheard
in the crowd stretching three streets down from the American
embassy: "You'll come with us," the father's voice was raised.
"I can't, I love her," the son declared. You saw the father
loosening his grasp on the son's wrist and turning towards the
embassy, the young man stumbling away from the helicopters
that could take him to safety.*

*You remember turning to Chú Hai. "If that was me and you
were the father what would you do?"*

*He'd looked abashed for a minute. Then, as if in blessing,
he'd run his thumb down your nose bridge and over your
upper lip to your chin. It was a gesture so intimate you had
to bite your lips to stop them from trembling. "Ah but I'm not,
am I?" he'd said, his left eye beginning to tick. He dug into his
shirt pocket, took out a pack of cigarettes and offered one to
you. "What a question!"*

*Indeed, what could have possessed you to ask it? You held
the cigarette to your lips, sucking in as he lighted it up. The
smoke, when you inhaled, burnt your throat and you began to
cough violently. He slapped you hard on your back until you
stopped. "I'm twenty-seven, and this is my first cigarette," you
said to him, bemused.*

He did not reply.

*The two of you walked away from the city under an
unusually dark sky. There were no flares shooting anywhere,
no sudden explosions of light to indicate a missile had found
its target. It was very quiet: no gunfire, no mortars, just the
whump-whump of the increasingly distant helicopters over the
American embassy. Entering Chinatown, you were surprised
how empty it was. The throngs of pleasure seekers, traders,
thieves and pickpockets had melted away. The whizzing red*

and yellow neon signs were switched off. There were no pimps in front of the gambling halls and cabarets. The shop fronts were either shuttered or shattered.

"Where's everyone?" you asked.

"Outside the embassy or cowering at home or here," Chú Hai pointed to the small thatched houseboats bobbing in front of you.

You'd wandered off the main street and deep down an alley to the river where the water people lived, where the opium boats were.

Chú Hai took you by the hand and pulled you towards one of the unpainted wooden sampans. "There's a first time for everything—a woman, a cigarette, a pipe. After tonight you'll never have another chance at it. Our masters will make sure of that," he said almost sadly.

His sudden mood change confused you. Why this shadow of regret? It should be a night for celebration. Or perhaps this was how Chú Hai celebrated.

Just once, you cautioned yourself, trying to forget how one thing always led to another; how one chicken had led to another and then to stained hands. You followed Chú Hai down into the den.

It was a small boat about a meter and a half wide and four or five meters long, with a deck in the front where you'd entered and another in the back facing the river, where the toilet was. The cabin was roofed over with thatch, the ceiling so low Chú Hai and you had to stoop once you were inside. The space was dark, with only a few small candles hanging in glass jars from the bamboo supports of the thatched roof. Wooden benches covered with reed mats lined both sides of the cabin. There was already someone else lying in the back of the boat, lost in dreaming, a candle flickering by his lax hand.

The place was a fire hazard.

"That man... the open flame," you said, taking a step back. You didn't want to give yourself over to the drug in the presence of a stranger. And you hadn't kept yourself alive up to this night to lose it in an accidental fire or a drug fuelled scuffle. You pulled against Chú Hai's hand, trying to back out. Instead of letting go, Chú Hai's grip around your wrist tightened. "Docile as a puppy, no danger at all," he said about the other customer. "He's in seventh heaven, just like we'll be," he chuckled with expectation, pulling you onto the boat with him.

The proprietress, a woman made so pale and delicate by her addiction she seemed to be constructed of paper and bamboo, greeted Chú Hai with a slight bow. He grunted and handed her some Southern currency notes. "No more of that," she said with a brittle twist of her neck. "It's gold now. Black if you have it to share, yellow if not." Chú Hai dug in his pockets. "Would you take dollars instead?" he teased. But she just twisted her neck again.

She had the infinite patience of one who'd smoked so many pipes time had no meaning, except to measure intervals between more pipes. Having just smoked, she had all the time in the world to wait.

"Hah! Even those who dream know this won't be any good tomorrow," Chú Hai grumbled as he put the piastres back into his wallet and dug out half a strip of gold instead.

The woman took the gold and tucked it inside her blouse. She beckoned the two of you to the benches nearest her. From a rack above her head, she took down two long pipes on which ceramic bowls in the bud shape of small boys' members were attached. She put these on a tray set with an oil lamp the size of a child's fist and a square lacquer box and shuffled towards Chú Hai.

"Give it to him first," Chú Hai said. "Be kind. He's a virgin."

The woman obeyed and came to kneel by you with the tray. She set the lamp's wick alight, then scraped out a tiny black pellet from the lacquer box with a needle and began to heat it over the flame. "For you, this will be more than enough," she assured, as if expecting you to complain about the little she was giving you.

You watched with fascination as she toasted the little pellet over the flame and sniffed at its pungent perfume before rolling it onto the edge of the pipe bowl and then plunging it in. She handed the pipe to you, helping you to steady it over the burning wick. "Once slowly but deeply and then again, a little faster," you heard Chú Hai's voice from behind the woman. You did as told and choked. You tried again, more slowly this time. After your third in-breath the pellet was all gone. And you were vaporized along with it.

You felt the bench underneath you soften, your own bones melt. Your body left you and you found yourself holding on to nothing but your thoughts, thoughts so crystal clear you couldn't find words for them.

"I can smell the stars," you heard yourself trying to explain to Chú Hai. It seemed quite obvious stars should have a scent to them like every other living burning thing in the universe, but how could you make him understand? "I'm not seeing them, I smell them. Seeing is nothing. Everyone can see stars. But to smell them takes effort. You have to breathe very hard. Or fly very far. After all, they're so very high," you said loudly, so Chú Hai would be sure to hear you from where he was, so far below you.

From up there, looking down, you saw everything. It was all laid out before you—the river, the city, the helicopters... Just north of the helicopters you saw the yellow starred tanks gathering at Tan Son Nhut Airport, getting ready for the next day's entry into the city. Further out, at sea, were the American aircraft carriers filling with more and more runaways. And in the heart of the city were the ones left behind, tearing the American Embassy to pieces in their rage and disappointment. Or was all this what you'd read off the report Chú Hai typed earlier?

Did it matter? The report was what the world, the stars, would see. So why shouldn't you, now, down here in this lightly rocking boat? It would be reality the way Chú Hai set it down. Because Chú Hai knew. He always knew.

How did Chú Hai know? You would have to ask him later when you came back down to earth. It was an existential question. The most important question as far as you were concerned. Otherwise, after following in his footsteps these many years, where would you find yourself when this dream ended?

You decided it couldn't wait. From where you were up in the sky, you shouted it down. "Chú Hai, can a master of deceit lead me to the truth?"

You thought you heard Chú Hai's voice answering but he was speaking to the man in the back of the boat. Actually two men, you saw now. The man, his companion and Chú Hai were having a convoluted conversation about wisdom and honor, courage and treachery. They didn't seem to be agreeing. Foolish humans... why not just live and let live?

"Never. We'll never surrender," you heard one of them say to the other. "Never," the other affirmed.

They got up to leave through the back end of the boat.

You saw them silhouetted against the early dawn sky, heroic in their Southern generals' uniforms with their peaked caps on and the stars glinting on their square shoulders. They put two long pipes into their mouths. Then they farted, just two little pops, before going over the edge.

You giggled to yourself. Generals farted in the same way lesser mortals did. How undignified, how uncontrolled... Or was it? Your face crumpled in distress. Had they done it to show their contempt for the wonderful new order soon to come? "They shouldn't have done that. You should've stopped them... stopped them..." you heard yourself sobbing to Chú Hai.

"Coming down," you heard him say to the woman.

She murmured something unintelligible. She was on her dawn pipe, drifting off. Chú Hai's worries belonged to him. They were none of her business. She was paid to provide dreams, not resolve problems.

You felt Chú Hai's arms around you, Chú Hai whispering meaningless baby words to soothe you. You felt your own tears soaking into his shirt. He was telling you, "A new birth always comes with pain. Just like you came, with blood and pain and into blood and pain. But you're living and breathing with a whole life before you, son, con trai. That's what matters. That's what's important."

His words beat painfully in your head as you walked out into the melancholy early morning with him, your head on his shoulder. The sunshine hurt your eyes. You were incredibly thirsty. Chú Hai led you down the boulevard, towards town, hoping to find a sidewalk coffee vendor on the way. But all of them seemed to have gone into hiding.

At the entrance to the Martyr's Square you saw a group of children in khaki uniforms. Bereft of its usual traffic, the roundabout was enormous even to your citified eyes. To most of these members of the Northern Army, recruited from hamlets in the Central Mountains, such an expanse must have been a new conception.

Chú Hai and you watched them circle the square once, then again, before making little forays down the six arterial roads branching out from the square. They always came back to the square's centre. Finally, while the majority of the group stayed in the roundabout, a small advance squad was sent up the side road on the market's east side. But, soon, they were back too. "There's nothing but a big wall there!" one of them shouted in an almost unintelligible accent.

You blinked. So this was the conquering army—a group of lost children barely one and a half meters tall.

Chú Hai called out to them from the corner where you and he were standing. "Comrades! Comrades!"

As one they swivelled around, their guns raised. No, these were not children after all, but a seasoned fighting force.

"Stop," a voice shouted from within the group. "Come forward," it said to Chú Hai.

He walked towards them, his arms at his side, his palms open. "Where do you want to go, Comrades?" he asked. "The Presidential Palace," the leader, indistinguishable from his companions in age and dress but with a crisp Hanoi accent, informed Chú Hai. "Do you know the way, Uncle?"

"It's just beyond the wall where your men just went," Chú Hai indicated with his hand. "We'll show you," he volunteered.

Your final memories of that day are of Saigon seen through the eyes of the teenagers from a Scout Platoon of the 324ᵗʰ Division. Your devastated city became once again your teenage Pearl of the Orient, a place of plenty, the object of

*a dream carried all the way South through the rain and the
jungle, through years of sacrifice.*

*"We raided a warehouse last night. It was full of medicine
and machines I never saw before," a stocky brown boy confided
to you. "We ate instant noodles from the supplies. There were
at least ten different flavors. And all we had to do was pour hot
water over them and they were ready," his friend contributed.*

*The first boy pointed to the nearly hundred year old trees
fronting the boulevard to the Palace, the black tarmac'd road
you were walking on. "Look at all this. You have so much, why
didn't you fight harder to defend it?"*

"We wanted peace," you told him.

*"For the sake of peace we handed it to them on a platter,"
you would say with true regret to Nina's father many years
later when you were seeking her hand in marriage. On that
morning though, all you felt was a shade of uncertainty. Yes, it
should not have been this easy—the Nationalist Army turning
into the guerrillas of old, melting away without even the
slightest resistance at the Northern Army's approach.*

.....

Now, the young soldiers from the North have become middle-
aged men with eyes clouded by greed. As for you, the scales
fell off your eyes a long time ago. What you see clearly is
that your city, which was dying when you left in 1979, is now
truly dead. You've not come back to celebrate a resurrection
brought about by *dời mới* but to mourn at a funeral.

You feel tears prickling at your eyelashes. Something rises
in your throat. It seems to be a bone from your heart... You
swallow, pushing the fragment back down where it belongs.

You can't afford to lose any more pieces of that organ, not even the rankling bones. And you can't disgrace yourself in front of this party functionary from the North.

"Please, will you help me with the check-in? I need to use the bathroom," you mumble to Minh the moment the van pulls up at the hotel.

Minh nods.

Pointing out your case to the doorman, he makes for the reception desk.

When you become better acquainted, he'll confess that when he went home to Hanoi from Moscow five years earlier, he too had broken down.

.....

It is the same hotel where Chú Hai had his office.

If you had eyes to see, you would notice it is also the same doorman, much thinner, guarding the portico. But you don't. You rush through the lobby to the men's room, thank goodness still in the same location, and into the plywood cubicle with the swinging half doors. Safe there, you sit down and let your ragged coughs loose, allowing them to pump salty slime up from your guts into your nostrils and your eyes and your mouth, to coat your shaking fingers.

You don't know how long you weep in the cubicle, or whether anyone comes in to use the bathroom, or to peek over the swing doors to check on you. But when your tears stop, as suddenly as they start, you are no longer the man who pined for this city and the Delta and the burial grounds of your ancestors for a decade. You accept, as you never did in the years you lived here after Liberation, that your homeland is a place in the past you can never go back to. This new country you've landed in is not the one you lost. You accept it as it is, without regret. And you will blame no one, not even yourself, for what it has become.

You want to share this realization with Minh, to surrender unconditionally and clear the air of any residual animosity he may be harboring, so the two of you can get on with whatever business is needed, to build a future for this place. But when you emerge from the bathroom, your swollen eyes dry, Minh is gone, leaving only an envelope with the receptionist.

You follow the bellman up to your room in a rickety wooden elevator, the same one you'd used so frequently years before. Once in your room, you tip the bellman over-generously and rush him away with rude haste. Locking the door after him and setting Minh's envelope on the dresser to review later, you go to the windows and wrestle close the creaky shutters and glass panes, then draw the curtains tight. You can't bring back your youth, but with the city's sad darkness shut out, the room now bears some semblance to the one you first slept in the year you graduated. If you are to be homeless, you determine, you will at least reclaim your memories to carry away with you.

Turning on the air-conditioner, drinking a warm beer from the selection set out on a shelf above the dresser, running a bath, you recall the evenings you spent with Julia Anderson in a room like this one.

.....

You'd been callow and young when it started, she less so. But the two of you had experienced your first fire-fight together, during a helicopter strafing in a Mekong Delta hamlet. You'd pressed her body to yours while running to safety. Later when you took her home, she'd fallen asleep with her buxom chest against your back. Something had been seeded, even if initially it was nothing more than wet dreams.

Chú Hai had sent you to Julia Anderson when you were eighteen. "A newly minted arrival who needs an interpreter for a visit to the Delta," he'd told you. "God forbid, you're turning me into an interpreter just like my father said you would," you had replied. But you went anyway. Because you were curious about American women... Because you'd promised to help Chú Hai in whatever way you could... Because he was interested in influencing American journalists, no matter how unimportant.

Chú Hai and you discovered very quickly, though, that Julia Anderson was one of those simple American patriots who would never report anything damaging about her countrymen on the ground, no matter how persuasive Chú Hai's arguments or evidence might be. The two of you wrote her off as soon as you could. So unimportant was she to Chú Hai and you, you hardly missed her when she gave up journalism and went home to America after the Tết offensive.

She had come back a year later, harder yet sleeker. Her dust colored hair was now tinted auburn and she was working in an undefined role at the Embassy. It was the role's ambiguity Chú Hai found intriguing. He sought her out and did his best to cultivate her trust and have her rely on him for information and opinions. Then in the year before your graduation, he set you at her.

It began innocuously, an envelope to be given to her personally at the embassy.

You didn't want to go. It was your final year at university. You needed to study. And there was Ai Nguyet, so moody, so sad, so beautiful, to take care of.

"But you offered to help. It's on your way home, just a quick stop," Chú Hai wheedled.

He pushed the envelope into your hands. He must have sensed you were ready, the woman ripe.

She didn't recognize you until you spoke. Then her eyes lit up and she folded you to her in a bear hug. "Why, you're all grown up," she said, holding you to her, pressing her round American breasts into your chest.

Her breasts, the objects of your febrile teenage nightmares... You remembered them carelessly rubbing against your back from the passenger perch of Chú Hai's motorcycle as she directed you on her errands here and there and back again; exciting and tormenting you the whole way. You took a step back. "Well, a bit older," you replied. You were self conscious, aware you'd grown centimeters taller and filled out across the shoulders and chest.

"Let me look at you," she said, her arms pushed out straight, her hands holding onto your shoulders. Like most of the foreigners you interpreted for, you knew she would still see a very young man, much younger than your age. But inside, so much older than them, you used to think, whenever you caught reflections of yourself and your clients in shop windows. They didn't have your shrouded eyes, the war-weariness around your lips, your closed defended face, your tense held-in posture. They didn't have a body that had spent a whole life in war.

You thought you were attractive. Ai Nguyet had told you so. And the Vietnamese staff at the hotel and cafés Chú Hai and you frequented always said you were. "Handsome, exactly like your Chú," they would gush, especially the older waitresses. But you did not know what Julia Anderson thought as she scanned your face, your neck, your chest and legs. Perhaps she felt a prickle of attraction, perhaps even more than that...

Suddenly she became shy and dropped her hands. "Well, let's see what he's got for me," she said, taking the envelope from you. She slit it open with the unvarnished nail of her index finger and peered inside. "I need to run these upstairs immediately," she told you. "Goodbye," she said, holding out a lightly trembling hand for you to shake.

You were so aroused you barely dared to touch it. When you met Ai Nguyet at the café a few doors away afterwards, and she leaned against you in greeting, you had to grit your teeth to stop yourself from crushing her against your chest to feel the swell of her tiny breasts on your body. That night your confused dreams of Julia Anderson began again.

Chú Hai kept throwing you and Julia Anderson together, sending you to her with messages, opinions, and interpretations. "Take her for coffee. Tell her my view of the situation is that it's untenable," he would instruct, rattling off a list of reasons you should communicate. Or he would excuse himself, "It's inconvenient for me to meet her. Just drop in and let her know I think they'll be changing the strategy soon." Or just, "Go. Tell her I'll be busy for the next two weeks. She'll know what that means."

You didn't understand how Chú Hai discerned what information Julia Anderson needed and when he should offer it. They were playing a deep game. Keeping track of the pieces of truth and untruth they traded was beyond you then. You were just their messenger, running between the two of them with your flesh thick and throbbing against your fly.

One day, in passing, she asked what you thought of the Vietnamese Army Chief of Staff. "Your own views, not your uncle's," she teased.

"Whose side should I pretend to be on?" you confronted Chú Hai later.

"Your own, naturally," Chú Hai laughed.

This ambiguity wasn't what you wanted just then. You dug your heels into the office carpet. "If it's for my own sake then I don't want to see her anymore. It's already complicated, keeping straight what you want me to tell her, what she wants me to pass on to you. Now having to worry about what I can or cannot say to her myself... She confuses me. She's just too sexy. It's difficult for me to be careful when I'm with her."

"Ahhh, fuck her then and get it out of your system," Chú Hai said, unexpectedly. "I set her aside for you, you know. So you can learn how to control what to say and not say, even while in the throes of passion."

"You set her aside for me. You mean... she... you..."

Chú Hai waved away your confusion with his elegant right hand. "Psssht, I'm an old man, forty-two. What I need is a sixteen year old who knows nothing, who'll cry out in ecstasy with a bit of probing here and there from a wet noodle. She's twenty-seven or twenty-eight, at her peak. How can I satisfy her?" he smiled. "But she's American. She's got a whole pack of them to choose from. Why me?" you asked. "Despite her hard shell, she's a romantic. She's in love with the exotic east, haven't you realized that? She'll take you over them anytime." He beckoned you to him. "Come. Let me tell you about what she needs."

This time, you didn't say you weren't interested.

It happened the night of your graduation. No one from your family could attend. It was out of the question for your blood-father who was in hiding after his defection. The road from the Delta had become too dangerous for your parents to come.

Oldest Brother-in-Law had finally moved out of his and Oldest Sister's house to live with his mistress. Oldest Sister, playing the tragic heroine, wanted nothing to do with your affairs. Loc and his family were in Nha Trang on the central coast. Worst of all, Ai Nguyet had refused to grace the occasion. Still trying to keep you and your plebeian background a secret from her family, she'd refused to show up at the commencement. Chú Hai was your one guest, and Julia Anderson, because Chú Hai had invited her.

Everyone else's families were there in full force— Binh's clan of coarse sisters with their American partners; Ly's unostentatious Chinese family and his girl friend, a fundamentalist Christian whose family had forbidden her to marry the agnostic Ly. Only you, the top student of the year, had no girl and no family to celebrate your success with. You would have felt unloved and abandoned if not for Chú Hai's efforts to make the occasion memorable—arranging for a colleague to photograph you in the graduation suit he'd gone with you to get tailored, jollying the three of you into the hotel's French restaurant where he'd ordered a magnificent dinner, leading everyone up to the rooftop bar later to watch the outgoing fires flaming on the horizon, plying you and Julia Anderson with drink.

You were both tipsy when Chú Hai got up from his chair to leave. "She's going to need help to her room," he whispered to you. "Let him take you," he advised Julia Anderson. "Au revoir, my children," he said, joining his palms in an oriental salute.

Sensing the rightness of the moment, Julia Anderson allowed you to take her to her fifth floor room, as you'd been ordered to. What happened next was a whisky sodden grope you have no clear memory of. But in the morning, after she'd shown you how to run a hot bath and you'd both soaked away the night's exertions and then showered, she let you see how it was done in the American way. And later allowed you to put into practice what Chú Hai had whispered.

This first then second then third time were a relief.

"You were right," you reported to Chú Hai the next evening, coming straight down to the office from her room. "I feel so much better now it's all out of the way." He guffawed. "Hah... I have bad news for you. It comes back. And then you have to do it again, and again, and again. Such is the nature of man."

And also the nature of women, American women anyway, you naively thought then. Julia Anderson invited you to her room again, and again, and again.

It was not as often as you would have liked. She was away from Saigon frequently. But you had Ai Nguyet, whom you could now love without the distraction of your body. And there was your new job and Chú Hai's machine as well. It was sufficient.

It was enough for Chú Hai too. With the positive developments in the field, there was no misinformation Chú Hai needed to pass to her and her superiors. He was satisfied, so long as there was someone to keep tabs on where she'd been and where she might be going.

"Laos and Cambodia. Up to the mountains, to meet Montagnards," you told him.

She had to be arranging Laotian and Cambodian clearance for the badly concealed 'secret' raids on North Vietnamese borderland positions, he guessed.

But you were unable to find out exactly when and where these raids would take place, and hence how they could be neutralized or avoided. "She's very careful. She comes and goes without notice. I only know where she's been because she talks in her sleep. After her trips she dreams in the language she last used."You didn't tell him she tossed and turned and sometimes cried out in fear, clutching you to her as if only you could save her. "I can recognize the languages. But I can't understand any of it," you said.

"You're useless. I'll have to send her a Montagnard or Lao in your place," he teased.

"As you like," you sulked.

You went off to Dalat to visit Binh.

When you came back, you didn't call in on him or Julia Anderson. You were still heart sore about Ai Nguyet and angry at Chú Hai for suggesting you were replaceable in Julia's bed by an aboriginal stud. Anyway, after the bacchanalia with Binh in Dalat, you didn't need her just yet. Let Chú Hai come to you when he ran out of Montagnards and Laotians.

He did.

This was your other life in Saigon for the next two years. Wrestling in the big French double bed with Julia, exchanging lies—she asking you questions you knew to be misleading, you passing on spurious facts; neither loving the other but each giving and taking from the other all you could. Through the skirmishes of the Christmas of 1971 and the preparations for another offensive the next year, all through the changing fortunes of the Quang Tri invasion, the attack on Kontum, the siege of An Loc...

You did well by Chú Hai. You learnt how to control what to say and not say even in the throes of passion. You kept your heart cool even as you confused her. Telling her as you traced your long fingers down her back, "He says they're thinking of waiting till next year, when you've all gone," when in fact the North Vietnamese Army came in March that year. Running your hands through her hair and whispering, "He thinks they'll do what they always do, come from the west," as the divisions flooded in from the north as well. Assuring her, "They'll never take Tay Ninh," which in fact the Northern forces didn't, but leaving out the essential tid-bit about the attack on An Loc. Even as you pulled her down to your face, opened your lips to receive her nipple like a young nestling, and let her suffocate you with her full, freckled breasts.

Yes, you did well by Chú Hai, feeding Julia Anderson the same false intelligence planted with her colleagues at South Vietnamese Intelligence and CIA surveillance, helping to confirm their mistaken beliefs, helping to cement the successful Northern incursions. True, there had been the return of the B-52s and thousands upon thousands dead in the countryside afterwards, retaliation Chú Hai and you hadn't expected, retaliation that compelled Chú Hai's masters to go back to Paris to negotiate. But they'd negotiated so cleverly there the settlement turned the tide of the war yet again, once more against the South.

.....

Yes, you did well by both Chú Hai and the revolution. At what cost, though? Not just to those who died in the B-52 bombings but to yourself and your relationships since? You set down your pen, leaving that karmic question hanging. You allow yourself to feel a pang of guilt at the mountain of deception you've heaped on Nina, how Nina has been made to live married to this person you so willingly allowed Chú Hai and Julia Anderson to shape.

.....

You uncap another bottle of warm beer, slip your recollections of Julia Anderson into a hotel envelope and date it, then turn to work.

Minh will meet you at 7 am the next day, his cover note informs you. Attached to the note is an annotated list of appointments—two deputy directors from the tobacco company, the chair lady of a government unit with rights to import machinery, someone from the national oil company and the directors of five small factories. All the factories are state owned enterprises except the very last, a soft drinks bottling plant belonging to an ethnic Chinese named Hua Cong Ly— your old friend Ly.

"Can we move Mr Ly's meeting forward? Also can we free up the back end of the week to allow for further developments?" you ask Minh at breakfast. "He and I go way back. It's more likely something comes out of this meeting than the others."

Minh is amenable to cancelling everyone except the two deputy directors—who are his superiors; and the lady with the import license—who, you later learn, is Minh's lover. After you finish with them Minh tactfully takes his leave. "Call me before you go to the airport so this rascal doesn't steal my van," he says, pointing to the driver.

.....

You want to see Ly first, because it's business Jerry has paid for. Once that's out of the way, you plan to visit your parents in the Delta before dropping in on everyone else including

Chú Hai and Oldest Sister. Unfortunately Ly is away till the next Saturday, you find out when you call to shift your appointment forward.

"Can Tho tomorrow then. First thing after breakfast," you tell the driver. That's your intention anyway. But instead of heading out to the highway after your meal you find yourself directing the van back into the city, towards the quiet cul-de-sac where *Chú Hai* had lived after Liberation. No matter the proper sequence for visits, the heart has its own orderings, you realize.

Chú Hai's lane, lovely before, has lost all its grace in your years away. Most of the pastel colored walls hiding the small French style houses have been demolished, their bricks sold to supplement household expenses. Rickety add-ons—wooden lean-to's, tarpaulin sheds, even cardboard partitions—stick to the houses like colonies of barnacles. The few walls remaining are crumbling, the plaster cracked, the crack lines overgrown with moss.

Thankfully, number five's walls are still intact and the painted gate is securely closed and sheathed with iron sheets, an indication the house continues to be occupied by an official in good standing. You peer through the spy hole, a four centimeter opening cut through the metal, into a cement courtyard filled with pots of bonsai and rooster cages. He's there, you breathe with happiness.

You call through the opening.

A scholarly man, now white-haired, straightens up from behind an ornamental pine and walks quickly over, lowering his head to the spy hole.

You place your palm against it to block Chú Hai's view. "Sheer stupidity, positioning an un-protected eye where god knows what can blind it," you scold, trying to suppress the laughter bubbling up from your gut.

"Damn it! Up to your tricks again, are you?"Chú Hai's excited voice says. He pushes a finger out through the hole and pokes your palm away with the hard end of a fingernail. "Move that hand, *con*. Let me have a look at you."

A bright thick lashed eye appears in the hole for a second. You hear the rattle of keys, then the gate swings open and for the second time in your life you find yourself enfolded in Chú Hai's embrace.

It is everything a son might wish a father's welcome to be.

11
Homecoming

THIRD SISTER, SEWING BY HER FRONT DOOR in Can Tho merely looks up and nods when you walk through the unlocked front gate and into her sunlit courtyard.

"You're here," she says.

"Third Sister," you reply in greeting, adding, "Father and Mother, how are they?"

"No different since I last wrote to you. He's alive; as for mother, she's getting more and more..." She puts down her needlework and leads you to the middle hall to see for yourself.

Your father, paralyzed by a series of strokes, is lying on his platform, propped on his side by pillows. Your mother, eyes closed, swings in a hammock strung beside the black wood divan. The windows are open, but still the room smells of old age, incontinence and impending death.

You kneel down on the floor between them. "*Ba, Má*, I'm home," you say.

Your father blinks. You think you see a momentary spark of recognition in his eyes. On your mother's face though there's only confusion.

"It's me, Youngest," you say, bringing her hand up to touch your face and hair.

"No Sir. Don't tease me just because I'm an old woman who can't see," she says. She traces her fingers around your eye sockets and across your softening jaw to show you she isn't as senile as everyone fears. "You have my Youngest's voice for sure, but my son is a young man and you're not," she explains. Bending forward, she sniffs at your nose and your mouth. "I never allowed my son to smoke or to drink. You, Sir, stink like a playboy. No, you're not my son. I won't let you trick me." She folds her legs back up into the hammock and closes her eyes.

On hearing this, a loud gurgle erupts from your father. He begins coughing in great bellows which turn his face purple. Your Third Sister steps forward and lifts him up to clear his airways. From behind, you see your father's face flopped loosely over your sister's left shoulder. His eyes are wide open. Tears are streaming down his cheeks.

.....

Your father's crying face hovers over you as you slip in and out of consciousness in the attic that was once your bedroom. Your sisters, who'd prepared your welcome feast, surround you, jostling to wipe away your sweat, quieten your thrashing limbs and cool your steaming brow. "It was something in the water... Perhaps in the vegetables... Just a stomach grown weak after years in America," they whisper.

"It's amoebic dysentery," a grim-faced Ba Roi tells them. He shoos them off and claims you to watch over as assiduously as he might a valuable prisoner of war, to keep death at bay so you can be saved for later interrogation. He hydrates you, dripping water from fresh coconuts down your throat through the stems of water-swamp plants. To kill the infection, he chews up ginger and jungle leaves and spits the concoction directly from his mouth into yours. With his own hands he wipes you clean after every eruption of your bowels and changes and carries away the soiled banana leaves spread under your aching body. And as you burn and mutter with delirium, he sponges down your hot body and hums old fashioned lullabies to you.

In your lucid moments Ba Roi assails you with questions about your life in America. He takes out your letters, saved through the years, and pesters you to clarify what you've written about the machines you came across there. And, in a startling confession, he confides his disillusionment with the Revolution and the Party. "I suspected as much. And now, talking to you, I'm sure. If we'd let the Americans win the war we'd all have been better off." He points with a sour grimace to the banana leaves lining your wooden bed. "Look at this. Fifteen years after the Revolution and we're still lying on leaves, the same bed sheets I had in the jungle hospital." His laugh afterwards is hoarse and laden with remorse.

.....

It's your turn to feel remorse when, nursed back to health, you return to Saigon and visit Oldest Sister and her husband.

.....

It was in Oldest Sister's and Oldest Brother-in-Law's well-provisioned house that you spent your high school years. In that house down an alley in Saigon's District Three, Oldest Brother-in-Law had first persuaded you to taste the wonders churned out by his cook—French charcuterie, explosive

Northern gunpowder pickles made from fermented baby eggplants, Southern grilled quails and other exotic birds, and an uncountable variety of dumplings and cakes from Imperial Hue. It was from that house that Oldest Brother-in-Law ushered all of the members of the household—you, Loc, Huong, your Oldest Sister, her five children, and the maids—into the fleet of American donated police cars at his disposal and ferried you all to the city's best-air conditioned theatre to enjoy the delights of Hollywood movies. It was in the dining room of that house, during the first Tết of Liberation, that you were forcefully reminded how badly you'd repaid that corrupt and cruel man's generosity to you.

You were twenty-eight that New Year. As always, you ate khổ qua, bitter gourd, for the Tết re-union dinner... So bitterness would pass you by.

That year the khổ qua was so sharp Oldest Sister was convinced bitterness would pass all of you by, not just for the next twelve months but for many years to come. She had simmered it plain in water. The meat, just the half kilogram you brought home from work, had to be set aside for the obligatory New Year stew. Sugar couldn't be found in the markets to make candied offerings, not even for the price of gold. You didn't have enough money for boiled head-cheese or saucissons. All your savings had been converted—not once but twice—your total stock of paper money turned in and each adult given two hundred New Vietnamese Dong in exchange. It was just enough for a week of Russian barley or six bowls of good white rice for your Tết dinner meant for seven.

You sat down around Oldest Sister's dining table, an incomplete circle. The head of the house, Oldest Brother-in-Law, was missing.

In the May following Liberation all former employees of the old government had been ordered to register for re-education. Not recognized yet as a hero of the revolution and still at your old job in the government machinery depot, you put your name down like everyone else. On the day itself, you and the few other engineers who hadn't fled were ushered into the hall of your former high school to listen to the new minister of heavy industry speechifying on the revolutionary government's policy of reconciliation. When the minister was done, you were sent home. In June, you were required to attend another course, ten days on the crimes of the Americans and their puppet regime. After the course all of you were corralled for another day to write essays on what you'd learnt. Again, after your essays were handed in, you were released. Re-education, you concluded, was time consuming but not life threatening.

When the directive for a third study session was announced in July, you had no qualms about signing up. Nor did you question Chú Hai's advice for Oldest Brother-in-Law to come out of hiding in the countryside and register too. "The cadres have interviewed the neighbors. There's no covering up your Oldest Brother-in-Law's position in the old regime. Sooner or later, he'll have to come home. Isn't it better for him to regularize his status now? All he'll suffer is a few weeks of re-education and then no more hiding, no more fear ..." he'd said, and you'd repeated to Oldest Sister.

The next day Oldest Brother-in-Law returned to go with you to the neighborhood pickup point. As stipulated in the announcement, both of you brought everything you needed for a thirty day stay—your own food, sleeping mats and towels, and enough money for incidentals. In addition, your bag contained two cartons of American cigarettes and a sealed envelope from Chú Hai. "Your status isn't certain until we get official recognition of your role in the war," he'd said. He pressed the cigarettes and envelope into your hands. "Use the packs in the first carton as gifts to the assistants. Tell them I've entrusted you with a personal message for the section head. When you meet him, present the other carton with my compliments and also this letter."

You exhausted the first carton during a nerve-wracking morning being passed from one dour faced thick accented soldier to another. When finally you were brought in front of the section leader, a jungle bleached man in plain civilian clothes, he was hostile. "My men say you've been agitating them non-stop to give me a direct message from my comrade Trung," he barked.

You forced yourself to lower your eyes, to be humble. You dug out the carton of cigarettes and placed it carefully on the man's desk with two hands. "He asked you to accept these," you said. Then you slid Chú Hai's envelope under the carton, "... and also to take a look at this."

The eyes behind the section head's puffy lids gleamed at the sight of the envelope but his voice remained contemptuous. "You Southerners think everyone's for sale." His hand reached out to take the envelope. The short rough fingers hesitated as they pulled out the letter inside, one page thin with no enclosures.

You held your breath.

The man's thick right index finger traced the lines of the message. Then he put the letter back into the envelope with more care than it was taken out. "Looks are certainly deceiving," he said. He leaned over and pushed the carton of cigarettes on his table back to you. "Take these back. I don't need them to know we can't overlook anyone's service for the revolution. Don't worry, Young Brother. I'll do what's right by you."

The section head was indeed a man who could discern right from wrong. When the cadres came in with their name lists late that evening, Oldest Brother-in-Law and you were separated. Along with a handful of other unlikely Northern sympathizers—an elderly engineer from the Port Authority, one of the former principals of the technical high school you'd gone to, and a group of Oldest Sister's colleagues from the Women's Hospital—you were asked to stand on the lead cadre's left. Everyone else, including Oldest Brother-in-Law, was asked to squat down on the other side.

You've never forgotten how Oldest Brother-in-Law's expression changed from confusion, to disbelief, to understanding and then to fury. How he jumped up and tried to scramble over the hunched down backs of the public works contractors, bank managers, hospital workers and post office supervisors, to get at you. And how he was knocked back with the butt of a soldier's rifle and hauled into the truck taking them all away.

After a week, the medical workers were sent back, their identity documents stamped with the words 'essential personnel'. After a month the neighbor opposite came home, thinner and more careful with his words, but otherwise healthy. But after six months, Oldest Brother-in-Law was still away.

In the third week, Oldest Sister had asked why you were let off when even the doctors were detained. In the second month, after having figured it out and cursing you for being a collaborator, she'd asked that you use your contacts to get Brother-in-Law released. In the fifth month, when her youngest son came home from school crying that he couldn't have a red neck-scarf because his father was a class enemy, she stopped talking about her husband altogether.

During your pre-New Year visit to Chú Hai, he shared that Oldest Brother-in-Law was fine. "Not to worry, it's just re-education," he'd said. It was an insubstantial tid-bit he volunteered to salve his own conscience, unlike the two kilo bag of short grain American rice he pushed into your hands."I'm a single man, what can I do with twelve kilos a month," he said, shamefaced that the rations he received as a party member were three times your allotment as an engineer. "It's not fragrant like our rice, but maybe your sister can use them for New Year cakes. Make a bánh tét to represent the South, a bánh chưng for the North."

You didn't remind him that Southerners rarely made the square Northern bánh chưng at home, or that Oldest Sister didn't have enough fuel to boil up two cakes. After all, even Chú Hai had to toe the party line. You accepted the rice gladly and handed it to Oldest for her to do what she could with it. You didn't repeat what he said about her husband to her. How reliable was his information these days?

Still, when everyone sat at table you were grateful Chú Hai had made it possible for you to have a rice cake for the New Year. It would have been too sad for the children if there was not even one. And Oldest Sister had tried her best. The children bit with gusto into the make-do roll she'd stuffed with a few unripe bananas scavenged from a neighbor's tree. But when you picked up a slice for yourself, you found the cake hadn't been boiled for long enough. The half-cooked grains of rice grated between your teeth and the unripe bananas stuck bitter against your tongue.

.....

The memory of that meal grates now as you push open the decrepit gate hanging loose on its hinges, and see your Oldest Sister hunched over a tray, sorting husks of broken rice with fingers bent from arthritis.

She doesn't notice you in the doorway. Her eyes are set on her task and she has two enormous ear-phones on, presumably to block out the martial music blaring from the community loudspeaker just outside the house.

"Oldest Sister," you go to tap her shoulder.

"*Trời đất ôi!* Heaven and earth!" your Oldest Sister screams, tearing the headphones off her head and setting aside the tray of rice to stand up and kiss you on both cheeks.

You take a step back. You've always had a low tolerance for Oldest and her grand gestures.

"You've gotten thinner," she says, clutching at your upper arm. "You've been ill?"

"Yes. I had a bout of dysentery," you confess with reluctance. "In Can Tho."

The goodwill disappears from her face. "You went there first without telling me? Surely you could have sent a messenger to tell me. I would have made an effort then to come to the hotel to see you, my own brother. I could have gone down with you in the van too, to the Delta. I haven't seen our parents in ages. Don't you know how difficult it is now to scrape the money together for a trip down?"

"I had work to do," you say. A lame excuse, you know. In truth, you delayed your visit to Oldest because you've always felt she housed you on sufferance all your teenage years, and even afterwards, when your contribution to the household became essential after Brother-in-Law left for his mistress' house. And then there's your guilt over Oldest Brother-in-Law's fifteen years in re-education...

"I didn't know if Oldest Brother-in-Law would welcome me," you say.

"Ah yes, your Brother-in-Law... I've told your Brother-in-Law that whatever you might have done before the war, he should understand it was because of your blood-father. And afterwards, when none of us could work because of his police background, he should be thankful your contributions to those people allowed you to keep your job."

She rushes on in a more amenable tone, anxious not to create ruptures in a relationship which has ensured her family's financial survival in recent years. "It's only because of you we managed to keep body and soul together during these terrible times." Tears begin to well up in her yellow tinged eyes. "Yes, only because of you..." she says, reaching over to pinch your cheeks with her swollen fingers.

Her performance is interrupted by a sudden loud keening from the back of the house.

"That man!" she shouts in exasperation. She bustles through the dining room and towards the noise.

You follow, curious.

The wailing is coming from the corner of the kitchen, from a lump of humanity hiding under a gunny sack.

Oldest Sister reaches down and flips the sack over with her foot. "Stop it," she says to Oldest Brother-in-Law. "It's just the music from the neighborhood propaganda loudspeakers. You're not back at the re-education camp, do you hear me?" She pulls her disoriented crying husband to a sitting position. "See. Youngest is home. What kind of welcome are you giving him?"

12
Estrangement

IN THE TIME YOU'RE BURIED in the countryside, Nina is wearing herself out, imagining you embroiled in all kinds of cloak and dagger situations. When finally she receives the laconic telegram you send from Ho Chi Minh City saying you've just been delayed with your family in Can Tho, she's so angry she tears it up and flushes the pieces down the toilet.

You don't know that then. You don't get a call back from her afterwards, screaming, to tell you. You find out three days later when you're in Bangkok with access to a direct dial line and can't get through to your house.

Worried, you contact Loc and ask him to drive up the Canyon to check on her.

"The phone isn't working," she tells him at the front door, chilly and distant.

"He was near death from dysentery," Loc has to plead before she agrees to go back with him, to speak to you from his apartment.

"After your stupid telegram, I disconnected the phone. I didn't feel like I wanted, ever, to speak to you again," she tells you when Loc puts her on the line.

Her voice is dripping icicles. She doesn't ask about your dysentery or express concern that you would've died but for Third's careful nursing. You can't know she crawled into bed with Tri the night she tore up the telegram and cried herself to sleep on his pillows.

She proceeds to tell you breezily that her supervisory board has finally approved the dissertation — 'The war for minds: links between individual susceptibility to enemy propaganda and the onset of post traumatic stress' — and she's now looking for post-doctoral positions in academia.

She doesn't seem to hear the panicked, "Why? I thought you promised to come at Christmas," that you try to interject into the conversation.

"No more veterans and no more counseling. I'm done with picking up after wars. Yours, Papa's and Maman's, anyone's... I'm not even thinking about collecting data from those new migrants flooding Little Saigon nowadays," she tells you.

You know the migrants she means, veterans on the Orderly Departure Program, released from re-education camps to go to America under US government sponsorship. Men with haunted faces, tense jaws and shoulders held into their chests. Men who've been kicked and beaten too long and now will hit back if they're even touched. Men like your Oldest Brother-in-Law in Saigon keening under a gunny sack in his kitchen. They're ideal subjects for a paper on the Southern view of the war, if Nina wants to write one. You can't believe she's choosing to ignore them.

"Cutting off your nose to spite your face?" you can't resist asking.

She ignores the dig.

Instead, she begins to tell you how well Loc's and Huong's manicure shop near Koreatown in Los Angeles is doing, and how Huong is hopeful that before long she and Loc will be able to move out of their Federal Housing Assistance apartment and back into a house of their own. "So sweet," she enthuses, venom in her voice. "Not like some of us who're being forced to dismantle our homes for no reason at all."

Talking to her is a waste of Loc's dollars, you think to yourself.

"Can you please put Loc on? I've got some things to tell him about Oldest's family," you say to her, hurt and brusque.

"I finally went to visit Oldest Sister the day before I left Vietnam. Oldest Brother-in-Law's in a bad way. After fifteen years of re-education, his nerves are totally shredded," you tell Loc. "The best option for him is the ODP program. I'll help with the processing and take care of the expenses in Vietnam and the flight out, but can you co-ordinate the paperwork on the US side?" you ask.

"Adding another hothead to the mess of hotheads already here," Loc says. "They've just set up a new front in California, an overseas resistance army, they call it. They're going to punish anyone found collaborating with Vietnam. You may not get a good return for your kindness," he warns.

"I owe him. I was the one who got him sent to re-education," you reply. You change the subject. "It's not him I'm worried about at the moment. It's my wife. She's on fire."

"Yes, the worst kind... cold fire," Loc agrees. He advises, "You should call her more often. These Americans, they're on the phone all the time. She talks to her mother twice a week. You're her husband. She expects more."

You've already passed your fortieth birthday, but still your brother feels it's his duty to tutor you on the behavior suitable for a married man.

"I suppose..." you reply.

.....

Nina is smooth with her denials when next you call, a short one day after your gall-spattered exchange.

"I wasn't angry. I just realized burrowing around in other people's wounds isn't the best way to understand myself. I'm always telling my patients they can't make something out of what isn't there. Your war isn't part of my experience. I'm not going to know myself any better even if I spend a lifetime digging around in it. What I need is to go into myself." She begins to throw out a jargon laden explanation. "There's a Jungian process for that. It's called individuation, bringing all the disparate parts of the self together."

"Mmm-hmmm," you say, careful not to commit to anything.

"Uh-huh. So I'm looking at post-doc training positions with that specialty."

You don't dare ask how she's going to do that and still join you in Asia with Tri. "You're still planning to come over for Christmas aren't you?" you venture.

"The tickets are booked," she replies.

It's a yes, but not quite. You decide to take the answer at face value. Perhaps at Christmas, without a long distance phone line to protect her, she'll chicken out. Perhaps she'll change her mind about this terrible path she seems already set on. You hope.

.....

When your family emerges into the spanking new second terminal of Singapore airport and you see Nina, you're certain your hopes will be fulfilled. She's standing tall and straight again, the pall of depression lifted from her. Her upper arm muscles are firm and the skin on her legs, arms and neck is shining with good health. Her face is relaxed, her eyes smiling the same way they had when she welcomed you in New York City. She's in good humor, her lips curved up at something Tri's saying.

She comes to hug you lightly after Tri's dutiful greeting. Yes, she likes everything, she professes—the airport, the flowers, your new haircut and your weekend polo shirt and khakis. "A new image," she says with approval. She likes everything... except the chauffeur driven company Jaguar which has hugely impressed your son. That elicits just a dismissive shake of her head.

Something is different. You search her face, wondering what has changed. "You've cut away your hair." You reach out to touch the short feathery ends. Is that it, what is not quite right about your wife?

She bends her head forward to show off an elegant white nape. "I wanted to look more like a PhD, grown up. How could you not have noticed? I thought, with all that practice, you'd be more observant," she raises a trimmed eyebrow at you.

Possibly, you worry, she hasn't forgiven or forgotten everything.

But that spark of acidity is the only sign she gives during the holiday of anything wrong between the two of you. During your months apart, Nina has relaxed and detached in a strangely positive way. She no longer frets about things going wrong nor becomes anxious and distressed when they do. While you remain gripped by the need for absolute harmony and order, even in the placement of the chopsticks on a restaurant table, without Nina responding to your every little burst of irritation, your little explosions of temper can only seem petty. They cannot hover, turn toxic or pollute.

"We are having the best time peacefully ever," Tri says on behalf of all of you, in the middle of eating an ice slurpy.

"Well I'm glad," you reply. You're more than glad, even if it isn't due to any improvement in your disposition.

"Yes you are." He nods, acknowledging the congruence between your words and inner state. He turns to Nina. "He's not telling lies for once."

You watch your son close his eyes, turn his face up to the sun and begin to carefully lick the syrup from the slurpy off his fingers. It is one of those rare instances when you can read the expression on his face. He is happy.

When night falls, Nina allows you to make love to her with a disengagement that drives you wild, letting you possess and punish her without compunction for all your time apart. If you feel any uneasiness about her curious new state of being, your insecurities are calmed when, decorating the plastic tree she finds in a supermarket, she produces the crystal star from your past Christmases in California and hands it to you to put up. All your residual fears disappear during a sultry midnight Christmas service when she pulls your face against hers and wishes you a Happy Christmas with an open-mouthed American kiss, in full view of the mostly Asian congregation.

It seems she wants your idyll to continue forever. Sitting in a coffee shop at the airport hours before she and Tri are due to fly, watching Tri browse through the shelves in the adjoining bookstore, you realize you haven't resolved anything at all about the family coming to Singapore.

"As intended. I'm not coming back. Not to stay, anyway." Nina says.

You've known all along this would happen. But, still, you're not prepared.

"I spent the fall sending out job applications," she confesses. "I applied for a therapist position in Manhattan that includes post-doctoral training at the Institute for Individuation. Although it was just a whim, I got it."

Your jaw goes slack. "New York City's dangerous. You won't manage. Not with Tri the way he is."

But the promise of that word 'individuation' seems to have imprinted itself onto your wife in the same seductive way the bone circlet on your thigh had so many years ago. "I lived there before. We'll manage," she says, her black eyes turning a dark determined jet.

You can't argue. When she had asked how she and Tri would cope with you flying away to Vietnam, that was the answer you'd given—"We'll manage."

"It's not that I've stopped loving you. And I don't have anyone else. It's just that I need some time to myself," she forestalls before you even ask. "I've spent all these years trying to understand you and it didn't even turn out to be you at all. I should have spent that time finding out about myself, why Vietnam and the war is such an issue with me. I'm going to take that time now." She raises her hand, then puts it down again in a gesture of helplessness. "I can't be around you to do it. I see you doing all the things you usually do, being the person I thought I married. Then it comes to me that it's Thong the communist spy saying this, thinking that. I need distance to see both of us clearly," she says. "And full disclosure from you," she concludes.

What she wants is your blessing, so she can go without guilt, you think. "Running doesn't help. It would be better if you stayed," you start to say. But would it really? Can you promise that if she stays you'll let her see you whole? To promise that, you'll have to tell her about Julia Anderson and Chú Hai and the chicken and more; about the life you've begun to reclaim and store in hotel envelopes; the life still waiting to be written into the empty pages of your journal. And if you do, how can you be sure she'll still love you, Nina the daughter of Hue, the Ai Nguyet look-alike?

"Are you asking me for a divorce? I won't give you one, you know," you say, as if what you want or don't, matters under California law. But you say it anyway.

"No. I don't want a divorce. I just want some time to myself, and to move to a new job in New York City," she replies. She adds, "We might need to sell the house, if you agree..."

"Alright. And you and Tri will still visit?"

She nods. "Full disclosure, that's what I need. Not right away, but over time. You can write it down in letters if it's easier that way."

"Are you sure? What about this morning, last night, all the other nights these two weeks?"

She smiles the saddest smile, bends across the tiny coffee table between you and brushes her lips against yours. "You, of all people, should know how easy it is to sleep with the enemy. The difficulty is living with a stranger."

You raise your hand to the unaccustomed coolness of her bare nape, so vulnerable you can separate the bones underneath with a single twist if you want to. You pull her face against yours and bury your nose in her flesh, a Vietnamese kiss... taking her essence in to remember her by.

You want to hold her there all day, but Tri's back from the bookstore.

"It's time," he says, pointing to the blinking alarm on his watch.

With him, it's futile to haggle for even an extra second. You let Nina go.

"I won't remain a stranger," you manage to whisper in her ear.

You don't know what full disclosure entails or even if you have the capacity to do it. You can't be sure who the self Nina's intending to discover will be. But going forward you will try to share what you can with whoever she becomes.

It's the only way you'll get your wife and your son back, you tell yourself, as you walk them to the departure gate.

THE PENITENT

13
Openings

YOUR FIRST LETTER TO NINA BEGINS—'You asked for full disclosure, let's start.'

In truth it's very far from full disclosure, only a description of a week in Vietnam—'being a wheeler and dealer, trying to arrange protection for a Chinese financier grown too big for his own good.' A simple recounting of your first meeting with Ly and the story of how he's gotten too rich for his own good and now needs an insurance plan. 'It's an audacious idea. But he's an old friend and I'm determined to help him,' you write.

"You didn't say what Ly's ultimate insurance plan was but it's a good start," Nina comments when next you speak on the phone. But anyway, she tells you, she's putting the letter into the box of papers she's packing for the move to New York. "Send more," she says. "I'm going to start a whole hope chest just for them."

.....

You send a second letter recounting how pleased Jerry has been with your first Vietnamese trip. Old news but...

He'd been waiting in the lobby of your Bangkok hotel, bouncing from foot to foot, when you got in from the airport. "I heard the first two persons you went to see after your official meetings were a newly promoted NVA general and your Third Brother-in-Law, a retired NVA colonel. And after that the Chinese soft drinks manufacturer with the soap distribution network in Russia, the biggest unofficial financier for the state owned sector. Are you on a roll or not?" He was so excited he could barely keep his voice down.

"And I have a deal from the Chinese guy," you said.

Ly's insurance plan is a single name — an American beverage company, the world leader in cola based soft drinks. "He wants a joint venture with them," you reported. "His reasons are first, simple ambition; second, to create jobs; and third, to help his country by introducing new machinery and methods."

You did not mention a fourth reason, the one that weighs most heavily with Ly. But it's something you share with Nina in your third letter.

.....

Except for ballooning from an average sized young man to a middle aged one of enormous proportions reflective of the fortune he's built, Ly hasn't changed. He's as blunt as ever. After walking you through his various businesses — his parents' fish sauce concern which he's turned into a lucrative export earner, a soap factory with distribution into Russia that earns him valuable Soviet oil credits, and his soft drinks factory — he asks about you in his old no-nonsense way. "Who do you work for now? Who asked you to come back?"

You try to answer as best you can. "Now the Soviets have collapsed, the Americans think Vietnam will welcome them back as a counterweight to China. Like before, they're throwing money around. But this time they're using it to pay for machinery and factories, not guns." You confess, "I'm supposed to be paving the way." You add, "But, regardless who pays me I don't take any sides now except my own. If I can help my family and friends, and put some rice into someone's rice bowl, that's enough for me."

It's a good enough answer for Ly.

He beams. "After all those years dallying with the communists, you've finally seen sense." He leans over and shares his fears.

Ly's partners owe him too much in foreign currency and have become too dependent on his ability to raise capital from his overseas dealings. The temptation to neutralize him and take control of the assets that feed his wealth is becoming irresistible. It's just a question of time when the axe will fall.

"Divide and rule, that's always the inclination of those in power, doesn't matter which type of regime. My mistake was to go full steam ahead, forgetting that. Don't ever stand in front, my father would've told me. I was too arrogant," Ly says. "My brands are so well known now, the companies so large, they can only be appropriated if I'm found guilty of grave crimes, ones for which the sentence will be death. It'll be like the old days again. Do you remember?"

.....

You'd forgotten about the executions until Ly asked the question.

On evenings before public executions, there would be sandbags built up in a U-shape in the Martyr's Square. If you saw the sandbags there, you avoided that route to school the next day. But one early morning, summoned unexpectedly by your blood-father for coffee at the market, you had no choice but to pass the site just as a convoy of green trucks pulled up. Hoping that noise and distance would shelter you from the sight and sound of the impending slaughter, you'd rushed into the market and made your way to the far end where the coffee stall was. Nonetheless, above the market's hubbub, you'd heard the boots of the soldiers, the shouting of the mob, and the fusillade of carbines as the bullets were discharged. The market had fallen silent momentarily after that. And then two piercing screams had come through the great door and echoed through the hall. They were from the two wives of the incredibly wealthy Chinese businessman who'd just been shot dead for profiteering, a paternal cousin of Ly's mother.

.....

"Go ahead, tell me what you're planning," you say to Ly.

"It would be more difficult to accuse me of economic crimes if I have a proper joint venture, with foreign board representation and international accounting," he explains. "That's why I want that particular partner. Although it's typically American, it's also powerfully global." He smiles at you then, an ironic smile. "It's the same strategy the old kings used, to protect themselves from their neighbors, sending their daughters off to new allies when the old ones got weak. The soap factory's already in bed with the Russians. Now I need an American. The soft drinks plant is small but it's the only marriageable daughter I've got." He isn't worried about losing his wealth. "We don't come with anything, and we can't take anything away with us." But he doesn't want to die just yet. "My children are young, and I'm still very fond of my wife," he says.

.....

You too are still very fond of your wife, the one who wants full disclosure.

You're tempted to reveal more to Nina, but you can't be sure that will help win her back more quickly. The memory of Ai Nguyet sitting at the café table in the ice-cream shop staring at you with unforgiving eyes still haunts you. Your letters, sent in nondescript envelopes from Hong Kong and Singapore, filled only with details of your working life, are all you can start with. Baby steps, you know. But you hope that with practice, they will eventually reveal more.

You send a fourth, a fifth, and then a continuous stream of letters detailing how you and Jerry are shuttling between Hong Kong and Singapore to make Ly's outrageous idea a success. How, between these trips, you go to Ho Chi Minh City to confer with Ly and keep the deal alive by playing interminable rounds of tennis with the directors of an obscure state body Ly has nominated as the government partner for his joint venture.

You write that after a few weeks, you've become inured to the wrenching transitions you experience between the glitz and bustle of Hong Kong, the self satisfied efficiency of Singapore and the wretchedness of Vietnam. 'I feel a sense of purpose again. Working towards the peak of my game, I feel I've recovered my identity,' you share.

You're worried about confessing this nugget, that you're happiest as a middleman working sides, a double-dealer, a spy. You wait for the backlash. But there's none.

'I'm glad you're happy,' Nina replies from California.

Much as you want her to, she doesn't add that she's thinking of giving up the idea of New York City and the pursuit of individuation, that she feels an unbearable urge to pack herself and Tri up and fly to you. Instead there's an enclosure with a comparison of New York City and California house prices and spreadsheets of financial scenarios if she rents in New York City or if you sell out on the West Coast and buy again in the East.

She's confused, she writes. The broker you've recommended, a referral by Ly's family in America, wants to show condominiums in Flushing, New York City's emerging Asia Town. Papa and Maman prefer the West Side of Manhattan, near Columbia University. 'You're so much better at these things. Will you come to New York to make the decision with me?' the words jump out from her letter.

.....

You arrive in California in late spring, then fly with Nina and Tri to Washington D.C., where Papa picks the three of you up in his new Mercedes. The old diplomat hugs his daughter and grandson but won't take your outstretched hand. When Maman comes to meet you all at the door, she looks past you to acknowledge Tri folding his arms in formal greeting, then walks away. "Come with Memé. I've made some nice snacks for you from the royal recipes," she tosses her head back and calls out to your son.

Maman has never forgiven you for presenting her the non-choice of a pregnant unmarried daughter or a willing but un-pedigreed son-in-law. And then there are the postcards, which she still thinks are to some woman in Asia.

"Now this..." you hear her sobbing to Papa out in the patio after dinner that night. She can't point her finger at what 'this' is. "It's just the whole catastrophe!"

Papa on the other hand is simply angry you've deserted Nina and are supporting her decision to move to a dangerous city with his only grandchild.

"I've got to do what I can," you justify yourself to him. "If this is how I can help my family and friends and fill someone's rice bowl, then I should. Anyway, New York City's just a train ride away. It's much more convenient for you to visit than Orange County. And Nina and Tri can come to you more easily too."

You don't want to battle Nina's parents but you have to make your position clear, to make space to accommodate the awkwardness of your first face to face with Nina since the tentative disclosures in your letters.

Who are you... who are you... you can see the refrain running through Nina's eyes as the two of you make love carefully in her childhood bedroom. As you kiss and sigh like teenagers learning the act for the first time. As you trace your fingers down her body, as she receives you, a stranger again but not quite.

Initially, Tri is more stand offish than usual, but after a while he forgives you enough to open up and ask about Vietnam.

"Vietnam's beautiful. You'll like it. But you'll need to change your expectations about cleanliness, efficiency and toilet arrangements," you tell him.

"Change by how much?" he asks, as always needing lengths and breadths and heights and mass.

To show him in pictures, you dig into your attaché case for the stack of photographs you mean to share with Nina, and spread them out for him on Papa's and Maman's *faux* Louis XIV coffee table.

There's a view of luminous green rice fields with a young boy standing on a padi bund, his piss painting a shining arc against the evening sky; another of a mountain peak shrouded in morning mist and a long golden finger lake surrounded by neat patches of vegetable fields. Then a third of a bonsai-filled courtyard and a man in his forties beside a younger man in a suit; and a fourth of a different man laughing behind a rooster. Finally, there's a landscape of a turquoise colored bay surrounded by a crescent of shining white sand fringed by a forest of beach pines.

"Toilet arrangements in the Delta. No smells. And you're doing the rice plants a favor because pee is full of ammonia and that will create nitrogen," you tell Tri, indicating the first photo.

You watch him nod with satisfaction at the thought of his upcoming contributions to the ecosystem.

You point to the mountain and the lake. "Lang Bian Peak and Golden Lake. It's in Dalat, where I'm going to build a golf course. My blood-father and blood-mother, your grandparents, went there for a holiday. I'll take you and your mother one day, if you like."

"Is it high?" he asks. "If I stand on the side of the mountain will I roll down into the lake and drown?"

You never succeeded in teaching your son to swim. And now you're too far away, you think with regret.

"It's jungle all the way down the mountain. You can't roll down impenetrable jungle," you reason with him as logically as you can. You add, knowing how he hangs on to an idea once it enters his head, "Don't worry. You're not going to Vietnam immediately. I haven't gotten your Mom to agree yet. You can just think about it for the time being."

.....

That night you share the picture of the boy in the rice fields and the story of the lost kite with Nina.

"I imagined it flying over unknown lands and across the ocean and I knew I had to follow it. I was only five but I knew I would be leaving."

You wonder if Nina of the Paris educated mandarin ancestors and D.C. upbringing can understand how far the outside world was to a young boy from the rice fields of Bac Lieu. How impossible his longing to see the other side would appear. Perhaps not, you conclude.

You move on to the photo of Dalat, relating your blood-parents' story, slight as it is. It was a happy enough time for them to commemorate with your name, you say. You tell her its true meaning for the first time, that Thong means pine, because your blood-mother thought they were the most beautiful trees ever. You wonder, as you say that, why you've kept this small thing from your wife for so long. There is no good answer, you realize. Hiding, even the most inconsequential information, is simply a habit with you, a bad one.

Now you hear Nina repeating your name, making the same sound she always makes. But does she see a different person? Someone who bends to endure? Someone who's resilient enough to remain himself despite the twists and turns of life? Someone whose love will remain evergreen through this cold spell in your relationship, until she comes around? Perhaps. You feel her lean over. You bring her hand to your chest, to where your blood-mother's bone circlet with its etchings of pine now hangs on a new black leather string. Caressing it, smoothing away the years, the two of you fall asleep in each other's arms.

The next night you show her the picture of Chú Hai and you in the courtyard of the hotel. "What do you see?" you ask.

"Two men in a garden," Nina replies. "I'd guess from the face the older man is your blood-father. I can't see the other face too well but I know it's you," she replies.

"It's interesting that we see what we expect to, and then we edit out the rest. I had that photo for years and never saw what you did until it was shoved in my face," you say. "Yes, that's me the day of my graduation, in the garden of the hotel where the ceremony was held... But that's not my blood-father." You pass Nina the picture of the man with the rooster. "That is my blood-father, the rooster master." You point back to the older man in the first photograph. "This is Chú Hai. He was my English tutor for many years. Nowadays in Ho Chi Minh City, he's better known as General Trung, the Chairman of the Institute for the Study of Foreign Relations. He used to be a journalist for an American magazine. Now he's recognized openly as a high-ranking party official. He was my boss and mentor, you might say..."

Nina picks up the picture of your fair skinned broad shouldered blood-father squatting with his rooster, his wide mouth opened in laughter, revealing large cigarette stained teeth. She points to the hands holding the bird, their solid square tipped fingers. She examines the picture of you and Chú Hai again. "He has an open face, not what I'd expect of a spymaster or a high-ranking communist," she says. She goes through the rest of the data you've presented. "Same tanned skin, same slim muscular build. But he's more relaxed. His hands are loose on his belt buckle, not like yours, clenched into two fists and pulling at your suit jacket. And his eyes are different—softer and more open, not shrouded."

She peers at Chú Hai's face, using a finger to trace the widow's peak beginning slightly off-centre of his forehead, the salt and pepper hair growing stiff and wild from it. She stares into your face and puts her finger on your forehead, at the point slightly to the left where your hair line dips down to meet skin. She runs her fingers through your rough hair, now streaked grey, and cups both hands around your pointed chin. "But how did he... you...?" she asks.

You recount the story.

.....

You'd asked him the same thing the first time you noticed the resemblance, when you went to say goodbye before leaving the country.

He said he'd been your parents' bodyguard during his training with the swamp guerillas, before he went to the city to do intelligence work. He'd looked after them for slightly less than a year, and during this time, he'd said rather ambiguously, they realized your blood-mother was pregnant. This was her first pregnancy and she was depressed. She was bleeding too. Your blood-father had her moved to a temporary camp on the river so she could go quickly to town and a hospital if she

needed to. He had also sent two bodyguards and a maid with
her. The maid, it turned out, was the sticky rice vendor who
became your step-mother later. Her husband was one of the
bodyguards. Chú Hai was the other.

"Do you know that old wife's tale about why children look
the way they do?" he'd asked you. "It's because they take after
whatever a pregnant women spends the most time looking at...
Well, at that riverside camp there was only your blood-mother,
myself, the very plain maid and an ugly Cambodian. You
should be thankful your blood-mother spent more time with
me than with the other two." And then, he'd laughed.

.....

You turn to Nina, smiling at how ingeniously Chú Hai had
sidestepped the issue. "After that, he just moved on and started
talking about my journey out of Vietnam, about how I needn't
put myself in danger snooping around for data to send to Ba Roi.
Anything out of the newspapers would do, he said, because
he was quite sure the country wouldn't be able to understand
or use anything I found technically interesting. I felt like I'd
dreamt the whole conversation. The only other thing is, when
I got up to leave, he hugged me for a very long time. And he
addressed me as *con trai*, son... He has never mentioned this
matter again. I visit him every time I go to Vietnam. We always
have a wonderful time together. I feel a great deal of affection
for him and he for me. There's the physical likeness. But how
he became my father, if he is, I don't know."

You open your hands, at a loss. "So, how is someone who
can't even say for sure who his father is, tell you who he is?"
you ask your wife.

"We'll do it together. Find the pieces bit by bit," she says, reaching over to take your hands in hers, and squeezing tight.

.....

Before solving the puzzle of your origins though, you have to find a home in New York City for your wife and son.

Surprisingly, it's Tri who discovers the gem.

Left alone with you to wander the Murray Hill District near the Jung Institute where Nina has dropped in for a meeting, Tri's stopped by a glimpse of a bright yellow landing and a rainbow colored staircase in a brownstone typical of that neighborhood.

"Colorful," he says to you.

You can see he's excited to find this burst of whimsy in no-nonsense black-red-and-grey New York City.

He points to the 'for sale' sign hung on the door fortuitously left ajar. "Can we go see?" he asks, disappearing into the lobby before you can reply. You follow him up the yellow, orange, red, violet, indigo, blue and green steps and find an empty stark white apartment with what Tri dismisses as a disappointingly normal arrangement of living spaces. But at one corner of the living room is another rainbow colored staircase, this time a spiral. He scrambles up it, calling down to you to be quick and come see when he reaches the top.

He's in a vast open attic, at the end of which is a floor which slopes gently skyward in gradually deepening blue steps to a moon hatch. The hatch opens on to a terrace just big enough for a built-in metal bench curved like a crescent. It's from this terrace that Tri and you see a section of the United Nations' Plaza and its flag poles. On that day, from a certain angle, what Tri glimpses is the red Vietnamese flag with its yellow star.

He points it out to you. "See that. It's not Papi's and Memé's old yellow flag with the three red stripes. It's the alive flag, where you are. As long as I can see that flag, we'll always be together. Cross my heart and hope to die..."

He turns and looks at you, quite decided. "We must live here," he says.

.....

Nina's charmed by the attic and the crescent balcony too. When she discovers a mezzanine under the attic's stair/wall which will be ideal for her study, the deal's sealed. There is no security or doorman but the neighbors, two respectably retired gay men, are around most of the day. "So near the Institute and not five minutes' walk from Tri's new school," she says. She pauses, waiting for you to object. But you don't, not even about the brownstone's hefty price tag.

You do grumble a little when you sign the check for the deposit. "I don't know what the world's coming to when I've got to give up a custom built split level, with ten thousand square feet of land and a swimming pool, for two floors in an eighty year old building." But that's the only time you complain.

In the late summer, before you go back to Asia, you and Tri climb up to the terrace once more to catch a glimpse of the yellow star on the Vietnamese flag. This, you tell yourself, is what's essential. No matter the price, no matter what Nina's father and uncles and the mad old veterans in Orange County might say about collaborators, the star is the most important

thing. It's a daily promise to your son that you will come
back, that one day you will all be together again.

.....

You have promised to phone Tri every week, a call just for
him. You've scheduled Monday nights when Nina goes to the
Institute to meet her supervising therapist and Kim, who's
conveniently moved to New York to be with her boyfriend,
keeps a watching brief.

It's Kim who picks up the phone the first time you call for Tri.

"He's out on the balcony," she tells you. "He spends a lot
of time out there on the crescent bench looking at the flag. He
thinks he's together with you when he sees the flag. He says it's
a communication channel," she reports. "I did discuss it with
Auntie Nina, but she said not to worry. It's just how he is."

"Well, he does see things a bit differently from other
people," you say. "Why don't you put him on for some real
communication with me? Maybe we can snap him out of that
fantasy while I'm actually on the line with him."

Tri comes on and says hello with his usual solemn gravity.

"I heard from Kim you can see and feel me when you
look at that flag with the star on it," you comment, careful to
say things literally so he won't misinterpret and go off on a
tangent.

"You heard wrong. You're not here for me to see. I just feel
you," he replies.

"Feel?" Is it something emotional he's conjured up, a
comforting illusion to keep himself on an even keel?

"Like, are you happy? Do you have a stomach ache?
Right now, you have a stomach ache. The kind you get when

you don't know what's happening, when you're worried, especially about me."

So your ten-year-old son thinks he's psychic. Besides all the rest of his weirdness, you're being asked to deal with this too?

"So do you just feel me or other people as well?" you ask.

"For other people I have to open the receiver first," he reports, matter-of-fact. "But Mummy is always with me. And you too, when I look at the flag. You used to be around more, when you were nearer. But now, you're too far."

He's certainly saying a lot for Tri. The strangest things, as if they're his everyday reality, a reality you don't know how to respond to. You move on to something more familiar. "So how's school?"

"It's harder than my old school, but not too hard for me," he says. "They're pushing me up a year for maths. But I have to stay where I am for language arts. And I need a counselor, they told Mom the other day." He repeats the diagnosis Nina has already told you about. "I am not interacting at an age-appropriate level."

"And are you trying to now?" you ask.

"It's not necessary." He seems quite adamant about that. Another dead end.

You sigh. "Well, try a little bit. It's important, learning how to communicate with people. And people communicate by talking. Promise me you'll try."

"I promise I'll try," he replies. But it's the robotic Tri talking, not the boy chattering about his alternate reality, where a flag provides a channel for communicating with his father.

"Thank you," you say anyway. "I'll expect lots of improvement when we meet at Christmas. We'll have long conversations, all three of us."

"Yes, long conversations, all three of us. At Christmas," he repeats.

.....

You do not ask Nina to visit Vietnam at Christmas, nor does she ask to go. Instead, you meet her and Tri at the airport in Bangkok and then spend December on an island facing the Andaman Sea. An island where in the mornings the three of you walk the beaches and in the afternoons you send Tri off to nature study classes, while Nina and you are massaged by sturdy Thai women. Where after dinner Nina takes Tri to fish for squid on a baroque jetty over an ink-black sea while you work or meditate among the red timbers of your holiday villa. And later, when Tri sleeps, the two of you make love deep into the night.

You don't ask Nina when she might come back to you. She doesn't discuss when you might end your assignment. The two of you are simply glad that Tri, seemingly wiser than his years, does not grow stranger despite the strange shape your relationship has taken.

When it's New Year again you say goodbye and Nina takes your son away, nothing between the two of you settled. You return to your work, a job that feels as essentially right to you as Nina says hers is apart from you; a rightness that doesn't allow the two of you to resolve anything. You can only wait and hope it will all fall neatly into place again as naturally as it has fallen apart.

14
Each line with trepidation

ALONE IN THE ANONYMOUS SERVICE APARTMENTS and hotel rooms you occupy up and down the western edge of the Pacific, you go back to reclaiming your life and setting it down on paper.

Nina is never far from your thoughts. Each memory you recall is written down with trepidation, in the knowledge that one day she'll see them. Each line is accompanied by an ache of longing for her, a throb in your loins you can't ignore. Over time, you begin to resent your wife for expecting you to manage without her, without a woman, for months on end. It seems especially unreasonable when you're surrounded by so many young women, all ready to trade their bodies for a bit of your time and the chance of a better life. It's a subject that comes up in conversation with Chú Hai one evening, before a night out with Ly.

"Do you remember Julia Anderson?" you ask him, looking into the cup of amber tinted tea in your hands.

He nods. "In fact she came to see me at the Institute the other day. She's in charge of East Asian Cultural Affairs at the American Embassy in Tokyo. But she seems to have forgotten you. She didn't ask after you at all." He checks to see if you're piqued about that.

You keep your face expressionless. You don't want him to know you bumped into her a month earlier in Japan, and that you are indeed hurt she hasn't mentioned that to him.

Chú Hai tsks-tsks at your pretended indifference. He squeezes your shoulder. "Doesn't matter whether I remember her or she remembers you. The important thing is you still remember her..." He brings his head down to you, so you're eye to eye. "It's alright you know, *con*. You always remember the first time. Or you should anyway, even if it didn't happen the way your heart would have wished." He taps his index and middle fingers on your thigh. "What you should remember with Julia Anderson is that the heart wasn't an issue then. It was first of all business, important business. What you should remember now, in these days of peace, is that the body may have its needs but you shouldn't put love at risk."

You're embarrassed but not surprised this man can read you so well. "So, why did you tell me that when I got to this age I'd need a sixteen-year-old for my wet noodle?" you tease, unable to hide the twinkle in your eye.

Chú Hai protests with mock anger. "Don't misquote me. I said I needed the sixteen year olds. You've had the benefit of American beef and seafood for ten years. I'm sure you don't have a problem with a wet noodle. And you're married to a beautiful woman whom you tell me you love dearly, notwithstanding your separation. I was free as a bird then, still am. The love of my life died years ago. Almost as long ago as you've been alive..."

He stutters to a stop, but only for a heartbeat. "What you do with your body, you're too old to ask me for permission," he says. "Just remember, do no harm and don't make promises you can't keep. And, bear in mind that children are a responsibility you can't just throw away."

You store his little throwaway about children safe in your heart. Can it be an admission of the other thing? You leave it at that and go off to help Ly with his amusements.

As long as you set limits, you tell yourself, Nina need not know.

.....

An engineer, an interpreter, a spy... A dealmaker. You wonder what the Chief Clerk and Commander would think about your activities these days. Exporting American capitalism via joint ventures and foreign currency financing; building business structures to protect a friend and his family from the government's envy; helping your family by arranging Oldest Brother-in-Law's migration to America, securing a soft drinks distributorship for a sister, placing this or that nephew or niece in a factory here and an office there; filling as many rice bowls as you can.

"For perfect virtue, practice five things under all circumstances... gravity, generosity of soul, sincerity, earnestness, and kindness," the Chief Clerk had often quoted from Confucius. You believe you're practicing well. If he were not incapacitated by those strokes, if he could still talk, if he were not already dying, he would give you his blessing.

But the Commander?

You can't know. He had died in 1979, a bad death. Your fault. You can't change the facts. How can you do enough to lay his hungry ghost to rest?

.....

*"Give out... Breathe in... Give out... Let go..." your mother
had soothed, rubbing the last of her pre-1975 cache of green
medicated oil onto your blood-father's chest, doing what she
could do to help.*

*There was no other medicine to kill the tuberculosis
hacking at his chest, the dysentery draining his fluids, the
jungle miasmas erupting from his seventy-year-old body
lying on the plank bed in your attic bedroom. It was 1979,
and the country was short of everything. Besides there was
too much fear and regret knotted up in the lean muscles of the
Commander's chest. Much as your mother cared about him,
there was nothing she could do to ease his going.*

*You sat with your father at the other end of the room,
watching her futile attempts. It was so hard to live when one's
time had come, you were thinking. Just drawing breath in
and letting it out again became as difficult as lifting Thai Son
mountain. Yet it was so hard to stop too. With the life your
blood-father had lived, what multitudes of retribution would
he be expecting?*

*"Too heavy," your heard him wheezing to your mother, his
breath dragging as if he was heaving a long-forgotten pack
across a jungle trail.*

"Hush," your mother brushed his forehead.

*"He's burning. He needs ice," she said to you. But she
knew as well as you did that the refrigerator had broken down
and there was no electricity anyway. "No help for it, he'll
have to draw breath by himself till his allotted time," you said.
She frowned at you, then turned back to remove the too-hot
towel from his chest.*

"Let go. Let go and breathe in," she told him.

His muscles remained tense under her hand, the skin rough and goose pimpled, a plucked chicken's skin like that of the roosters he'd sent to death in the cockpits...

"Will he be reborn badly?" she looked to your father, the Chief Clerk, hoping for reassurance. But he had none to give.

"Well, no matter. We just have to do the best we can to help him," she said.

She placed her hand firmly above your blood-father's heart and said an 'Amitabha'. Come what may, you knew she would try to will him back to her, so she could guide him properly on his way with the peaceful heart prescribed in the Buddhist scriptures.

The weight on his chest and across his shoulders and back wouldn't lift, though. He continued to shout and rant, lost in his nightmares. You wished you could reach into them and pull him out. But he was trapped in the hallucinations haunting him from his warring life. All you could do was follow his mutterings and hold his hand as he walked his fevered path.

You tried to understand his disconnected whispers. It was his twenty-seventh day crossing the Pleiku plateau, he was saying. He was heading south, leading a convoy of supplies towards the camp hidden outside the US air base. He and his comrades had avoided the napalm. But its acrid residue continued to rise from the barren ground into the jungle canopy, cutting into his lungs. More than two thirds of the convoy was dead. Now each man, even himself, carried triple loads—three rice belts across their waists, powder packed in six bamboo tubes on their backs.

Now he was moving downhill, he said. The air was warmer, heavy with chemicals. He tried to remember the clear cold of the highlands, but its texture escaped him. His breath dragged with each step into the depths.

He was on yet another trek, he pulled at your hand to tell you. It was a different time. He had a comrade across his back. The man's breathing, ragged with shrapnel, was tearing into his nape. The man's remaining arm beat a tattoo against his left breast, swinging with each lurching step. He heard artillery coming nearer. The man's weight pressed against the circlet strapped to his back. The pine cones carved around the bone rubbed against his skin, chafing it.

They'd caught him, he shouted to your mother. Through prison bars he saw her turned into a wizened hill-tribe shaman dressed all in black. She was offering him a bowl filled with darkness. She was telling him to drink it, to allow it to strengthen him.

He swallowed and choked on the bowl of medicine your mother was coaxing him to drink. The medicine had turned to blood, he moaned.

He pushed your mother away. He had more important things to attend to, he managed to stutter. For, between the thighs of a woman, a child's head was emerging covered in muck. Could she not hear its newborn wail, like a siren, he asked your mother. It was the son he'd waited so long for, the one who would feed his ancestors. He'd done his duty by his father and his grandfathers.

You saw relief rush over his gasping, clutching-at-life body. He had bent down to thank his wife, he said in a whisper. But she had looked away, he muttered, shaking his head in bewilderment. There had been tears on her cheeks.

It wasn't his first wife crying, he opened his eyes wide suddenly, to announce to the room. It was his second wife, the sticky rice vendor he'd married after they both defected. She was telling him she couldn't go back to face his first wife's family because she'd stood by and done nothing when his first wife was killed. She'd been too happy to have his first wife dead, to have him free for herself, for her to give him real descendants... not that boy, that pretender...

He put his fists against his ears to block out the slander. But, he groaned, her voice kept going on and on...

Your mother looked up at you. You could see she had no heart to tell him it was his own voice confessing everything to her, the one he'd mistaken for a witch with a bowl of blood.

She put a hand against his lips. Then she turned to push you away. "This is not for you to hear," she said. Tears were rolling down her wrinkled cheeks, yet, still she was composed enough to protect his dignity, to spare him the humiliation of others seeing that he, the old swamp fighter, had broken. You wondered what there had been between them to engender such care, what secrets you were not privy to.

From across the room you heard him ask why she'd grown so old? It couldn't be, he screamed.

He called her name and shouted for her to run out into the night with him, away from the sirens and his old comrades coming to punish him. The river was nearby, he said. It was broad and brown, swollen with the waters rushing down from Cambodia. He would go there, he whispered to her. He would dive into the flood. His first wife was out there in the waters somewhere, buried on an islet in the delta clay, he explained. He had to get to her, to get the truth from her.

But he'd taken too long, forgotten where he placed the trail marks. And the river was flowing too fast, the current too strong. He couldn't keep afloat.

You saw his eyes close. He cried out that he was sinking...
That his body was plummeting like a stone... That the mud was
closing over him.

.....

He died on the first day of the seventh Lunar month, the
month of hungry ghosts. You buried him in the black soil laid
down over generations by the river, beside his father and his
grandfathers before him, seven generations in all. You hadn't
been able to afford a headstone but you saw it in your mind,
white marble, inscribed with the words—'The Commander,
provincial notary, village headman, swamp fighter, fallen hero
of the revolution, fugitive, Blood-father.'

Now, twice a year, during the Hungry Ghosts Festival and
Thanh Minh, you perform the sacrifices for your blood-father
and his parents and grandparents before him, at the gravesite
in Bac Lieu. But knowing what you do now about your origins,
you can't say you do them honestly, with all your heart, your
mind totally focused. And you can't promise that Tri, your
American son, will continue the pretence after you. You have
abandoned him in New York with American-born Nina, a
Catholic who doesn't care about ancestral anniversaries and
will never remember the lunar dates, much less pass them
on. No, you can't be sure at all if the Commander's pleased
with you.

.....

You don't need to wonder what Chú Hai thinks, though. He's
told you. "It's just money. It comes. It goes. Why get so excited

about it?" he waves away with amusement the sums you show him so proudly. Your business affairs interest him only because at this moment in history, factories and machinery are the new channels for diplomacy. Chú Hai remains a staunch believer in the party and in international dialogue. "The Institute is my mistress now," he jokes. And indeed he attends to it like the most devoted of lovers—going there at the break of dawn, conscientiously training successive intakes of party members, assiduously hosting international visitors, constantly lobbying for an international re-visioning of the war and the reasons for the fall of the South.

"Still the propagandist," you mock in jest.

But the two of you do not quarrel.

When you meet, it's no longer to analyze policies or dissect current affairs, but simply to have a cup of tea and update each other on your latest activities. For you to tell him how your son is, to speculate what Nina's latest state of mind might be, your conversations meandering broad and steady like the maturing Mekong that nourishes your Delta.

It's because of Chú Hai that you continue to have hope for your long distance marriage. If fate can build a relationship such as Chú Hai's and yours from a mysterious beginning he will not talk about, a chance meeting on a kite field and another in the back garden of a villa, then surely fate will also determine a day when Nina and you come back together. You hope against hope, against the weight of your karma.

15
Karma knocking

BUT NINA IS STUBBORN. Full disclosure is what she wants. Yet even as you allow your letters to fill with more detail and ready yourself to send her the envelopes and journals thick with memories, something in her simply won't bend.

"We're both fine the way we are," she says on more than one of your visits to the brownstone. "Although things could be better if you came home to New York to stay, it can't be. This is the best we can do."

And it's not a bad life the two of you have.

You have the intrigues you knit together for Jerry— intrigues she now knows something about. And on top of that there's the gravy, the rich rewards Ly's given you for your labors on his behalf—shares in the soft drink joint venture and a bank Ly's started, distribution rights for consumer goods across the delta, other smaller manufacturing concerns—all producing earnings compounding inexorably in proxy bank accounts scattered across South East Asia.

"It wouldn't be fair if I forced you to come home," she says.

Disingenuous daughter of Hue, you think.

"As for me... My patients engage me quite as much as your deals. You see that, don't you?"

And indeed you can. There's always someone in the waiting room of the ground floor apartment she's bought over from the widowed gay owner and turned into consulting rooms. She's so successful she's stopped accepting new patients.

"I make a good living. I help people just like you do. How can we want more?"

She has a point. It would not be wise to tempt the gods or to disturb karma.

So the two of you go along the way you've grown accustomed to. Through the ups and downs of Saddam Hussein's increasing isolation in Iraq, a ground breaking for a golf resort in the Central Mountains, Nina's appointment to the Management Committee of the Jung Institute, Tri's year-in year-out presence on the International School's honor roll... Through public upheavals and private triumphs...

But your fat bank balances, Nina's psychological balance, even the two red dots on your soles that your mother believed kept your fate in balance, can't shield you from consequences once karma shudders.

In 1992, after the opening ceremonies for the Dalat golf course Jerry hopes will become a magnet for the elite of Vietnam, as you hurtle down the mountain roads towards the coast and Nha Trang, karma awakes. In a Monkey year full of mischief, a jury in Los Angeles hands out an extraordinary verdict, a decision that engulfs the city in flames and takes with it Loc's and Huong's nail salon and their youngest daughter Thi.

You see the horrific images replaying in airport lounges in Ho Chi Minh City, Hong Kong and Tokyo on your journey back to Southern California to be with your brother and his wife. You see men and women being beaten up on the corner of Normandie and Florence, the mob running up the broad Los Angeles roadways to Koreatown and then being repulsed at the Olympic intersection by vigilantes with hand guns and flamethrowers. You see the tide turn back to South Central. You see the windows of the one-storey shop fronts there being smashed, the buildings by the roadside torched. You can almost smell the smoke rising thick and black in the dark wake of the crowd all the way from Koreatown to the Santa Monica Freeway; smoke and flames like those at the burning fuel depot in Nha Trang, where you and Loc and his family once shared a seemingly golden time.

It was to be just a minute, you learn from Kim and Nina, who come off the plane from New York City and are waiting at John Wayne Airport to drive with you to Little Saigon... Just a quick run from the alley for Thi to pick up a term paper she left in Huong's office at the back of the salon. But in that moment, the Molotov cocktail flung from the dusty street finds a way past the iron-bars and through the front window. In seconds, the acetones, the polishes, the removers and the polyester carpet are burning. The glass partition separating Huong's office from the salon is no barrier to the fire. It shatters. The pressure from the heat is so intense Thi can't pull the door open from the inside to escape, nor can Loc hammer the door in from the alley to get her out.

The sprinklers turn on as they're supposed to. The fire trucks come almost immediately. Still it is too late. Even though the helicopter evacuates Thi to the best burn unit in the Southland and the doctors work on her skin and her lungs and her face through the night.

When you arrive at the apartment, Loc is still at the Torrance Burn Centre where Thi's been taken. He's been there for the last three days. First to watch Thi being wheeled into emergency, then to hover outside the ICU watching her mummy-wrapped body struggle for breath and finally today, navigating bureaucracy to bring her body back to Orange County.

It isn't till Sunday, the fifth day, that Loc brings his daughter home. He and Huong bury her on Monday after a service attended by more people than they can count. She's in a closed casket. Her burnt face has been too awful for Loc to contemplate for more than a few seconds and he's refused to let Huong have a last look at it. "Better to remember her the way she always looked," you hear him say as he bars her entry into the mortician's room, standing aside only after they've closed the white gilded casket and put the screws in the cover.

"It's *vipaka*, cause and consequence," he tells you after the funeral, letting himself fall into your arms, forgetful that he's the shining hero of your childhood. "*Vipaka*," he repeats, shaking tearlessly against your shoulders and chest.

You hold your brother tight against the storm of emotion, the self blame, the payback for everything he and you and Oldest Brother-in-Law and uncountable men of your generation did and never acknowledged or asked pardon for.

He mumbles, "Nha Trang."

You understand. "Every month I'll have a hundred kilograms of rice distributed to the temples and churches in Nha Trang, to give to the poor," you promise him.

The next day you swap your trans-Pacific ticket for one to New York City, to go to your only son, left temporarily in Papa's and Maman's care. So you can hold him tight against your chest.

"Loc is right. We're marked by karma because of that war. Even if he and I only harmed people because of things we

didn't do, there were consequences. This is why..." you try to
tell Nina during take-off.

But all she does is nod and rub your shoulders.

She hasn't lived through the war. How can she understand?

.....

*It was in the mountains beyond Dalat and on the coast in Nha
Trang that karma began piling up for you and Loc.*

*It started because you were not to let anyone else have
even an inkling about your true loyalties. "Do whatever
needs doing so your anti-government tail won't show," Chú
Hai had ordered. After the Paris Accords and the ceasefire-in-
place, after the North had been allowed to remain in Southern
territory, what was necessary was for you to join other
Southern army reservists in the remotest parts of the country.
To plant as many Southern flags as you could on tribal land.
It was what the South had to do to prove its claims to as much
territory as possible, a bright young official had told President
Thieu. And so, you went.*

*It was at the flag-planting exercise that Binh and you met
up again. You were seconded to a regular unit in Ban Me
Thuot. Binh, who couldn't wriggle out of active duty at this
time of national need, turned out to be the commander.*

*Binh knew how to enjoy himself and take care of his men.
The normal routine was to remain a couple of nights in each
village, making day trips out to the surrounding hamlets—half
a day in to plant the flags, half a day out again. Binh always
arrived at the villages with crates of beer. Inevitably, because
of the beer, the headmen would invite all of you to stay in
the long house, high up on stilts, protected from wandering*

animals and sheltered from the cold night mists rolling down the mountain peaks. The day marches were not too bad either. Although the squads had to watch out for mines and possible VC ambushes on the trails, the weather was cool. As it wasn't time for the monsoons, you didn't have to cross slippery streams or hack through rain-drenched jungle. And after your marches, you would always come back to parties with a roasted pig or dog and bare breasted tribal girls afterwards.

But despite everything, including the two lucky red dots on your soles that were supposed to protect you, you developed a blister on your big toe which became infected. After a few days, it became tortuous for you to walk the ten to fifteen kilometers in and out of the hamlets. Binh finally decided you needed medical attention. On a quiet weekday morning, after the rest of his men had been sent on patrol, he hitched a motorcycle ride with you down to the town at the bottom of the mountain to find a clinic.

There was no doctor in town but there was beer, three crates which the two of you took back up the mountain in a decrepit tuk-tuk.

The tuk-tuk blew a tire halfway. The tribal driver, claiming he didn't have a spare, went back down the hill to get the tire patched. Unwilling to abandon the beer and climb the mountain on foot, Binh and you opted to stay put and wait for the driver to come back.

"A nap while waiting," Binh said, stepping into the bush and settling his back against a tree. "You keep watch. Commanding officer's instructions," he laughed, hugely thrilled he could finally boss you around.

You went to hide behind a bush with a clear view of traffic, some way from the tuk-tuk. About half an hour into your watch, you saw some Ede tribesmen come out from the jungle a few hundred meters away and walk up to the vehicle. They were modern Ede, dressed in ragged shirts and pants, not their native loin cloths and black wrappings. Only the leader, a dark man with straight hanging hair cut blunt at his ears, had kept his ear piercings. But even he had abandoned his traditional blowpipe and arrows. You saw the handle of a small revolver protruding from the waistband of his trousers. A bright new hunting knife shone from a leather holster strapped to his right calf. The holster was marked with Chinese ideograms. Not a group of simple hill people, you decided.

You watched as the leader motioned to a small boy lugging a large pouch woven from jungle vines. The child climbed into the tuk-tuk's carriage. To steal the beer, you supposed. But he merely rifled around as if he was looking for something he'd dropped, then clambered out. His pouch looked a little flatter, but you could not be sure.

You watched as the whole group turned off the road and disappeared back into the trees. You didn't know what to make of them. But if they were your enemy's enemy then you would be their friend, you decided. You didn't mention them to Binh when he awoke. They hadn't done anything worth reporting, you justified to yourself. So it seemed. Then.

Your driver came slouching back quite soon after Binh awoke. He had the repaired tire in his hand and a new hat on. He nodded at the two of you, went to fix the tire back on the wheel and then motioned for Binh and you to board.

When you arrived at the village, the two of you got off the vehicle and made for the longhouse, expecting the driver to unload the crates of beer. But he hurried away in the direction of the jungle. "Nature calls," he shouted, clutching his stomach.

"Lazy sod," Binh grumbled as he walked back to the tuk-tuk.

Hampered by your bad foot you followed more slowly. It was as you were shambling after Binh that you noticed the driver watching from behind a stand of bamboo, just where the jungle began. His face, under his wide brimmed hat, was unusually tanned; his eyes, staring from a fringe of straight hair cut bluntly above ears pierced through with black bone plugs, were strangely intent. It wasn't your original driver at all but the leader of the Ede group who'd stopped by earlier.

You should've called out to Binh right then. But you didn't. You hesitated for a few seconds to consider what your blood-father or Chú Hai might do in the circumstances. It was a few seconds too many. Before you could open your mouth, Binh was already inside the carriage of the tuk-tuk lifting up the top crate of beer, and the booby was exploding between his legs.

You saw Binh bounce onto the dusty roadway in a shower of sparks, pieces of khaki and jelly-like blobs of red flying away from him. Then he was screaming curses, his upper legs a mash of bone and bloody flesh loosely attached to two straight shins still encased in black army boots. You ran to him and began to fashion a tourniquet from the sleeves of both your shirts. Before you were finished, he'd blacked out.

The tribal guerilla had disappeared. The tuk-tuk was a pile of mangled metal. The traumatized villagers would not help. The explosion had been a clear warning from tribal secessionists not to offer further assistance to government troops. You could not wait for your squads to come back. You carried Binh on your back down to the town, your big toe throbbing the entire three kilometers.

From the town, Binh was evacuated to the army hospital. The doctors there managed to save his legs but the shrapnel was so deeply embedded in his genitals, they couldn't be repaired. That booby hadn't meant to kill, but it took something more valuable than life from Binh.

Binh couldn't thank you enough for getting him to town. He told everyone what a hero you were. When he got out of hospital he threw a party for you, one you couldn't refuse. You got so drunk at that party you nearly hit a lamp-post with your motorbike on the way home. But you didn't. Vipaka, you remember thinking as you swerved back onto the pavement in the nick of time. You'd escaped. But like Binh, only barely.

Still karma didn't seem to be in any hurry to punish you. After the flag planting mission, you were sent on yet another plum assignment—to Nha Trang.

Everything glittered in Nha Trang—the city with its shining beaches, the American lipsticked bar girls, the money pouring in. At twenty-five, you were in charge of rentals and maintenance of the gigantic Rome Plows used to bulldoze through jungle, as well as the quarry, the rock crushing plant, the gravel plants and over a hundred men. As the plant manager, unmarried, living in the company villa and driving a company pick-up truck, you were the best catch around for the girls left to fend for themselves in the aftermath of American disengagement. And how puppy dog eager you were to let them get at you.

Besides the girls, a spring tide of money was also running into your life. You were finally in a position to approve tenders. As Ly had predicted, white envelopes stuffed with cash arrived without fail at your two storey villa after the signing of each contract, incentives for you to give the successful contractor's next bid the same priority.

A waste of time, you'd chuckle to yourself, as you slit open the envelopes and took their contents to the jewelry shop to convert into gold. You hadn't abandoned your misgivings about letting bribes determine the award process. You always assessed the bids according to an eligibility checklist left behind by the Americans, and usually you awarded the tenders to the most qualified bidder. Once or twice a month though, Chú Hai's 'friends', bidders who would never qualify if you used the checklist, would call to request access to a bulldozer. Then one and all would notice you'd allowed someone patently unqualified to win. This seeming randomness confused the bona-fide contractors who simplistically assumed you were willing to do anything for enough money. Ever more bills were stuffed into your envelopes.

It was ironic. You were lending the Southern bulldozers to the Northern Army so they could clear jungle for the invasion and at the same time getting richer by the month doing it. It was a win-win situation for you, a lose-lose one for the government. No wonder the war's outcome.

At the time, Loc and Huong were in Nha Trang in their own little house by the sea, Loc heading a propaganda unit, Huong tending to a girl and three younger boys with one more on the way. It was the finishing touch to your good fortune in Nha Trang. It was like old times with Loc except that now he could no longer play the anti-war ballads you'd both loved in Saigon. And now, both of you were more careful with your conversation. It would not do if the two of you became too knowledgeable about each other's activities.

At this stage of the war, many Northern squads were already hiding in the surrounding hamlets. As part of his propaganda and pacification role, it was Loc's job to seek out and destroy the hidden clusters. He was your brother and he had six rice bowls to fill. You couldn't blame him.

Your responsibility was to keep the large Northern units in the jungles hidden by passing on the clearing schedules, so they could move out of the way and remain undetected until the actual invasion. Like the allocation of the bulldozer tenders, instructions about this had been left in the villa your second day in Nha Trang. Every Friday, before going out to lunch, you were to leave the following week's schedule out on your desk. When you got back, someone in the network would have read and memorized the information and you could lock it back into your drawer. If Loc knew about what you were doing, he didn't interfere. You were his brother.

It was a rare privilege—to be able provide intelligence and to supply equipment to hasten the end of the war without staining your hands. It didn't last.

One Friday afternoon you came back to your desk to find a slim envelope on top of the clearing schedules. Inside was a note asking you to leave the fuel depot's keys out overnight. Fuel prices were sky high and you'd just awarded a tender to one of Chú Hai's 'friends'. You assumed 'the friend' needed to tap some fuel. You left the keys out as instructed, without a second thought, and hopped into your pick-up to go to Loc's and Huong's for dinner.

You had made a mental note to go in early the next day to adjust the fuel meters, so no one would guess the tanks had been tapped. But you didn't think to tell the night guard to go off duty. The young boy, from a small hamlet west of Nha Trang, was dozing in front of the fuel tanks when the sappers crept in. He was a very good guard, a light sleeper, his colleagues told you later. But he had no chance against the half a dozen men who overpowered him, knocked him unconscious and then set the station on fire.

You were across town with Loc, barbecuing cuttlefish to go with your beer, when you heard the explosions.

It was 1974. The communists had just sabotaged the main oil facility near Saigon and burnt up fourteen million liters of gasoline. The Americans had cut the country's aid again. World oil prices were sky high. It didn't surprise you the neighborhood guerrillas executed a copycat action. But if you'd been less careless, if you'd taken the young guard off duty, he need not have died. You would not be looking at a boy shaped patch of stickiness on the blackened floor of the station when you went to inspect the damage later that night. It was one more karmic setback.

And Loc's part?

It began with a series of thefts. US aid had plunged. Taxes had been hiked. Prices had tripled. Loc himself couldn't make his salary last more than half a month. It was much worse for those he commanded. To keep morale up, he'd begun to divert some of the propaganda rice issued for poor hamlets to his own men. He had three squads, twenty-four families, plus another four or five families of widows and children; almost a village in all. Why support the Northern army at the expense of his own people? Better to starve the communist supporters into submission. All it involved was skimming a few kilos from a 'good' hamlet occasionally and punishing whole 'bad' villages once the evidence was in.

The headman from one of the punished hamlets went to the authorities, accusing Loc of misappropriation. To clear himself, Loc got a friend from the local army post to sweep the hamlet. They netted a whole squad of Northern saboteurs hiding in an underground cubby. After the sweep, the villagers found the headman's body in a stream, strangle marks black around his water bloated neck.

It turned out that Loc's friend had an only son, the boy on duty the night your fuel station was blown up. Loc and you could not know if the attack on the fuel station was a simple act of revenge or part of a grand strategy of attrition. Who was more responsible for that boy's death? Was it Loc? Was it you? All the two of you could do was wait, haunted by the boy's ghost, until time revealed the answer.

.....

As you fly to New York City towards your only son, your wife beside you, what's evident is that karma has exacted its due from Loc. What about you, though, you wonder. When will you be asked to pay back and how? And what about that act of omission against Binh?

"In war we all end up killing, one way or another," you raise your head to tell Nina. "It's difficult not to, even when you're neutral. Once you take sides, it's impossible. But karma can follow, all the way to America. Like these riots and what's happened to Thi." You turn to Nina to plead your case. "You shouldn't do this to me, Nina. Don't send me back there alone worrying about you and Tri. It's time the two of you came to be with me."

"Anything can happen anywhere. What you need to do is forgive yourself," she counsels you like one of her patients. "You did the best you could, in the circumstances. There was nothing else you could do better, nothing..." And, she concludes, "I love you."

Love is what levels the scales, Nina, the returned to her roots Catholic, the believer in a redeeming god, hopes.

You do not have her faith, you fear.

16
But...

NINA MIGHT LOVE YOU. She might have forgiven you. She might ignore the small infidelities you succumb to when apart from her. But she won't yield to the country that made you.

She flies willingly with Tri to meet you in Tokyo, in Hong Kong, in Bangkok, in Manila, most often in Singapore. Yet each time you ask her to go to Vietnam, she balks. She only ends up going because your father the Chief Clerk is dying, and she, his daughter-in-law, has to pay her long overdue respects.

Even then, she has excuses. There are patients she's responsible for, and appointments that need rescheduling. There's Tri and his peculiarities—what if he can't cope with the dirt and the noise in Vietnam? He's been doing so well lately, become almost totally socialized. She doesn't want any setbacks. And there are the anti-communist factions still so vocal in America... "I'm afraid of demonstrations outside my clinic and people flooding Papa's house with hate mail," she confesses over the phone.

"Nina, it's 1997. The US trade embargo's been lifted for three years. Ly's received official visitors from the soft drinks company. It's all over US television. Have Loc and

Huong told you about anyone who boycotted their colas in Little Saigon after the visit? I heard even Oldest Brother-in-Law continues to mix his Bacardi with it. Don't use that as an excuse. Please."

"You're over there. You have no idea how virulent they are. I've heard Loc talking about the cell-groups your Oldest Brother-in-Law's joined since he arrived. And Binh's in them as well. I talk to my father and my uncles in D.C. too. I know what feelings are like on the ground."

"If you wait another year it'll be too late. Do you want to be a daughter-in-law or not?" You hope she hears your other unasked question. Does she want to be a wife?

"Alright," she says finally.

"Good," you say. You let her know, "Loc, Huong and their children have already agreed to come along. You'll have company."

.....

Rural Vietnam is exactly as Nina imagines, she's happy to inform you. The rice fields and wayside villages are the descriptions in her textbooks brought to life, the skinny brown children in T-shirts and baseball caps modern reincarnations of the urchins she saw in 70's magazine articles. Your family fits her preconceptions of long-suffering war-battered Vietnamese too—reticent Third, stringy and brown like the old jungle fighter he was; your Can Tho and Bac Lieu sisters and brothers-in-law, the Vietnamese farmers and farm wives of her imagination.

But reality is not a stage set. After the kind greetings and platitudes, Nina finds she has nothing to say to any one of them. The women's soft welcoming caresses on her hands and forearms, the way they draw her in close to their sides to exchange this or that confidence, their pats of admiration on her white smooth skin, are too familiar too soon. "I need a safe New Yorker's arm's length" she confesses.

Your father, wheezing and gulping for breath, repulses her. His painful struggle, so different from the morphine-cushioned passing of terminal patients in the US, is simply unacceptable. "Why isn't anyone giving him anything?" she berates you once you're both away from everybody, in the attic you gutted entirely a few years ago to make a new air-conditioned retreat for yourself. Her big eyes blink with outrage at the cruelty your family is inflicting.

"He needs to be aware," you explain, repeating your father's wishes yet again. "He has to be mentally present to hear the monks guiding him through the *bardo* to where he can achieve a good rebirth. If he's drugged, all his years practicing will be thrown away." You assure her, "It's what he wants."

She won't accept this. "It's inhumane," she says. She bangs her fist against the wall, then gets up and goes downstairs.

You watch from the attic window as she emerges from the ancestral hall and crosses the courtyard to the new house you've built for your parents next door; the house your father will never move into; the house where your mother lies, blind and demented, unaware your father's dying.

"She was swinging in the hammock muttering," Nina tells you later, after dinner. "She was telling some kind of wandering disjointed story about a rape, and a baby, a murder and a stolen bangle. It was tantalizing, even if it didn't have a head or tail to it."

"Well, did you piece it all together, Dr Analytical?" you ask, shifting your head against her belly to make yourself comfortable.

"Not yet. Perhaps in a few more days," she says. But, she's still sitting beside your mother puzzling it out when a few days later a wail rises from the main house, Third Sister's message to everyone that the Chief Clerk has departed at last.

.....

The courtyards fill with visitors—regional party members who want to show respect for Ba Roi the retired Colonel and Party District Secretary; the large Southern families of the other brothers-in-law; your business associates from the city; curious neighbors who want a look at Loc and Huong and their children, finally back after nearly twenty years away.

Loc and you stand in traditional sack cloth beside the magnificent three-prowed hardwood casket bought with your American dollars. You bow your thanks to the visitors and bow your thanks again. Your backs ache. Your feet are sore. But you're both grateful, indeed overwhelmed, by the respect showered on your father, this provincial Chief Clerk who's done nothing more than look after his family and bring up his children while reading the classics.

Nina is not among the crowds. She's hiding in the air-conditioned attic. She hasn't found a place for herself like Loc's boys and Tri. A generation removed from their Delta roots, they're fitting in much better than she is. Loc's boys are mingling in the courtyards below, serving refreshments and chatting with their cousins. Even awkward Tri has found his place, sitting behind his grandfather's casket, meditating with the monks, chanting when they chant.

The funeral hall, with its smell of incense seeping into the hot moisture laden air, makes Nina feel sick. There is no room in the kitchen for her tall body, long elbows and American ignorance of wood fires and kerosene fueled stoves. She's gone there to help. But the women laboring at the endless rounds of meals for the visitors have no time to tell her what to do, not even Huong and Kim. "They simply moved me out of the way," she complains during a break, when you've gone up to the attic to cool off for a few minutes.

"Go sit with *Má* then and send the maid to the kitchen instead. At least, they'll be able to use her extra hands there," you snap. You can only tolerate so much of that American penchant for sharing every insecurity. You're still not as American as Chú Hai in that respect, notwithstanding all your years there, all your years married to Nina.

She's upset at the tone of your voice, too imperative, too much like any other Vietnamese husband. But she obeys. She showers and goes back downstairs into the heat and the crowd, her head held high like a princess in a procession. She stops, makes the customary three bows at your father's coffin, deep and reverent bows exactly as her Maman has taught her, then she sails across the courtyard and into the little garden next door.

She's there now, you know, even as you stand by Loc, bowing, saying thank you, bowing again. She'll be in the courtyard filled with the fragrant orchids for which you've paid a fortune, to bring down from the mountains to scent your blind mother's days. She'll still be trying to decipher your mother's ramblings about a murder, a baby, a rape, an ivory bangle...

.....

Nina thought she'd like Ho Chi Minh City better. But the rundown city filled with beggars and overhung with the stench of rotting fruit and sewage is a disappointment. Still dirt poor in 1997 despite more than ten years of *dời mới* and three years after the lifting of the US trade embargo, it is more awful than she expects. Her reactions, pity for the inhabitants and relief she's managed to escape living there, shame her; shame her so much she doesn't even share them with you until years later.

The only time she feels at ease is with Chú Hai.

You know she falls for him immediately when he greets Tri with an openly welcoming pat on the shoulder and not the formal folded arms her Papa and Maman require. She does not fail to notice how he accepts Tri's introduction gift, a complex drawing of a mandala made at the funeral, with genuine appreciation; how he spends time asking Tri for the meaning behind each of the concentric bands of designs he's so carefully rendered; how thoughtfully he comments on Tri's answers.

Then it's Nina's turn. Now for the most important one, his bright quick eyes seem to say. He takes both her hands in his, in palms that have the same feeling against the back of her hands as yours, and then he smiles his seductive wolf's smile. "Ah yes, the great love of my boy's life," is the first thing he says. "I've waited a long time to meet you," are his next words, with just a hint of gentle recrimination. A warm welcome but not too familiar, Nina will feel. Just right.

Just as his farewell is when the three of you come to take your leave for Hue—a handshake for Tri, a squeeze on the upper arm for you, a kiss on both Nina's cheeks in the old French style. You hear him whisper to her, "Don't take too long before you come back again, my dear." Then releasing her, a more public statement, "And when you get to Hue give my regards to your uncles. "

"He's a charmer. Little wonder you've been under his spell all these years," she has to concede. She wrinkles her nose like she used to before you made her sad. "He trained you well. No wonder I've been under your spell all these years."

.....

There is much less to charm in Hue. Her uncles in the flesh, the ones who chose the Viet Cong, are not the bony determined communist generals of her youthful imagination. Except for their bad teeth, the two urbane eighty year olds who now do business with you and Ly are clones of her Papa and her uncles in America. There's nothing ancient about the family temple she's heard her father reminiscing about all her life either. Restored with the two generals' business takings and contributions from relatives abroad, it is over-large and gaudy with gold. Even in discreet and snobbish Hue, the generals' children, who supervised the rebuilding, haven't been able to resist showing off.

"But it's all *façade*," she says to you in the privacy of the guesthouse next to her cousin's brand new French-style villa. "The toilets at the back were leaking. And there were termite droppings at the base of the wooden pillars, even though they're supposed to be hardwood and lacquered with a hundred layers of oil." She hesitates, fingering the German satin bedspread you are both sitting on, before voicing her next thought. "I wonder how much of the money people sent back went into my cousins' pockets?" she asks.

You raise a surprised eyebrow at your wife's question.

"Wow!" she puts a hand to her mouth. Her big eyes are wide. "That's the kind of thought you would think. I've only been here a month and I've become as cynical as you." She tilts her chin to run the situation through her analytical head. "You know, Vietnam can't be a good idea if it can turn me sour so quickly."

You look around the over-the-top guest quarters your family's been given, the sitting area with its collection of *ormolu* clocks in an intricately carved display chest, the floors inlaid with colored marble chips, like a Roman mosaic. "They probably have lined their pockets. You're only being realistic. It's better than being deluded, isn't it?" you comment.

"But to live in a place where you have to constantly doubt everyone's trustworthiness..." she protests.

.....

"I can't," she writes you from her study, when she's back alone in New York. She's longing for you and missing Tri, who's shocked the two of you by deciding to spend the rest of the summer in Vietnam with Chú Hai. But, in the years of self-analysis, she's finally learnt to discern what she needs and what she doesn't, what she can do and what she can't. She can't go to live in Vietnam.

As for full disclosure, she no longer needs the rest of the story. What you've shared so far is more than enough. All she wants is you, living with her in New York City. Haven't you told her Asia's in the midst of an economic crisis and all the deals have dried up? Isn't this the best time for you to take a sabbatical, to see if you might like living in New York? She's tried this past summer in Vietnam. It's your turn now.

No, Nina can't forgive the country that spawned you.

ENDGAME

17
Full disclosure

THERE'S NO POINT BEING POLITE NOW, no point rationing the disclosures about your life. You send a telegram to Nina—'You promised to say yes if you got full disclosure. I'm giving it to you. Be ready for the express mail deliveries.'

You send five boxes by air-express, paying six hundred and thirty dollars in postage. They contain the life you've reclaimed during your time in Asia, eight and a half years worth of journals and papers stuffed into hotel envelopes. They're not everything. You've crossed over sentences, torn out pages and even shredded others. Some sins, you've decided, are not for confession. Still, it is a mountain of secrets, revealed.

In the cover letter accompanying the boxes, you write down a line from an old Vietnamese saying—'*Công cha như núi Thái Sơn...* The labors of a father are as heavy as Thai Son Mountain.' You hope she'll understand. You've had three fathers—the Commander, the Chief Clerk and Chú Hai. Five boxes are nothing against the weight of their labors, shaping you into who you've become.

You also send separately, in an overnight package, a few sheets of paper, a photograph and a plain note card.

On the note card you've written—'This is full disclosure, who I am, who you married. It's why I can't live in a country where everyone's trustworthiness is taken for granted. I will understand if you can't keep your promise. But I hope that love, as you always say, can conquer.'

It's unreasonable to ask Nina to bear the whole burden of reconciliation, to hope that love will indeed prevail, that it can lighten some of the weight of karma. But it's too late for caution. Now you must gamble everything.

.....

This is your final wager:
One page, beginning with the sentence—

'I said goodbye to Julia Anderson in July 1974.'

The excerpt continuing in this way—

'Although we spoke occasionally over the phone, I hadn't seen her since I left Saigon. During that time she'd been busy establishing a support network of American advisors meant to remain after the US withdrawal; an undercover network, in contravention of the Paris Accords.

'The endgame was near. I was occupied balancing the rising demand for bulldozers from both sides, from the South to keep the roads cleared to prevent attacks, from the North to clear away jungle so the attacks could take place.

'During a week when I had to cover up 'losing' one of the bulldozers I'd sent out to Ban Me Thuot to open a mountain path for the Northern tanks, Julia Anderson phoned me from Saigon. She was leaving and wanted to say goodbye in person, she told me. I was flattered. As she requested, I made arrangements to meet her for the weekend.

'I went by plane, paying for the ticket with some of my commissions. It was my first time flying. I'd just turned twenty-six and on the flight out, I felt truly a man — an adult with commissions turned into gold safely under my bed and an American woman to meet in the city.

'When I arrived at the hotel, I went to see Chú Hai at his office first, then proceeded up to the fifth floor to meet Julia. She was packing. She hugged me in greeting like she always did but, unusually, she didn't tease me about how well I was looking. Perhaps, like her, I too appeared older and sadder. Certainly I was more street smart, more full of sin. Her hugs didn't arouse me as quickly as they used to, but I was happy to see her again. We went down to the bar for a drink, then dinner. After that we spent the night together.'

A yellow post-it with the line —

'If you want full disclosure, then I unfortunately will have to tell about the kisses'.

And a drawing of a small circle with two ink smudges for blushing cheeks and a downward curving mouth.

Another three pages —

'In the morning Julia Anderson asked if I wanted her help to leave Vietnam. I didn't reply for quite a while. Why might she want to help me, I asked finally. She was evasive. We were going to be overrun, didn't I know? Then, anyone involved in any way with the Americans would be dead meat. Dead meat, she repeated. Chú Hai would be taken care of because he worked for the magazine. But I didn't have any official affiliation with the Americans, although I'd done so much work for them. She didn't want to leave me to suffer the consequences.

'I was ashamed at how successfully Chú Hai and I had hoodwinked her. It didn't stop me spewing out more pro-American nonsense, though. Yes things were getting desperate, but Nixon would never let us down, would he? He'd promised to send the B-52s if we needed them. The country would come through. I was quite sure I would be safe, I told her. I didn't say why I was so confident. It wasn't a lie, just an omission.

'She became very angry and called me a stupid boy. Nixon was a good man, a staunch ally of South Vietnam, but the Supreme Court had ordered him to produce all of the Watergate tapes. Soon he'd be impeached. What would his promises be worth then? Would the next President care that Thieu had helped Nixon win his first term? She didn't think so. Congress had cut Vietnamese aid again. The country was now at the very back in the line for aid. Did I know our aid for the whole year was only one fifth what Israel received for the three week Yom Kippur war?

'We're abandoning you and not coming back, she said. You should get out before it's too late. She started apologizing, for her country, for having to leave herself, for letting a young boy like me get involved in the first place. I kept telling her it wasn't her fault. But she didn't seem to want comforting. She began to cry. It would be cruel to tell her the truth, that I was impatient for the invasion and would rejoice at the inevitable rout of the Southern army. I reached over and did what I usually did with her. It seemed to help. She calmed down.

'In the middle of that night, she again asked me to leave. She said she would get my name onto one of the employee lists, or failing that, as a family member. As her husband, she whispered into the dark.

'It began to dawn on me that perhaps what had passed between us since we first met when I was eighteen meant more to her than I'd assumed. I held her very tight and told her I was more grateful than I could ever say. Inside I felt like a double- headed snake.

'We spent the next day riding around Saigon. The day after, she asked me to take her to the Delta, where we'd gone on our first assignment. There were beggars everywhere we went, many more than before. Around the markets we saw one-legged men, one-armed men, men with no legs... Those without legs were sitting on pieces of cardboard attached to their necks with strings, dragging themselves along with their hands in the filth. In the hamlets the beggars were children, light haired with sharp noses or dark skinned with African features, the offspring of American soldiers and Vietnamese women. Even then, before the war's end, they were being treated very badly. I saw people cuffing and kicking them. At a shop, I was almost hit when the owner threw one, a tiny dust colored girl, out into the street like a sack of rubbish.

'You see—Julia Anderson said after I'd steadied myself against her, and the child had scuttled away—you see what's already happening to the children of Americans? What do you think the communists will do to their lovers?

'People, especially in the countryside, did look at us in an unfriendly way. But I didn't worry. When the war was over, it would be known that I was a hero of the resistance. Or so I believed. I would be lauded then, not attacked or assaulted. I told her this was my country. I could be myself here. How would I live over there, where I would have to constantly explain myself?

'I must have thanked her at least fifty times that weekend. We were closer and more at ease with each other those two days than at any other time in the eight years we'd known each other. Aside from covering up my true loyalties, there was no misinformation I had to convey to her, nothing I needed to pry from her. We were simply a Vietnamese man and an American woman, riding around on a motorbike.

'I was sad when it came time for me to fly back to Nha Trang. I'd discovered a deep feeling for her, one I hadn't been aware of all those years. It wasn't love exactly. But when I said goodbye to her at the airport, I felt I was saying goodbye to a part of me. Not the best part perhaps, but still a piece of myself. I hugged and kissed her out in the public gallery in front of gawking Vietnamese and Americans who looked aside. I lied and told her my heart would be with her and I would think about what she had said.'

An interruption here. You'd torn away the rest of that last page. Your writing had been unsteady. Some lines had been smeared with wetness. Nina did not need to see your last emotion-laden moments with Nina Anderson, how the feelings rushed over you in your solitary hotel room when you reclaimed those moments more than twenty years later.

Another page—

'In Nha Trang, things seemed far worse than when I left, although I was away only two nights. Perhaps I was in a heightened state of sensitivity. Perhaps what I saw in the Delta and Julia Anderson's warnings made me more aware of how the people were suffering. For the first time I began to feel dread at the prospect of the oncoming invasion, and the inevitable killings and repercussions that would follow.

'Loc came to see me. His morale was at a new low. His budget was being cut again and the rice distribution program scaled back further. With the suppliers creaming off their share, there wasn't enough rice now for even the men on active duty. Still, rice wasn't the most important thing on his mind. What concerned him was his fate once we were overrun. All his working life he'd been on what would soon be the wrong side. No one could protect him, he said. But if I could manage it, he would be grateful if I could take care of Huong and the children when he was gone.

'I told him not to be so pessimistic. After he left, I wrote to Julia Anderson telling her I'd changed my mind and would do what she suggested. I gave her all my personal details. Then I sent the letter to Chú Hai to forward to the US embassy in Israel where she'd gone. Already, I feared, it might be too late for her to help. But she called me a month later from Tel Aviv. Over the line she told me how pleased she was I'd agreed. She'd managed to put me on the evacuation list for American associates. I should expect someone from the embassy to contact me through Chú Hai when the time came. I thanked her. I would forever be in her debt, I told her truthfully. Then I told her I missed her, which was a lie.

'After the call, I went to Loc and explained the plan to him. I gave him my identity papers for him to commission fakes with. Then I briefed him on the story he should tell when the embassy called. And I swore to him I'd make sure Huong and the children could follow.'

Next, the photograph—a scene of a turquoise colored bay surrounded by a crescent of shining white sand fringed by beach pines, the East Beach on Phu Quoc Island—nothing written on the front, nor on the back, nothing about that harrowing trip with Huong and her children from Nha Trang to that bay as the Northern Army poured in.

This is what you wrote in the journal pages that should have accompanied the photograph, pages you put through Chú Hai's shredder—

'The two lane highway to Cam Ranh was jammed with seven lanes of traffic fighting to go south. The vehicles could move no faster than the refugees plodding along on foot. I feared it would take a day instead of an hour to get to the wharves.

'Among the convoy were cone-hatted men and women carrying children and baskets, setting one foot in front of the other with their eyes down, nothing to look forward to. Amidst them, better dressed city people wheeled bicycles and motorbikes piled with suitcases. Hawkers walked along, selling their leftover wares. Accompanying them, a solitary booklover pushed a barrow overflowing with loot from the city library.

'Some, like my driver, the driver's girlfriend, and myself, sweltered inside the cabs of our pickups. Like many others, Huong and her children, including newborn Thi, dozed under plastic tarps in the flatbeds of the trucks. The even wealthier lounged in their motorcars, inscrutable behind their sunglasses. In the car ahead, I saw a mother passing around packages of imported biscuits to her fat white children.

'It was a determined flight, fuelled by rumors of the routs in far off Quang Tri and Hue, the televised image of the general overseeing those northernmost regions landing in Danang seasick and dishevelled, the almost absolute news silence on local TV thereafter. All of us were driven by sights we imagined, fed by BBC accounts that the yellow starred flag was being hoisted once again over the Hue citadel, that Montagnard platoons had rebelled on the retreat from Kontum; that they were engulfing the highlands in a tribal uprising.

'The rumors became wilder as they were passed from mouth to ear to mouth. I heard two women walking beside the pickup, so near my open window I could have reached over and snatched the half-hidden gold chains around their necks, discussing the Montagnard uprising—They got hold of a young girl and took turns with her. When they were done, she was ripped apart... My husband said they attacked the relief forces we sent up from Nha Trang. Poor things, not soldiers at all... They fell on them, cut out their livers later... Yes, I hear they eat them raw.

'I looked through the glass pane separating the cab from the flatbed to see if Huong had heard the ghastly stories, and if so, how she was bearing up. She'd gathered her sleeping children close to her like a comfort blanket and bent her head towards the baby's, rubbing her ear against the barely there fuzz to block out the women's horror stories.

'I pushed the pane open and asked—Sixth Sister, are you alright? She obviously wasn't, but she nodded anyway—I'm worried about the children. It's so hot and the air's so heavy. They're all flushed already. What if they get a fever?... We'll get to the sea soon, it should be cooler in a few hours—I said. I must not have convinced her. She turned away to look at the sky. I slid the window pane shut.

'Overhead, above the clouds, planes roared and helicopters thrummed their way north to relieve the troops fighting there. But on the road itself no mortars fired, no anti-aircraft missiles whistled up to the airborne machines to bring them down in flames onto our human train; there were no soldiers waiting to fall on all of us, nor to surround us with protection. Everything that mattered was happening somewhere else, to someone else—a brother, an uncle, a father, a son, a husband of a sister-in-law.

'Brother-in-Law! Youngest!—Huong tapped on the glass pane. I slid the pane open again—Yes?... She said—I just wanted to say that you were right. I was fretting about Sixth. I didn't say because I didn't want you to worry about me. You have enough to think about already, getting all of us to Cam Ranh, onto the boat, and then from the port down there home to Saigon...

'What she'd confessed was all true, but could any of her realizations lighten my burdens on this final journey south? She continued—I want you to know that I'm going to pray. I'm going to beseech the Virgin of La Vang to help Sixth make it home safe. No matter his anger when he finds us gone and just your message on the door. As long as he gets home safe, with his liver and his heart intact and finds that address you left for him, that's all I need. That's what I'm going to pray for. It will be one thing you won't have to worry about.

'It must have been the Virgin of La Vang. It was not the Buddha in any case, as I hadn't offered him even a sigh. Whatever the prime or motivating cause, Loc did manage to get on a US plane out. And, at Cam Ranh, I managed to negotiate the passage south for all of us.

'It cost me six strips of gold, more than a month's pay, to secure places on the Navy ship meant for high officers and their dependents. The officers and dependents were hidden below deck, safe inside their cabins. Everyone else not meant to be there, including our little group, were given passage above deck in the rain. No one complained. Everyone knew fish rotted from the head first. The government was already rotten. The army wouldn't survive for long. Better to be going south, out on deck at the mercy of the monsoon, than to be left in the city to become cannon fodder when the hordes descended.

'I found a space for Huong, the children and myself in a nook under the life-boats, and rigged a small tent with the tarp we'd brought along. Then I went to look for access into the ship's bolted down insides to replenish the food we'd already depleted.

'I brought back bread, half a boiled *saucisson*, a nearly full can of condensed milk and a plastic container of water... It was all I could get for three strips of gold. I didn't want to spend more—I told Huong. I didn't know how long it would take us to get home. The crew member I'd bought the food from said the boat wouldn't be allowed to enter Saigon and we would have to dock further away, I reported.

'Huong told me I'd done my best. She helped me put all the food, except for the condensed milk and water, into a basket far inside the shelter of the tarp. Taking a bowl, she mixed some milk with the water. She sipped a mouthful and brought Thi's mouth to her own. The baby rocked her head from side to side looking for the teat and making small whines of frustration against the fleshy knob made by Huong's lips. Then, realizing there was sustenance coming from this unfamiliar source, she opened her mouth wider and began to swallow. Satisfied that all would now be well until our next meal, I lowered my head against the huddle of the three boys' backs and closed my eyes.

'To the left, hidden by a tarp indistinguishable from ours, I heard a woman telling her children a story about the ancestors of the Vietnamese people—the dragon king, the mountain fairy and their hundred children; how fifty of these children had stayed on the mountain, as their family had; how now, they were following the other fifty siblings out to sea... But I liked our mountain and our house—one of the children protested... And so did I, I liked our house too, the house we built from nothing—I heard Huong say to herself just before I drifted off to sleep.

'In deep night, the darkened ship powered its way through the heaving waves. The rain stopped. Beneath the tarp the boys slept in the protective enclosure of my body. Behind them, Kim huddled by the food basket. Outside the safety of the tarp Huong, giddy and nauseous, paced the deck.

'She wouldn't have wandered far. It would have been too dangerous. She would have kept to the ten or fifteen meters on the left and right of our nook. She would have stepped carefully, taking care to avoid the little pools of vomit beginning to collect on the metal floor. And she might have stopped to cough every now and then, to clear the smell of the half-digested rice and fermenting bread and fish sauce from her nostrils. To comfort herself, she would have held Thi close to her, letting her suckle even though there was no milk left.

'Others too were restless in the dark—some hungry and harmless, some crazed, still others on fire with the anger and shame of defeat, and then some who'd just taken advantage of the chaos to break out of the prisons and walk free. It was Huong's fate that one of these escapees happened to see her sipping from a rice bowl, her thin blouse and trousers damp and clinging to her body, Thi's tiny hand stroking an exposed breast.

'Huong screamed just once as the hard rough hand clamped over her mouth. The bowl she was holding fell, breaking against the metal deck.

'I awoke and pulled the tarp open. Paces from me, I saw a man holding Huong to the deck, heaving over her. I wrestled him off Huong, exposing her nakedness. The two of us grappled with each other, rolling on the deck at Huong's feet. The prisoner managed to straddle me and pin me down against the metal flooring of the ship. He bent his face into my neck, ready to bite through to the jugular. In that moment, Huong reached for the gold she'd hidden in the sling under the baby's bottom and threw it over the man's shaved head to the far end of the gangway... Five taels, go and get it—she shouted. The prisoner was off me and gathering all the gold up before she even finished her sentence. By the time I pushed myself up from the deck, he'd disappeared into the dark. There was no one about except Huong and me. If anyone heard anything, they were minding their own business.

'I disentangled myself from Huong's trousers, which had gotten caught on my body during the fight, and handed them to her. Then I picked Thi up and walked back to our shelter, leaving Huong to follow.

'Huong didn't know what I'd seen, but her eyes would not meet mine when she came back under the tarp to take Thi from me. The two of us did not speak until the next day when the boat docked in Phu Quoc Island, off the south western coast of Vietnam... Sixth Sister, I should have taken more care. I don't know what to say to Sixth—I began to apologize. She stopped me short—Nothing, he doesn't need to know. You came in time to stop everything. Nothing happened... She didn't know that when I pulled the prisoner away from her by the hips, I'd felt the man's penis against my forearm, slick from penetrating her.

'I considered the coast line, the white beach fringed by bluish beach pines... Alright then—I said. I took her hand and pressed two taels of gold into it. Just in case—I told her... She nodded and tucked the sheets into Thi's sling, where the first five taels I'd given her had been. I looked away, out towards the refugee camp that was growing before my eyes behind Phu Quoc jetty. I tried not to think of the twelve months worth of wages she'd thrown away to save my life.

'We'd arrived in Phu Quoc in the middle of the morning, but weren't allowed to disembark until all the officers and their families alighted. As we waited up on the ship, Huong and I saw a contingent of military police officers march through the crowded dock to form a cordon. A line of men tied, together with metal chains, was led through by two more MPs, followed by a crowd of shouting and cursing passengers.

'I heard a woman from a neighboring group tell Huong the bound men were robbers and extortionists, the shouting group their accusers... If you've lost anything, just report it to the officers down there and they'll arrest the person responsible and get your things back for you—she said.

'I knew Huong wouldn't acknowledge the woman or the hint. Even if there were eyes in the dark that had seen something, she'd continue to pretend nothing had happened, just as she'd pretended with me. So nothing could ever be said about it later. Her future life with Loc depended on that. It was worth more to her than the five princely taels of gold she'd thrown at the escapee. She'd do nothing to get the money back.

'But I learnt Huong could do a lot worse to keep the matter quiet forever.

'As I filed between the two ranks of military police towards the dock gates, I noticed Huong's attacker pushing through the crowd until he was directly behind her. He began to rub himself against her back. When she turned around to see who it might be, he leered and ran his tongue around his lips. I jostled to get between her and the man. But before I could reach her she'd already slipped towards one of the MPs forming the cordon.

'I saw her whisper into the young man's tired innocent face, then turn to give the rapist a jubilant smile before melting back into the crowd and moving on into anonymity. I saw the MP turn to stare at the rapist with the dazed look of someone who'd just won a lottery.

'That evening after we'd registered and been given our places in the refugee camp, Huong informed me she was going to the beach. She needed a good wash, she said, and there was only drinking water in the camp.

'It was natural a woman who'd just been violated should need some time for reflection. But there was a set to Huong's chin that bothered me. I climbed onto the top of a truck and followed the path she took until she disappeared around a knoll and into a thicket of trees. She was going to the East Beach, I noted. Once I found someone to look after the children I'd follow, I decided.

'Huong had gone down to the beach where the MPs carried out their executions, I learnt from an acquaintance who arrived a few days before. It was not a place to frequent, my acquaintance warned, especially at sunset.

'When I reached the beach later, an hour before sunset, Huong was nowhere to be seen. But I was quite sure she was somewhere nearby. I hid myself up a beach pine and waited for what might happen next.

'The MPs finally came, at about 6 pm, when the tide was at its highest. First the older MPs filed down, each carrying a rifle. They were followed by a group of younger MPs, dragging along a gaggle of bound men, Huong's attacker among them. The older MPs stopped to form a line on the sand. The bound men were made to splash shin deep into the waterline, pushed onto their knees and blindfolded. Then the MPs with the rifles stepped backward.

'Up in my tree I heard the clicks of the rifles being cocked. Someone counted to three. The rifles fired. I saw the bound men topple one against the other into the water, their mouths opening to take in the sea. When the last man had fallen, some of the younger MPs were ordered to untie the bodies and push them into the outgoing tide.

'The young MP Huong had tipped off was among those in the disposal squad. When he was done, he came up from the water, went to a tree not far from me and bent over to retch. In the hip pocket of his sodden pants, outlined against his skinny buttocks, I saw a stack of gold leaves at least five thick.

'I stayed up in the tree until the beach cleared and it grew dark. Then I went looking for Huong. She was neck deep in water some distance from the shore, looking here and there as if she had lost something. I shouted her name but there was no response. I had to undress down to my boxers and my blood-mother's bone circlet to go to her. She was totally naked and desperately turning around and around. Her skin was wrinkled and water logged. I took hold of her shoulders and turned her towards me. Come Sixth Sister, let's go home now—I said... She struggled away from me. Her eyes were feral, flickering... I have to find that man and bury him—she muttered—They killed him and then just floated him away. How's he going to find rest? The way the tides are he'll never know where he is. He'll be a wandering ghost forever. I shouldn't have told the MP he had the gold. It was my fault, all my fault. Holy Mary Mother of God have mercy on me, St. Joseph intercede for me— she began to pray.

'It's not your fault. It's war. Things happen in a war—I said. I took her by the hand and led her up to the shore, then wiped her dry with my undershirt.

Unresisting, she allowed me to thread her feet through my trousers and pull them up her legs before tying them tight around her waist. I put her arms through my shirt and buttoned it up. And then I combed her hair dry with my fingers and plaited it. The last thing I did was throw her clothes into the sea, the ones she had on when she'd been raped... See, there's nothing left from last night. You're all washed now, totally clean—I comforted her.

'She didn't seem to hear. I bent forward in front of her and heaved her onto my back. She allowed me to carry her piggy-back all the way to the camp, she in my dry outer clothes, and me in dripping boxers. On the way I sang her a lullaby—under the new moon my little child all will be well, and all will be well. Everything brand new.

'I did not feel all would be well, though. Not for Huong anyway. She'd thrown away half the gold I had—the five taels she'd scattered at the rapist that was now with the military policeman, the twó extra taels I'd given her that she'd left somewhere on the beach. I had only seven taels left after the expenses on the ship out from Nha Trang. With defeat imminent, I didn't know if seven taels would be enough to buy all of us out of Phu Quoc and pay for Huong and the children's escape from Vietnam.

'As Huong and the children slept, I sat and fretted.

'I left our tent and went to look for my acquaintance from Nha Trang to find out what he might know about a young MP with a tired face.

'At moon set, I sneaked into the enclosure where the electric generators were and pulled at a wire and then another. The machines sparked. The whole camp plunged into darkness.

'It was something I had to do, the only way I could guarantee Huong's and the children's freedom, I said to myself as I walked towards the nearby bushes to pick up the implements I'd set aside. It was necessary, I kept telling myself as I made my way out of the camp in the ink black confusion towards my five taels of gold. I needed the gold to fulfill the promise I'd made to Loc, to get his wife and children out of Vietnam once the South fell. It was the best way to protect Huong's and Loc's marriage from repercussions. Who knew what the rapist had told the young MP, and whether he could keep the story to himself? If he were silenced, there would be no rumors, none at all.

'My bare feet picked their way quickly and surely down the path I'd already walked twice that day. At the end of the path, I turned towards the military police quarters at the top of the East Beach. Carefully, I crawled in the direction of the tents set up just a few days ago, tents, I noticed, that were only flimsily protected by rolls of concertina wire and one patrolling guard.

'I squatted and watched with my heart in my mouth as someone lighted an oil lamp and the dark triangle of the main tent came to flickering life, then relaxed as the rest of the encampment remained in darkness, asleep. I waited for the patrolling guard to pass my way, and trip over the leather string I'd strung up between two bushes. I pounced on the guard and knocked him on the head with the long heavy tree branch in my hand.

'He fell with a thud. Before he could regain consciousness, I muffled his mouth with a rag I'd scavenged, and tied another over his wrists and ankles, binding them together to keep him immobile when he woke; everything done exactly as I'd been taught during my reservist training in the losing Nationalist army.

'I went back to retrieve the leather thong and threaded it through my blood-mother's bangle, which I'd tucked temporarily in the waistband of my trousers. I tied the circlet back flat around my stomach and touched it once for luck. Whatever my mother the Chief Clerk's wife might think, I was going ahead. My blood-mother, who had protected my blood-father all these years, she would be the one looking out for me.

'I lifted up the bottom of the concertina wire fence with the tree branch and edged myself under the spikes.

'There were only two fresh MPs, I'd been told. They slept in the last tent, in the worst location near the latrine pits. I made my way there guided by the stink, and lifted the tent flap. There was only one man asleep in the tent. The other recruit must have been the guard I'd just knocked down. The young man's white uniform was hanging on a peg attached to the ridge pole. I ran my hands over the clothes, hoping to feel the hardness of the gold sheets. Perhaps, I hoped, I might not have to take things as far as I was prepared to. But the gold was not on the uniform.

'I set my jaw. It couldn't be any harder than strangling a rooster, could it? And I hadn't felt anything when I did that, had I?

'In war one must take sides, I heard my blood-father's voice saying. All was fair in love and war, I heard Chú Hai scolding. The war had found me when I killed the chicken. Later there had been Ai Nguyet, Julia Anderson, Binh, the boy-shaped patch of burnt stickiness in Nha Trang. This would be just a feather on the weight of all that karma, I told myself.

'My right hand reached out and slipped under the young policeman's pillow, where the gold would most likely be. The young man sighed as my fingers brushed against his hair. His hand reached up sleepily to caress mine. He must have been dreaming about a lover, I realized. Then his eyes opened. He could not see me in the darkness but he must have known immediately that the fingers he'd just touched were not his beloved's.

'Before he could open his mouth, I pulled the rough military issue blanket covering his body up and over his head. I pressed down as hard as I could. For as long as I needed to. It was the best way, the best way, I kept telling myself as I stumbled down to the sea to wash.

'When I'd cleaned away all traces of what I'd done, I hoisted myself onto a rock and waited. Sunrise came, as always. The pitch black nothingness before my eyes changed into a turquoise colored bay surrounded by a crescent of shining white sand. Perched on the rock, I let the sun's rays warm me. I tried to forget the night.

'Huong and I never mentioned those two nights ever again, not to each other, not to anyone else, not while in Phu Quoc, not after.

'I bribed our way off the island with part of the twelve taels of gold I now had, and bought our journey

back to Can Tho. There, I appropriated a boat from
the company's shipyard, provisioned it and found a
pilot, then put Huong and the children in the care of a
colleague who was also escaping, and sent them away.
My promise to my brother was fulfilled. It wasn't my
responsibility what happened to Loc and Huong after.
How that one small incident on a ship escaping from
Nha Trang might reverberate through the rest of my
brother's marriage.'

All that is left of the night is the picture you and Nina had
never got around to discussing when you first began to share
your past. If Nina replies to ask you for the story behind this,
then it means fate intends to separate you. This is your hard
limit. What, you've come to realize, you can never disclose.

What you disclose instead is on a single page, freshly written—

'A few years ago, I met Julia Anderson again at an
American Chamber of Commerce cocktail party in
Tokyo. She was whispering intimately to an attractive
Eurasian man, a very young man. Aside from that only
her voice was the same. She'd gained weight, dyed her
hair a dignified dark brown, and had work done to her
face. As for me, she initially mistook me for Chú Hai
because I looked so much like her memory of him—a
middle aged Vietnamese man. She told me she'd
worried when I didn't turn up among the evacuees in
1975. I said I'd only left in 1979, giving the impression
there'd been a hitch. Perhaps she suspected. Near the
end of our conversation she asked if I'd sold my place

on the lists to someone else. I said no, the truth minus a few significant omissions. She let it go. We promised each other we'd catch up, but of course we didn't.

'She visited Chú Hai subsequently, bringing along her son whom she wanted Chú Hai to mentor. She did not ask Chú Hai about me. I didn't tell you about both meetings. The habit of leaving out facts, especially when the telling is not to my advantage, is one I haven't been able to give up.

'You see my aversion to the daylight, even now. You say you don't need more revelations but do you truly understand the kind of opportunist I was? Looking at how good I am at Jerry's work, I'm probably still someone you must always suspect of being untrustworthy. That's the reality about this country and about me. As I said to Julia Anderson those many years ago, I can be myself in this country. How can I live over there, where I would have to constantly explain myself? But I can't see a life without you either. It is presumptuous to ask, but for love's sake can the mountain move to Mohammed?'

.....

You receive Nina's reply in an email the next day—'Not here and not there but perhaps common ground elsewhere?'

REDEMPTION

Part Three

GIVING BACK

18
Reconciliation

YOU'LL BE WANDERERS TOGETHER until you find common ground, Nina and you agree. Practically speaking, it means six months in New York so Nina can close her practice, *Tết* in Vietnam and half a year there to see if Nina might possibly feel better about the country, then Christmas in France, for Nina to reconnect with her Nguyen cousins, and after that a blank check. It's a better compromise than you have a right to expect.

You arrange a meeting with Jerry in Hong Kong, to negotiate a sabbatical. You'll come soon, you tell Nina over the phone. As soon as you can settle things with Jerry. Before the end of this Tiger year, you assure her.

.....

You return to your wife and son, with Chú Hai in tow. After an interval of nearly fifty years, Chú Hai is in America again as the leader of a forward team preparing for the first visit by a Foreign Minister of the Socialist Republic of Vietnam to the United States of America.

You invite him to Tri's high school graduation and when he arrives in New York, you tempt him to sneak away from the delegation to attend a wedding.

Loc's daughter Kim is finally marrying Jake, the Jewish boy she's tried to hide from her parents for so many years. Loc and Huong have refused to have a Vietnamese celebration. Not because they disapprove of a non-Vietnamese son-in-law— they're thankful thirty-one year old Kim is finally marrying— but because 1998 is another year of the Tiger and they don't wish to attract its attention.

"Something quiet. And better not in Orange County, so we don't have to explain," they tell the young couple.

Jake and Kim are secretly pleased. "A small Jewish wedding in the Catskills then. In Jake's parents' country house," they offer as a compromise.

Chú Hai is thrilled to be part of it. "I have to pinch myself to feel it's real. I feel like I'm in my favorite movie, *The Fiddler on the Roof*," he says to you. "Although that's not an entirely acceptable communist story," he confesses, his lips twisted half-regretfully like Papa Nguyen's when he lights up his Cuban cigars. He gushes, "It's so wonderful, your niece the beautiful black haired bride, that ruddy faced groom in his yarmulke and white shawl, the canopy... And especially the part when the groom steps on the goblet," he sucks in his breath, full of anticipation.

"Why?" you hear Huong whisper with consternation to Loc as the rabbi places the wine glass on the ground and Jake's shoe crunches into the crystal.

"Because we need to remember..." the Rabbi intones in a Hebrew your Vietnamese family can only follow from the English prayer booklets in their hands.

"How unfortunate, beginning a marriage to the sound of shattering glass, just so they can commemorate something two thousand years old," Huong grumbles to Loc, Nina, and you later, during the dancing. "Why don't they leave it all behind?"

"Because they're Jews, that's why," you hear Loc saying as he leads her to the dance floor.

.....

It isn't just Jews who can't let go. Among others holding on are men like Oldest Brother-in-Law, Binh and their compatriots, the veterans of the South Vietnamese Army in the Orderly Departure Program cell groups. Men who have their uniforms altered to accommodate their widening girths and shrinking shoulders so they can be properly dressed at the April 30th commemorations. Men who line up to lay wreaths at the Little Saigon Memorial Statue to the Vietnam war dead, then salute the triple striped flag and sing the old anthem. Men whose hearts are still afire, those whom people like you, doing business in Vietnam, try to avoid.

They find you anyway, standing beside Chú Hai, the two of you smiling from behind a Vietnamese bride and a Jewish groom on a wedding video Loc is showing your Oldest Sister's family.

Oldest's family had not gone to the Catskills. Still not comfortable among Americans, they opted to watch the replay of the ceremony in Loc's and Huong's apartment instead.

"Oldest Brother-in-Law asked to stop the video when he saw your face," Loc calls you in New York to caution. "He recognized your tutor as the leader of the preparatory team for the Foreign Minister's visit. Now he and Binh are talking about killing you because you're a collaborator."

"Why Binh?" you ask. "He's not the violent kind."

"Oldest wound him up. He asked if Binh was quite sure you didn't call up that attack on him the time you were planting flags together."

You repeat the story you've put out from day one. "I didn't call up that attack. I was right there with him. I might just as well have been blasted myself."

"I know," Loc says. "But you should have seen Binh's face when Oldest posed the question. You need to remember what Oldest is like, pure spite with a snake's tongue. He'll never change. And Binh is so easy to set on fire..."

"Well, I'll make sure I keep out of their way."

"What if they come looking?"

"Sixth Brother, you worry too much. Don't worry. I'll be fine."

.....

And for the moment, you are fine. You're spending your first full summer in eight years with your whole family, Chú Hai included. And Chú Hai is amusing himself injecting whimsy and light into everything happening at the brownstone.

"Tri's finishing high school two years ahead with a full scholarship to Cal Tech, and all you can think of is dinner at a Chinese restaurant?" he says, raising his eyebrows in disbelief at the arrangements Nina and you have made. "We must come up with something better."

The something better turns out to be a candle lit celebration at the impossible to get into Tavern on the Green, at a park-facing table conjured up at short notice through a friend of a friend of a friend. It's a fantastic evening of wonderfully crafted food followed by a near miss with a mugger because Chú Hai insists on a stroll around Central Park afterwards. Still, who can fault the climax? The four of you on a wild run through the mid-summer night, whooping and screaming like teenagers all the way back to the safety of the town car.

He's creating more homely magic too. He's the one who engages Tri in all the celebrations—showing Tri how to capture his own graduation from behind the safety of a camera lens; later coaxing Tri to write down all the positive and negative feelings he experiences during the ceremonies in mathematical equations, then helping him translate the equations into words for the family to share.

"Just like how he made me translate from Vietnamese to English years ago," you tell Nina. You lean over to squeeze Chú Hai's shoulder, touched by the attention he's giving your difficult son.

"But there's a difference," Chú Hai points out. "You were totally self-centered . Your son on the other hand is amazingly insightful about what everyone else is feeling and what their motivations are. He'd make a great journalist. Or with that dead pan face, even a spy."

"Not on my life," Nina retorts before she can help herself. "An astronomer?" she suggests.

"A physicist rather," you say.

"Heaven will decide," Chú Hai interrupts, averting the awkward moment.

He waves his conjuror's wand over your fiftieth birthday celebrations, plotting a week long family fiesta for you—planned excursions to places he, Nina and Tri want to share. "Our own special pieces of New York City; individualized, un-replicable birthday gifts," he announces on the day itself. "Five gifts—two each from Nina and Tri, one from me."

Nina gives you an evening at her Institute's Thursday night open-house. The reason why she'd come to New York City in the first place; after the brownstone, the second most important building in her New York City life. The next morning, she takes you to sit in the garden at Jefferson Market in the West Village, a tiny patch of green with only twelve trees. Unknown to you, she's volunteered there every autumn since you've been in Asia. Digging in the ground to prepare it for winter and smelling the last summer roses, she confesses, somehow helped when she missed you after your summers together.

"I'm sorry." You brush your thumb against her fingers.

"My fault," she answers.

"Ours," you say, picking up a fallen rose petal from the bench and placing it on her cheek.

Tri gives you the rooftop balcony. "For obvious reasons," he says, an unconscious rebuke for your years of absence.

You thank him, your heart cracking a little.

"I have two more because Great Uncle says this doesn't count. It should be someplace out in the city, not in the house."

The first of his two other gifts is the astronomical ceiling over the main concourse at Grand Central Station. "See the back to front sky like how God might see it," he points up. The next is the New York City Library, because it's where he spends most of his time, and it has one of the city's oldest pneumatic messenger systems.

At Grand Central Station, you don't tell your son you aren't a believer. It's important to him, that's what matters. At the library, you sit in his favorite place and try to imagine him there on winter afternoons, reading esoterica and listening to the pneumatic cartridges whizzing through the ceiling. You wonder if he might have been less eccentric, this lonely brilliant child of yours, if you'd been at home. Probably not, you excuse yourself.

Chú Hai's own gift to you is the Statue of Liberty. Because it's the first place he visited in New York City fifty years ago and he remembers the wonderful view.

"It's also the best way now for an old noodle to get inside a lady," he whispers to you in Vietnamese when you're halfway up to the viewing platform.

It's the best part of the celebrations, the sound of Nina's laughter high and clear like tinkling water, the echoes rising all the way up to the tiny opening at the top.

.....

And so the 1998 Year of the Tiger passes.

"A paper Tiger," you tell Loc and Huong on New Year's Eve when Nina and you join them for Tết.

"Shhh," they reply together, instantly.

"Yes, it was a good year but perhaps you shouldn't proclaim it so loudly," Loc says.

"Let me break a leg then," you laugh, throwing salt over your left shoulder to appease his ghosts.

But the Tiger year rolls smoothly into the year of the Cat with no untoward developments. In the late summer, after one last trip to Vietnam, Jerry finally lets you off the defense industry's leash and you go to work full time regularizing Ly's businesses and transferring the assets you, he, Minh and your other partners have accumulated into off-shore holding structures. Preparing representative companies in the US from which business can be transacted worldwide. Finally completing Ly's insurance plan, envisioned so long ago.

By winter, you've wrapped it all up. "Everything's out of Vietnam now, most of it in Singapore. All the Special Purpose Vehicles in the tax havens are set up. We're operational in the US," you tell Nina. You've asked Kim to join Ly's nephew in the New York City offices, freeing yourself from state-side work. You and Nina can fly away free.

You take Nina to the Delta for *Tết*, travelling under a new year moon slim as a harvest knife, a silver blade against the black sky.

The two of you have made your peace with each other. Like the Paris Accords, it's a cease-fire in place. Neither of you can go back to where you came from, your days as a young couple in Laguna Canyon. Your soldiers and bases— your confessions, your abandonment of her and Tri and your desperate holding on to them, Nina's sacrifice of her illustrious career, her abandonment of her patients—are explosives scattered deep in your hearts and psyches, ready to be re-activated at any moment and thrown into each other's faces as evidence of how wrong or right each of you have been, how much you've both given up.

But unlike the North and the South, Nina and you have genuinely good intentions. Already in the middle of your lives, you can't afford to waste years in recrimination like the communists did after Liberation. As you sit together in the back of the plush new car borrowed from Ly, the driver making his way between the rice-fields underneath the New

Year moon, you feel Nina's hand press lightly into yours and press back as lightly, in return.

.....

After Tết, Nina and you spend six months visiting non-profits in Vietnam.

The street children in Ho Chi Minh City, the sex trafficking in the Mekong Delta, the terrible effects of Agent Orange in Central Vietnam, the lack of drinking water, the over abundance of flood waters... You hope at least some of these needs will touch Nina's bleeding American heart.

"If my wife wants to help with even ten in a thousand of these issues, she'll be here for a lifetime. And if I can help her, I'll be generating a significant amount of good karma, enough at least to redeem half my sins," you tell Ly during a stop-over in Ho Chi Minh City on your way to visit yet another non-profit.

"It's a waste of time," Ly retorts. "Just do business and create more employment. Once a man has a job he gets back his self esteem. He stops drinking. He stops beating his wife. He has no time to gamble or whore around. Forget this running about and come back to work. You've taken a long enough break. I've so many ideas."

"But I promised my wife," you protest.

"I'll lend you my wife to help her. My wife's church is involved in all kinds of good works. There must be something for your wife to pick up. They're both Christians, aren't they? Even if one's a Catholic and the other a Protestant, surely they can work together?"

"She hasn't decided if she wants to live here full time yet. Give me six more months to soften her up. After that I'll see if she'll allow me to come back part time."

You're reluctant to give up the hook that might keep Nina in Vietnam with you. You're still apprehensive about the toll karma might exact. You don't want to lose a son to karma like Loc has lost his daughter. You leave Ly hanging and go to Hue with Nina, to a pediatric program run out of the hospital Binh once worked at.

.....

You'd ended up at the Hue hospital in 1977 after three months in the ravaged countryside, repairing the bombed-out bridges of the North-South railway. Wracked by malaria and stomach trouble, you were looking to trade some Bunsen burners and gas canisters you'd pilfered from the company warehouse with the hospital pharmacist. But the pharmacist at the hospital didn't need your burners. She didn't have any malaria pills or antacids anyway, she told you. She directed you to the laboratory, where she thought you might have better luck.

The laboratory was hidden behind frosted glass doors, through which you saw shadows gathered around someone lying on a bench. When you slid the doors open, you heard a familiar voice coming from the prone figure. "You need to ask what they actually mean when they say what they say. For example is it really liberation, giải phóng, or is it just double speak for phỏng giái, a burnt crotch? Maybe they're burning our balls to free our spirits from desire, to liberate us from our machismo. Or maybe they just want to kill all possibility of us standing up and resisting."

It was Binh.

"Comrades, think! Never believe what you're told without careful examination!" he was saying. He sat up. "Stand up for yourself and for your manhood!" he shouted. He jumped off the bench and gestured with his hands below his belt, before completing the speech with a sweeping bow to acknowledge the other men's applause.

It would not be good if Binh saw you just then, you decided. You slid the door shut as quietly as you could, then knocked again with a loud rat-a-tat.

"Excuse me, I'm looking for the laboratory manager," you said.

"Heavenly mother-fucker! What the fuck are you doing here?" Binh rushed up, grabbed your shoulders and hustled you out of the hospital without introducing you to his colleagues.

It turned out he was now Mr Dinh, he told you once he settled you in his favorite bar.

"And how did that happen?"

"Eh, you got to survive, right? So... new name, new identity," he said, looking down at his flat home-brew. "You can become a new person quite easily in a rout. There's no shortage of discarded identities lying around dead on the wayside. Of course, it's somewhat harder to find some poor sod with an ID picture and name that resembles you. More luck if you find someone in the same line of work." He stretched out all ten of his chubby fingers and examined them for a moment. "Sometimes though, they might need a bit of help with their journey to a better place..."

You knew what he meant. Neither of you needed to hear each other's confessions. "So what do you do as laboratory manager here?" you asked instead.

"Not lab tests, for sure. We've run out of chemicals. What keeps us going is processing the still-borns. We pickle them in formaldehyde and seal them in plastic bags, then send them along." He frowned. "There are way too many of them dropping out too soon. All deformed... Not mine to wonder why, though, is it? I leave that to the card-holding politically acceptable researchers up in Hanoi. My responsibility is just to seal the bags with an electrical element and send them there. But the electricity isn't reliable anymore. It's getting crowded in the store room, all those pots stacking up full of unwrapped pickled babies. Your Bunsen burners and gas are just the thing. I'm quite sure my boss will part with some malaria tablets for the goods."

Binh was as good as his word. He turned up at the dormitories of the Hue warehouse the next morning with thirty-six precious malaria pills. But there were still no antacids anywhere.

.....

Now there are antacids aplenty at the hospital. As for the deformed babies, they've found the cause.

"Agent Orange," Nina's doctor cousin, the founder of the program, says as she leads the two of you through a ward full of listless hole-in-the-heart babies. "The boys and girls with cleft lips are Agent Orange too," she points to another ward full of broken faced babies. "As are the miscarriages," she says striding through the drained women staring blankly, lying two to a bed, feet to head. "Infertility also. Although that's probably a blessing, no matter what the old folks think," she observes with a quick shake of her head as you walk past the men squatting outside the corridor of the fertility centre.

Nina nods, silenced by the suffering she sees.

"So much to do," Nina's cousin shares the next day on a home visit to a spaghetti limb child, one of yet another group of Agent Orange victims."The hospital facilities are getting much better with international donations, and will improve even more if you can help us bring in American money and expertise, as we discussed," the cousin says. "But there's no cure for this child." She indicates the boy with arms and legs growing in clockwise waves, lying helpless on a grass mat at your feet, protected from the chickens wandering around the other half of the house by a thin wire net. "His parents are farmers. They need to be out in the fields. This is the best they can do for him."

"Aren't the Vietnamese and American governments negotiating compensation for children like these?" Nina asks. "The US government will be making payouts soon, won't it? It's a matter of principle. If US veterans are getting assistance, so should these kids. In addition to direct assistance, we should also tap government-to-government compensation. Maybe I could help do that, as well as the foreign fund raising," she turns to ask you, her eyes blinking with excitement.

"It's better to fund everything directly. There'll be so much leakage from a government-to-government settlement, these kids won't see any of it," you remonstrate. You want to remind your wife that only the day before she was considering spending more time in Vietnam if you could put together a country-wide network of meaningful social projects to involve her in. But you see Nina already back in New York City writing letters to senators, planning campaigns to mobilize housewives, filing class actions against the chemical companies. You see her slipping away from you and back to America, if you don't hold on tight.

You say to Nina's cousin, "We'll set up an office here in Vietnam to help collect the data needed for government-to-government negotiations." You tell Nina, "I'll see about setting up a US foundation to help with the lobbying stateside. We can get Kim to look after the US part. That would save us having to travel back and forth. But if we need to, I'll go along with you." There, that's settled. You've reined in your wife, you hope.

"If you want it that way," Nina says, giving you an indulgent smile.

So it's agreed, the two of you will spend more time in Vietnam to set up the Agent Orange project. But before that, there's the interlude in Paris.

19
Renunciation

IN PARIS, NINA AND YOU have the honeymoon you couldn't afford twenty years before. You spoil yourselves in expensive hotels, you drink too much wine and Nina buys too many clothes. You don't begrudge yourselves anything. But at Midnight Mass on the outskirts of Paris, watching a Nativity performance, your stomach heavy from *foie gras* and Christmas Eve *canard*, the over-indulgence suddenly weighs on you. Well-wrapped up against the cold, a man with everything it seems, your wife and son on either side of you and enough leisure and money to travel where you wish while you're still young enough to do it, your thoughts turn unbidden to the past, to the time of your greatest hunger.

.....

There was always an ache in your belly. The family was eating barley porridge almost constantly now, mixed with swamp leaves and fermented shrimp when available, with lemon grass and salt when not. The children had been told at school that Uncle Ho ate lemon grass and salt on the trail south, that it

*made him strong. You couldn't imagine a more abrasive mix
for bloating the stomach and scouring it. It was all part of a
dastardly plot by Ho Chi Minh's followers to bring anyone still
resisting to their knees in the latrines, you thought miserably.*

*It was eighteen months into Liberation. You'd gotten your
heart's desire. But you'd never felt more wretched.*

*It was better in the beginning, when Chú Hai was still
around. Then your meager rations had been supplemented
by the packets of rice, dried beans and even fresh meat he
bundled into the basket of your bicycle whenever you stopped
by for a visit. But now Chú Hai was in Hanoi.*

*He'd greeted you with a lopsided turn to his mouth the
last time you saw him. "I'll be going north for a refresher in
Marxist dialectics," he'd said.*

"Even you," you couldn't help voicing your dismay. "When?"

*"In a few days," he answered. He wouldn't say more.
Stuffing three big plastic bags into your hand, he hustled you
onto the back of the motorcycle he could still afford to run
with his party member's fuel allocation. "We have time for one
last shopping trip," he told you.*

*You putt-putted through the desolate streets to the old
American PX, now converted to a special privilege store for
high government officials. The stacks were less than half-filled,
the cadres having helped themselves as quickly as they could
to the goods left by the Americans. But there was still some
American rice and flour left, as well as a fair amount of newly
stocked Russian millet, Chinese cooking oil, and the ubiquitous
barley. Chú Hai loaded up on his full quota of rice and oil
before leading you on a zig-zag wander through the aisles to
see what else might be found. He uncovered a half open bag
of sugar, three small capsules of gas and, miraculously, four*

dented cans of condensed milk. He also had special coupons for some chicken and two cans of braised Chinese pork. That evening, you went home with your bicycle laden.

That was the last good meal the family had, you reminisced, fingering the ridges of your ribs. That was your last conversation with Chú Hai too. It had been months now and not a word. No doubt he'd gone to Hanoi by air, the way respected party members went. But still you worried what they might be doing to him. Were they making him write repeated essays on the same subject, as they did at your own twice-weekly political sessions? Were his treatises destined to become toilet paper, as yours were? You would ask him to write this into a funny story when he came back. If he came back. If he escaped the re-molding they intended for him.

You had found yourself missing other people too—your blood-father, Loc, your parents, Ly, Binh, Julia Anderson...

She was invading your dreams again, re-enacting your last time together in multiple variations—the two of you riding down the hotel elevator together, she crushing herself against you to press the 'up' button when you reached the ground floor, and leading you back to her room; her body against your back on the way to the airport, her arms wrapping around you to turn the motorbike into a side road, then hurrying the two of you through an alley; she pulling you down an airplane aisle, and pushing your back against the wall of the tiny toilet. Each time you saw yourself protesting, "I've run out, we can't." Each time you saw her shaking her head and whispering, "Come."

You didn't understand your inexplicable longing for her. But as if she'd heard you, a care package arrived from France many months after the Christmas she intended it for. It contained fabric and medicines that could be resold and a tentative guarded letter stating only the hope that you were well. She also enclosed her new mailing address in Paris and a greeting card. Underneath the generic seasonal wishes, she'd typed that Christmas was now so much more meaningful because of the child given to her in Israel. She'd said how motherhood had changed her unexpectedly and indescribably. You felt a nagging disquiet about her circumstances when you saw the message. But she was a woman of the world, with an American dollar paycheck. She would manage if... As it was, you had enough problems feeding yourself and taking care of Oldest and her lot. You remember scrunching up the card, choosing to see her message as an offensive and unnecessary boast that you'd already been replaced by someone else, and a child out of it to boot! You kicked the care package under your bed and didn't bother to look at it again until one of Oldest Sister's children begged you for its contents to trade in the black market.

.....

Now as you watch the children of the French-Vietnamese community re-enacting the Christmas myth—the tiny black haired Mary led by a taller half-French Joseph, the poodles pretending to be sheep, the great St. Bernard meant to represent a Magus' elephant, the untidy gaggle of shepherds and Magi with their mix of pure and mingled French and Vietnamese features—you wonder idly what Julia Anderson's child born of some union with a man from the Middle East might look like; how your son's face might be different if you hadn't aborted your future with Julia Anderson by giving Loc your place on that list of evacuees.

You steal a glance at Tri sitting on your right. He looks as he should, his face a recognizable re-combination of Nina's and your own Vietnamese features—her oval-shaped face with your olive skin, your high nose, her large eyes. Tri is deep in prayer, his eyes closed, his wide forehead and pointed nose raised towards the God he believes in so profoundly. He's come a long way from that awkward boy with tantrums. He's learnt to adjust to the world and work with it. Not comfortably, but well enough to manage, well enough that now it's clearly evident he's not an idiot but unbelievably bright. So bright that at nineteen he's in a Ph.D. program in theoretical physics at Stanford. "We give our children life but heaven gives them their dispositions," your mother, the Chief Clerk's wife, used to say. Well this son of yours is definitely his own person.

You catch Nina also looking sidelong at Tri, in her eyes the same bemused mixture of wonder you feel. The two of you exchange glances, complicit and congratulatory, that this beautiful young adult is your flesh and blood. If you believed in Nina's God, you would fall on your knees in praise and thanksgiving at the miracle.

.....

How are you to know how mistaken it is to feel so secure about Tri? You only find out much later how unhappy he's been, the lengths he'll go to for relief. You only find out when everything falls apart.

Then, Chú Hai remembers how Tri reckoned the sum of Nina's and your debts in his emotional balance. Love, Chú Hai had been trying to explain to Tri the first summer he stayed over in Vietnam, was additive and sometimes even multiplicative.

Tri understood immediately. He gave Chú Hai an example—Nina loved you, she loved herself, she left you; that was two pluses and a minus for her. He had a similar calculation for you. Added together, he concluded, your long separation still equated to two—a positive for both of you. But he confided to Chú Hai, that wasn't the case for himself. For Tri it had been a case of him loving both of you, and both of you leaving him, two pluses against two bigger minuses—a big zero at best.

Chú Hai continues with the stinging tail of the story, Tri's conclusion later, when both of you began your wandering life. You'd always been his selfish runaway parents, he'd said; one escaping to Vietnam and the other running to New York City, each to increase your own net happiness; and then, still uncaring, you'd both run away again to be together, leaving him alone in America. He'd concluded then that everyone had a right to their own pluses, just as you and Nina did. If he had to hurt the two of you to follow his own inclinations, well it couldn't be helped, Chú Hai remembers him saying.

You begin to understand more when Nina shows you an article in a psychology journal on the human oddities called empaths, people who feel and absorb the emotions of others around them, like sponges.

"How do they do it? What's the scientific explanation?" you ask, disbelieving.

She reads out a quote in the article from one of them, coincidentally a theoretical physicist—'In physical terms, I suspect it's simply a wave frequency I can access that's not accessible to less sensitive human beings. But it's impossible to explain the actual experience, the immediate apprehension of the complex webs of conditioned causality from which everyone's emotions rise and into which they ebb. It's a sensation that can be so intense I'm buffeted into impassiveness. It's why I work with theories and equations. They're so much quieter.'

She turns to blink at you. "So much like Tri, no?"

Indeed. A switch flicks on. But by then, understanding can't help. You have to deal with what Tri has decided. To accept his choice.

.....

Your son will be depriving his ancestors of any further descendents, and offering himself as a sacrifice to a possibly non-existent god, Kim tells you by email; a message Nina and you receive fifteen days late because you're both out of range, setting up a community health program for an upcountry hill tribe.

"He's decided what?" you shout over the crackling line between Brooklyn and Chú Hai's living room.

"To become a Trappist monk," Kim pronounces each syllable slowly, to make sure you hear. "He's going into a one-year observership and he won't be talking to anyone until he's finished with the first three months of it."

"Not talking to us until what's finished?"

"His observership," Kim repeats.

"Without consulting us?" You refuse to believe anything she's saying.

"Because he says it's between him and God," your niece replies.

And that is that.

But there's history and your karma before that. And between the weight of your karma and Tri's decision, the intermediate causes.

Unknown to anyone in the family, Tri had been spending weekends at a Trappist monastery in the Sacramento Valley. Apparently, Kim had found out, he had also read that interview about empaths and the quote from the theoretical physicist. But he'd learnt that logic could only go so far. To go beyond required something more than mathematics or physics. A letting go he thought only the Trappists could teach him.

"He wants to see if they can show him the way to an all encompassing reality. He thinks they're his best chance because they're guys who want God more than anything else in life," Kim tries to explain. "I don't understand it all, even now. Something about how God is infinity, and if he merges with infinity he'll be able to silence all the voices that are buffeting him and driving him crazy."

"A nervous breakdown," you mutter. You can understand that. Your somewhere along the autistic spectrum son Tri has had a meltdown.

"That's not what he'd say," Kim replies. "Although it sure looked like that to me too when I first saw him."

.....

Six months ago, a year after you and Nina left France to return to Vietnam, the monks had called Kim.

The call came late in the evening. Flying out on the red-eye to Sacramento, Kim had driven as fast as she could through bucolic farmland to find Tri in a plain room with a curtain for a door, a window overlooking the monks' vineyards, a sink in a corner and a cot bed against a wall. The sound of men singing vespers echoed through the corridor. The Brother Director, sitting in a straight wooden chair by the window, was following from a breviary in his hands. Tri was on the floor, curled in a fetal bundle, quite still.

The Brother Director had risen to greet Kim and give her the essentials. Tri had been attending the monastery's life discernment weekends for almost a year. He'd been doing well and getting clearer about his vocation. But the one thing he wanted, to silence the voices of the world by melting into infinity, still eluded him. What he'd been given instead, that particular weekend, was an encounter with his self. Apparently too much too soon, the Director commented. That's why they'd called her.

"An encounter with himself?" Kim had stared at Tri's scrunched up body, slowly pulling itself into a tighter and tighter ball, before becoming scarily immobile again, as hard and quiet as a block of wood. "What did he see in himself that did this?"

"Time will tell," the Brother Director replied. "Perhaps he'll share it with us when it's all over. Now we can only pray."

Although convent school educated, Kim had not been sure how to pray. She had looked out the window at the straight rows of grapevines marching up the slopes, the California winter afternoon bright and clear, and sighed.

"His parents are away..." There was a question in the Director's comment.

Kim had ignored it. She had questions of her own. "Are you sure we don't need to take him to the hospital? To a psychiatric facility?" she had forced the words from her mouth.

The Brother Director shook his head. "The doctor's sedated him. And as you can see, he's no longer rocking. We're past the critical stage. What he needs tonight is just our presence, to watch and to pray."

He left before she could ask her hundred other questions. Why was Tri considering a religious life? Was the Director sure he hadn't a clue whom or what the self Tri encountered was, the self that caused this?

Kim had sat with Tri through *vespers*, a solitary dinner brought to her on a tray, *compline,* and then the night bells. She confessed that as she watched her young cousin repeatedly fold himself smaller, unfold and tighten again, in the same way he sometimes did as a child, she was sorely tempted to call Nina, the expert on breakdowns and crises of the spirit. But Tri, inscrutable and private since childhood, would want to keep this from both of you. She decided to respect his wishes unless things went badly wrong, she said to you later, defiant and unapologetic. She made that decision, she said, because at midnight she noticed that Tri had finally unwound fully and was lying on his side, breathing regularly.

She had stepped over him then and crawled onto the narrow single bed to stretch herself out too.

Kim was woken at 3.30 in the morning by the monks chanting *vigils*. There was a weight on her right shoulder. Tri had crawled into bed beside her, just as he used to when he came to sleepovers at her parents' house as a toddler. He'd tucked his body against hers, his head on her chest, his longer torso and legs in a curve around hers. His eyes were open and luminous, looking past her chin at the wall beyond.

"Hey, you okay?" she asked.

Tri nodded, his chin bobbing against her shoulder.

"What happened?"

"I felt. I felt everything I've not wanted to feel since I was born, I guess. Everything I stuck down a black hole and tried to forget about—fear, resentment, anger, grief, the human condition, fallen man..." he said, wonder in his voice. "It was during *vigils,* between the readings on the burning bush and the book to Autolycus by Saint Theophilus of Antioch. The world stopped. All the heart beats—Dad's, Mom's, other people's—they disappeared from my chest. And then my head got really quiet." He explained to Kim, "There was always this really interesting pattern of thoughts in my head, about why people felt what they did, a whole set of decision trees full of causes and consequences. That was gone too. There wasn't anything for my brain to decipher, no infinite permutations and combinations of anybody's concerns." He burrowed his head deeper into Kim's shoulder. "All I could feel was my own heartbeat, going tic-toc, tic-toc, like a metronome. All I could feel and think about was the information streaming from my own single body into my one mind." He swallowed. "It was too much. I just buckled under."

Later, Kim would tell her father, Loc, what Tri said he experienced. How his own feelings and fears so flooded into him, he had to struggle to open his eyes to escape from them and wrap his arms around himself to protect his body from the onslaught of memories. How he slipped from his knees onto the floor. How, to comfort himself he began to rock and rock and rock... To hold at bay the loss and the abandonment— you squeezing his hands in farewell at LAX, the door of his Laguna Canyon bedroom being shut for the last time, the sun on the linkway in the morning becoming only a memory. How he rocked and continued rocking to calm his rising fury at how you and Nina had left him, the two positives in your lives stolen from his happiness, leaving him those infinite negatives.

Kim understandably does not share any of this with you or Nina. It's Loc who does, when none of it matters anymore, when all it serves to do is make you feel guiltier. All Kim says to you is that Tri was unusually talkative that night. And all she finally asked him when he paused for breath was, "So... you think you need to go into therapy when we leave here?"

She remembers the bell for *lauds* ringing then, morning breaking again as it always has. "It wasn't growing up with a therapist that led to this breakthrough," she remembers Tri saying, before going to the sink in the corner of the room to wash out his mouth and splash water on his face and hair. "Time for morning prayers," he said to her, crossing himself as he left the room.

Even though that was six months ago, this was the moment when Kim knew Tri would be spending the rest of his life in the monastery.

.....

That is the story, and you should leave it at that, Nina advises. "At least, now, you'll have someone permanently praying to save you from that karma you're always worrying about," she says, unable to hide her pleasure at having a priest for a son.

"We can't live all our lives on the sidelines," Chú Hai adds.

"I don't call hiding in a monastery living," you say.

"We all have our own paths, Tri's, yours, mine, Julia Anderson's," he replies.

"What has Julia Anderson got to do with it?" you snap. It's such a pointless thing to say just then, when the future of your son is the issue.

He doesn't answer your question. Instead he bends down to rummage under the coffee table. When he straightens up, he's holding the earthenware bottle of Japanese sake and two small cups Julia Anderson brought him as a gift on her second visit.

"Come," he says pouring for you and Nina.

This is how it was with Chú Hai and you in the worst months after Liberation—Chú Hai pouring cheap home brew from a brown glass bottle, you downing one cup after another until you'd drowned all your disillusionment and nodded off to sleep on his sofa. This time though, you do not drink the bottle to the dregs. Nina and you down only a single cup each. And then you go back to your service apartment near the city centre where the two of you have your own bed.

"That child has been running towards a monastery since he was a thought in God's head," Nina says to you. "Like you say all the time, we gave birth to him but heaven's responsible for his disposition. If he's meant to be a monk, then he'll be one."

Nina's reminder doesn't make you feel better. You get up from the floor where you've been sitting, re-editing your hundredth email response to Tri. "I need a smoke," you say, stepping out onto the balcony and shutting the sliding door against your wife and her good sense.

You can feel Nina looking through the glass at your back. She'll be upset that, as usual, you're attributing Tri's decision to the karma from your previous lives, the post '75 one you've just retired from, the pre '75 one you've lived, the ones you've left behind in the hundred thousand cycles of reincarnation she claims you're haunted by.

You hear her sigh as she clambers into bed.

She's praying aloud so you can hear—a blessing for you, then one for Tri. You envy her ability to leave it all to someone she can't see, up there, somewhere. You're envious how she can be so comforted she's already snoring softly before she can begin to pray for herself.

Four floors below your balcony, the motorcycles continue to cross Tao Dan Park, their lights creating constantly changing criss-cross patterns on the roadway. The floor you sit down on is tiled with terracotta. The century old trees you look down at are highlighted by newly installed spotlights. Things are better in Vietnam now, at the beginning of the millennium. But you do not feel better. Now you finally understand your mother's pain when Loc joined the militia, when you threw in your lot with your blood-father and Chú Hai, when you decided to leave Vietnam on a leaky boat.

You lower your eyelids and will the burning in your belly to disappear from your consciousness. It feels as bad as in the worst days of '76, when Oldest, her children and you could think about nothing but your empty growling stomachs. Surely you'd done enough, feeding those children, to be spared this wounding by Tri you think. You rub both your fists against the soft flesh beginning to gather under your rib-cage, trying to knead the pain out. Obviously there's more to repay.

You breathe in, then out again, remembering your transgressions. You think about what might be if you'd been wiser, more caring, more filial... the thousand possible futures lost.

You imagine your mother free of worry, your father and blood-father full of expectation. You imagine a demure Delta wife gradually growing plump and assertive, fine-boned dark-skinned children sprouting into wiry young men and pliant young women, a gaggle of grandchildren. You imagine living in a world rooted in the delta clay of your birth, circumscribed by rice paddies and fruit orchards. No refugee boat to America, no flying over the Pacific like a lost kite, no stealthy passing of aerospace secrets, no business deals with Ly, no Nina, no Tri, no heartache.

You lean back against the glass doors that separate you from the air-conditioned room where Nina sleeps. You look up at the sky and realize it's nearly Mid-Autumn again. More than a quarter century has passed since your war, and here you are, still running. You're an earth rat with travelling feet who will never settle, Ly's astrologer has said. But there's no running away from life's pains, especially those inflicted by children tearing away. It's inevitable. They must be let loose, to worship whom they wish and embrace whatever illusions they will.

You go into the bedroom and wake Nina.

"We should be in California when Tri finishes his observership, to give him our blessing," you whisper into her ear.

20
Reparation

YOU GO TO MAKE YOUR EXCUSES to Ly. You'll be leaving
Saigon to spend a few months in California, and won't be around
for his next big triumph, the stock market listing of the bank you
helped him start. "I've to go to my son. He's just made a crazy
decision. God—that's his beginning and end, that's what my son
told my niece to tell me. He's going to become a priest."

"Is that better or worse than my son studying painting, and
art being his mistress?" Ly muses, referring to his youngest
son, who's pursuing an MFA at Parsons. Practical as always,
he opts for the complexities he can control. "There are sons
and there is business. Business, we can do something about.
Sons?" He shrugs. He looks around the brand new boardroom
you're both in, and turns to a pile of papers on the conference
table, the draft announcements for the listing of the bank.
"Here, take a look at these for me and tell me if we need to
make any corrections," he says, passing them over to you.

You slap the announcements back down on the table. It's a
trivial event now, it seems to you. "What's the point of building
all this up if our children aren't interested in taking it over?
What have we been working and struggling for all these years?"

Ly ignores your tantrum. "In the beginning, we did it to survive. Later to give our children all the good things we thought they should have. And in part to do what we could for our countrymen. Now, because we have nothing better to do that's more profitable or easier," he says.

"But I only have the one son," you tell your friend.

"All the more reason you shouldn't get bogged down by his doings. You have no diversification. It's a sure fire way to heartbreak. My position is they're grown up, and fortunately or otherwise, I've given them the means to do what they want, without having to worry about filling their rice bowls. My good fortune is I can occupy myself doing what I like best, building businesses." There's an expression of genuine contentment shining from his face. "As for you, your good fortune is to help me by doing what you do best, making the connections that allow me to keep my money and my family safe. And, if it makes you feel better, I'll let you count that towards the positive karma you're always chasing after." He grins, then shakes an index finger at you. "You shouldn't look down on money. It's just paper but it does give us the wherewithal to do good. The more of it we make, the more chance we have of rebalancing karma."

He motions for you to follow him into the office adjoining the boardroom. You see a new diagram on the white board behind his desk. He points to it. "I've noticed imports are rising much faster than exports. Soon we'll be back in a situation where everyone's scrambling for foreign exchange. So, I have this new idea for the bank and our trade financing business. What we need is a source of dollars independent of the country's ability to export—the remittances from the overseas Vietnamese. They're all sending money home under the table. Imagine how much better it would be if there were an official and secure channel. Think about a joint venture with someone like..." He names a global money wire service. "We keep the dollars received in the US there, pay out in Vietnam from the cash flow we generate in country and profit from the float between the pay-in and the pay-out dates in both currencies." He can barely keep from rubbing his fleshy palms together in glee.

"Clever," you grunt. Ly's ingenuity still amazes you. "I'll get Kim to do some work on the regulations," you say.

"It will be something to distract myself with," you tell Jerry, retired and signed on to work with you and Ly.

"It will be something to worry about besides Tri," you say to Nina.

.....

You postpone your visit to Tri at the monastery and go to the East Coast to see about Ly's new idea.

"Not a problem. It can be all American corporations on this side, so long as you have enough Dong in Vietnam to make the payouts there," Kim reports when you meet her in Brooklyn.

"Just three degrees of separation," Jerry says when you have lunch in Washington D.C. to discuss the 'in' for the American partner Ly wants.

"A walk in the park," you tell Nina, back in Papa's and Maman's house.

But she's worried. "Be careful. People like my uncles, your Oldest Brother-in-Law, Binh and the Veterans Associations won't take kindly to it."

"Old men," you dismiss them.

"Yes, with nothing to lose. Didn't you tell me once, when you've nothing to lose and heaven to gain, you can do wild things?" she reminds you.

"I was talking about the Viet Cong, not these guys." These are the losers. You won't let them stop you from making the money you need to do good, the wherewithal necessary to re-balance your karma. Anyway, what trouble can come out of that barren ground of lost time and disappointed hopes that Oldest Brother-in-Law, Binh, and their buddies occupy?

.....

More trouble than you can imagine.

You learn that they're infiltrating the second generation's Vietnamese language societies and church groups when Nina and you attend a fund raiser organized by the Coalition for Agent Orange Reparations, a D.C. non-profit the two of you fund anonymously.

The meeting, held in a church hall in Virginia not far from where Nina's parents live, sports a good turnout of students from nearby colleges. The speaker from the coalition has convincing facts and figures, and the students are engaged. "Money well spent," you say to Nina from the back of the room, where you've inconspicuously seated yourselves.

Money spent so well it invites trouble. For just as the speaker opens the forum for questions, there's a disturbance. A plump middle aged man heaves himself up to the front and commandeers the microphone. "I'm from the Vietnamese Armed Forces Veterans Association and I'd like to correct some factual errors," Binh says.

"Time to go," you whisper to Nina.

"No. If we stand up now he'll see us. Let's just sit till everyone leaves," Nina replies, unfortunately a little too loudly.

Binh's head turns and his eyes narrow as he recognizes the two of you.

He gives you a threatening nod. He will deal with you later, the nod seems to say. Then he turns his attention back to the room.

"There's no scientific basis for claiming that Agent Orange causes birth defects," he begins. "There are deformities, it's true. I myself was there at the hospital when the mothers started coming in with their monstrous babies. But we only began to see these cases after the war, after the communists destroyed the water system and people had to drink and wash out of ponds and rivers poisoned by Northern chemicals. Before that, there were no problems at all." He goes on the offensive. "The only reason why some among us are working with the occupiers to get compensation for so-called Agent Orange related problems is because they want to line their own pockets. The money won't be going to the victims, it'll go to corrupt government officials and their friends, liars who were given shelter by this great country and allowed to get rich on the fat of this free land."

"No one's working to line their pockets. We're working to make life better for our fellow Vietnamese. It's you old men who are depriving innocent victims of their rights. And all because of old grudges," a young woman in the audience springs up to object in English.

"Young woman, show a little respect. It's a representative from your father's and grandfathers' generation you're talking to," Binh replies in Vietnamese.

"It's a representative from a group of losers who won't admit they lost. It's someone who failed to build a country and begrudges the next generation a chance at building a better one. It's someone who refuses to see the reality of the world as it exists," the girl shoots back.

Jaws drop around the auditorium. Hands rise to mouths. This is America, and most of the young people in the room are American-born, but very few of them would have dared to say what she just has.

"You're mistaken, young woman," Binh says. He looks towards where you and Nina are sitting. "You've been misled by people like that man and woman over there," he says, pointing to the two of you. "Those two hiding in the back are exactly who I'm talking about when I mention people who are lining their pockets. He's a collaborator who skims money off American joint ventures to share with the corrupt government over there. It's dirty money like his that's funding the Agent Orange lawsuits in America. And why? So they can get more money for themselves. Who's the one with the agenda? Us old veterans who risked life and limb to defend the country and spent years in jails and re-education camps after that, or this draft dodging collaborator making money off our poor country?"

Eyes swivel to examine Nina and you.

Nina stands up to defend herself in her best Vietnamese. "Neither I nor my husband are collaborators. My father was a member of the Nationalist diplomatic corps stationed in D.C. before '75. I grew up in this community. Everyone in D.C. knows how hard my father worked for the South Vietnamese government. My husband and I don't have any agenda in Vietnam except helping our brothers and sisters there. It's the same agenda the founder of this church had—feeding the poor, helping the deaf to hear and the blind to see, sharing goodwill, nothing more."

There's scattered applause at this.

Nina continues. "Anyway, this isn't the proper arena to discuss my family. We're here to listen to the Agent Orange Reparations Coalitions' claim that Agent Orange has caused birth defects in Vietnam, and now the counter by this gentleman representing the Vietnamese Armed Forces Veterans Association. Let's get on with that. If anyone wants to discuss the kind of social work we're doing over there, my husband and I will be around and happy to answer questions afterwards."

The applause is louder this time and Nina sits down with a satisfied smile.

The wind taken out of his sails, Binh shuffles back to his seat, glowering. Later, through the crowd of young people who gather around you and Nina to talk about your initiatives in Vietnam, you see him hauling his swollen body out the hall and into the dark parking lot. He is alone. But you wonder, how many others like him hide in the shadows?

.....

"You shouldn't have stood up to him like that, in public," you say to Nina on the way back to Papa's and Maman's.

"He's only one person," she says, foolishly hopeful.

You don't tell her what you know from personal experience, how much a single person can do. A lot, you think, looking at your hands on the car's steering wheel. Your skin prickles with foreboding.

.....

You would feel worse if you were omniscient; if you could hear the conversation afterwards between Binh and your Oldest

Brother-in-Law in the Orange County shopfront that serves as the Vietnamese Armed Forces Veterans Association's HQ.

"It would have gone perfectly if not for that woman," Binh is saying to Oldest Brother-in-Law.

"They're a nest of vipers," Oldest Brother-in-Law is replying.

"Good thing the constitution in this country still gives us the right to bear arms," Binh says.

"But we must be patient. It's got to be at the right time and place," Oldest cautions.

"Yes, to make sure it makes a splash."

"The thing's how to get away after that?" Oldest asks.

"No problem. We'll let them catch us. Then, we'll claim diminished responsibility at the trial," Binh answers with bravado.

"Yes we both can, can't we?" A spark flickers in Oldest Brother-in-Law's eyes. "After how he parcelled me off to re-education and what they did to me there, no jury in this State is going to believe I haven't gone mad. That'll make another splash, the story of his betrayal. That dog and his wife and son, we'll make sure they're all wiped out. So there's no one to mourn them." His eyes turn fiery with anticipation.

But you're not omniscient. You see and hear nothing. It's only the smallest prickling of foreboding you feel, not enough to stop your do-gooding in Vietnam, your attempts to reduce your karmic debts.

.....

"What we can do is keep out of their way," Nina says.

But you're going to California to meet Tri at his monastery, and before that, stopping in Little Saigon to celebrate Loc's birthday. It is 2001 and Loc is turning sixty, a major transition in his life. You've promised to be there with him, a duty you owe him as his younger brother. It will be impossible to avoid Binh, Oldest Brother-in-Law and their friends at the party.

.....

Karma has been impatient with Loc, paying him back with more blows than can be considered fair. On his sixtieth birthday Loc feels the accounts are more than even. But even if there's something still owing, it's the end of his cycle, your mother has come to tell him in a dream. The book is closed. Anything else will be carried forward into his next incarnation. This lifetime he can start afresh again. "It's something to be happy about," he says when he shares the dream with you.

You see Loc scanning the restaurant, noting who's come to celebrate with him, who has not. He's sitting next to Binh at a table well away from yours. Binh is going through the whisky at his table as if it's a pitcher of water, and complaining about President Clinton's visit to Vietnam. "A mistake, a very bad mistake," he's slurring loudly for all to hear.

"All that anger pickled in liquor," Nina whispers into your ear, careful to keep the comment from the others at your table—Kim and Jake and Loc's three sons and their wives. You nod. At the rate he's going, Binh won't last long enough for a sixtieth party.

"Let it go," you hear Loc cajoling Binh, raising his voice to send the message to anyone else who needs reminding. "That visit was a year ago. We've got a new President now. The war's been over for twenty-five years. It's time we all moved on. It's so poor over there. If the US wants to mend fences and help the economy, why begrudge the country?"

"Because those assholes stole the country, don't you remember?" Binh's face, already flushed from half a bottle of whiskey, darkens an even deeper crimson.

"There are people living there who aren't communists. They deserve a future just like you and me," Loc holds his ground.

"Ahhh, you and your brother," Binh points his chin towards your table. "Don't the two of you know there's more to life than just filling rice-bowls?" He turns from Loc in disgust to fill a glass for Oldest Brother-in-Law.

Oldest Brother-in-Law raises his glass unsteadily to Loc. "It's your big birthday so we'll let you off this time. But watch what you say if you don't want Binh here and our other buddies to teach you a good lesson."

"A former militia man, we're ashamed of you," Binh scolds, pointing a finger into Loc's face. He looks directly now across the restaurant towards you. "Not much of an improvement over your brother at all," he shouts, so the whole room knows which brother he means.

Oldest Brother-in-Law follows his glance. "That one's always acting as if blood never stained his hands. As if he can erase all the harm he's caused by pretending he didn't do it. But one of these days he'll get what's coming to him."

You see broken glass, upturned tables, and Loc's children losing their security deposit if things don't calm down.

But Loc is pouring out another round. "Cheers, guys. As you said, it's my sixtieth. Give me a break."

And they do.

The party ends with a rousing rendition of the old national anthem, led by Oldest Brother-in-Law. Everyone goes home peaceably, in various stages of drunkenness. Should your brother expect life to be even kinder?

"This morning, with that dream from mother fresh in my mind, I was positive about it," he confesses to you back in his apartment, in front of another made-in-America Vietnamese musical video. "But now, I'm not sure... I already got my break in '75. Do I deserve another one just because our mother said so in a dream?" he asks, his head knocking tipsily against your shoulder.

"Let me think," you mutter at him, pushing his head off your chest and towards Huong, sitting on the other end of their sofa.

.....

It's true Loc got off easy then. He hadn't been killed, he hadn't been captured, and he'd managed to escape on an airplane. His journey to Saigon was a simple matter of bribing his way into the Nha Trang flying school and stowing away in the back of a Chinook helicopter transporting corpses back to the capitol. It wasn't pleasant but Loc had ridden this way many times before on missions. It shouldn't have bothered him.

Once he reached Saigon, Loc had sneaked into the deserted officers' quarters, bathed, then stolen a bicycle and ridden downtown to meet Chú Hai at his office in the hotel.

He hadn't liked Chú Hai, you'd found out when Loc and you were reunited in America. "He talked constantly. And he was so tactless. He didn't even bother to hide his happiness about the state of things. It burnt me up, here." Loc had gathered his fingers together into the shape of a grenade and dug into his stomach to show you.

But it hadn't been unbearable. Loc had to tolerate Chú Hai only for one night. The next day they received a call with instructions for Loc to go to the meeting point. At around midnight, he'd been taken to the airport in a bus and shepherded across a darkened airfield into a transport jet. In the morning, a mere three days after leaving Nha Trang, he was safe in Guam.

.....

You belch whisky fumes into your brother's face.

"Yes, it was undeserved good fortune, Sixth Brother. And no, I can't say if you've done enough or been punished enough to make it even now..." you slur. The alcohol makes you too frank. You lean across from Loc to Huong. "What do you think, Sixth Sister? Are we all paid up?"

She gives you a jaundiced look. Whatever's past is past and should not be brought up again even when drunk, the look says.

"That's the question isn't it?" Loc mumbles. "That's the worry. Do I deserve another break? Or might life throw me a last one just to spite me?"

You sit up, suddenly sober. Indeed, that's the question. And what might life throw you? You, the one who's been given and given and yet has barely paid back a mote, notwithstanding all the charity work you're funding.

.....

You're still troubled when you and Nina arrive at Tri's monastery in California's central valley.

The setting for the monastery is as beautiful as Kim has reported. The guest rooms, built in a Spanish style around an old-fashioned garden, remind you of your first home in Bac Lieu, low slung, yellow stuccoed, with red tiled roofs. The monastery is separated from the guest quarters by a high wooden lattice, over which purple passion flowers climb. Peering through the fence, you see men in cassocks walking past you towards a building on your right, to what you assume must be the chapel.

Nina and you have been invited to attend the service, entering through a separate door to sit behind a screen where you'll be invisible to the monks. You've refused. "Incense and chanting isn't going to put me in a better frame of mind. And the first time I see Tri after this decision of his, I want to see him face to face, not through a screen," you tell Nina. She's gone to the service alone. And so it is that you're by yourself when you catch your first sight of Tri through the screen of passion vines.

He's on the other side of the lattice fence, walking towards the chapel with the other monks, his brown-hooded head bent, his eyes looking downwards at the path in front of him. His sturdy fingers, so unlike yours, are fingering a string of wooden beads.

Tri's face has the look of blissful surrender you saw on the faces of the generals who'd walked to the end of the floating opium den, put their pistols into their mouths and blown their brains out in 1975; the look of men ready to die for lost causes.

The awful doomed expression is still on his face when the monastery's Brother Director brings him to you later, now dressed in an ordinary beige T-shirt and khaki pants.

"Ba," he says, letting you hug him.

You see him searching your face, looking for clues as to how you might be feeling, how he should connect with you. You realize with a start that the son who claims his heart line to yours has been severed, is reaching out to you.

You put your hand out to touch his head, newly shaven and as smooth and un-scarred as the day he was born. Both your eyes lock. Yours are wet. His, you see, are quizzical... As if he's trying to grasp what they mean, your tears.

"It's alright, Dad," he cups your cheeks in both his hands. He touches his forehead to yours, trying to re-establish that in-the-body connection he used to have. "I'm happy. This is right for me."

You pull him to you, as close as you can, so he can feel your heart beating against his chest. "Do what you have to do," you say to your son.

"Not that I can understand any of it," you tell Nina afterwards, after Tri has retreated back to his brown-robed brothers behind the lattice fence, and the two of you are alone in the dusk-tinted garden.

Karma has exacted its ultimate spiteful price from you, you realize. You won't be physically punished nor will your son be taken away from you in flames like Loc's daughter Thi. Instead, karma is taking away your sense of possibilities. What you feel now must be the same shock, dismay, and alienation that overcame the Buddha when he realized the futility and meaninglessness of his everyday life.

How complacent and foolish you've been to think that how you've lived so far has been enough, to do what one man must—to keep himself alive, to help his family and countrymen to the best of his ability, to hold on to his loved ones and give himself to them as honestly as he can.

.....

When Nina and you return to Vietnam, you find that the two of you have entirely different stories to tell Chú Hai about Tri.

Nina says, "He looked wonderful. He was so at peace with himself and so centered I envied him."

You tell Chú Hai, "Marx was right about religion being an opiate. He looked like someone on a drug high. It's just as the astrologers predicted. There'll be no more sons to make sacrifices for my blood-father and his family. So much tilling, and in the end it's all turned out to be barren ground."

It's flogging a dead horse, worrying about your blood-father's descendents. Whether Tri enters the monastery to be a priest or not, the clues suggest your blood-father's line stopped before you were born. As for Chú Hai, he obviously doesn't need to lay claim to any descendants, you included.

"It isn't that I believe the ancestors are literally hanging around waiting to be fed. But for them to have lived and labored and then have no one to remember them. It's pitiful. Children should have consideration for the memories of those gone before," you say.

Chú Hai makes light of the situation. "Young people will be young people. I don't recall you caring about your ancestors when you came to tell me you were leaving for America," he reminds you.

.....

It's true. You hadn't cared then, hadn't even taken in his warning that you'd sold your future to Ba Roi for your ticket out. All you'd wanted was to be off. And to have his blessing.

"Ah, don't be like that Chú Hai," you'd fawned when he'd called you a foolish boy and turned his face away that day. "I'm not you. I can't think of everything like you do. But come on, I'm still your star pupil. You told me so yourself many times. You can't just look away and let me leave you like that."

Chú Hai didn't turn around.

You gave a mock sigh. "Well, if you won't let me look at your face or give me one last smile, at least let me leave you a photo." You'd taken out your old ID card, which you wouldn't need any more now you had a fake one, and slid it across the coffee table into Chú Hai's line of vision. "And maybe you can give me one of yourself, for me to remember you by?"

He'd kept his head turned. "I haven't got one," he said. He was gruff, a frog in his throat. "Anyway you don't need one. You'll be back soon enough. Eventually, the communists and the Americans will make up. And we'll find ourselves just the way we are now, sitting side by side in this room here."

"Oh please," you had insisted, pushing your ID card further across the table, drawing your chair in towards him. It had seemed the most important thing to have his picture, now you'd asked for it, now you wouldn't be seeing his face again for who knew how long.

"Oh for god's sake!" he'd exclaimed, before slapping his own ID card on the table next to yours. "Fool. All you have to do is look in the mirror."

This was the first time you saw your two faces side by side, as like as two peas from the same pod. Except for the long eyes, which everyone told you came from your blood-mother.

. . . . .

Your forebears and their mysteries...

It isn't enough helping the living; the dead also need their dues, you realize. If you have nothing to look forward to, then you'll look back, you decide. You'll imbue meaning into your life with filial piety. Even if someone else seeded you, you'll do what your blood-father and blood-mother intended for you when you were just a thought in their heads. You'll provide for the ancestors. Not just for the rest of your life and Tri's, but beyond.

And if you do enough, a voice deep in your heart whispers slyly, perhaps karma might even give Tri back to you.

SACRIFICES

21
Bones

YOU'LL ENDOW A FAMILY TEMPLE in Can Tho, you share with Nina; a memorial for the Commander and his ancestors, and a gathering place for the Chief Clerk's Vietnamese descendents, and Oldest's and Loc's American children.

"It'll divert energy from our projects," Nina warns. "They've just started, and need tending. I don't think we'll have the bandwidth to take on something else." She adds, "You aren't even sure you believe in an afterlife. Who'll pray in it? You're not expecting any more descendants from the male line, are you? And Loc's children are all in America and not likely to come back."

You dismiss her protests. "If there are no sons around, then the female line will have to do it. As it is, Third Sister's the one taking care of the sacrifices for my father's and mother's ancestors, not Loc. If I put aside the money, Kim will surely see to it we have an endowment that goes beyond forever. It's daughters you rely on ultimately."

You pull Nina to you and rest your head against her shoulder.

"It's something that needs doing. If I don't, Tri certainly isn't going to. Even if my blood-father's line ended before I was born, it doesn't mean I should forget him. But, he might well be forgotten eventually, buried away in Bac Lieu. If I exhume his bones and bring them to Can Tho to a joint family place, then there'll be just one destination for everyone to visit, a single gathering place in Vietnam that Tri, and Oldest's and Loc's children can identify with."

"What about that training centre I was going to set up with Ly's wife for post-traumatic stress counselors? And that land mine disposal program you wanted to take on?" Nina asks.

"I promise you, we'll manage. I'll tell Ly I have less time for him," you assure her. "And when the temple's ready and my father and blood-father are moved in, we'll go look for my blood-mother's grave and bring her back too," you tempt.

You see Nina smile. "A quest," she says, her black eyes glittering.

.....

"The pieces are a rape, a baby, a murder and a stolen bangle," this much Nina has gathered from your mother, blind and senile, almost ready to meet her maker. "The rape comes before the baby, naturally. And from appearances..." Her eyes check to make sure you won't be offended at what she'll say next... "The rapist is Chú Hai even if he makes it sound like a love affair in the version he told you." She points at you. "You're the baby of course. But what's next?"

You drum your fingers against the glass of the attic window and look out across the courtyard to the other house where your mother's dying. You let Nina play with her hypotheses, and go back to the package of information Chú Hai's students have compiled for you on the new appointees to the politburo, central bank and ministries.

"Does the stolen bangle come first, or the murder?" Nina asks. She decides, "Murder last. Murderer? Your blood-father. That's the most likely scenario. Possibly in a jealous fit after he discovered the affair." She pauses. "But why doesn't he kill you then? Why does he carry the bangle as a talisman on his back and pass it on to you after that?" She turns to you. "You never felt he treated you like anything other than his true son, did you?" she asks.

"No, never," you answer.

"That's a complication then," she says, rubbing the bridge of her nose.

She attacks the puzzle from a different direction. "Not Chú Hai. No motive. Rape or love story, your blood-mother seems to have kept it a secret. Your blood-father never suspected him, so he didn't need to protect himself." She lies back against the bedcovers, happy with that piece in place. "The bangle keeps flitting through your mother's story—first there were two, now there's one in the grave, the other lost then found and hanging around your neck. But it might be a red herring. Maybe it doesn't even matter." She circles back to the rape. "Chú Hai could be the suspect, but only if your mother's wrong about the rape. Only if Chú Hai's version, a love story, is correct. Then, perhaps, Chú Hai might have killed your blood-mother out of desperation, because she refused to come away with him after you were born. That might explain his departure from the camp and his leaving behind the bangle she gave to him, because he was too guilty to hold on to it. But, to lose his cool like that... It doesn't sound like the Chú Hai we know, does it?" She sits up. "What do you think?"

She's interrupted your thoughts about how the trade minister might be persuaded to issue a license to develop an industrial park near Saigon, on land Ly's managed to pick up cheap.

"It's not a Ph.D. dissertation, *cưng*. You can't solve everything in the world with hypotheses and counterfactuals. My mother would need to tell you and she can't. That's a fact. It'll always be a mystery," you tell her. You don't add that perhaps she might like to corner Chú Hai. That's forbidden territory, not a place you're prepared to let Nina go with her hows and whys and whens.

Nina goes down to your mother. You see her from the attic window, kneeling beside the hammock, staring at your mother, willing her to provide the answers.

But your mother can resolve nothing for Nina now. In no pain, life simply ebbing away from her, your mother's contemplating the next stage, not the past. She's leaving everything behind—the rape, the baby, the murder, the stolen bangle. If she knows anything about the murder, she hadn't been in a position to stop it. As for the baby, she's done more than enough by you.

Not that any of it matters at this point in her life, you think. The lessons she'd taught you and Loc and your sisters—the need for a good thought to offset a bad, for an atonement to wipe out a sin—wouldn't they pale to nothing against the voices calling her, the white light... Perhaps a broad tall shape beckoning?

.....

You send your mother off just as the new family temple is completed—Loc and you, Huong and Nina, your sisters and brothers-in-law, her grandchildren and great-grandchildren. Flesh and blood signs of a life well spent and blessed, all of you are there, except Oldest and her family, who do not have US travel documents yet, and Tri, who's locked away as a postulant.

Dry as a leaf, your mother leaves easily on the pyre of kindling scented with sandalwood and incense sticks. Loc and you shed tears but you don't shudder at this burning. Her passing and cremation are part of the cycle of life, a cycle which sees Loc and Huong going home to America to welcome another grandchild, while Nina and you remain behind to settle your mother in her resting place, and begin the search for your long abandoned blood-mother.

.....

You do not find your blood-mother till 2006. Even though you remember your blood-father's directions almost word for word, even with your money and resources.

You'd been anxious through the hunt, but you feel nothing when they lift her up from the black delta clay, what remnants there are after nearly sixty years—bits of hands and feet, crushed pieces of rib, arms and forearms, upper and lower leg bones as tiny as a child's, a delicate jaw bone, her cranium broken in half, the pelvis collapsed.

It would sadden her, what you're thinking: That she wasn't the one who cradled you when you were colicky, who rubbed mosquito balm on your legs before you slept, and let you nuzzle her breasts during nightmares, who saved the best pieces of pork fat for you, although she ate no meat herself. That you have no memory of her, just the stories from your blood-father, an allusion from Chú Hai and your own almond-shaped eyes in the mirror. It would sadden her, but it can't be helped.

The laborers hoist up the pieces from her grave, one basket at a time. You carry the baskets to a makeshift plank table with an attentive Tri, who's come to Vietnam specially for the occasion. Then, scooping from a barrel filled with rice-wine brewed for the purpose, your son and you wash away the years of mud encasing her.

The retinue of monks you've brought along lay out the washed bones again as best they can, while chanting prayers to release whatever might still be trapped in the remains. You watch dry-eyed as your son chants along with them, his face still carrying its blissful religion-deluded expression.

As the monks and Tri pray, you seek the dead woman's forgiveness for taking so long to come for her. "But now I'm taking you home to the new temple I've built, where Blood-father and Father and Mother are waiting to receive you," you whisper to her bones. You pick them up with chopsticks—you, Nina and Tri—then layer them into the celadon jar Nina has commissioned specially from a potter in San Francisco. Just before the monks cap the jar, you take out a flat package wrapped in red silk from your shirt pocket. It contains the bone bangle you've worn on your body since your blood-father gave it to you. The bangle is yellowed now from long contact against human skin; your blood-father's, then yours. The etched pattern of pine needles on its surface has almost completely worn away. Still there's a gleam to it. You rub it gently between your thumb and index finger one last time, before placing it in the jar and fastening it with red string to the cracked earth-stained one you found by her left wrist, the one that identified her to you.

"She has both of them now. Now she can rest," you say to Nina.

Nina doesn't reply immediately. She looks up at the trees, at the sky between the leaves. Across the river she sees a kite fly by, floating to freedom in the stark blue delta sky.

She points to it. "See, isn't that a good omen?"

.....

You install your blood-mother's jar next to the Commander's. "It doesn't matter who I am or how I came about," you pray to both of them. "I am a son of your spirit. I lay you to rest."

.....

Nonetheless, your blood-mother does not rest. Whether the physicists believe in it or not, there remains a quirk in the time-space continuum allowing connections to be made between the here and now, and the there and beyond, a channel through which a spirit can cry out if she wishes.

Whether it's from the shock of the new aluminum frame window clattering shut, or Third Sister's fingers becoming shaky with age, the jar containing your blood-mother's remains slips out of Third Sister's hands when she's cleaning the altar. The celadon pot bounces away from her like a ball before falling onto the rust brown granite floor with a sharp crack and breaking cleanly into two. The red cloth holding the bangles falls out and unfolds itself, revealing the two circlets of bone loosely tied to each other.

"An accident," Third Sister explains away the white porcelain replacement jar when next you visit with Nina. "I didn't want to bother you two with it. The monks came and said all the proper prayers for reinstatement. Everything's fine now."

You do not know that when you go out to the fields with your brothers-in-law for a look at their new fish ponds, Third Sister corners Nina. "How is it this was in Auntie's jar?" she asks, opening her palm to show Nina the less worn circlet.

"It's Thong's. His blood-father gave it to him years ago and told him to put it in the jar with the other one when he found her," Nina answers.

"Well, it shouldn't be there. That's why the jar broke. Auntie was telling us she didn't want it with her."

"Why?" Nina asks, hopeful that the last piece of the puzzle will fall into place at last.

.....

This is what Third Sister tells your wife, a story Nina recounts reluctantly only after the perpetrator himself has confessed.

.....

It started with a treat before Mid-Autumn, a cinema show on the hospital grounds. It was a screening of The Three Musketeers, the old fashioned kind where people sat on mats in the open to watch the moving images projected on a piece of white cloth hung between two trees.

In those days, that had been a special occasion. Everyone in town went to see the film, including a day laborer your

*father had assigned to guard the government store-rooms...
Inevitably, there was a break-in. As punishment, the Chief
Clerk thrashed the man, accidently laming him.*

*At Mid-Autumn, the guardians of the oppressed, a Viet
Cong guerrilla squad, came to teach your father a lesson. But
your father had gone with your mother to a wake in a nearby
hamlet. Oldest Sister and Third Sister had been left to look
after the younger children, supervised by your blood-mother,
who'd come to town for the festival.*

*Third Sister was twelve, Oldest was fourteen, your blood-
mother still quite a young woman. It is easy to imagine what
might have passed when the vigilantes found the Chief Clerk
missing and only children and three young women at home.
But it hadn't.*

*Your blood-mother had stepped forward and asked them to
take just her, lying that she was the Chief Clerk's oldest daughter.
She'd said her sisters were too young. An eye for an eye, one
daughter for one man lamed, she'd argued. She convinced them.
They hustled her into a room and sent in just one young man.*

*Third Sister and Oldest Sister couldn't see anything. But,
standing outside the front room they'd heard everything
through the wooden walls. Your blood-mother had fought
the rapist most of the way, until she didn't have any strength
left, your Third Sister said. When she came out, her eyes
were red but she was dressed and still walking straight, still
whole. It was only the bangle missing from her right wrist that
suggested something had happened.*

*Nine months later, your mother was called into the salt
marshes and came back home with you*

.....

"I haven't seen this for more than half a century," Third Sister tells Nina. "I've no idea how Uncle got it back. But I believe Auntie would never have wanted that thing resting next to her bones."

She presses the circlet into Nina's palm. "Oldest saw the face of the young man sent in to Auntie. She always thought Youngest looked remarkably like him. She also said the general in Saigon whom Youngest calls Chú Hai has the same face." She notices that Nina isn't surprised by this revelation. "I think you should give this back to him," she says.

"But what will I say to Thong?" Nina asks.

Third Sister bends forward to clasp Nina's free hand in both of hers. "Nothing. Don't say anything, ever. His mother sacrificed herself to protect us. To honor her, my mother said we were never to tell him what happened, never to let him know he'd come about through an act of violence." She looks at Nina sadly. "Sometimes, it's best to hide the truth."

And Nina agrees. Who can benefit from this sorry tale, when Chú Hai and you are as close as thieves, each holding a central place in the other's heart? She will not be the first one to break this awful truth to you, she decides.

But there's the problem of where to hide the bangle. The two of you have been living in each other's pockets since coming back to Vietnam. She digs in your wallet for small change for the beggars. You raid her handbag for wet wipes and sunscreen. Often, both of you travel with only one suitcase and a single toiletry bag between you. It's a closeness Nina couldn't have imagined in your long years apart, an unanticipated joy. But now it's an obstacle to something she needs to do to protect you.

She finally stuffs the bangle into a box of tampons, a box she knows you'll never investigate. She's right. You only suspect later that the circlet has passed through her hands on its way back to Chú Hai and then your son, because of her uncontrolled curiosity. For inevitably, when puzzling over how to hide the bangle from you, Nina also begins to wonder how you originally took it out of Vietnam undetected.

You've told her about the checks on those allowed to escape the country then. How your documents were scrutinized and re-scrutinized before you could board the rusty freighter. How you were all frisked and relieved of any gold and valuables you were attempting to carry out. How your orifices, especially those of the young women, were probed. And how, when you got on the high seas, the pirates who accosted you tore apart the boat, searching under and between every single board and probing every cubby when they found nothing on your bodies. But if Nina wants more of that story...

"I let my hair grow to my shoulders. Then Chú Hai braided the bangle against my head with it. He put the bangle between the two whorls of hair here, on the flat of my skull. And he attached my Father's and my Mother's gold wedding bands here at the two hollows above my nape." You indicate the positions on your head for Nina to see. "After that, I stopped washing my hair. At one point, there were lice in it. If you'd seen me then, you'd never have invited me back to your apartment."

"But how were you allowed to walk around with a head full of un-Socialist Rastafarian locks?"

How she always needs details!

"It was Chú Hai's idea. I was already pretending a nervous breakdown so I could disappear from work to help with provisioning and stocking the boat. When I presented him with the problem of the circlet and my parents' wedding rings, he came up with the hair as the final touch. He said no one would try to get too near a crazy man with a stinking head of hair, let alone stop him from leaving."

"So, Chú Hai saw your mother's bangle after she died?"

"Mmm-hmmm," you say. "He recognized it. But he would have thought it was the one she usually wore on her wrist. I don't think he'd know about the one that was lost and then found."

"Do you remember if he was nervous, or emotional, or anything out of the ordinary when you showed it to him or when he took it from you to attach to your head?"

You don't understand why Nina's asking such questions, especially when everything's settled and the bangle is safe where it should be, but you humor her. "This was just a few weeks after Chú Hai put our ID cards side by side, just as I was preparing to escape the country. If he was nervous, or emotional, or anything out of the ordinary, it would all have gone over my head. Anyway, you know him now. If he swallowed an elephant and didn't want you to know he had indigestion, well, you wouldn't, would you?"

"So true," Nina says. "But he's the key, the chameleon piece that pulls the whole puzzle together. Everything goes back to him." She's insisting on this as if it's a fact you need to understand. As if you haven't grasped his full measure already.

.....

Nina decides to unlock the mystery the next week, when you've left her in Saigon and flown off to the Central Coast to assess an oil refinery project for Ly.

"I'm running out to visit Chú Hai," she tells you when you call to touch base. "I'm going to corner him."

You are too pre-occupied with the spreadsheets from the feasibility study to ask her why.

In any case, Chú Hai isn't there to be cornered. He's gone to the hospital for an operation, his sister informs Nina at the gate. She doesn't know what kind. Her brother never tells her anything, she complains. He's been coming and going as usual. Then suddenly, the other day, he calls from the office to tell her he needs a medical procedure. It's nothing serious, she's been told. And he hasn't asked her to visit. But if Nina wants to, it's the hospital for cadres. She gives Nina his ward and bed number.

Chú Hai's room at the end of a grey carpeted corridor air-freshened by ionizers is bright and modern.

"Wow! They've recreated a Singapore hospital in Saigon just for you cadres," Nina shouts into the room when she arrives.

Strangely, there is no answering retort or laugh.

Nina has to push aside the curtains around Chú Hai's hospital bed to see his response.

'But the doctors are still no damn good,' Chú Hai lifts a magnetic doodle pad for her to read.

He's propped up on pillows, his neck and lower jaw wrapped in bandages. Nina sees him try to greet her with his usual mischievous grin, but something has happened to his jaw muscles and his lips merely wobble.

"What's happened? Why didn't you tell us?"

He scribbles— 'Cough... Sore throat... Scratches.'

Nina finds out from the newly recruited Vietnamese-American doctor that it's not just scratches. There are irregular growths in and around the throat. They've found malignant cells. There's a tumor wrapped around the voice box. They've taken out the bits from the inside of the throat and mended it. But the voice box is gone. Chú Hai won't speak again.

Chú Hai is at his most vulnerable, face to face with his mortality, his defenses down. If Nina wants to get information about the bangle, now is the moment. But she can't. It's a time for forbearing, not confrontation. Instead, she scolds Chú Hai gently for not telling the two of you, then goes to call you with the bad news.

Like her court ancestors, Nina has the art of timing in her bones. She doesn't know it then, but there will be a better time to confront Chú Hai with the circlet, to leverage it for more than just a story.

.....

They find another hotspot. Not in the throat they've been scanning and torturing with radioactive waves for the last year but in the prostate. Probably unrelated, the doctor tells you, just something that happens in old men. Nonetheless, it ought to be investigated.

'Not enough exercise down there,' Chú Hai types on his new mini-computer. He adds a smiley icon, then continues, 'It's telling me the down-there exists. I need to pay attention to it and give it some fun before it's too late. I'll be fine if you find me a sweet sixteen.'

You don't say anything. Instead you take his left hand in yours, and point to the age spots on its back, and the wrinkles around his knuckles and wrist.

After a while he punches out, 'So you don't think you can find a sweet sixteen who'll touch skin like mine? So I've no choice? It's off with it or I'm gone?' He bites his lower lip and turns to examine the pattern on the curtains the nurse has drawn to block out the sun.

You pat his knee, the bones sharp against your palm, even under layers of blankets, and adopt the roguish tone he used to put on. "It's not the balls, you know. The wet noodle will still work. Anyway, before we worry about the sweet sixteens, let's do a biopsy first. Then we can decide."

After the last near miss, Nina and you had sent Chú Hai to Singapore for follow-up radiotherapy. 'No need. Everyone has to die anyway. Why prolong the agony?' he'd written on the doodle-pad then, trying to brush you off. But against his inclinations, he'd gone, and has been flying out for quarterly checkups since.

'No need for a biopsy. The more they check, the more they'll find. Just fly me home. Quick and sharp is how I said I wanted to die last year. Quick and sharp is what I'm thinking I want this time,' he bangs on his keyboard now.

It's not what I want," you shout.

'It's not your life... It's not your death... It's no concern of yours,' the reply flies off Chú Hai's fingers.

"Oh yes it is!" You grab the computer and fling it across the room to the opposite wall. Its plastic parts break and clatter to the floor as you stalk out.

But Chú Hai sticks to his guns. He won't sign the consent forms for the biopsy. He turns his face to the curtained window when Nina and you visit.

"You still have so many good years. Don't let them go just like that," you beg.

"Prostate cancers are slow growing, very controllable if they're treated early," Nina tries to appeal to his logical side.

"I told you already, you're not losing your balls," you raise your voice in exasperation.

"Prostate cancers tend to spread to the bones if they're not caught. Extremely painful once they get there," Nina threatens.

"And by then it will undoubtedly be too late, far too late" you shout.

He will not bend.

You imagine him laughing at the two of you, silly children trying to shake him with empty words. Yes, you haven't forgotten he spent the twenty-five years of the American war leading a double, even a triple life. Yes, you know that although he always lived in fear of discovery he never once veered from his purpose.

"But this is foolish bravado," you plead with him.

He keeps his face turned to the curtains. You see him mouthing the Analects to block you and Nina out, "The superior man lies under arms and meets death without regret, how firm is his energy. When good principles prevail he does not alter his stand, how firm is his energy. When bad principles prevail, he maintains his course to death without changing, how firm is his energy."

.....

"If we can't do anything for the general, we'll need to release the hospital bed to someone else," the doctor informs you.

"We're paying, damn it!" you say, losing your manners.

"Still, we're a hospital. We have a waiting list. And most of the people on it seem more interested in getting better than the general."

"Give us one more day," Nina placates the doctor. She breathes in your ear. "Let me go and talk to him alone."

"You think you can convince him?" You're skeptical.

"I don't know, but it's worth trying. I backed away from confrontation before, when he was at his weakest and afraid to die. Now when he's at his most foolish, I'm hoping I can bring him back to his senses by showing him how much he still owes the living," she replies.

.....

You learn this from Nina after Chú Hai dies:

He shuts his eyes when he sees her come in and heaves himself over so he's facing the curtains again, his back to her.

"Hey Chú, I thought you'd like to know the hospital's kicking us out. They say we should be giving your bed to someone else who's more interested in living," she whispers.

She waits to see if there's a response from him, but there isn't. He isn't a spy trained to withstand all manner of torture for nothing. Finally, she strokes his right hand gently. "You've won. And seeing as you're determined to go, I thought you should have this to take along," she says. Then she opens his hand flat and presses the bone circlet into it.

His hand trembles as it closes around the circlet. After some time, he brings his thumb and index finger together and tentatively caresses the old bone.

Nina says in her softest voice, "Thong put it into his blood-mother's jar with the other one, like his blood-father asked him to. But the jar broke. She wasn't ready to take it back. I think, she wanted you to have it, to remind you of your obligations...

The Confucians say we have children so they'll take care of us when we're old and to make sacrifices to us when we're dead. The Buddhists say we have children because we owe them their lives. What do you think, Chú?"

Nina turns around to draw open the curtains and let the daylight in. She climbs onto Chú Hai's bed and closes both her hands around his, wrapping her fingers and his around the circlet. "There are so many things you still owe my husband. So many explanations why things turned out the way they did. And even if you don't want to give him those explanations, still he needs an acknowledgement of what he is to you and what you are to him." She raises his hand, still holding the circlet, up to her lips, and kisses it. "Just an acknowledgement before you die. You owe him that, don't you think? *Ba?*"

She's obeyed your Third Sister. She's given back the circlet to him. She hasn't asked him for any secrets. She isn't any clearer how the jigsaw fits. But she thinks she's said enough. He'll never tell, and therefore he'll have to live.

She slides off the bed and leaves the room.

He remains where he is, facing the window, his back to her, his eyes shut. But now light is pouring in.

.....

The bangle's muteness beating against his palm must have moved him.

You imagine him now, taking up a pen from the table beside the hospital bed, trying to fashion the story. It isn't the truth he finally left for you in a formal white envelope, written on onion skin paper in his and your mother tongue, Vietnamese. These are scraps, what you find on pieces of hospital stationery when his sister gives you the keys to his safe after his funeral. They're his starts and stops, written in English, the language he liked to hide behind.

'How should the story start?'

'Should it begin in the first person? I was a young man and foolish, also foolishly in love. Or the second and third? You may have forgiven him for keeping silent about the past, but can you forgive him for keeping this last one from you... No, the second and third don't work. It keeps coming back to the first person, myself. It appears it must be written that way then. But not as a confession. Never.'

'So, I start again. If I told you it happened one way, I would become a rapist. Or I could cast your blood mother as the adulteress and her husband as the unwitting cuckold... Hardly edifying. As for what happened after, would you rather she died in child birth, separated too soon from a longed for child? Or would you prefer the version where her husband killed her in a jealous fit? Or a third, where I suffocated her with my palm to stop her from smothering you, the unwanted offspring of an unfortunate encounter? Would you rather believe I sought you out to nurture you? Or that our first few encounters were accidents of fate, the heavens deciding I should have a hand in your life regardless of how much I wanted to put it all behind me?'

'After reconsideration, I realize this isn't a story to be told from a single point of view. There are too many threads, too many characters. Why work with only one voice? I'm a journalist, a rapporteur. Perhaps, I should assume the omniscient, be like God, all knowing... But I'm not God. I'm mortal, dying. And still there are the secrets untold. I can only hope it will somehow all be redeemed—my sins as monumental as Thai Son Mountain, the consequences flowing like water through to endless generations. In the end, all I know is to spin a story from the facts, taking into account my audience. And yes, perhaps beyond that, there is one last thing...'

22
Flesh and blood

CHÚ HAI WANTS TO GO TO AMERICA. It is 2008 and your sixtieth birthday. It's a full cycle, the perfect occasion.

He picks the text out on his clamshell, an all-in-one device on which he receives and sends phone messages and chats with the world at large. '4 ur b'day. Havent c'n Tri 4 ages. Not getting youngr... N can stay 2 watch prez elections aftr.'

"All this text-speak. What happened to everything you taught me about writing in proper sentences?" you grumble.

Chú Hai ignores the reprimand. 'Best thing abt losing voice box is freedom not 2 respond,' he'd typed for you the other day. Now he shuts the clamshell and simply raises his eyebrow in a question.

You give in. "We'll have my sixtieth birthday in America then. But just a family affair, not the big business bash we planned for Ho Chi Minh City."

"A business bash won't do in America," Nina concurs, still worried about the South Vietnamese veterans' lobbies there.

It's true, they haven't cooled off. Instead, they've become increasingly vocal. In Hawaii, a wealthy fish importer you know dies. Among the wreaths sent to his wake is one from a Vietnam based fish processor. Three months later a letter arrives at his widow's home. 'Stop dealing with Vietnam fish processors or you'll find your son in the freezers, neatly wrapped, next to your communist fillets,' it says. In Little Saigon, the publisher of a newspaper featuring the Ho Chi Minh Mausoleum in Hanoi is sent a cartoon of a man strangled at his desk. A week later the publisher's office is broken into and two plastic hands stained with red ink are left on his keyboard. 'If anyone should write even one sentence praising the Monster Ho...' a post-it note stuck on the computer screen warns.

It isn't personal. The victims' activities just happen to turn up on the veterans' radar. Like the Vietnamese doctor in Seattle whose clinic is ransacked after helping Nina recruit volunteers for the Hue hospital. Or the Agent Orange non-profit in D.C., which receives anonymous hate mail regularly. Even Loc and Huong have been confronted because it's gotten out that Kim works for a Ho Chi Minh City businessman.

The lobbyists haven't done any real harm, but the malevolence of their threats is a worry. A family bash but not in Orange County. Far away in New York City, and you'll fly over anyone from Orange County who wants to come, Nina and you agree.

"We can expect Loc and Huong and the boys, and maybe their wives; Oldest and some of her children; Kim with Jake and the two little ones; Ly and his wife, who'll be visiting their son at Parsons; and Jerry of course," you count.

"My parents too," Nina reminds you.

"Yes. But only for form's sake," you agree, reluctantly.

"Binh?"

"No. Preferably not Oldest Brother-in-Law either."

"We have to ask Oldest Sister. We can't avoid asking her husband."

"You're right. We can't. We'll just have to give him the pleasure of refusing."

"We can all fly to California after the party, then take a road trip up the Coast to Tri's monastery for his final vows and ordination," you tell Chú Hai, "Good scenery on the way up, good wine from the monks' vineyards when we get there, good bye to Tri at the end."

Chú Hai ignores the complaint about Tri, and simply gives you a thumbs up. 'All set 2 go when ur rdy,' he taps.

Kim makes the arrangements. A one year old restaurant in a Brooklyn Chinatown building the company owns, she emails. Just above a bank in your remittance network, and serving excellent food at great prices. Better still, there's a good value hotel just a block away, that the folks from California can stay at. Not Vietnamese food, she admits, but then New York has never been a good place for Vietnamese food, as you all know.

No, you won't find good Vietnamese food in Brooklyn's Chinatown. In Brooklyn though, you'll be safe from the anger of the old soldiers from Orange County and free from any mischief they might want to foment. Kim won't need to hire security guards to protect you or Ly or Chú Hai from gatecrashers. Although the one square mile along Eighth Avenue is filled with new runaways from communism, the Chinese immigrants in Brooklyn have no politics. Like the majority of those from China taking to the sea and air for the Golden Mountain, all they care about is their rice bowls.

Still, there are trade links between the Chinese in Brooklyn, and Vietnam, China's former vassal state—imports of frozen shrimp, Delta catfish, dried squid, the ubiquitous fish sauce, sweatshop clothing and imitation electronics—goods for which greenbacks have to be paid. Ly's foresight has ensured that the greenbacks are sent through your remittance agency. The flows are a blip compared to the cash going back to mainland China through other banks. But together with the money leaving Orange County to support families left in Vietnam, it's enough for Ly and you and your families and friends to make a good living. It's enough to make the old soldiers burn.

.....

Loc reports that Oldest Brother-in-Law has been extremely disagreeable about the invitation Loc hand-delivers to him at the Veterans' Association.

"The cheek of it, using his black money for a party and then inviting us to celebrate with him," Oldest Brother-in-Law had told Loc, dismissing the correctness of your etiquette and the respect implied by the personal delivery of the red and gold envelope.

To show his disdain, he'd turned away from the computer where he was downloading news from the Association's network of internet watchers, and coughed and spat out a globule of green gunk through the window.

"Not us. Just you," Binh had corrected Oldest Brother-in-Law from the donated velour easy-chair he was lolling in. "Some of us have been forgotten," he'd said, his face glowering.

Loc hadn't anticipated Binh's presence. "Well, it isn't his fault. You're the one who said you wanted nothing further to do with him," he'd replied.

"Even so, he shouldn't have forgotten Binh," Oldest Brother-in-Law had said. He'd flashed a malevolent look at Binh. "Maybe it's time we make sure he doesn't forget?" Adding, "A full cycle birthday means completion, doesn't it? Why not one final symbolic act of resistance from you and me just to show him what completion really means?"

"And if we do it during a Presidential campaign, we'll have the world as an audience," Binh had completed the thought for his friend, his hand moving unconsciously to pat the dull ache in his crotch.

"It sounds like trouble," Loc warns you.

"They're just windbags," you say to your brother.

You dismiss it. A thing not thought of and not brought into the open has no power, you tell yourself. You don't mention it to Nina. You don't even remember to ask Kim to arrange some security, just in case.

.....

Now the party is upon you, you must reassure yourself that not having security isn't a problem. Nothing will happen, you say to yourself. And if anything does, well, there are enough nephews and friends to keep it all together. You hope.

"Forty people is just right," you say to Nina as you zip up the bodice of her new navy blue lace dress.

"Yes, it'll be intimate. All close friends and family," she replies. She nibbles on her freshly manicured little finger, then examines it. "Except for that analyst from the State Department Chú Hai invited."

Chú Hai's unlikely guest is Jules Anderson, Julia's son.

You apologize. "It's awkward for you, I know. But she and I are just an old story. It's all about Chú Hai's obligations. She did go to see Chú Hai when she was dying of cancer to specially request he keep an eye on the kid. Chú Hai couldn't not invite him when he's just down the road in D.C."

"I know," Nina says, giving you a kiss on the cheek. "It's not Julia Anderson or her son I'm uncomfortable about. This is New York. Everyone runs into everyone's ex all the time. It's just that Chú Hai was so transparent about wanting him at the party. It's out of character, our Chú Hai showing his hand like that. And then there's your Oldest Brother-in-Law's strange birthday greeting..."

A telegram from Oldest Brother-in-Law had arrived at the brownstone in the morning with the message—'Now that you're at the end of a cycle, what next?'

"Well, we can't worry about it now. Everything's arranged and we must just go through with it," you tell her, shrugging away her anxiety and yours. You sniff the side of her neck. Chanel, the perfume she always uses. You take her elbow. "Come. The town car's here and Tri's already waiting outside."

.....

Tri has been allowed to attend your party before starting the thirty-day retreat preceding his final vows, a special dispensation from the Brother Director.

Nothing will change his decision, he's told Nina. That's why he decided to ask for the permission to come. And indeed after two days in New York, he hasn't presented you with the ultimate birthday present, he's not given the slightest hint that his commitment to a religious life is wavering.

But something has changed, apparently. After seven years, the heart lines have been restored, he's confided to Kim. The buzz of other people's thoughts and feelings is back. And now it's even more confusing than before, because he can hear and feel his own emotions accompanying everyone else's. He's no more a selfless observer. He's become a separate Tri, participating.

Kim feels compelled to share this development with you and Nina in the ante-room beside the restaurant's main dining area, when she notices Tri becoming unsettled as the guests trickle in.

"Well at least we know now, if anything happens," Nina replies. She bites her lip and puts a restraining hand on you, just in case you lose it.

But you have no heart for an outburst at Kim, a rant that she might have told you sooner so you could have given Tri the choice to remain quietly at home.

Kim is defensive. "He said he wanted to come. He said he'd manage. After getting over that first shock of emotion from you when you hugged him at the airport, he said he'd be fine with everything else."

"What shock? What did he think I felt?" Now you're the one being defensive.

She hesitates before replying. "He said there was a lament in your gut. That it was as sorrowful as the Absalom his brother monks sang at the *Nones* he attended before going to the airport."

You shake your head, at a loss.

She gives you a disbelieving look. "The Absalom. You don't know it?"

"No," you confess. Your mother had not been like Huong, a staunch Catholic who sent Kim to a Catholic school till she was sixteen.

Kim enlightens you by chanting the words, "O my son Absalom. O Absalom, my son, my son..."

"That's enough, dear," Nina holds her palm up and presses it lightly against Kim's lips. She turns to you with a bright false smile. "Well, if he could get over that, I suppose he'll be alright out there."

.....

Tri is standing by the restaurant foyer, looking a little dazed. When you, Nina and Kim come out from the side room, relief crosses his face.

You go up to him and touch his chest.

He puts his hand over yours and gives you a crooked smile. "It's alright, Dad. God does help, you know," he says.

He can only ever say the truth, no matter how it hurts. No matter how much of your pain he feels. You nod, moving away, hoping even the smallest bit more distance might protect him from your sorrow. It isn't his fault, this empathy he bears. This suffering only the monastery can cushion him from.

You see him watching you walk away, then close his eyes to offer whatever is clamoring in his body to his God.

"Be still, my soul," you see the words forming on his lips before he walks out into the gathering of his cousins and uncles and aunts, the gathering of other souls.

.....

Nina follows Tri into the crowd. This is what she remembers of their conversation:

"Are you okay?" she asks.

"I'm surprised I'm still distinctly me even though I'm hearing and feeling everyone else," he says. He closes his eyes and shares what he feels. "Overflowing joy—that's from Great Uncle Chú Hai. An undercurrent of anxiety flitting through Kim, also you—both of you need it to be perfect tonight. Papi and Memé are upset about Dad's politics and having Great Uncle here, but they're really impressed by Dad's success, Memé especially. She's full of grudging admiration." He opens his eyes and scans the room. "The rest—envy, affection, pride—you can see it well enough." Then, Nina remembers, he rocks a little and leans into her.

"What was that?" she clutches at his arm.

He puts his hand up to his breastbone. He whispers, "Just something warm here, what's not seen, the pain behind the laughter and congratulations, the hidden hopes and fears. There's too much of it."

Nina feels him press against her a little harder, the way he used to when he was frightened as a child.

But he brushes her hand away almost immediately and straightens up. "If I were Jesus, I'd heal them. I'd multiply the five loaves and two fishes of my limited heart to feed their heart hunger, to make them whole," he says with urgency. "But I'm just me, a son on a father's special birthday," he allows, giving Nina a smile filled with the peace of starry vineyard nights.

It is he who takes the lead after that, Nina recalls. He who pulls Nina back to the entryway so he can stand beside the two of you to shake his cousins' hands, to fold his arms and bob his head to greet his elders formally, to behave as he should.

"Who is that?" he asks Nina, his eyes moving to the stocky man with sun-bleached hair and a faded tan greeting Chú Hai.

"It's Great Uncle's guest, someone from the State Department whose mother worked in Vietnam during the war," Nina tells him. "We must go say hello."

"Of course we must," he replies.

And then, Nina recalls, your son takes her hand and leads her towards you and the man closest to your heart, and the stranger.

.....

As you, Nina and Chú Hai, cluster around Jules Anderson, Tri stands a little to the side, listening.

"Jules, the son of ..." Chú Hai is saying.

"Ah yes, your mother married in the Middle East," Nina comments.

To which Jules replies, "She never married. I'm adopted."

And then he's shaking your hand and telling you, "I think we met briefly once in Tokyo."

With his heart lines restored, Tri will know how your emotions are bouncing high and low, you suddenly feel with unusual certainty. He'll have noticed that flash of wounded pride running through you when Jules was introduced, and after that, the wave of nostalgia and regret when you realize Julia Anderson has remained alone most of her life. Like you, Tri will be confused by the questions about Jules's parentage that suddenly bubble through your mind. His brain waves will be racing like Nina's, his mental lights turning on the way Nina's do when she finds interesting new pieces of data. He'll also have absorbed Chú Hai's nervousness—Chú Hai's tightly reined in hope, the rigidity of his jaw bone, the flutter in his left eye.

You see Tri close his eyes as he struggles to understand the complex interplay of feelings between all of you and the stranger in your midst. You close your eyes too, and inexplicably, you begin to feel with your son. As if you've fallen into a deep tunnel and emerged on the other side, you and Tri are one, absorbed in the strangeness of your own feelings and Chú Hai's and Nina's and Jules' and Tri's own... Your son and you, a single entity trying to make sense of the mystery's dimensions.

Then from within the web of Tri's and your entangled perceptions, you hear a loud "Happy Birthday!" and a guttural "Hello!"

"Uncle Binh and Oldest Uncle," you feel Tri choke. "They're not meant to be here," he voices the tsunami of panic surging through the room behind him.

Whether you hear the rest of it in your heart, or with your ears, you will never know. "Gates down—Dad; soldiers in place—Great Uncle. Hate and hunting dog hearts sending out whooshes of anger—Uncle Binh and Oldest Uncle. A mad urge to kill making for Dad and Great Uncle. Fire seeking a target..."

What you do see with your eyes is your son turning his head blindly, trying to locate the source of the fire. Still locked in his own other dimension, he doesn't realise that the short snouts of Oldest Brother-in-Law's and Binh's guns are pointed at you and Chú Hai. "There," he decides. This, you know, you hear in the depths of your heart. And then, without thinking, he steps forward to deflect the flames, straight into the bullets Binh means for you.

"Something warm here," you hear his voice coming through the air, surprisingly loud. You see him open his eyes to find out what it might be. "Carnations just like those on the altar at Easter," he says to you with a pleased smile. "There's one on the floor," he points to the patch of blood slowly pooling there.

You watch paralysed, as he bends forward to pick up one of the drops of red for Nina. He buckles. To cushion his fall, his hand reaches out for Nina's ankle.

You hear a dull thump, then Tri's voice in your heart echoing your heart's cries, comforting you even as he leaves you... "O my son Absalom. O Absalom, my son, my son."

.....

It happens much faster for Nina. What she recalls are Tri's arms swinging back as the bullets from Binh's micro-Uzi spray into him, Tri falling in front of her like a broken puppet, his body jerking onto the ground by her feet. She hears an animal howl escaping from you, then sees you leaping out at Binh, just in time to miss the bullets from Oldest Brother-in-Law's gun. She sees another spray of bullets going towards Chú Hai, and at the same time Jules Anderson lunging into Oldest Brother-in-Law. Then Chú Hai is pulling her down onto the floor with him. Peering from the plush carpeting, she sees Jules Anderson grappling with Oldest Brother-in-Law, you rolling on the floor with Binh, eight arms struggling for two guns.

.....

You manage to scramble on top of Binh and catch hold of his gun. Pushing and pulling, you turn the nozzle towards him. He's looking into your eyes. You're staring into his. Both your hands are tight around the gun's grip. Then Binh relaxes. His arms, which have been pushing hard against the gun and at you, soften. His elbows fall back onto the floor. The Uzi's snout falls towards his mouth and red rimmed eyes. Your face moves closer to his.

"Go on. Shoot. You've got the balls. Now show me you have the guts," Binh taunts.

Your index finger moves a fraction up the grip to the trigger. All you have to do is move it a centimeter more, wrap it around the hooked metal and then squeeze, and Binh will be gone. His head will jerk back like Tri's, his blood spray out like Tri's, his brains and skull explode the way the generals' had when they blew their brains out the night the country was unified and lost. Your son's killer will be neutralized and wiped off the face of the earth, no longer a threat to your wife or yourself. You'll have kept what remains of your family safe, like you kept Huong safe in 1975 in Phu Quoc. Your finger creeps up half a centimeter...

"Go on. Do it. If you don't have the guts, do it from your heart. Put me out of my misery," Binh says, his voice a hiss. "I want to die a hero's death. After taking away my balls you can bloody well give that to me can't you? You motherfucker!"

Binh's hold on the gun tightens again. His fingers under yours struggle to move up the magazine chamber. His hand reaches yours and curls over it. He crushes your finger down on the trigger. With all your strength, you straighten your arm and push, pointing the gun towards the ceiling. It goes off, the bullets pock marking the ceiling, the back-kick from the shot ricocheting down your raised forearm and biceps.

"Damn you!" Binh chokes out. He lifts his head and bites your armpit.

You drop the gun.

Binh struggles under you, trying to crawl out from beneath your weight to get at the weapon. You throw yourself bodily over him, your legs pinning him down with an animal strength you've just discovered you possess. Your elbows dig into his shoulders.You move your hands to his neck, prepared to tighten them all the way.

Binh is tense, the pulse on the side of his neck beating hard below your fingers. Your fingers tighten. Your right and left hands move closer to each other. The stink of fear wafts up from Binh's body into your nose. You can smell his sweat, his cologne... Brut. You'd inhaled that same mix of syrup, musk and man on the young military policeman who'd kept Huong's gold. His scent had floated up to you strong and hot that blacked-out night on Phu Quoc when you pressed the blanket over his face, pressed so hard his heels had started to drum, then pressed harder until his heels stopped drumming, and the room filled with the stench of shit so strong the cologne couldn't mask it. You'd killed him. Not in anger and not in fear, simply for five taels of gold.

You remember the rapist's lips pressed against your neck the night before that and how you'd prayed to be saved, and been granted mercy in exchange for five taels of gold. But you'd taken the gold back, and a life along with it. A life Tri has now paid for. You can't kill again.

Your body sags into Binh's. Your cheeks rub.

Your cheeks had pressed against each other's in the same way once before, when you were boys, on Binh's first and only visit to the Delta. He'd talked you into climbing a *longan* tree to raid the juicy fruit after a morning bicycling along the rice bunds. Going up higher than you should have, you'd slipped and fallen on him, knocking the wind out of his chest. You remember how you scrambled onto his prone body to feel his heartbeat, how you continued to lie there, your cheek against his, willing him to come back to life. How thankful you were when finally his eyes fluttered open.

And here you are again, grown apart once, together again. You're even now—both men who will have no sons. You're back where you were before—cheek to cheek, both come to your senses.

You lift your weight from Binh and sit up. There's warm blood trickling down your armpit where he bit you. You see finger marks and bruised skin around his neck, where you almost strangled him. "No guts or no heart, whatever, I can't do it," you whisper to your friend.

.....

You push yourself up to your feet and go to your wife, who's kneeling by your child... your only child. His hand, still warm but too heavy now, is tight around her ankle.

"He must have grabbed it as he fell," she tries to explain the data to you, her big black eyes unfocused, flooded. "So frightened he must have been with all the noise, the confusion. He was always such an easily frightened child. Always..."

She strokes his hand. "There's nothing to be afraid of now," she tells him "You can let go of my ankle now. The fight's over. It's over. You can let go and get up now. It's safe to get up now."

She says it over and over. It's safe. He can let go of her ankle now. He can get up. But he can't.

"Why?" she asks his God and hers.

A FULL CYCLE

23
What remains

FLATBUSH SLIDES SILENTLY PAST the town car, the midnight hulks of the old houses ominous, their dark fronts occasionally opening, to reveal dimly lit rectangles outlining human shadows. It's a landscape of dark blues, greys and blacks. There are no reds, no blood that you can see.

"There's no blood and gore, no rape and no torture," you remember Nina saying while reading your journals. And indeed, in the recollections of the war you've set down on paper, there are no memories of bodies falling into the sea when boarding the ships at Cam Ranh Bay or people being ripped apart by propellers after the ships start. There is nothing about prostitutes being gang raped by the incoming army, or runaway Nationalist officials shot by their subordinates. You had tried to protect Nina from all that. But now the gore and the blood are all over the sleeves and front of her dress. Now she knows what it means—the loss, the pain, the sorrow. And there are no lies you can tell to make it better for her. No lies at all.

Even Chú Hai, that master of words, has nothing for Nina on this night. He's sobbing soundlessly into his chest. Quick and sharp is how he wanted it, he'd told you before, a simple wish for an uncomplicated death for himself when the time came. But not for your son Tri. And not this quickly. Not so sharply. 'If I hadn't tried to play God... If only I hadn't tried to play God...' his fingers tap out the voiceless incantation on his clamshell over and over, the ticking of his nails against the keys the only sound in the car.

His lament means nothing to you. What has he been playing at? Whatever, it's too late now for regret.

You know there's still a wife for you to take care of, and the hunched over old man on your left, with his head on his knees and his shoulders shaking, as well. But you have no reserves of anything left to take care of anyone, even yourself. To go the way of Tri, to sleep the sleep of the dead, to rest in peace... that's what you crave.

You lean back against Loc, your brother who seems to have materialized from nowhere to anchor you firmly against his body. You give in to the sedation somebody has shot up your arm.

.....

A dog is whining softly. It's you, whimpering. You're rolled up in a ball on the floor, the blood stained shirt you had on the evening before is covering your head, two small pieces of crumpled paper are in your fisted hand.

It is night again, you notice without noticing. You've slept the whole day in forgetfulness as someone, perhaps Loc, perhaps Kim or Jake, has gotten the necessary formalities done with the police and the medical examiners and the morticians. It's been a whole day since Tri...

"Dear," you hear Nina call from the bed.

You cannot face her sorrow, cannot allow it to resonate with your own, to multiply and amplify what you feel. You raise yourself into a kneeling position, wrap the sleeves of your shirt around your neck and begin pulling them tight and then tighter until you feel yourself choking.

Nina pounces on you. "Stop it!" she shouts, slapping your hands and your head. She pulls on your arms. "I'm not going to lose you too, do you hear me?" she says as she tugs at the shirt sleeves.

The sleeves tear, releasing both of you. Nina falls onto your curved back. Both your shoulders are heaving. She cradles your head in her hands, then moves them down to your shoulders and rolls both of you over till she's flat on the floor and your head is on her belly. You turn your face into her body and let your tears soak through the blood-stiffened bodice of her dress onto her flesh. You hear her tears drip in little plips from her white cheekbones onto the wooden floor.

.....

Nina and you are curled spoon-like against each other, both staring out at nothing when Huong comes in with a pot of tea the next morning. You sit up, take it from her without speaking, and pour. You sip. There is nothing to say. It is morning again. A second night has passed since Tri...

Huong crawls across the floor to pick up the two pieces of paper crunched in your hand the evening before. "They were folded in the scapulars Tri hung on his chest and back," she tells Nina.

Nina smoothes out the two sheets and reads the messages Tri has left for the two of you. The first piece of paper contains two lines from a hymn—'All the beauty I see, he has given to me. And his giving is gentle as silence.' On the second is a verse from the Gospel of John—'Unless a grain of wheat falls upon the ground and dies, it remains but a single grain with no life.'

You look away. You do not want to hear any more about Nina's and Tri's faith or their God. Without comment, Nina folds up the messages and tucks them into her bra.

"Where's everyone? Are they okay?" she asks Huong.

"The General's in the basement with Loc. The boys are awake and in the kitchen. Kim and Jake just phoned. They'll be here in a bit. Your friend Ly and his family are coming too. I don't think anybody's okay, but everyone's up and about," Huong says.

"And we should be too, shouldn't we?" Nina turns to you to ask.

You look at Nina over the rim of your teacup, then down again into the pale green tea, half gone already. You drink the rest, swallowing the bitterness in a gulp. Like the story Tri told you once about how his God too had not been able to let the cup pass him by, there is no escaping the night that has been, the day already upon you.

You put the teacup down. "Yes," you say. "There's work to be done."

.....

One evening, after the wake, after the funeral and the cremation, before you fly over the North Pole and down the western edge of the Pacific to install Tri's remains in the family temple, Nina and Chú Hai go to look once more at the astronomical ceiling over the main concourse of Grand Central Station.

"Do you remember what he said about it? Why it was painted back to front?" Nina asks, as the two of them tilt their heads back to look at the intricate pattern of stars and planets.

"Because the artist thought that was how God would see it," Chú Hai mouths, soundless.

Nina gives Chú Hai a watery smile. "Well, I guess he's seeing it the same way too, isn't he?"

Chú Hai looks out into the crowd of New Yorkers getting on with their lives, coming here and going there, then digs into his trousers for a tissue pack, gesturing that a piece of dirt seems to have gotten into his eye.

"Mine too," Nina says, reaching into her purse.

And suddenly they're holding on to each other—an old man hacking chest-breaking coughs, a middle aged woman with flooded black eyes—making a spectacle of themselves, crying in the middle of the main concourse of Grand Central Station, under a ceiling painted the way one of God's angels might see it.

.....

You aren't with the two of them, grieving in full view of one and all. As far as you're concerned, there's no god sitting in heaven, contemplating the world from the right side up. Why be reminded that Tri gave away a good part of his life for this delusion? If anyone needs a metaphysical explanation, you'll give them the one about pay-back for a military policeman you killed in Phu Quoc while retrieving five miserable taels of gold. You'll remember Tri in other ways, you've told them, and they've respected your wishes and left you at home to do just that.

You climb up the faded rainbow spiral staircase into the attic where Tri lived most of his childhood. The box the Brother Director sent back from Northern California, the pile of condolences faxed and mailed in from across the country and the Pacific, the anonymous hate mail and the newspaper reports about the incident are all piled in the far corner near Tri's old bed. It's been two months and no one has been able to face them. With no one in the house to see if you break down and cry your heart out, you decide it's a convenient time to begin sorting out what remains.

Nina had asked that your ordination gift to Tri, the chalice and ciborium hand-turned from Pacific madrone, be cremated along with him. Tri's box contains just two brown cassocks, a pair of sandals, his breviary, a bible, three sets of regular clothes and a photo of a young boy standing on a padi bund pissing into the evening sky. That's all you have to hold on to, the sum of your son's twenty-eight years. No last letter, no journal. It's a pittance compared to the five boxes you reclaimed and sent to Nina, documenting your first thirty-one years. It's so much like Tri to leave so little behind, the boy who would let nothing in this world touch him, the young man who refused to lay claim to anything from the world. Looking at the little box with its meager contents, you feel cheated. But by whom, you can't say.

You sift through the pile of condolences slowly. They are from all over—business associates, friends, even one from a racist German-American machinist who'd worked with you in your first job. 'A death causes one to stop and think, to want to reconnect,'—the man's message shines out from a gold and white card with doves. You should be grateful for the kind thoughts, but all you can think is how useless it is.

What do you care about reconnecting with someone you never connected with in the first place?

This exercise isn't helping. You are numb and will remain numb for many more days and even years, you realize.

You flick through the hate mail with indifference. If they must hate, then they must. It's nothing to do with you, their hate, even if they've killed your son. They've just been instruments of karma. But the ever watchful operative in you does wonder how they've gotten your address. And now they have it, is it finally time to let go of the brownstone? You've used it so little these past years and now will probably use it even less. In time, you think, suddenly feeling very tired. You'll come to that decision in time.

You go to the pile of newspaper reports someone, probably Kim, has cut out and clipped together. The local papers, in English, Chinese and Vietnamese, have the most extensive coverage, with full color pictures of the carnage, the victims and the perpetrators. In the nationals, you see terse reports picked up from the wires. Then there are the op-ed pieces from the specialist press and international editions, much like the ones Chú Hai had you practice writing in Saigon so long ago. One in particular catches your eye, an article titled 'The War Continues' by Julia Anderson's son Jules.

It isn't the article but the black and white photo attached to the by-line which holds you. "We see what we expect to see and filter out everything else," you recall telling Nina once. If one expects a child born of Julia Anderson's union with a man from the Middle East, then what's seen is her dusty hair, the presumed father's dusky skin. If the man introduced is a child adopted in the Middle East, then his dusty hair, his high nose and his long amber eyes are simply indications of Central-Asian ancestry. But in a black and white rectangle the size of an ID photo with all traces of color removed, what is obvious is a shock of strong straight hair starting from a widow's peak slightly off-centre, a high nose, a pointed chin, long suspicious eyes. A face like the one you see in the mirror every day, like those in the two ID pictures placed side by side on Chú Hai's coffee table so long ago... A pea from the same pod.

.....

After dinner that night, you leave Nina to wash up and follow Chú Hai down to the basement guest room to show him the newspaper article.

"How?" you ask.

He doesn't pretend to misunderstand the question. 'Your last meeting with her in Saigon,' he types out in full, this being too important a conversation to leave to text-speak.

"Why didn't you tell me?"

He answers. 'It was for her to tell you and she didn't seem to want to... She didn't tell me either, but I guessed the first time she brought him to me, after that meeting you finally told me about in Japan. When she came the second time to ask me to keep tabs on him, I became quite sure. There was no need to travel half way around the world just to tell me he was an Asian specialist at the State Department. Why mention that she was an orphan and he would have no one else after she died? But both times she didn't speak of you. So what was I to do?' He hesitates, looks down at his fingers, then starts to type again. 'Anyway, sons can be a burden, especially sons who haven't been told you exist. They've done fine without a father for so long, why should they welcome a stranger? One might be judged and found wanting... I didn't want to saddle you with all that.' His eyes begin to water. 'Finally, when I thought you might be ready and tried to play God by conjuring up a meeting on your birthday, look what happened. After that, I didn't think it was my place to ask you to risk loving another son, a stranger,' he concludes, the sadness and guilt over Tri still fresh on his face.

"Did you think twice?" you ask, finally daring to bring up the elephant that has lurked in your relationship all these years.

Chú Hai's long fingers hover over the phone keys for what seems to you like an eternity before they begin to tap again. 'Many times more than twice. On the kite field, when the Commander brought you to me, each time you came to the office. From the day you were born I've thought about it and counted the cost. Even today, now, still I count the cost... But sitting here with you, the two of us together, how can I regret it?'

You see him smile as he raises the screen to show you this last sentence.

"If that's the case, why shouldn't I take the risk, Chú?"

Much as you want to, the word *'Ba'* will not form on your tongue. Still there he is, your true father, finally acknowledged. What does it matter how you address him?

Indeed, he nods. He reaches out and covers your hand with his own. Yes, his eyes say, why shouldn't we?

You feel the numbness in your chest thaw a little. Losing Tri has fissured your world. Nothing can mend that. But something remains—a wife, family, friends, even a lost friend who might one day forgive you. And something has been given for what's been taken away—a son discovered, a blood tie finally acknowledged. It is much more than karma should allow.

Your heart skips a beat. There might be no gods but what you've been offered is nothing less than redemption.

24
A legacy

YOUR FATHER CANNOT ACCOMPANY YOU in the body
to redeem the time you've lost with Jules Anderson. Chú Hai
dies a few weeks after Tri's ashes are installed in the family
temple. As he so much wanted, his going is short. Blessedly
it isn't sharp and it isn't painful. He slips away one night in
his overstuffed armchair, a day old copy of the International
Herald Tribune in his lap. It is his beloved roosters, unfed at
dawn, that alert his sister with their crowing.

He isn't buried in Delta clay in the unfortunately positioned
graveyard of his forefathers. You aren't given a chance to explain
to his sister why you should be allowed to lay him to rest in the
family temple you've built for your ancestors either. As befits
his contribution to the country, his masters memorialize him in
the National Cemetery for Revolutionary Heroes.

His sister finds the instructions for orchestrating your
meeting with Jules in a plain brown envelope on his desk next
to a square package. Each step is listed as precisely as those
he'd given you for courting Ai Nguyet more than forty years
before. 'Write to Jules a month after my funeral. Tell him I've
died, with a simple description of the funeral. Remind him of

my promise to his mother. Then ask him if you can personally hand over some mementoes I've left for him. Let him determine the time and place. If he doesn't reply after three months, send him a gentle reminder.'

Nina isn't surprised when you tell her about Jules and about Chú Hai's instructions. She simply pats your hand and says, "Let's find him then." And she volunteers to go with you, if you need her, once he's found.

Your wife's love, you realize, will always flow. Something else more than your karma should allow.

.....

Jules has moved from Washington D.C. It takes Jerry a year to discover he's in the US Embassy in London, his exact responsibilities there difficult to ascertain.

You imagine he must be more than a little concerned when he receives the letter from that stranger whose birthday party turned into a shootout. Still, he agrees politely enough—'In London, at your convenience. Otherwise I shall be in D.C. in the summer.'

In the middle of winter, a month after receiving his reply, a week after completing the sale of the brownstone, Nina and you fly from New York to meet him.

"The café in the National Portrait Gallery off Nelson's Needle just after lunch," he suggests, when you call to make the appointment. A neutral place at a neutral hour, he's learned his tradecraft well, you think. Chú Hai would approve.

He's seated in the corner of the room near an emergency exit, his back defended, with a wide view of the comings and goings, and a quick way out if needed. The only man in a grey suit among English matrons in twin sets and tourists in layers of sweaters, he's at a café table jiggling a teabag in a cup of hot water, and looking at a museum catalogue.

He stands up when he sees the two of you, dropping the teabag abruptly and splashing hot water over the table.

You reintroduce yourself and Nina.

Everyone shakes hands.

"Cold out isn't it?" he asks, becoming suddenly British.

"Nice and warm in here though," Nina replies, just as British.

"What was it like in New York?" he counters.

As he and Nina make small talk, you examine your son, Julia Anderson's son. You can't help noting he's big boned like his mother, that he is the color of dust, like the little girl you saw kicked about in the Delta the last time his mother and you were together, that he has eyes shaped like yours but amber like a lion's, no one's eyes but his own. When Nina places the package from Chú Hai on the table, the hand that reaches out for it has scholar's fingers, just like yours. Like yours, the fingers are delicate but strong enough to kill. It is a hand that can potentially crush a heart, yours.

You see Jules touch the package tentatively. For all your discomfiture as you pass it to him—Nina blinking furiously, your eyes sliding this way and that—it might be a letter bomb. It isn't inconceivable, considering the circumstances of your last meeting.

His hand hesitates. Perhaps he's wondering what this last gift from his mother's friend is; that man who his mother said was someone very important in his life, someone to keep in touch with, someone who would look after him when she was gone.

Jules does not look to you like someone who needs looking after. This tag-along son of that solitary peripatetic woman would have learned to take care of himself soon enough.

You've been told how well he's done in the international schools he was shuffled in and out of, the honors he received in college, his reputation in the State Department.

"And anyway, now the old guy's dead too," he says suddenly, his fingers drawing back to the edge of the table. "Is it a memory I should even hold on to?" he asks.

You don't reply for a while. Finally you lie. "He said he'd always felt a certain sympathy between the two of you, an undercurrent of understanding."

Jules' hand comes back to the package. "May I?" he asks you.

You look at Nina and then nod.

Jules unties the package to reveal an airmail envelope outlined with blue and red stripes, and a grey silk pouch. He lifts the flap of the envelope. It contains two ID cards and a newspaper cutting of his own face pasted on cardboard. You reach over, and silently fan out the ID cards and the cardboard piece on the table. Then you push the silk pouch towards him.

Barely able to take his eyes off the three almost similar faces looking back at him from the table, Jules unties the pouch. The ivory circlet and a sheet of paper folded in the shape of a kite fall into his hands.

He unfolds the tiny kite and reads—'One day I shall be gone. And my life, what of it will remain? The consequences of what I did, both bad and good; a son of a son who carries the image of what I was on his body; a circle of bone too mute to explain itself; a story, if you are looking for one, about beginnings.'

Your son raises his amber eyes to you—a stranger with a face like his own. He looks at Nina—a woman who is not his mother. He picks up the circlet, his hand trembling, and closes his thumb and index finger over the worn bone.

Epilogue

EARLY MYTHICAL HISTORY

The beginnings are shrouded in history. There is no record of the date and time the Dragon King Lac Long Quan emerged from the Eastern Seas to couple with Au Co, a fairy of the mountains. What the people remember are the hundred sons who hatched from the hundred eggs and the manner of their separation—half to follow their father back to the sea, the others to remain with their mother, to guard the mountain passes. Even then there was the suspicion of a woman raped. Even then there were brothers alienated one from the other, two separate peoples bound only by turbulent blood.

It is said that around 3000 BCE one of Lac Long Quan's sons founded Van Lang. It is said that the Hung kings of his line ruled this kingdom on the plains and coastal regions of the Red River for 18 generations until 258 BCE. That year Thuc Phan, leader of the mountainous Tay Au defeated these plains-dwelling Lac Viet. Taking the name King An Duong, he established the kingdom of Au Lac, with a capital at Co Loa, north of today's Hanoi.

CHINESE DOMINION

Au Lac came to an end in 203 BCE in the chaos after China's Emperor Qin Shi Huang's death. An opportunistic general of the Wu State sealed the passes leading into China, and established his own fiefdom, proclaiming himself King Trieu Da of Nam Viet.

A hundred years later, a resurgent Chinese court under the Han Dynasty re-conquered the country. Thus began the years of Giao Chi, the thousand years of Chinese domination and intermittent insurrections that incubated the Confucian-Buddhist Vietnamese society of today and hatched the rebels that inspired Vietnam's twentieth century guerillas and swamp fighters.

The first of these rebels were Trung Trac and Trung Nhi, two sisters who rose against the Han in CE 40-43. Following them in CE 243 was Lady Trieu, an elephant- riding heroine still honored in cult-worship today. In the sixth century, a man named Ly Bi managed to establish a brief period of autonomy. But once China was re-unified under the Tang dynasty, the region was again drawn into the Chinese orbit, this time as 'Annam', the 'Pacified South'. Annam was to remain a Tang protectorate for over three hundred years (CE 602–938).

AUTONOMY

Political transition in China finally allowed the Vietnamese to gain independence. In CE 938, a genuinely independent Vietnamese sovereign, Duong Dinh Nghe, ascended the throne in Dai La (present day Hanoi).

Although Duong Dinh Nghe was assassinated in the sixth year of his reign, his general and son-in-law, Ngo Quyen, succeeded in defending the country against punitive action from the Chinese. His victory, involving the use of metal-tipped wooden stakes to barricade the Dang River, signals the definitive start to a period of autonomy.

Ngo Quyen took the title of king in 939 CE, with his capital at Co-Loa. After Ngo Quyen died, the country was plagued by factional disputes. Strong men gave way to weak sons, who fell prey to usurpers. Notable rulers during this time included Dinh Bo Linh, who re-unified a fractured country, and Le Hoan, who defeated another Chinese attempt to re-occupy the country around CE 981 and ruled until 1005.

Four years after Le Hoan's death, Buddhist interests were moved to depose his despotic son and install the religious advisor, Ly Cong Uan, onto the throne. Ly Cong Uan took the reign name of Ly Thai To and founded Dai Viet—and the country was ruled by the Ly and Tran dynasties (his descendants) from 1010 to 1400.

While the Chinese did try to re-establish control over Dai Viet during the Ly and Tran dynasties, most importantly in 1076 by the Sung and again in 1288 by the Mongols, they were repulsed. In the first instance, General Ly Thuong Kiet sent the Sung packing. In the second, Tran Hung Dao, the great general of Tran replicated Ngo Quyen's strategy at the Bach Dang River to vanquish the Mongols. It was a feat that many other Asian and Europen nations could not manage.

EXPANSION, DIVISION AND REUNIFICATION

The period of Ly and Tran saw a flowering of Buddhism and the rise of Zen court poetry. It was also during this period that the Nam Tien—the southward expansion of the territory into present day Central and South Vietnam—began.

This southward movement continued under the Ho Dynasty and the Later Tran Dynasty, halting for only twenty years during the Chinese occupation under the Ming dynasty (1407–1427). But after Le Loi drove the Ming out in 1428 and established the Later Le dynasty, this southern drift resumed.

The slowly lengthening country was administered by a mandarin bureaucracy schooled in Confucian ethics, one which grew in strength as the Dai Viet lands spread to Qui Nhon in Central Vietnam. By the 1500s the Le kings were being squeezed by the various mandarin clans, among them the Nguyen. Things came to a head in 1524, when the Le king was forced out of the capital by a rebellion subsequently quashed by General Mac Dang Dung, who established himself as ruler of Northern Dai Viet. The Le, supported by the Nguyen clan, remained nominally in charge of Southern Dai Viet, with a seat south of the Mac capital. The country was essentially divided in two.

In 1599, the Trinh clan, in co-operation with the Nguyen, restored the Le to their capital in present day Hanoi. But henceforth, the Le were kings only in name. The Trinh now ruled northern Vietnam. Meanwhile, the Nguyen held and continued their expansion southwards into Cham and Cambodian territory, as well as the Mekong Delta lands settled by Ming Chinese refugees in the thirteenth century. By the eighteenth century, the Trinh and Nguyen clans, as proxies of the Le, had taken over most of what is recognized as present-day Vietnam.

Administered by mandarins who abused the system for personal gain, the country was constantly plagued by famine. Peasant revolts multiplied. In the late eighteenth century, one such revolt led by Nguyen Hue, a peasant from the southern province of Tay Son, finally toppled the triumvirate of the Le Kings and Trinh and Nguyen clans.

The 1779–1803 reunification under Nguyen Hue is celebrated by the Vietnamese till today.

FRENCH ENCROACHMENTS

The Tay Son did not last. In 1789, even as Nguyen Hue busied himself with land reforms in the north, the last remaining scion of the Nguyen Lords, Nguyen Anh, was already seeking assistance from the French to regain his patrimony.

In 1802 Nguyen Anh entered Hanoi and inaugurated the Nguyen Dynasty, using local troops trained by French adventurers. For that assistance, Nguyen Anh ceded Condor Island to the French and granted them a trading concession at Danang. Those were the first steps towards the eventual carving up of Dai Viet into Cochin-China, Annam and Tonkin, and handing the pieces to the French one at a time.

The French might have been content with Condor Island and Danang, leaving the country to missionaries, were it not for the successes of the British in China and Burma. Hoping to access China from the South, the French began to plan their conquest of Dai Viet, using as pretext the need to protect French missionaries in the country.

In 1858, the French attacked Danang and moved south to capture Saigon in 1862. Despite strong popular resistance, the Nguyen court decided to adopt a policy of negotiation, and ceded three of the six southern provinces—Bien Hoa, Gia Dinh and Dinh Tuong—to the French. These provinces became the initial constituents of the new French colony of Cochin-China. In 1867, Chau Doc, Ha Tien and Vinh Long, along the Mekong delta, were added to the colony, a fait accompli recognized in the 1874 Treaty of Saigon.

The French then turned their attention to Hanoi. The Nguyen court sought help from the Qing dynasty in China. The Chinese sent 10,000 troops, who took up positions north of Hanoi but did not fight. Meanwhile, the Nguyen emperor had died without an heir. In-fighting amongst court officials to control the throne diverted the court's attention from the defense of Hanoi.

In 1883, the French secured Hanoi. An ultimatum was then given to the Nguyen court to surrender. When the Nguyen court failed to react, Hue was bombarded. In exchange for a ceasefire, the Treaty of Hue, recognizing a French semi-protectorate over the north and a protectorate in Annam was signed on 25 August 1883. The whole of Dai Viet was now once more a vassal of a foreign state.

FRENCH RULE

Over the next 70 years the French, supported by a court and mandarin class interested only in preserving its privileges, exploited the land and forced the peasants into indentured servitude on rubber plantations, in mines, and on rail-road and canal projects, so as to develop the country's natural resources for export. By the 1900s, as the colonial administration tightened its grip and the peasants' economic lot deteriorated so that their chief concern became survival, armed resistance against the colonists all but ceased.

Three events in Asia—Japan's victory over Tsarist Russia in 1905, Sun Yat Sen's proclamation of the Chinese Republic in 1911, and the 1917 October Revolution in Russia—made the Vietnamese aware that neither European domination nor monarchy were inevitable. Moreover, the French introduction of *quốc ngữ*—a Romanized alphabet which replaced *chữ nôm*, the traditional Chinese character-based script—had undermined the hold of Confucian thought on younger Vietnamese intellectuals. They were ready to grapple with new concepts such as equality, fraternity, liberty, democracy, socialism and communism.

Vietnamese who had gone to study in France or been conscripted there as laborers and soldiers to assist in France's defense during World War I returned and spread the new thinking. Growing literacy, due to the French imposed *quốc ngữ*, allowed the masses to read and understand these ideas. By the time of the Great Depression, a grass roots force for independence had spread from workers in the cities to previously Confucian provincial petty bureaucrats like chief clerks and assistant notaires. Many signed on to underground independence movements.

WORLD WAR II AND THE AFTERMATH

Despite grass roots resistance and intermittent uprisings, the French maintained their hold on Vietnam until 1940. Then, following France's surrender to the Germans, the Vichy government and the Nguyen Court were forced to let Japanese troops enter Indo-China. The region became a Japanese base and supplier of food and raw materials for the Japanese war effort.

The heaviest burden on the Vietnamese was the compulsory delivery of rice to the Japanese army at the same time that rice-fields were being forcibly cleared to plant jute for sacking. In 1944, when US bombing disrupted the transport of coal from North Vietnam to Saigon, the French and Japanese requisitioned rice and maize to use as fuel for power stations. The famine, which began in the North in 1943, escalated.

Discontent spread among even merchants and rich peasants. It was at this time that Ho Chi Minh, who had returned secretly to Vietnam in 1941 after 30 years in exile, founded the Viet Minh Front, a pro-independence movement whose main aim was to liberate the country from Franco-Japanese domination.

In 1945, when it became obvious that the Axis powers would be defeated, the Gaullist party began to deploy troops to safeguard the French presence in Indo-China. But on 9 March 1945, in a counter-putsch, the Japanese disarmed all French troops in Dai Viet. The Nguyen court immediately proclaimed independence under Emperor Bao Dai, abrogated all treaties signed with France, and aligned itself with the Japanese to form a Greater East Asia military alliance. In June, Bao Dai adopted the name Viet Nam for the country. Bao Dai's Viet Nam however was shortlived. When the Japanese surrendered unconditionally in August 1945, Bao Dai was forced to abdicate.

Separately, in the north, Ho Chi Minh was also preparing for an independent Viet Nam. But to no avail. Although Ho Chi Minh immediately proclaimed the independence of Viet Nam in Ba Dinh Square in Hanoi on 2 September 1945, the same day that the Japanese signed the surrender agreement in Tokyo Bay, he was ignored.

Vietnam's fate had already been decided in Potsdam. In July 1945, following the defeat of Germany, the World War II Allies including the US, Britain, and the Soviet Union had gone there to plan the postwar world. To disarm the Japanese, the Allies divided the country in half at the 16th parallel, with the Chinese Nationalists moving into the north and the British into the south. Although no Vietnamese parties were at the conference, it was also agreed that Vietnam would once again become a French colony.

By virtue of the Potsdam agreements, 150,000 Nationalist Chinese troops entered North Vietnam, looting Hanoi and villages along the way. British troops arrived in Saigon on 13 September 1945. By 22 September, all French soldiers imprisoned by the Japanese had been released. They proceeded to go on a deadly rampage against both the Viet Minh and civilians. By October 1945, 35,000 French soldiers had arrived to restore French rule in South Vietnam.

In February 1946, following the departure of the Chinese Nationalists, Ho Chi Minh allowed the French to return to Hanoi in exchange for recognition of his Democratic Republic of Vietnam. But the French were treacherous and prevaricated. Instead, in June 1946, they established Cochin-China as a separatist republic, with Bao Dai as President.

Hostilities between the French and the Viet Minh escalated. By November 1946, the French had re-occupied Hanoi, and the Viet Minh were forced to retreat to the jungle. It was from the jungles that the Viet Minh began the war of attrition which resulted in the 1954 French defeat at Dien Bien Phu and the Geneva negotiations, dividing the country into North and South Vietnam. With this, brother would fight brother once more.

But that would be in the future. What is important in the years between 1946 and 1954 is that many patriots in both the north and south slipped through French lines to join the Viet Minh in their fight for independence. Among these would be an assistant notary from a small Mekong Delta town who would become a Commander of swamp fighters. A few years later, the son of a civil engineer would follow, a youth whom the re-organized Viet Minh Front, the Viet Cong, would send to America to train as a journalist and a spy. This would be the young man who would break into a petty bureaucrat's home on a moonlit night and, mistaking a young woman there for the bureaucrat's daughter, rape the wife of his new Commander.

About the author

AUDREY CHIN works with numbers as a financial steward by day and with words at night. Her mission is to tell the Southeast Asian story to an international audience from the point-of-view of a multi-cultural Peranakan woman in Singapore. Her debut novel, *Learning to Fly*, was a coming-of-age story set in the rainforests of the region. She is contributing co-editor of *Singapore Women Re-Presented*, which tells Singapore's social history from the perspective of Singaporean Women.

Audrey is married to Minh and has been a daughter-in-law of the Vietnamese diaspora for thirty years. *As the Heart Bones Break* is distilled from the many diasporic stories she heard over that period.

Find out more at www.audreychin.com